THE HANGING CHEAT

*Lady Fan Mysteries
Book Ten*

Elizabeth Bailey

Also in the Lady Fan Mystery Series
The Gilded Shroud
The Deathly Portent
The Opium Purge
The Candlelit Coffin
The Mortal Blow
The Fateful Marriage
The Dagger Dance
The Unwanted Corpse
The Vengeance Trail

THE HANGING CHEAT

Published by Sapere Books.

24 Trafalgar Road, Ilkley, LS29 8HH

saperebooks.com

Copyright © Elizabeth Bailey, 2023
Elizabeth Bailey has asserted her right to be identified as the author of this work.
All rights reserved.

No part of this publication may be reproduced, stored in any retrieval system, or transmitted, in any form, or by any means, electronic, mechanical, photocopying, recording, or otherwise, without the prior written permission of the publishers.
This book is a work of fiction. Names, characters, businesses, organisations, places and events, other than those clearly in the public domain, are either the product of the author's imagination, or are used fictitiously.
Any resemblances to actual persons, living or dead, events or locales are purely coincidental.

ISBN: 978-0-85495-195-6

CHAPTER ONE

November, 1796

From the comfort of a cushioned chair positioned to catch the warmth from the fire, Ottilia Fanshawe watched her husband examining his new crop in the mirror above the mantel. Lord Francis turned his head this way and that, the dark locks that now just brushed his collar flicking his cheek. Their wave was more pronounced, with a tendency to slip across the forehead from his brow. Ottilia found it disorienting.

It was all of a piece. This whole unavoidable excursion to her previous home had thrown life out of kilter. Not least due to being back in Ash Lodge. Her old house felt cramped after the spaciousness of Flitteris Manor. Even this main family room in which she had passed numberless hours, was not much bigger than her private parlour at home. Besides the few chairs and a small sofa, it boasted only a side table and a neat writing bureau. Moreover, with the growing bump of her advancing pregnancy, she seemed altogether too big for the environment. Under any other circumstance, her careful spouse would not have allowed her to travel at all, just as the weather was turning too, with November upon them. But there had been no gainsaying necessity on this occasion.

"We will have to go, Fan. I must be there for poor Patrick and the boys. With their mother gone, Ben and Tom especially will need me."

The express announcing her sister-in-law's death had saddened Ottilia, but the shock had been minimal. Sophie Hathaway had ever been sickly. She had succumbed, so Patrick said, to the worst of her various ailments, her taking off sudden, if not unexpected.

Francis had thankfully concurred. "Naturally you must go. But we'll go alone. I refuse to take the children on such a melancholy visit. Let them remain comfortable and warm at home. Besides, as I remember, your brother's house would scarcely accommodate the entirety of our retinue."

With which Ottilia had been obliged to agree. In the event, only Joanie and Tyler accompanied them, the maid (without whom Ottilia could not manage in her present condition) travelling with them in the coach and the footman taking the seat up behind. As well, since both were obliged to share rooms with her brother's servants while the coachman and groom were accommodated above the stables.

The funeral had been well attended, attesting to Doctor Patrick Hathaway's popularity in the district. But there was no rushing away directly since Ottilia had all to do to comfort her nephews. Francis had taken it upon himself to do what he might for his brother-in-law, accompanying him on a necessary trip to Salisbury, where he had also been persuaded to emulate Patrick's more fashionable hairstyle. He was frowning at his reflection.

"What do you think, Tillie?"

Mischief entered Ottilia's breast. "Other than it has taken years off you?"

He turned from the mirror, throwing a glance heavenwards. "Be serious."

"I am. I doubt Pretty will recognise you when we go home. For my part, it makes you look rather dashing."

"You are a teasing wretch, woman. Shall I grow it back?" He returned to contemplation of the new crop, sounding decidedly disgruntled. "I should not have listened to Patrick."

"Fiddle! My brother looks younger too. Look upon it as having provided him with a much-needed distraction."

"What, in making me look a fool?"

"You don't look in the least bit foolish, Fan. I confess it was a trifle of a shock to begin with, but I am already becoming accustomed."

"Yes, well, it's a shock to me seeing myself in the mirror." He thrust a straying lock back with an impatient hand. "It is too unruly, what's more. It will drive me mad."

"You will settle into it, my dearest dear. I think it may look well when we are home again and able to put off our blacks."

The funereal garb presently worn by members of the entire household was necessary in the doctor's house, so Patrick had averred. "With patients and well-wishers likely to drop in at any moment, we must be prepared at all times. It must be uncomfortable for you in your present state of pregnancy, my dear sister, and I am sorry for it."

Ottilia had at once disclaimed. The high-waisted gown had been made up at speed in black poplin, the material's silk and worsted mix being suitable for winter's cold, and its full petticoats allowed for her expanding belly. The elderly dressmaker in the village who had been used to make up her gowns when she lived with the Hathaways, had been pleased to have her custom again and copied one of Ottilia's own for the pattern.

Francis only grunted in response to her encouraging remark, but at last turned away from the mirror and drew up a chair. "How long must we stay, do you think?"

"A little longer, if you please, Fan. Ben was tearful again last night."

"He looked to be in fine fettle at breakfast."

"He is putting on a show for his father's sake. In any event, he and Tom have gone off to hunt rabbits in the woods."

Truth to tell, Ottilia had suggested the sporting jaunt in hopes it might distract her bereaved nephews. She had comforted both, severally and together, and thought their initial strong grief had perhaps been expended. She was less certain of her brother's state of mind. She reached for her coffee cup and found it empty.

Her husband had noticed. "Shall I ring for a fresh pot?"

"Better not, Fan. I shall only be obliged to retire to the chamber yet again." Her bladder was apt to behave inconveniently, the more so as the weeks went by. She followed her earlier thought. "How did you find Patrick?"

An odd look crossed her spouse's face. "How do you mean?"

Ottilia eyed him. "Did he confide in you?"

"What about?"

She clicked her tongue. "Pray don't be obtuse, my dearest. Patrick's stoicism is almost superhuman. I have not seen him shed one tear."

"You could scarcely expect him to make a parade of his emotions, for pity's sake." He was studying his nails, brushing at the newly pared ends.

Ottilia grew a trifle uneasy. "Is there anything I should know, Fan?"

His gaze flew up and met hers, a frown creasing his brow. "What, why?"

"You are being evasive."

"I'm not at all."

"What did Patrick say to you?"

He hesitated, his glance flicking away and back again. At length, he gave an exaggerated groan. "If you must have it, he confessed to some slight feeling of relief."

Ottilia relaxed again. "Is that all?"

"You don't find it reprehensible? Patrick supposed you might."

"It is perfectly understandable. Sophie's various ailments have plagued him for years. I dare say his sorrow is tempered by the thought she is no longer suffering."

"There is that."

Her husband sounded relieved. Ottilia was about to enquire further when the clatter of running feet interrupted her. "That sounds as if the boys are back."

Sure enough, within a matter of seconds, her two nephews erupted into the room, evidently in a state of great excitement.

Ben, who at fifteen and clad in mourning garb had been hitherto conducting himself in an adult manner, looked at this moment much more like the little boy Ottilia had cared for in his early childhood, blond locks flying, face flushed, blue eyes sparkling. He made straight for Ottilia's chair.

"Auntilla! You've got to turn back into Lady Fan!" Came the ghoulish voice of his brother, a year younger and still chubby cheeked, but quite as blond, as handsome as his deceased mother, and looking even more like the rambunctious nurseling Ottilia remembered. "We found a dead body," said Tom. "It's been hanged in a tree!"

Ottilia's response was automatic. "Where?"

"In the woods."

"We nearly shot it, Auntilla, only Ben saw it just in time."

The elder boy took up the tale. "We didn't realise he was dead at first. But the moment we got close there could be no doubt. I checked for a pulse nevertheless."

"I told you not to bother, Ben," scoffed his junior. "He was cold as a fish."

Ottilia intervened. "You did quite right, Ben. It is always best to be sure. Do you know the man?"

Tom took this. "'Course we do. It's that horrid Justice Penkevil. No one will cry for him, Auntilla. Everybody hates him."

His brother nudged him. "Shut it, Tom. You ought not to prejudice Lady Fan. Not but what it's true he's pretty much disliked, Auntilla. Don't you remember him?"

"If you'll give me a chance to say so, I believe I have a vague recollection, assuming it is Mr Hector Penkevil you mean."

"That's him. A brute, he is. Wouldn't surprise me if it's not old Petrus Gubb who did for him."

Before Ben could again admonish his brother, Francis cut in. "If I might edge in a word, you gabsters, ought you not to fetch your papa rather than your aunt? He is best placed to take charge of this business."

Aware of the note of irritation in her husband's voice, Ottilia hastened to encourage this notion. "Yes, indeed he is. Tom, why don't you —?"

"Yes, but Papa won't be able to find out who killed him, Auntilla," objected her nephew.

"It does not sound as if anybody did," said Francis. "He was hanged, you said, which is far more likely to be a suicide."

"Very true, Fan. Tom, go and find your papa. He will be in his examining room, I expect."

"Yes, he will. I left him there," said Francis.

Tom groaned. "Well, I'll go, 'cause Papa will want to know, but it's not suicide, is it, Ben?"

The elder stripling's eyes took on the sparkle which had died a little. "It's not, Auntilla, I can tell."

"How?"

"He'd have been still hanging, but he wasn't. He'd fallen to the ground. Or someone cut him down."

"Then how do you know he was hanged in the first place?" Thus Francis, evidently keen to avoid any prospect of yet another murder landing in Ottilia's lap.

She could not blame him, considering the dreadful events at Dalesford Hall in the summer which had very nearly put paid to her existence. Her husband was yet haunted by her near escape. There were nights of troubled dreams. Francis dismissed her anxious queries, but Ottilia was not deceived. Her nephews, having scant knowledge of those difficult days, were naturally all too eager for her participation.

"That's easy, Uncle Fan," Tom said on a triumphant note, taking the question. "He's still got the rope round his neck."

"That's not all," pursued Ben, portentous now, his gaze fixed upon Ottilia. "He ought to be pale in the face and he's not. That's what Papa told me."

Since Ben had been apprenticing under his father during school holidays for the past couple of years, Ottilia was inclined to accept his observation. Nevertheless, a familiar sliver of anticipation went through her at the prospect of an intriguing puzzle. Guilt swiftly succeeded it and she refrained from speaking of her desire to see the corpse, guessing at her spouse's likely reaction, instead rounding on her younger nephew.

"Why are you still here, Tom? Fetch Patrick at once!"

Her tone provoked a startled look in the boy's face, but he obeyed, shooting out of the room.

True to her prediction, Francis put in an instant protest. "You'd best leave your father to sort this out, Ben."

"But Auntilla needs to see —"

"Your aunt is in no state to be traipsing through the woods. Especially at this season. It's cold out."

"It isn't all that cold, Uncle Fan. If she wraps up well —"

"Wraps up be damned! She is pregnant. These dratted woods of yours are likely strewn with fallen branches and all manner of obstacles. Not to mention icy patches."

Ben looked crestfallen — not half as much as Ottilia felt, the niggling disappointment a thorn in her ever-wakeful conscience. "I know it's not the most suitable for Auntilla, sir, but there isn't much ice, I swear."

"Nevertheless —"

Ottilia made a hasty intervention. "Pray don't argue, Ben. Uncle Fan has always a care to my health. I am sure your papa is far more competent than I to determine how the poor man died."

Ben let out a frustrated sound, hopefully missing the mixed emotions in her husband's face. Ottilia read there both guilt and exasperation and was thankful she had not shown an interest he clearly felt to be inappropriate. But her nephew was not similarly reticent.

"He's not a poor man, that's just it, Auntilla. Mr Penkevil is well to do. Only he's mean too. He never gives a farthing more than he must and that wife of his, Mama was used to say, has been wearing the same gowns year after year. She could tell under the attempts to refurbish, Mama said."

It was the first time he had mentioned his mother without recalling his grief and Ottilia fleetingly rejoiced. It occurred to her that this discovery of the body might be considered providential. Nothing could more surely ease the prevailing gloom than a delve into a possible murder. Might she persuade Francis by this means?

"Should we not perhaps take advantage of the occasion, Fan?" His brows drew together and she added on a light note, "No doubt there is nothing in it, but need we disappoint the boys? I must take my daily walk, and if we accompany Patrick —"

"Tillie, no! You are not fit for it."

He did not sound as curt as he looked and Ottilia took heart. "How if you were to give me your arm and help me over any obstacles? We need not rush. I doubt poor Mr Penkevil is going anywhere."

A crack of laughter from Ben served to lighten the disapprobation on her spouse's face and his lip quirked. "That is the truest word as yet spoken on the subject, I suspect."

Was this tacit permission? Ottilia did not pursue it, turning back to Ben with the question she knew to be essential in any observation of the kind. "Was there anyone else about? You did not move anything, I trust?"

"We knew better than that, Auntilla. As a matter of fact, Willy Heath was wandering the woods and he came up just as I was checking the pulse. I set him to keep watch."

Anxiety wafted through Ottilia and her interest burgeoned. "Did Willy understand he must stay and not touch anything?"

"Oh, I repeated it several times and made him go over it too. He won't fail."

Francis cut in at this point and Ottilia detected the impatience behind his words. "Who is this individual? Some simpleton?"

"He's on the parish, Uncle Fan. All the locals look out for Willy, feed him and that. Papa gives him odd jobs he can manage. He's good with accounts."

"Good with accounts?"

Ottilia hastened to explain, feeling that any distraction from the main issue was of value. "He is something of a savant with numbers, Fan. The poor fellow is not truly a simpleton. He has some malfunction of the brain, Patrick thinks, which prevents him from understanding the exigencies of day-to-day life."

"He likes the woods, sir," added Ben, "and goes about estimating how many leaves are on the trees and such like. Old Petrus Gubb keeps him at the farm, not just to do odd jobs, but because he can take one look at a field and knows straight off if any sheep are missing."

Approaching footsteps signalled the return of Tom, accompanied by Patrick's heavier tread, bringing discussion of Willy Heath's remarkable abilities to an end.

CHAPTER TWO

The corpse was lying in a crumpled heap, just as one might expect had it fallen from the stout branch above. Despite his misgivings, Francis had been persuaded to allow the expedition by his brother-in-law who, rather to his surprise, proved amenable to having Tillie's opinion.

"If nothing else, my sister's corroboration will serve to stop my sons going further with this ridiculous notion of murder. I set it to Ottilia's account that they must needs jump to such conclusions so she may as well wear the character of Lady Fan and set their minds at rest."

Tillie had not taken issue with her brother's half-teasing remarks, merely eyeing him with a hint of that mischief Francis valued. He was loath to quash it, anxious never to resurrect the spectre of the horrid estrangement that had sprung up between them at the worst possible moment in the fateful aftermath days of his niece Lizzy's wedding. That Tillie was equally anxious on that score he knew only too well. Upon their return to Flitteris, once her health had improved and the early weeks of morning sickness had dissipated, his darling wife had thrown herself heart and soul into their domestic affairs, from overseeing the housekeeper (Mrs Bertram's astonishment at this unprecedented interest notwithstanding) to supervising Pretty's education, visiting the nursery with frequency, and ensuring the well-being of tenants who had fallen upon difficult times. She even enquired into estate matters that were wholly the province of Francis and his agent Pether.

Francis found her new-found enthusiasm both gratifying and, to his chagrin, dispiriting. She was doing it for his benefit and it showed. The activities in which she engaged held little true involvement for a mind used to intricate puzzling and the way his beloved wife had begun to defer to his judgement grated more than a little. He had more than once urged her to desist from too much action, on the score of her pregnancy, but the truth was Francis preferred her natural behaviour. He could only marvel at the perverseness of his own character after the fuss and bother he had stirred up in complaining of her lack of interest in a life of domesticity.

The enforced interlude to attend the obsequies of Tillie's sister-in-law had come as something of a relief, if he was honest with himself. Whether he was prepared to endure the exigencies of another murder hunt, however, remained a question. Nevertheless, once the party arrived at the scene in the woods where the corpse lay, Francis found his attention irresistibly drawn to the markings on the bough which indicated the rope now looping on the ground had indeed been tied around it.

His wife, who had endured the walk pretty well, he was obliged with some reluctance to admit, was engaged in examining the body alongside her brother doctor. Ben, who was standing over them, was paying eager and close attention. Willy Heath was still in attendance, standing at a little distance with Tom, the younger boy barred from crowding those around the body.

Doctor Patrick Hathaway, a tall and rangy man, very like Ottilia in feature with his sister's grey eyes and an easy-going way with him, had greeted the fellow Willy Heath with kindness and his usual bonhomie.

"Well done, lad, well done. I trust none have sought to interfere with matters here?"

The youth had looked blank.

Patrick slowed his speech. "No one came by while you were watching Mr Penkevil?"

Willy shook his head. "I seen Master Ben and Master Tom just."

"No one else?"

"You just. And them two." A vague wafture of his hand encompassed Francis and Ottilia.

"Good, good. Stay, Willy, but stand off now, there's a good fellow." He turned back towards the body. "Now then, let us see what we have here."

Tillie was already on her haunches examining the dead man's head when Patrick joined her. The first observations concerned the length of time the body had been there.

"Well, his limbs are not stiff," said Tillie. "Rigor mortis has passed."

"Or it has not yet begun."

"How so, Patrick?"

"In this cold, it will be delayed."

"Then it will be hard indeed to estimate just when he died."

"I fear so. He's ice-cold, but that is to be expected in this weather. I may be able to judge better from lividity and other signs when I have him naked on the slab."

"May I watch you do the autopsy, Papa?"

"I might not need to cut him up, Ben. Indeed, I hope I won't. The way he died seems eminently clear even from this cursory examination. Let's straighten him out and we'll be able to see better. Take the legs, Ben."

His help was not requested with this operation and Francis felt he was making but a poor addition to the conference. He shifted away and concentrated his attention on the immediate environment. At which point, he noted the branch above the corpse. He heard but indistinctly the murmured conversation as he squinted up to examine the spot where the rope had been tied. The markings showed it had been slung over the branch rather than tied around it. Then it must have been tied off elsewhere. He began to follow the rope which was lying loosely along the icy ground.

"Petechiae are present in the lips and eyelids."

"What are they, Papa?"

"See those coloured spots, Ben, in the tissues inside the lips? These are bleeding sites. On the eyelids too, if you look closely."

"What does it mean then?"

"It indicates strangulation, but whether from being hung or some other cause is not clear."

"But did you not say his face would be pale if he was hung, sir?"

"He may have fallen before life was fully extinct. He was awkwardly placed as you saw. Hard to tell yet where the blood may have pooled."

Just as Francis located the place he was seeking, his wife spoke.

"We ought to remove his neckcloth and look for the mark of the rope, do you not think, Patrick?"

His brother-in-law agreed and the discussion faded in Francis's ears as he located the end of the rope partway curled around the bottom of the tree. He again checked the branch, noting how grooves were gouged into the wood. The rope had certainly taken the man's weight. How had the fellow bungled it? Had he tied too loose a knot at the neck, which had come loose as he dropped? The rope had indeed been around his neck, as Tom had said, until Patrick removed it.

Summary executions by hanging had been a feature of his long-gone army days. Cruel and horrible. Francis had hated such affairs and had tried by all means in his power to avoid condemning any soldier to such a miserable end. Better a firing squad and a quick release. In his experience, stringing a man up in that way gave him a slow and painful death. A loose knot ought to ensure a man lived, though he might well lose consciousness. Had this particular suicide been too far gone when he fell to the ground to pull his neck free before he suffocated?

Another feature surfaced in Francis's mind. He shifted back and examined the tree trunk. Where were the grooves, if any? The rope must have been tied off for the suicide to hang himself at all. Recalling those far-off executions, a vivid image came to mind of lines rubbed into the bark when the dead soldier had been brought down, the rope untied. A minute examination of the trunk revealed only a light scuffing instead of the expected indentation.

Another thought struck him and he looked about the area around the body. If the man had hung himself from a branch this high, from what object did he launch to accomplish his purpose?

As Francis reached an inevitable conclusion, he became aware of an altered tone in the discussion behind him and turned to find Tillie confronting her brother across the corpse, both now standing.

"Where have your wits gone begging, Patrick, to be insisting it is indeed a hanging? I grant you the V-shape at the back of the neck, but what of these abrasions about the throat?"

Patrick let out an exasperated sound. "Are you telling me my business now? The fact he is on the ground shows it was a mangled effort. He struggled against the rope. That in itself would account for such abrasions."

"These, Patrick?" Tillie pointed to the dead man's throat. "These bruises were not left by a ligature. They are finger marks."

"Impossible to tell with the effects of livor mortis."

"Well, I can clearly see them, if you cannot."

Tom had moved closer and the doctor's two sons were looking from one to the other of the combatants, the younger clearly bursting with suppressed excitement while the elder was as obviously dismayed. Had they not before seen brother and sister at outs? Now Francis thought about it, he had never seen it either. His brother-in-law was customarily the most even-tempered of men. Was this present curmudgeonly attitude symptomatic of his grief? Francis had every reason to think otherwise after the conversation they'd had earlier, but perhaps Patrick was more affected by his wife's passing than he had hitherto allowed to appear.

He was visibly holding in his temper as he spoke now, his voice clipped. "You are so apt to see murder everywhere, Ottilia, you can no longer view an ordinary death without seeking to complicate matters."

"A suicide is scarcely an ordinary death."

"Aha! So you admit he may well have taken his own life."

Tillie gave an audible sigh. "Pardon me, but I said nothing of the kind. You are being deliberately obtuse when you know perfectly well —"

"What I know, Ottilia, is that if Penkevil was indeed murdered, the consequences to this parish are legion. Do you not know how many people will be affected? It is bad enough he killed himself, let alone having half the county suspect."

At which point, Ben chimed in. "Yes, but that's just it, Papa. I told Auntilla that nobody liked him."

His father raised a finger. "You keep out of it!"

"But —"

"Quiet, I said!"

As Tillie opened her mouth to enter another protest, Francis took a hand, moving to join them. "Give me leave, Patrick."

Patrick's grey gaze came around to meet his, his brows drawing together and impatience in his tone. "What is it, Fan?"

Francis flung up a hand. "Loath as I am to add to your frustration, my friend, I am obliged to state that I agree with my wife."

He caught an astonished glance from Tillie and threw her a warning look. Patrick was eyeing him with ill-concealed annoyance.

"Your reason? Do you also propose to argue with my medical knowledge?"

Francis felt himself stiffen and made a deliberate effort to rein in his own rising irritation. It would not help for him to quarrel with Patrick as well. "I wouldn't dream of it. I do know something of the mechanics of a hanging, however."

He went on to explain his observation of the lack of severe indentation on the tree trunk as opposed to the gouging on the branch above, and was gratified to see Patrick's ruffled feathers settling as interest entered his features. He entered a caveat nonetheless. "Then he tied it off too loosely. Which would account for his dropping to the ground."

"Well, if he did attempt to kill himself, I can see no means by which he could have launched onto the rope. That branch is high. He would have needed a tree trunk or some such thing to climb up on, so that he could kick it away."

"Indeed, Fan." Tillie was in again. "One cannot suppose he could tie the rope around his own neck and then pull himself up."

"Nor, I regret to say for your sake, Patrick, is it feasible to suppose someone removed such an item since the body was only discovered this morning."

A deep and heartfelt sigh came from Patrick and he put his hands palm up in a gesture of defeat. "I concede. Not that I will thank you, Fanshawe, for demonstrating that it could not be a suicide."

"A deliberate attempt to make it appear so, Patrick," said Tillie on a conciliatory note.

Her brother was not appeased. "Which fooled neither of you, it would appear."

"We have a good deal of experience, my dear brother."

"Don't I know it."

Tillie's features fell into mischief. "You are disgruntled, Patrick, so I had better not remark upon how clumsy was this an attempt to deceive."

Patrick gave a shout of laughter. "You wretch, Ottilia!"

Relieved at the lightening of the general mood, Francis found he was instead inwardly cursing at the mischance that brought them to this district at this precise time. He foresaw that his wish to return home at the earliest possible moment was blasted. Despite his desire that his wife would return to the conduct natural to her, the thought of the inevitable end to this discovery was anathema.

Tillie would not be persuaded to leave until she had solved this puzzle.

CHAPTER THREE

By the time the party returned to Ash Lodge, Ottilia was more tired than she had bargained for. She refrained from informing Francis, aware that he was already distempered by this burgeoning adventure, notwithstanding his conclusive contribution.

Her brother, she was relieved to see, had regained his customary insouciant manner. The immediate necessity to inform the authorities and the dead man's family had taken precedence over his misgivings about the consequences of the event.

"I must certify the death and write a note for Marden," Patrick said, heading for his study which was situated adjacent to the examining room on the ground floor.

"Who is Marden?"

Ottilia did not answer Francis immediately, instead calling after her brother. "Should you not inform Sir Hugh Riccarton, Patrick?"

He halted at the study door, turning back into the hall. "The devil! Yes, I must. Penkevil was himself a justice, of course, but that's no use now." He threw Ottilia a quizzical look. "No need for you to involve yourself, my dear sister. We may leave the matter in Sir Hugh's hands." He then slipped inside the room and shut the door before Ottilia had a chance to respond beyond a protesting exclamation.

"Do I take it that fellow is the law around these parts?"

"Just so, Fan. Sir Hugh is the nearest magistrate, and Mr Marden is the coroner. He will have to see the body for himself, but I doubt Sir Hugh will take the trouble to tramp through the woods for the purpose."

Her elder nephew had accompanied them back to the house, leaving Tom, at his father's request, to stay with Willy Heath, once again detailed to guard the body.

The notion had not sat well with Tom. "Must I, Papa?"

"It will not be for long. I shall send someone to relieve you both within the hour."

"But I want to see what Auntilla is going to do."

"She'll be doing nothing for the moment. There are formalities to be undertaken before anything in that line can be attempted."

Ottilia did not gainsay her brother, casting a faintly apprehensive look at her spouse. How was Francis taking this? Would he, like Patrick, be eager to veto her taking anything further? She could not withstand a fervent hope that he would be more amenable than her brother, for she had every intention of discovering what she might of those who may potentially benefit from this death. She naturally had familiarity with certain families in the area, but her acquaintance by no means encompassed all who might be involved. She hoped to rely on Ben for enlightenment. Assuming her spouse entered no objection.

As it chanced, her nephew began the process without realising it, for upon his father closing the study door, he drew close and spoke in a lowered tone. "You won't abandon it, will you, Auntilla? I doubt Sir Hugh can do better than Lady Fan."

Ottilia had to laugh. "You flatter me, Ben. I know Sir Hugh for a sensible man. I don't think he will give me any trouble."

She made for the stairs, glad of the support of the banister. Her slow progress was plainly noted by Francis.

"You're exhausted, aren't you? I knew it." He caught up and gave her the support of his arm about her back.

"Thank you, Fan, but I shall do very well when I have rested a little."

"You ought to lie down upon your bed."

"I will be perfectly at ease in that comfortable chair. Coffee will set me up nicely."

"I'll tell Betty to make some, Auntilla," said Ben. He had been following up the stairs, but turned instead and clattered down again in search of the Hathaway cook-cum-housekeeper.

Ottilia continued on up. "I hope he comes back afterwards. I need his knowledge of the Penkevils." She spoke unguardedly and upon the instant looked to see how Francis took this.

His face gave nothing away and his tone was noncommittal. "You are determined to pursue it, I see."

"Pray don't be upset, my dearest dear. We were going to remain a little longer in any event." Not that this aspect was likely to weigh with him as much as the fact of carrying out an investigation at all.

Francis grunted, but thankfully said nothing further until he had escorted her into the parlour and settled her in the chair, fetching a footstool. "Feet up, my loved one. Remember Patrick's warning about swollen ankles."

"I have not suffered from them as yet," Ottilia said, allowing him to lift her feet onto the cushioned stool. But she sighed in content nevertheless as she sank into the seat and rested her head against the high upholstered back.

The chair had been especially made for Sophie; the purpose of its well-stuffed cushioning intended to ease the many aches from which she so often suffered. Ottilia had no qualms about using it, believing that her deceased sister-in-law would not begrudge it to her. Besides, she had it from Patrick that Sophie had often these last years been too unwell to leave her room, preferring to languish on the day-bed set near the window, which afforded the welcome sight of flowering shrubs in the rockery and, in summer, a steady invasion of butterflies and birds. Not being in the least superstitious, Ottilia appropriated the special chair almost as soon as she stepped into Ash Lodge.

Francis took up his usual stance at the mantel, casting a pained look at his reflection before he turned to address Ottilia again. "I suppose it is quite pointless to think this business might be ignored?"

She eyed him for a moment before she spoke. "Do you dislike it as much as ever?"

He shrugged in that way he had which signalled discomfort. "I can't say I am delighted at the prospect."

He paused and Ottilia's nerves betrayed her. "But? There is a but, is there not, Fan?"

A faint lift of his eyebrow came. "It is not the one you are expecting."

"Tell me, my dearest. I would not for the world put you through this all over again."

The short laugh he gave did nothing to reassure her. "My loved one, you won't be able to help it, will you?" He threw up a hand as she opened her mouth to answer and Ottilia held her tongue, waiting. In a moment, his face softened and a rather crooked smile appeared. "You will think me perverse beyond reason, Tillie. I think I am almost glad this has occurred."

Ottilia's heart jerked. "You are not serious!"

"Indeed I am." He came across and dropped to his haunches beside the chair, taking one of her hands and bringing it to his lips. The kiss upon her fingertips was balm. Then he looked up. "You have been assiduous in trying to please me, have you not?"

"Fan!"

"No, let us be truthful with one another, my dear one." He released her hand and stood up, his gaze rueful. "I never meant to force you to change. I love you for making the effort, but it's not you, Tillie."

She sighed in her heart as well as aloud. "I hoped I could make a better fist of it, my dearest dear, but it seems I was wrong."

"You were not wrong. You have done well as far as it goes. But your heart isn't in domesticity, my dear one, and I should never have led you to think you must act as if it was."

"It has not all been vain, Fan, I promise you. I do enjoy the company of the children and it has given me pleasure to ensure Pretty receives an education she can enjoy. She loves stories and is beginning to read them for herself, you know."

He laughed. "I do know. She as good as informed me I am becoming redundant, saying I should instead start reading to Luke." He wafted a hand. "But that is beside the bridge. What I am trying to say to you is, go to it."

Ottilia's eyes pricked. "Do you mean it, Fan? You will not regret it? Or worry I might be endangered?"

"I shall make sure you are not in any position to be endangered. Just be the woman I love, Tillie, that's all." He grinned. "For a start, you can tell me how you intend to proceed."

Half disinclined to accept this whole-hearted support, Ottilia was nevertheless instantly diverted to the problem now confronting her. "That must depend upon who is likely to become involved."

"Can you make a stab at a guess? Tell me about the dead man."

She watched him retire to his customary post at the mantel, feeling a little as if the wind had been taken out of her sails. But the question set her off thinking. "I was very little acquainted with Hector Penkevil. He has acquired a wife since my time, according to Ben's account. He was helpful in pointing out those who came to Sophie's obsequies whom I did not know, if you recall."

"It is no use asking me. Strangers, the lot of them, for my part."

"Well, Patrick attends the Penkevil women, Ben said, and most of his patients came in support. There is, if I remember correctly, a Penkevil brother. A clergyman, I think, but I don't believe he was present. But one need not, as we know, necessarily confine oneself to the family of the deceased."

"Your nephews seem to think there may be any number of persons willing to dispose of him. Was he an unpleasant man?"

Really, her spouse was almost too forbearing. Was this real? Despite a niggle of doubt, Ottilia conjured a vague recollection of the man when alive, which differed somewhat from the condition of the corpse. "As I recall, he smiled little. He was not ill-looking. Handsome perhaps if he had not tended to sport a sour expression. At least, I do not ever remember to have seen him otherwise than looking as if he suppressed an ill temper."

Francis let out a groaning sigh, reminiscent of his attitude during earlier incidents. "This promises to produce a plethora of suspects."

"I fear so, if Ben's reading of Penkevil's standing in the neighbourhood is to be believed."

At which moment, before she could again worry at her husband's unexpected acquiescence, her nephew himself walked in. "Your coffee is on its way, Auntilla. Tyler will bring it, he said."

Ottilia was about to answer when Francis hailed the lad instead. "In good time, Ben. Your aunt is desirous of hearing all you know of this Penkevil's family and associates."

Nothing loath, Ben moved to join him at the mantel. "I've got it all at my fingertips, Uncle Fan." Stripling he might be, Ottilia reflected in passing, but already he almost matched Francis in height. "At least half of them are Papa's patients and I've been a-visiting with him often and often so I'm pretty well up on who is who."

Ottilia did not immediately put him to the trouble of reciting names. "You accompany Patrick? What of Mr Wickenby? I thought he was apprenticed to my brother."

Ben waved away his father's medical assistant with an airy hand. "Oh well, of course John goes along when I'm at school. But he's got his own patients now too. He won't take over Papa's practice because that's for me to do."

"Later on, Ben," said Ottilia, distracted from the main point. "Surely Patrick intends for you to spend some time at one of the London hospitals, does he not?"

"Not for a year or two yet, Auntilla. I've still much to learn of him. But John will set up on his own when I am ready to become Papa's partner. One doctor can't service the whole district, you know."

Francis cut in before Ottilia could enquire further into her nephew's prospects. "Can we leave off discussing your medical future, Ben, and concentrate upon the present problem?"

"Auntilla asked me!"

Ottilia gave her spouse a rueful smile. "You are very right, Fan. We'll talk of it another time, Ben." She felt strangely unreal, as if she participated in a scene in a play. She hoped the sensation would not persist and summoned her attention back. "Tell me about Mr Penkevil's family. Is his brother not in the clergy?"

"You mean Reverend Penkevil. Alexander Penkevil, that is. He has the vicarage at Ebbesborn." Ben became eager. "I should think he'd be only too happy to kill off Hector. They are forever at outs."

"Would Alexander inherit the estate?"

"Not unless he takes off Hector's son as well. Mind you, he's only a boy."

"How old?"

"Five or six, I should think, as he's breeched now. There's a girl too, but younger."

Ottilia's sympathies were at once stirred. "Oh, dear, poor children."

Ben snorted. "Lucky children more like. Tom's seen him several times thrash the little fellow soundly and he don't care who's watching. And for nothing, Tom says. All he did one time was break a toy and he didn't mean it. I should think he'd be glad to be rid of such a papa."

Ottilia, though she heartily disapproved of abusive punishments upon children, felt it politic to rein Ben in. "You cannot know how the child feels about his father, Ben. One should never jump to conclusions."

"Well, but —"

"What we can deduce, however, is that there will be some sort of trustee. If that turns out to be the reverend Alexander, I fear we cannot rule him out."

"Ah, you mean I dare say, my love, that he might still look forward to several years of benefitting from his brother's estate."

"Just so, Fan." He was truly taking this at his word and Ottilia was beset with an unsettling thought that she had disappointed him.

Ben was staring at his uncle. "How could he do so? Wouldn't he be bound by the law?"

"To a degree. An unscrupulous man with control over the finances of an estate could readily take advantage to his own betterment."

Ben brightened. "Then Alexander Penkevil must be the main suspect, sir."

Ottilia dissolved into laughter. "Premature, Ben. We have as yet no notion who else might be considered. Didn't you talk of Farmer Gubb at the outset, for instance? Or was that Tom?"

"Not to mention all these other people whom you claimed disliked the man," put in Francis. "*Everyone* seems pretty comprehensive."

An interruption came in the person of the Fanshawe's footman, burdened with a tray upon which were the makings of Ottilia's favourite beverage. She was relieved at the prospect of a normality to which she might cling.

"Your coffee, my lady." Tyler looked to Francis as he set the tray down on the side table. "I ventured to bring Doctor Hathaway's Madeira, my lord, as Master Ben suggested."

"I thought you'd be glad of it, Uncle Fan, after being out in the cold."

Francis thanked him and moved to pour himself a glass, what time the footman prepared a cup of coffee to Ottilia's taste, larded with cream and sugar. She accepted it with a word of thanks and sipped at the welcome brew. The interlude had the effect of dissipating the fogginess that had beset her. Once the footman had retired, she felt herself to be a trifle more natural as she returned to the subject of the murder.

"Tell me about Hector Penkevil's wife, Ben, as I cannot have met her."

Her nephew, having lost the argument with Francis in a spirited attempt to be permitted to partake of the Madeira — "Not without your papa's permission, Ben!" — gave in with reluctance and turned to respond.

"She's called Ruth and she don't like him either. By all accounts she's afraid of Hector."

"Who says so?"

"Everyone, Auntilla."

"Specifically, Ben."

He chewed his lip. "Well, it's her mother who set it about. Papa tends Mrs Poyle and she's forever complaining about it."

"Who is Mrs Poyle?"

"Margery Poyle she's called. It's Ruth Penkevil's mother, as I said. She don't like Hector either, for all she lives in his house."

Ottilia had no chance to enquire more particularly into the nature of Mrs Poyle's dislike because her brother entered the room at this moment.

"I've sent the notes with Ford," said Patrick. "However, I think I'd best go myself to Aston Park to break the news to Mrs Penkevil."

"If your groom has gone off, I can send Ryde and Williams to relieve young Tom and that other fellow," offered Francis.

"That's good of you, Fan."

"Not at all. Ryde has experience of these things and will keep all safe until the authorities can get there."

"I've asked Marden to arrange for undertakers to collect the body and bring it to my outhouse. They can remove it from the woods once he's seen it for himself. I doubt Sir Hugh will come out. He will rely on the accounts given by Marden and myself, I suspect."

"Ah, that's what Ottilia supposed. Then if Ben will kindly show them the way, I'll get my servants on to it immediately."

Francis left the room on the words, followed at once by Ben upon his father's command. Patrick turned to Ottilia with a rueful look.

"I dare say I am interrupting your preliminary foray, my dear sister. Were you pumping Ben?"

"Horrid brother of mine you are, how dare you?" But Ottilia was laughing, beginning to find the old enthusiasm burgeoning in her breast. "I was, of course."

His mouth creased in a smile. "I know you rather too well, Ottilia. You ought to be resting in any event."

"Yes, Doctor. As you command, Doctor."

"Obstinate female. I cannot imagine how Fan bears with you."

"He is a saint." Which, at this juncture, she was inclined to believe was indeed the case. Her brother, evidently not of the same opinion, snorted his amusement. She let it pass. "Have no fear, Patrick. I shall rest indeed and ruminate while I enjoy my coffee."

He left her with a word of farewell and for a short while Ottilia did indeed relax into the cushions as she savoured the taste of her coffee. With leisure at last to think over her husband's extraordinary encouragement, she found that her recalcitrant mind chose instead to return to the matter of the mangled attempt to conceal a murder by a show of suicide. Reflecting that, do what she might, her personality as Lady Fan would not be suppressed, her thoughts began to centre upon potential suspects. Or perhaps those who might be better acquainted with the persons surrounding the victim. Roving across her various acquaintance in the district, the name of one of her closest friends popped into her head and she straightened in the chair.

"Esther! The very woman I need. If there is anything untoward about these people, she will undoubtedly know of it."

CHAPTER FOUR

Mrs Esther Winning, a matron some dozen years Ottilia's senior, had been nevertheless one of her closest friends and allies. A comely woman, possessed of several children, now widely scattered, and a lawyer husband of whom she was inordinately fond, she resided in a pleasant house situated on the outskirts of Kington's Ash. The day being cold but free of any sign of snow, Ottilia, suitably cloaked, was thus able to walk there upon the following morning, with Tyler as escort, without fear of tiring herself unduly.

Francis had elected, at Patrick's invitation, to watch his more detailed examination of the corpse, a decision which seemed to Ottilia to cement his insistence on her going ahead to scout out the villain of the piece. The remains of Hector Penkevil were now resident upon the slab in the makeshift mortuary Patrick had some years past caused to be fashioned out of an outhouse.

"I can't keep doing post-mortems in the examining room," he had declared. "Too messy. If Marden will keep commandeering my services, I must have a more suitable location."

In truth, as Ottilia knew, such requests formed a generous source of income for the Hathaway practice, besides being useful training for Patrick's assistant. And now Ben, too, it would appear.

Having no desire in her present condition to see a cadaver cut up, Ottilia chose instead to begin upon her enquiries. She had long ceased being sick on a regular basis, but her stomach was still prone to be delicate.

Esther Winning was no fashion plate, but she had gravitated to the current mode for high-waisted gowns and was wearing a modest ensemble of blue kerseymere with sleeves to the wrist, augmented by a Paisley shawl and a pretty cap half concealing dark locks streaked with grey. She greeted her visitor with acclaim.

"My dear Ottilia, I have been hoping for one of our cosy chats, but I hardly dared suppose you might be at leisure. Did you not say at poor Sophie's funeral feast that you must hurry home to your little ones?"

Ottilia had taken the hands held out to her and now leaned in to kiss the elder lady's cheek. "I did, but circumstance has intervened, I fear."

Her friend's intelligent gaze raked her. "Oho! You are on the hunt, are you?"

"I might have known you would find me out directly."

Esther joined in her laughter, but made haste to usher her into a chair close to a cheerful fire. "Sit down and be comfortable. Did you walk here? If you had only sent to me, I would have come to you. I am astonished your husband permits you to jaunter about in that state. How far gone are you? Nigh on seven months, I should guess, or more perhaps."

Startled, Ottilia eyed her hostess as that lady re-settled into the seat from which she had jumped up when her guest was announced. "Heavens, Esther, no! It cannot be more than six. I admit my maid and I had some difficulty working out the time at the outset, but…" She faded out.

"I beg your pardon, my dear. I did not mean to alarm you. I must be mistaken."

"Unless we have gauged it wrong."

Esther tutted. "Don't look so distressed, Ottilia. If it troubles you, I am sure your brother may set you straight. He is an excellent physician. How is he faring, by the by?"

Ottilia's thoughts were drawn from her pregnancy to her brother's state of unnatural calm. "Surprisingly well, as it happens."

"Ah, indeed? Well, that is — er — good news."

A riffle of puzzlement ran through Ottilia as her hostess glanced away, almost as if Esther did not wish to meet her gaze. Something flitted across her memory but it vanished before she could catch it as the matron turned back with a smile.

"I have relied upon Doctor Hathaway's skill any time these many years. As you well know, he saw me through that dreadful fever and I cannot even count the occasions upon which I have called him in for one or other of the children."

Ottilia banished the little niggles at the periphery of her mind and focused on her hostess. "No longer, I trust. Did you not see off the last of them a year ago?"

"Oh, indeed. They have all flown the nest at last." She gave Ottilia a quizzical look. "But you did not come here to discuss my brood. Is it the Penkevil affair?"

"Just so, Esther. Although I had not expected the news to travel quite as fast."

Esther all but snorted. "You know what these villages are, my dear. Hector Penkevil is an important man in these parts. His taking off in such a fashion is bound to cause an immediate stir. Was it suicide?"

"I strongly doubt it." Knowing her friend was entirely to be trusted, Ottilia did not hesitate to relate the circumstances which had led to a very different conclusion. "What Sir Hugh will make of it is another matter, however."

Esther threw her an amused look. "You know very well Sir Hugh will take your part. If I have heard him boast of your prowess once, I have heard it a dozen times. Anyone would suppose he had trained you!"

Astonished, Ottilia eyed her. "You cannot mean he has heard of my involvement in these sorts of events?"

"Everyone has, my dear. Your fame runs before you."

"Even here?"

"Especially here. We may claim you for a former resident, you know, and boast of our acquaintance with the notorious Lady Fan."

Ottilia broke into rueful laughter, sparing a flick of gratitude for her spouse's encouragement. "An appropriate word, Esther. Fie on you for a teasing wretch!"

Esther joined in her amusement. "Well, I exaggerate perhaps, but word of some of your exploits has reached our quiet backwater. Suffice to say, Sir Hugh will be only too delighted to accommodate you."

"Then I trust he may prove more useful than I anticipate. But at this present, I am happy enough to pick your brains, if you are willing."

"Pick away, my dear. What is it you wish —?" Esther broke off as the door opened, revealing a middle-aged woman armed with a tray whom Ottilia recognised for her hostess's housekeeper. "Ah, here is Sally with our coffee." She cast one of her knowing glances at Ottilia. "You see, I have not forgotten."

"You are an angel, Esther. My husband calls me an addict."

The housekeeper was busily setting the contents of the tray upon a round table situated close to her mistress's chair. "There's fresh-made jumbles and macaroons too, ma'am, as I hope her ladyship may like."

Ottilia instantly acknowledged this. "I shall indeed. I well remember your delicious baked goods, Sally, thank you."

Sally disclaimed and set about providing both guest and hostess with cups of coffee and a small platter for the sweetmeats. As soon as she withdrew, Esther requested Ottilia to ask her anything she needed to know.

"What I am chiefly after, Esther, is anything you can tell me about the members of Hector Penkevil's family. I have gathered a little about his wife and mother-in-law from Ben, but I would be grateful to know just how those relationships stand. The clergyman brother too, if there is anything there."

Esther took a thoughtful sip of her beverage before answering. "I am not well acquainted with Ruth. She is years younger than I and we have not come very much in each other's way. If you scrape acquaintance with Nancy Meerbrook, however, I believe they are bosom bows."

A vague recollection surfaced. "Spinsterish female? Thin and somewhat vapid? Has she not yet found herself a husband?"

"Sadly no, poor thing. She is quite desperate and inclined to set her cap at any remotely eligible male to appear in the vicinity. One cannot blame her. She lives alone but for one maid and her income must be inadequate, judging by her appearance."

Her sympathies caught, Ottilia nevertheless pursued her purpose. "But you feel she may be of use to me?"

"If, as I suppose, Ruth has confided in her. The poor woman cannot entrust her secrets to her mother. Margery Poyle is a blabbermouth."

"Such women can be valuable when one is digging into the whys and wherefores of a killing."

"Not that woman, my dear Ottilia. One cannot believe the half of what she says. If her perceived wrongs bear any relation to the truth, you would be obliged to write off Hector Penkevil as the cruellest creature alive."

Ottilia's ears pricked up. "Indeed? In what sense?"

"Oh, in every way. He is known to be parsimonious to a fault, that is well established. According to Margery Poyle, however, he adds to this a vicious temper and a vengeful heart. He loses no opportunity, she claims, to insult and belittle her because of her inferior station."

Unkind, and gave some credence to the dissent existing between Margery and her son-in-law. But there were other options to consider.

Ottilia changed tack. "What of the brother?"

Esther brightened. "Now there you have a distinct possibility. By all accounts, the very reverend Alexander Penkevil positively loathes his brother. One cannot be much surprised. Hector never hesitates to demonstrate his contempt for Alexander, saying how ill-suited he is for the cloth and bemoaning the fact their father managed to secure for him the rectory of Ebbesborn."

"While Alexander in his turn covets the elder son's inheritance, I take it?"

Esther pursed her lips. "Envies perhaps. He could gain nothing from Hector's death. There is a son, you must know."

"So I gather." Ottilia remained unconvinced of Alexander gaining nothing but she kept the thought to herself. "You said he loathed Hector. Did he say as much?"

"Oh, it is obvious. He uses his sermons to needle his brother, choosing texts wherein he might make pointed observations against Hector's ill temper and unkind rulings in his magisterial role."

"Was he unfair?"

"His victims thought so. I am bound to admit he lost no opportunity to administer such penalties as were open to him. Sir Hugh has even been known to step in when Hector went too far upon occasion. Mercy was not among his qualities."

"He sounds to have been a most unpleasant man, this Hector."

"Oh, he is. Or was, I should say now. A number of people will bid him good riddance, I imagine."

Ottilia pounced on this. "Such as, Esther?"

"There speaks Lady Fan." Her hostess trilled with laughter, but refreshed herself with a gulp of coffee and the last of her macaroon before giving her answer. "You will be looking, I dare say, for those who might bear a grudge."

"Are there many?"

"Offhand I can think of two, but I should doubt of their being alone."

"It is a start, Esther. That is all I need."

Esther set down her cup. "Then I suggest you visit Brigadier O'Turk and Lady Carrefour. Though I doubt of the latter having murderous thoughts. But Brig, despite his age, is more than capable of despatching a man like Hector Penkevil."

CHAPTER FIVE

"Remind me not to make an audience of myself at another autopsy," said Francis on a distinctly acid note.

He was indeed looking a trifle pale but Ottilia could not resist the temptation to tease. "Was it not entertaining, my dearest dear? I had supposed your stomach to be stronger."

"Be quiet, you wretch!" He slid into a chair. "If you must have it, once Patrick had examined the naked corpse from head to toe, I supposed he would be satisfied."

Ottilia had once again settled into the comfy chair in the parlour and was in the act of raising her feet to rest upon the footstool, but she looked up at that. "He opened Hector up?"

Francis grunted. "Patrick insisted he must check the contents of the stomach. I've seen vile wounds on the living and the dead, but I don't recall anything quite as revolting."

Ottilia hid a smile, feeling her amusement at this juncture would not be taken well. She was still a trifle wary of appearing to be too deeply embedded in this fresh adventure. For all his generous dispensation, she did not fully trust that Francis would not succumb to feeling disgruntled in the way he so often did when she was involved in these things. Already the post-mortem had put him out. Yet her desire to know would not be denied. "Did Patrick find anything?"

"In the stomach? Nothing untoward, he says."

"Not poison then."

"He seems convinced the slaying was accomplished externally."

Triumph lit in Ottilia. "Hector was strangled then?"

"Patrick said he is forced to agree the throat was somewhat mangled, but not enough, he thinks, to state positively that strangling killed him."

Forgetting caution, Ottilia clicked her tongue. "He is not still supposing the death was caused by hanging, is he?" She regretted her impatience at once, but thankfully her spouse did not seem to be troubled by it.

"A combination of the two, hastened perhaps by exposure to the elements. Since he cannot positively identify the time of death, he is ambivalent about the actual cause."

"He really does not wish to believe it is murder, does he?"

"As to that, the business about the rope and the lack of anything to stand on he finds more convincing."

Ottilia could not resist. "Gratifying for you, my dearest. My brother is far more inclined to take your word than mine."

Her spouse accorded the sally a flicker of a smile. "There is a new aspect that may well support your theory. Patrick thinks Penkevil may have been unconscious throughout."

Ottilia leapt on this. "Aha! No signs of a struggle then, I surmise."

"Precisely. The fingernails were intact and there were no telltale skin scales under them. No defensive wounds, Patrick says."

"No wonder he opened the stomach then. He must have been looking for the means by which Hector was drugged."

To her astonishment, and indeed gratification, Francis became suddenly eager. "Could he have been drunk? Patrick said he smelled stale alcohol in the mouth." A grimace crossed her spouse's face. "At that point I had reason to be relieved I am not a medical man."

Ottilia's mind was working. "If he drank on top of taking a drug, he most certainly could not have been conscious, which rather rules out suicide, don't you think?"

"I think that is already established."

"Then we are looking for a person strong enough to pull up an unconscious or dead body to look as if he had been hung. Most likely a man, although a woman could have administered the drug."

"But there wasn't anything in the stomach."

"The traces could well have dissipated. There are several substances that might be used to induce a comatose state. I expect Patrick will feed a sample of the stomach contents to a frog."

"Unfortunate frog."

She had to laugh. "True, but at least it is not poison. It should only suffer a period of unnatural sleep."

"Which would confirm a drug rather than alcohol?"

"Just so, Fan."

At this moment, Tom bounced into the parlour, his announcement coming pat upon the discussion. "The frog is dead to the world and Papa is fuming!"

A questioning glance from her spouse urged Ottilia into speech. "Poor Patrick. He does not need a murder on his hands as well as … everything else."

Tom failed to pick up on her hesitation, his eyes a-sparkle as he came up to her chair. "But it's not on Papa's hands, Auntilla. It's on yours. Besides, it's tremendously exciting. We've not had a murder in these parts before. I'll wager I know who did it too."

Before Ottilia could refute this assertion, for how in the world could her nephews know, Francis intervened. "Who, then, if you know so much?"

Nothing loath, Tom crossed to his chair as he spoke. "At first, I was sure it must be his brother — Reverend Alexander, he is — because he's almost as horrid as the dead man. But it couldn't be him."

"Why not?"

"Because, Uncle Fan, he was away. Willy told me."

That made Ottilia cut in. "How does Willy Heath know that, Tom?"

"He likes to stand at the milestone on the Salisbury road and count who goes by. Willy can remember exactly who came and went, and when too. He says Reverend Penkevil drove to Salisbury the day before yesterday and didn't come back, so he wasn't at home the night of the murder."

An impatient expletive came from Francis. "One can't take that for gospel, Tom. This Willy cannot possibly have remained at his post at the roadside all the day and into the night."

"Well, he's often there for ages. Besides, John lives at Ebbesborn and he hadn't seen the reverend about that day either."

"Who is John?"

Ottilia took this. "Patrick's assistant, Fan. John Wickenby."

"All very well, but this John not seeing Reverend Penkevil is hardly conclusive."

"Ah, but you see, Uncle Fan, there's another reverend who is a much better prospect."

Ottilia was obliged to conceal a smile at her nephew's eagerness. "But do we need another reverend, Tom? Surely this is not another Penkevil relation?"

He moved back to her chair. "No, but I'll wager we do need him, Auntilla. It's the Reverend Bruno Pidsea and the graveyard of his church at St Leonard's abuts the woods.

Nothing easier than for him to drag Hector to the place where we found him and haul him up to look like a suicide."

"Yes, but why?" Francis struck in. "Has he a grudge against Penkevil?"

"Everyone has one, Uncle Fan. We keep telling you. He was horrid and nobody liked him."

Ottilia intervened, a little concerned that her nephew's enthusiasm might alienate her husband, although she had to admit Francis appeared to be wholly accepting of the affair. "That may be so, Tom, but it does not therefore follow that any of these would murder him. It takes a strong motivation to proceed to the extreme of killing someone. We do not live in a lawless country."

Tom looked decidedly disgruntled, but he was evidently not yet ready to relinquish his conviction. "I'll wager Hector did something evil to Pidsea. After all, he prosecuted the Hexworthies and he's always fining Farmer Gubb. Ben thinks it must be old Brig who did it because of his long-running feud with Hector. But what about Roland Huish?"

Several of this battery of names were known to Ottilia, but not the last. "Who is Roland Huish?"

"And why should he murder Hector?" added Francis on a dry note.

Tom's smile was triumphant. "'Cause he's got a huge *tendre* on Hector's wife and he claims Hector beat him to a pulp because of it. He limps now and the word is he even sued Hector."

Ottilia slipped this titbit into her memory even as her spouse gave forth a bark of laughter.

"According to Tom, my dear one, you now have a multitude of suspects. I hope you can keep them straight in your head because I am perfectly bewildered."

So too, if she was truthful, was Ottilia. Relieved Francis was taking this so well, she ticked off the names in her mind. Brigadier O'Turk was already on her list, alerted as she had been by her friend Esther Winning. Likewise, Esther's words made her chary of ruling out the Reverend Alexander Penkevil. His comings and goings might not necessarily be witnessed, especially since the murder had been carried out at night. Now it seemed she must add this Roland Huish to the mix, let alone the Reverend Bruno Pidsea, unlikely as his involvement was. Moreover, there were the wife and mother-in-law to be tackled in addition to Lady Carrefour. It began to seem an impossible task to unravel the culprit. She interrupted Tom's reiteration of his suppositions by which means he presumably hoped to convince Francis.

"Let us not jump to conclusions, Tom. We must proceed step by step."

Tom had broken off, but started up again at once. "Give me a step to do, Auntilla! I promise I won't jump to anything if you do."

She was doubtful of his ability to assist in any material fashion, but she could not deflate his enthusiasm by saying so. "Let me ponder on it, Tom. I am sure there will be an avenue for you to explore for me."

"Ben too. He wants to help."

No sooner were the words out of his mouth than her older nephew made an appearance, accompanied by Patrick, who looked both annoyed and defeated. He spoke as he entered. "You will no doubt be delighted to hear that your theory has at least partially proven out, my dear sister. The wretched man was indeed strangled as well as hung. Drugged beforehand, moreover."

Ignoring the sarcastic note, Ottilia gave him a deprecating smile. "So Tom has been telling us. I wish it had not fallen to your lot, but I hope we may be able to unravel it all."

"You had better," Patrick said, turning grim. "Half the suspects are bound to turn out to be my patients. I dread being called out by anyone at this juncture. I shall likely send John in my stead if I know them for a garrulous gossip."

Ottilia opened her mouth to offer a soothing response but her husband was before her.

"Garrulous gossips are what Tillie particularly prefers, Patrick. She finds them inordinately useful because they can't help but let out a deal of information."

Patrick snorted. "She's welcome to them. You'd best talk to Nancy Meerbrook and Margery Poyle, Ottilia. Neither of them can shut their mouths long enough for me to do the necessary examination. Not that either truly needs me. Hypochondriacs, both of them, with nothing more interesting to do than to invent ailments."

Ottilia's teasing nature got the better of her. "From all Esther told me, I imagine this Nancy will be the more eager for your ministrations now, my dear brother. You are, after all, a widower."

Too late she realised her error as Patrick's complexion flew colour.

Francis cut in fast. "Ottilia, that was uncalled for."

But it was the stricken faces of her two nephews rather than her husband's reprimand that pricked her conscience. She pushed up from the chair and went at once to her brother. "Fan is right, Patrick. An ill-timed jest. Forgive me, pray."

He grimaced, but took her proffered hand. "You always did pick the wrong moment, Ottilia." But, avoiding the bump, he drew her into a brief hug and then released her, smiling a little.

"I ought to be used to your ways, but we've been so long apart now, I had forgot."

"I do wish we had met more often. Never mind. This passage will make up for it." Ottilia gave him a quizzical look. "You will not be rid of us as speedily as you might have hoped now."

He sighed. "I trust you may not be too long about solving this mess. At least Sir Hugh writes that he is eager enough for your intervention."

"Is he so? How gratifying. May I visit any whom I wish to question?"

"I dare say you can take that as read."

A thought struck Ottilia. "By the by, Patrick, have you any notion what drug it was? Could you tell?"

Patrick's professional look came over his features. "Not opium, since it would have entirely dissipated. I can't be absolutely sure, but since it rendered Hector comatose, I suspect it was valerian."

"Then, for the sake of simplicity, let us go with that. We have time to plan our campaign today and begin tomorrow."

"The sooner the better." Her brother frowned. "You can't do much in one day, can you? People won't appreciate your badgering them on the Sabbath."

"Well, we have the whole of Saturday ahead of us. We may accomplish a great deal if we divide the work. Fan, I hope, will take his turn with some of these potential witnesses. He is invaluable and I rely upon him absolutely."

A snort from her spouse took Patrick's gaze to him. "She has roped you in, has she? I cannot say I envy you."

"I have not roped him in, Patrick. He is a willing participant." She threw Francis a look both hopeful and deprecating. "Are you not, my dearest?"

"Don't forget us, Auntilla," chimed in Tom before Francis could answer. "We'll do anything you ask, won't we, Ben? If you don't want to, Uncle Fan, you needn't."

Her husband quirked an eyebrow. "I'll hold you to that if occasion arises. However, I am a most accommodating husband, you must know, and will perform my part for fear of your aunt's nagging."

"Fie, Fan! I never nag. After all, you did bid me proceed."

At that, he gave a rueful smile. "I did and I can therefore scarcely refuse to assist."

"Well, you can nag us as much as you like, Auntilla. Can't she, Ben?"

His elder entered the lists at last. "Do shut it, Tom. For my part, I should think Uncle Fan is far more qualified to help than either of us." Yet he turned his blue gaze on Ottilia, the sparkle back. "But if you think there is anything we could usefully do to help, Auntilla…"

"I don't doubt there will be, Ben. In fact, it occurs to me that you must know this Farmer Gubb well. If I guide you in what to ask, perhaps you might question him for me?"

Both nephews assented with eager voices and when Patrick had departed, saying he must write up his autopsy report, Ottilia spent a somewhat trying hour or so attempting to instil a few useful tips into the heads of her two nephews. The interruptions made it tricky and when they went off at last to write up a list of her instructions ready for the morrow, she declared to Francis that she was astonished not to have a headache.

"More coffee is what you need, my dear one." He glanced at the case clock on the mantel. "And I am in need of sustenance before you decide where you wish to despatch me likewise."

"Betty will make you a sandwich, Fan. I could do with a snack myself."

"We'll give order for it when someone appears." He moved to the bell-pull and tugged. "What would you wish me to do by way of assisting you, Tillie?"

Her heart leapt and her eyes pricked. This despite his wish to eat first. She gave him a somewhat tremulous smile. "Are you sure, my dearest dear? I have no wish to plague you. I know deep down you feel it to be the horridest inconvenience."

He came across, brought a chair forward and sat down, taking her hand in his. "I cannot subscribe to the same drive you possess, my darling, but I stand by my decision." His lip twitched. "Shall I confess to being somewhat intrigued?"

The urge to weep receded as amusement crept into Ottilia's breast. "You had better perhaps. I had noticed."

"When did you not? I can't hide anything from you, witch of a wife."

"I hope you won't wish to, Fan." She hesitated, meeting the dark gaze as the question she longed to ask surfaced. "We are better together now, are we not?"

There was warmth in his smile. "Much better. Only promise me you will be careful of your health. That is my son or daughter you are carrying." He leaned in and kissed her and Ottilia's doubts faded as she gave the required promise. "Now, to return to the res, have you anything you particularly choose to parcel out to me?"

Ottilia pondered, but it did not take her long. "Perhaps you might follow up with the Hexworthy couple of whom Tom speaks. They run the White Horse at Norrington. But first, I would be grateful if tomorrow, you could at least tackle Brigadier O'Turk."

"Then you'd best tell me all about him while we eat. What about you?"

Ottilia gave him her impish smile. "Who else but the garrulous gossips?"

CHAPTER SIX

"Telling me that abominable feller is dead, are ye? Glad to hear it. Man's a presumptuous jackanapes, nothing but arrogance and bluster. Can't abide him."

Brigadier O'Turk, despite his great age, had still the soldierly bearing familiar to Francis from his army days. By good fortune the two men had met on horseback as Francis, on a hired nag, was riding down the lane to which he'd been directed in search of the brigadier's home turf.

"You'll find Brig's estate just short of Tolland Royal here," Patrick had told him, sketching a map as he spoke. "To the north of that is Penkevil's land. Their estates border right along this line, according to Hector. Brig holds that the boundary falls short and he is entitled to several more acres."

Francis studied the makeshift map. "They've gone to law?"

"Several times. Brig sued old Penkevil who imbued his son with a like obstinacy. Neither will give way, with the result the disputed land remains uncultivated and benefits neither."

Armed with this information, Francis was less surprised than he might have been to find the brigadier patrolling the edge of his property. It was easy enough to recognise that the greybeard sturdily upright in the saddle must be his quarry. When Francis accosted him, he was met with a fierce gaze that reminded him strongly of his former commander. Brigadier O'Turk might be ancient, his grey locks confined behind as Francis's own had so recently been and tied in a pigtail queue, but his old bones still carried him well and his mind was yet keen.

"Who are ye? What d'ye want?"

The introductions disposed of, Francis explained his purpose and discovered that the news of Hector's untimely demise had not before reached the brigadier's ears.

"The difficulty is, sir," he pursued after the old soldier had delivered himself of his condemnation, "that Mr Penkevil's death is far from natural."

Brigadier O'Turk blew out a contemptuous breath. "Not in my dotage, young feller, of course it's unnatural. Too young for it to be anything else. What did he die of? Spleen, I shouldn't wonder. Bad-tempered enough. Apoplexy, was it?"

Francis smothered a laugh to think how sublimely unconscious the brigadier was of irony in his criticism of the other man's temperament. "It's worse than that, sir. He was murdered."

A sudden movement of the brigadier's hands set his horse in motion, hooves shifting on the turf and a restless tossing of the head.

"Whoa there, boy, whoa! No need to take a pet." In a moment, the old man had regained control of his mount and his gaze returned to Francis, his white brows drawn together. "Murdered, you say?" His head reared up on a sudden, much in the fashion of his horse before him. "Why've ye come to me? Think I shot him, do ye?"

Francis bypassed the question. "He was not shot, sir. He was strangled and then strung up on a branch in the woods."

"Ha! Make it look like he did away with himself, eh?" A snort escaped him. "Not my style, I'd have ye know. Kill a man fair and square, if ye kill him at all."

A point of view Francis could appreciate. He was much inclined to accept the old man's word there and then, but he was mindful of his wife's methods. Tillie never took a judgement at face value. She would expect him to question any such assertion. Besides, she wanted to know more of the feud and he had promised to elicit what detail he could. Having given her carte blanche to do whatever she must to untangle the mess, he was determined to back her to the hilt. Her hesitant question as to the state of their relationship had cost him a pang. He had not before fully realised how his past recalcitrance had hurt his darling wife. He could not again give her cause to be reticent with him.

"I believe you, sir," he said. "However, I wonder if you would object to answering a few questions."

"About?"

Despite the belligerent tone, Francis took the plunge. "Your dispute with Hector Penkevil over land, sir."

"Upon what authority do ye ask?"

"Sir Hugh Riccarton's authority." Better at this juncture to leave Tillie out of it. He could not suppose a man of the brigadier's stamp would relish enquiry from a woman, no matter her reputation as Lady Fan. His wife had warned as much.

"He will remember me as a slip of a girl, Fan, if he recalls me at all. I had only recently attained my majority when I came here to live with Patrick and his family."

He therefore said no more and endured Brigadier O'Turk's piercing gaze on his for several moments of silent rumination.

At last the old man gave a nod. "Better come to the house." An odd grin twisted his lips. "Keep a good cellar. Ye can sample my claret." With which, he wheeled his mount and cantered off down the lane.

Francis urged his horse after him, wishing he'd been able to ride one of his own good horses instead. But Patrick Hathaway kept only a pair of horses and he needed his phaeton. Since the stables had only space for two more horses, the team that pulled the Fanshawe's coach had to be accommodated at the Stag, the only hostelry in Kington's Ash, exchanging instead this slug of a stallion Francis was keeping for his own use at Ash Lodge. Tillie having commandeered the coach for her enquiries, he'd had no choice but to ride. As well, since his coachman, Williams would have deplored the state of the narrow lane they were traversing, rain in the night having rendered the ground soggy.

A large building presently came into view, its proportions rather long and low than imposing. It looked to be old-fashioned in the style of at least a century ago, if not more. This impression was borne out after Francis, dismounting alongside his host, and handing his reins to a stable lad who came running up at sight of his master's horse, entered through a heavy old oak door into a dark panelled hallway. He followed the brigadier along a corridor and into a library, surprisingly bright despite the dark wood shelving that lined the walls. For this, two large leaded casement windows were responsible, letting in the sun from a south-facing garden.

The brigadier had shouted commands to unseen servants as he stomped through and within moments of settling into one of the two leathern chairs in front of a blazing fire, a footman entered. The tray he presented to the brigadier bore a decanter and two glasses. A testy command was thrown at the man. "Pour it, pour it! Give my guest a glass."

The footman set the tray down upon a convenient table and Francis was supplied with a glass of one of the finest clarets he had ever tasted.

"Your cellar is indeed of good quality, sir, if I go by this."

Brigadier O'Turk waved the compliment away. "No sense drinking at all if ye don't drink a smooth wine. Never waste my palate on rough liquor." He swigged from his own glass and settled himself more comfortably, stretching out his legs and crossing one ankle over the other. "Get to it, man. What d'ye want to know?"

Francis took a breath, not relishing the old man's probable reaction. "Your quarrel with Penkevil is of long-standing, I gather."

"Well? Well? What of that?"

"Has there perhaps been a worsening of relations between you of late?"

Brigadier O'Turk snorted. "How worse? Told you. Man's a serpent. Slithers behind your back and bites your ankle when you ain't looking."

"Has he bitten your ankle recently, sir?"

The brigadier appeared to ruminate, nursing his glass as he gazed into the deep red liquid. At length he looked up. "Trying to make out he drove me to the limit, are ye? Catch cold at that. Lost my temper with him times out of mind. Very sight of the feller makes me boil."

All very fine but it did not move them further forward. Francis tried plain dealing. "What happened, sir?"

The white head reared, the eyes again fiery. "Challenged him, didn't I? Told him we'd settle it once and for all."

Startled, Francis let out a laugh. "You met him?"

The other blew a contemptuous breath. "Tchah! Refused me, lily-livered poltroon. Made out it would break the rules of honour if he met a man my age, but I know better."

"At the risk of drawing your fire, sir, I must say that he is right."

His host became testy. "Know that, ye lunkhead! D'ye think I haven't been out more times than ye could count? Made no bones about it in my day. But that don't mean Penkevil wasn't hiding behind it for his own convenience. Tried to have me up before him for threatening to breach the peace."

With difficulty, Francis refrained from giving in to the laughter bubbling in his throat. "Did he summon you then?"

"Summoned me and had the brass to fine me in my absence."

"You didn't appear then."

"D'ye take me for a noddy? Of course I didn't appear. Refused to pay the fine into the bargain. Told him to set the constables on me if he dared. Knew he wouldn't. Told him the next time he set foot on my land I'd meet him with my fowling piece."

There was glee in the old man's voice now and he threw Francis a look of triumph before he tossed off the remaining wine in his glass.

In a puzzle how to proceed, Francis said nothing for a moment, sipping his own drink. It did not seem credible that a man of the brigadier's stamp would stoop to the pretence involved in Penkevil's murder. On the other hand, despite his great age, he looked to be strong enough and, by way of character, eminently capable of strangling a man to death. It was clear he had become enraged by Penkevil using his position as magistrate to trump up a spurious charge against him. But had his rage been enough to plot a secretive revenge?

His thoughts led Francis into speech. "If I may hazard a guess, sir, you don't seem the type to have carried out this particular killing. Nevertheless, I am afraid you cannot yet be ruled out."

The old man grunted. "Ye sound like a man of the law."

"I am merely a sceptic, sir. It happens that I have had reason to learn to mistrust what people say in cases of this kind.

Rarely do we meet with true honesty. Most witnesses turn out to be hiding something."

"Ah, a witness, am I? Who do ye mean by *we*?"

The man was sharp. Francis cursed his slip, but opted for truth. "If you must have it, sir, I am referring to my wife." He hesitated as the brigadier frowned. "You may remember her as Mrs Ottilia Grayshott. She is Doctor Hathaway's sister."

Brigadier O'Turk raised his brows. "That's what brings ye, is it? Wife died recently."

"Mrs Hathaway, yes. We came for the funeral."

His host had nothing to say to this. He rose abruptly, went to the table, and picked up the decanter. "Want another?"

"Not for me, I thank you." Francis got up too, feeling there was no more to be gained here. "I will leave you, sir."

Brigadier O'Turk swung round. "Stay where ye are!"

Francis eyed him. "Sir?"

"Sit ye down. Not done yet."

Francis felt his bristles rising. "Unless you have more to add, I see no reason to remain."

Testy again, the brigadier waved him down. "Sit, sit, man! Got something to say."

With reluctance, Francis retook his seat, watching as his host refilled his own glass and brought it with him to his chair, sitting down heavily. His gaze became steely.

"Ye can tell that wife of yours she's stirring up a hornet's nest."

So he did know of Tillie's exploits. Francis could not withstand a grimace. "She knows it. You are not the only one to dislike Penkevil."

"Wheels within wheels. Outlived my natural years I may have, but I ain't in my dotage. Wheels within wheels. You tell her."

Fortune favoured Ottilia's quest. Opting to seek out Mrs Margery Poyle first, she found Nancy Meerbrook visiting the newly made widow. She was shown into a formal drawing-room on the first floor of Aston Park, a somewhat grand title for an establishment not much larger than Flitteris Manor. The room was furnished in the old-fashioned style, sofas with matching straw-coloured cushioned seats placed around the walls, themselves papered in stripes of cream and gold, and adorned with classical paintings.

Neither of the two women in the room were yet in mourning garb. Hardly surprising within three days of the death. Ottilia recognised neither. As it chanced, once the introductions were made, Mrs Ruth Penkevil was found to be absent.

"She is laid down upon her bed, my lady," disclosed her spinster friend in a hushed tone, "and indeed one cannot wonder at it. I have just left her, you must know, for I could not reconcile it with my conscience not to do my utmost to ease her distress. Not that anyone could and who shall blame the poor thing? She has been perfectly distraught. A terrible tragedy!"

She whipped a handkerchief from the sleeve of her round gown of a muslin decidedly unsuitable for the season — although augmented with a black shawl, token to the dead — and dabbed at her eyes, what time Mrs Poyle, a dame as stout as Nancy Meerbrook was lean, burst out in a fury. "Do hold your tongue, Nancy! Tragedy indeed! As if Lady Francis don't already know as Hector was a mean piece and no loss to anyone."

Ottilia had no chance to respond to this blunt remark since Nancy at once took it up.

"How can you, ma'am? When your own dear daughter is prostrate."

"She ain't prostrate with grief, that I can vouch for. Shocked she may be, but if she sheds a single tear for my beast of a son-in-law you may call me a Dutchwoman."

Intrigued by the evidence of the woman's origins in her speech, Ottilia recalled her friend Esther's disclosures. Meeting the woman in person made it clear that the murder victim had married out of his class. If he belittled Mrs Poyle on that account, it explained her apparent and reported belligerence against her son-in-law. Could it also have proven a strong enough reason to release her daughter from a difficult marriage?

Nancy evidently thought it proper to gainsay the matron for Ottilia's benefit. "I beg you will not heed her, my lady. She does not know what she is saying."

"I know quite well what I'm saying, thank you, Nancy."

The spinster ignored the interruption. A creature of a spindlier figure than Ottilia remembered, with a manner both deferent and irritatingly smug, leaned close as she adopted a confiding air. "It is the shock of it that has rendered poor Mrs Poyle quite unlike herself. She is not in general apt to speak in such terms of Mr Penkevil."

Ottilia could not let this pass. "Indeed, ma'am? I had heard otherwise."

"So you might," broke in the matron. "I'm never one to be close-tongued. Nor it ain't no use trying to pretend I thought Hector anything but the greatest beast in nature for I'll wager the whole county knows it."

Ottilia almost laughed. "Since I gather you have been at pains to inform all and sundry of it, I cannot say I am surprised."

A snorting laugh escaped Mrs Poyle. "There's for your pretensions, Nancy." The spinster looked pained but made no comment. "It's a good thing you haven't come to offer condolences, my lady, ain't it?"

"You know why I am here?"

The matron waved towards a sofa placed to catch the warmth of the fire. "You'd best sit down, my lady. Your good brother came here with the news of Hector's taking off. As soon as he told as it were murder, I knew you'd come a-calling. It stands to reason."

"Does it?"

"They call you Lady Fan and tell of you finding out murderers left and right."

Despite the generosity of her husband in fostering the hunt, this reminder of her acquired reputation could not but prick at Ottilia's conscience. She had no answer to the comment, but Mrs Poyle continued without a qualm.

"You was sure to come nosing after Ruth and me, my lady. Nancy too, I shouldn't wonder. If no one else did, Doctor Hathaway would have told you how none for miles around could stick Hector at any price. Half of them might wish him dead, and that includes me."

"Mrs Poyle, how can you?" Nancy again had recourse to her handkerchief as she once more turned to Ottilia. "I can assure you, my lady, I had no reason to wish Mr Penkevil dead, none at all."

"Then you have nothing to fear, Miss Meerbrook," Ottilia soothed. Suppressing the guilt, and determining to pursue her purpose to the full, she produced a smile as she took a seat on the sofa indicated by the matron. "Do join me. You may be surprised to learn that Mrs Poyle is perfectly correct. I had every intention of seeking you out."

The spinster, who had been about to perch beside her, shot back up again. "Me? I cannot think why, my lady. I can have nothing to say of the least use to you."

"Allow me to be the judge of that." She waited, keeping her gaze on the woman until she sat down, her pose prim, hands tightly clasped in her lap. Noting how Nancy's cheeks lacked the bloom of youth, her lips pinched and her bosom non-existent under the bodice of her gown, Ottilia urged her better self to be charitable. The woman might be irksome but the signs of poverty were unmistakeable. The muslin gown was, on closer inspection, a little worn in places with yellowing lace at the flounce. Her thinness bordered on skeletal. Purse-pinched she must be, and likely desperate enough to set her cap at any potential suitor.

Her hurried ruminations were interrupted by Mrs Poyle. "Was you meaning to ask if either of us did away with Hector then?"

Ottilia brought her gaze to bear on the matron. "I was rather wondering what you might be able to tell me about his activities in his role as magistrate. I understand he did not often temper justice with mercy?"

Mrs Poyle snorted. "Forget often. He never did. If he could send some poor devil to the assizes or fine him into the ground, he'd do it. He's even been known to order the lash after confining a lad in the lock-up for days. Willy Heath is one of his victims."

Startled, and at once distressed, Ottilia jumped on this. "Willy? What did he do to him?"

"He beat him, what else? Only because the boy was stood in his path on the lane and made his horse rear. Thrashed Willy on the spot." Mrs Poyle frowned. "I'm surprised the doctor never told you. He had to tend the boy's wounds for that beast drew blood on him he whipped him so hard."

A frisson of dismay ran through Ottilia. Could Willy Heath have taken revenge? He was not much more than a stripling, but he was by no means incapable of the necessary strength. The bungled murder might well signal the work of one who had not all his wits. But would Willy think of drugging his victim first? Unlikely. If he had been responsible, Ottilia could not think it was premeditated.

"Why do you bring that up, Mrs Poyle?" Nancy's voice quavered a little. "Do you mean to accuse everyone?"

"Who's accusing? I'm telling her how Hector was."

"You are making it out that there are people whom her ladyship might suspect. It is unfair of you. Even if someone was not fond of Mr Penkevil, it does not follow they might stoop to such a dreadful act."

The already familiar snort escaped Mrs Poyle. "What, are you afraid I may speak of Alexander? How he hated his brother? Are you troubled for him, Nancy? Or are you really and truly afraid he might have done it?"

Nancy uttered a shriek, her complexion growing pink. "Wicked! How dare you speak so? The reverend would never… He is a man of the cloth!" She turned to Ottilia, so eager as to be almost tearful. "My lady, pray don't heed her! The Reverend Penkevil is a good man, a most God-fearing man. Whatever his feelings, he would never ever do harm to his brother. Mrs Poyle does not like him, but —"

"Who says I don't like him? I've nothing against the man beyond he's prosy and apt to look down his nose at those he considers lesser than himself. But you won't deny he'd give a lot to stand in Hector's shoes."

"What nonsense! How could he when there is little Jason?" Again, Nancy addressed Ottilia. "He is a minor, and you will see how well the reverend will take care of the poor fatherless boy. He has already told dear Ruth that she need not fret for Jason's future."

Ottilia cut in before Mrs Poyle could take up the cudgels again. "The Reverend Penkevil is the boy's trustee, I take it?"

"Oh, yes. He is joined in the task with Mr Hope. He is the Penkevil's lawyer."

"You seem very well informed, Miss Meerbrook?"

The spinster's cheeks again flew colour. "Ruth is my particular friend, you see. She has been used to confide in me."

Ottilia pounced. "She has discussed with you what must happen after her husband's demise?"

A pair of apprehensive eyes gazed at Ottilia. "Why, yes... I mean, yesterday — the reverend was here and ... of course I came the moment I heard for I knew Ruth would need my support."

"You are telling me you discussed these matters only yesterday, Miss Meerbrook," Ottilia pursued, relentless. "When your friend Ruth had been given this terrible news a mere four and twenty hours before? When she has been as distraught as you have described her?"

The spinster's colour drained from her cheeks and then came again as Ottilia kept her gaze fixed upon her. She was aware in the periphery of her vision how Mrs Poyle stared, her mouth at half-cock.

In the silence, a case clock on the mantel ticked away the minutes. At last Ottilia relaxed the tension, smiling a little. "Come, Miss Meerbrook, it is better to be open with me, do you not think? Otherwise, I may imagine much worse than the truth."

The spinster let her breath go in a rush. "Well, it — it is not what you think."

"What do I think?"

"Ruth was not planning anything." It was coming out faster now. "The matter came up quite naturally in conversation. It is not as if she was anticipating her husband's death. I see that as matters have turned out, it looks bad, but it was not meant. You must believe me. No more than the reverend would dear Ruth contemplate such a hideous thing. Why, she would have made her children orphans! She would never dream of harming her little ones. She is the most devoted mother."

"Ha!" Thus Mrs Poyle. "So devoted she leaves them to the nurses while she gallivants off the Lord knows where day after day."

Nancy turned on her. "She only does so to escape your constant complaints. Yes, and to get away from a husband who can think of nothing better to do than to criticise —" She broke off, one hand flying to her mouth as her gaze again popped at Ottilia. "I did not mean that! She is devoted to Hector. *Was* so."

"Balderdash! Ruth was afraid of him, the ninny. I told her she ought to stand up to him, but would she?"

"The way you do, Mrs Poyle?" The spinster was in again. "You know well such conduct only succeeds in making him angry and he takes it out on poor Ruth. Often and often I have heard the reverend complain of your attitude. He says you make bad worse and he is right."

"As if Alexander can talk? If I have heard him quarrelling mightily with Hector once, I've heard it a dozen times." Mrs Poyle's gaze returned to Ottilia. "You see how the wretched man has put everyone at outs? I'm glad he's gone and I don't care who hears me say so." She thrust up her chin, but Ottilia noted how it wobbled. Was she nervous underneath the bluster? "And if that makes you think as I had something to do with sending him to hell, so be it. You can have me up before Sir Hugh Riccarton, but I'll tell you this. I'd get a fairer hearing than ever anyone got from Justice Hector Penkevil. Justice! A less fitting title for that stinker you couldn't invent."

Ottilia had allowed the give and take between the two women to flow freely. What better way to have either make a slip? Nancy had made several apparently untoward remarks that could well incriminate her widowed friend and tried to mitigate the damage. Yet a niggle of doubt crept in. Might these have been deliberate? Best to test the ground.

The spinster was sitting tight-lipped, her disapproving gaze on Mrs Poyle, who looked triumphant after delivering herself of that comprehensive denunciation. One could not entirely trust her either since she had made it obvious that she and her deceased son-in-law had been at outs.

Ottilia went into the attack. "May I take it you are well-acquainted with the Reverend Alexander Penkevil, Miss Meerbrook?"

The spinster's gaze whipped round and a trifle of pink stained her cheek. "Why should I not be?"

"No reason in the world, ma'am. I merely supposed you might be able to give me a reliable account of him."

Was it suspicion in the eyes? "In what respect?"

"What sort of a man is he? Am I to understand he does not resemble his unfortunate brother?"

The wariness deepened. "Why do you wish to know?"

"I wish to know about anyone close to Mr Penkevil." Ottilia adopted a conciliatory tone. "Come, Miss Meerbrook, you must see that it is of the first importance to understand the relationships of the deceased. You can help me, if you will."

The spinster's expression did not suggest that she was willing to do anything of the kind. She hesitated long enough for Mrs Poyle to lose patience.

"God save us, woman, speak! Free enough with your rabbiting earlier, you were."

Ottilia intervened. "Thank you, Mrs Poyle, but pray allow Miss Meerbrook to answer in her own good time." But she turned at once to the other woman and applied a spur. "The longer you hold off, you know, the harder it will be, my dear."

A little sigh escaped the spinster and her stiff pose relaxed slightly. "It is very hard. I would not wish you to think Alexander — I mean, the reverend —" correcting herself in a hurry — "could be in any way to blame in this horrid affair."

"You are giving me to understand his character does not of itself apportion blame? Is he a man of easy temperament? Mrs Poyle speaks of him quarrelling with his brother, but it usually takes two to make an argument."

This point of view appeared to make an impression. Nancy leaned in a little, once more adopting her confiding air. "That is just it, my lady. The reverend is not given to disputation. He is in general so very kind. You may enquire of any of his parishioners and they will all say the same." She sucked in a snatch breath. "There is no denying Mr Penkevil's moods were uneven. The reverend is apt to deplore his brother's lack of restraint. The reverend thought it inappropriate for a man in his position to be unable to control his temper. Aware how Ruth suffered, the reverend took it upon himself to remonstrate with Mr Penkevil." She sighed in a mournful fashion. "To no avail. His words went unheeded. One cannot wonder at it the brothers became estranged."

Ottilia leapt on this. "They were estranged then?"

Mrs Poyle took this. "Pooh! Estranged indeed. When Alexander took his pot luck in this house four days out of the seven?" She threw a contemptuous glance at the spinster and turned her gaze on Ottilia. "Don't you take nothing she says for gospel, my lady, with her the reverend this and the reverend that. Had her sights set on Alexander for an age."

"How dare you!" The spinster was up, balling her fists at her side. "It is nothing of the kind. My sole desire has been to comfort Ruth. If I have spoken to the reverend in private, it has only been on her behalf."

"On her behalf, is it, you find excuse to visit when you think Alexander will be here? Or did you seek him at his rectory and find him absent?"

"I did no such thing! I would scorn to conduct myself in that fashion. I am quite reconciled to my single state, I will have you know."

"Don't tell me, Nancy. You pounced on Roland Huish the minute he settled in the county and when you failed to snare him you returned to your siege of Alexander."

Nancy's voice rose to a shriek. "Wicked! How dare you talk so, Mrs Poyle? When I have devoted myself to your daughter's welfare — a thing you could never do for bellyaching on your own account to any who would listen. Ingratitude!"

Mrs Poyle snorted. "Who asked you to devote yourself? Ruth don't need your sycophantic whining. Never did no good anyhow."

The spinster dissolved into hiccupping sobs. Or was it a refuge? Ottilia was nevertheless about to scarify the older matron before attempting to soothe when a youthful-looking woman ran into the room, crying out as she came.

"What is amiss here? Why are you shouting? Gracious heaven, Nancy, what has set you off weeping? Mama, have you upset her again?"

A cacophony of protests, tearful explanations and argument ensued. Ottilia, tempted to put her hands over her ears, could not but wonder if the deceased Hector Penkevil was altogether to be blamed for his ill temper if this was the sort of scene he was obliged to endure in his home. The commotion gave her an opportunity to take stock of the woman who must be Hector's widow.

Mrs Penkevil was in semi-deshabille, attired in an open-robed negligée gown of sprigged muslin but missing both apron and cap, clutching to her bosom a large shawl set about her shoulders. Hair of light brown, loose and in some disarray, fell upon her shoulders. It was obvious she had not yet had time to adopt the black garments suitable to her widowed state, and equally so that her first grief had dissipated. Her face was pretty enough even in its pallid condition and her eyes were not reddened from a bout of weeping. Or had she not been as distraught as Nancy Meerbrook described?

In due course, the spinster was soothed into quiet, the matron called to order and Mrs Ruth Penkevil made aware of Ottilia's presence.

She greeted this news with a pretty air of apology. "Do forgive me, my lady, for I did not see you at first. It is kind of you to call, but I confess I am not truly up to receiving visitors."

Mrs Poyle cut in. "She ain't a visitor, Ruth. Not if you suppose she's here to make you condolences."

Ruth blinked and bent an enquiring gaze upon Ottilia. "Is it not so? Do forgive me, but I don't understand." She put a hand to her head. "I am none too clear in my mind at this present, you understand."

"I understand perfectly," Ottilia said, taking the hand that was half put out and half wavering before her. "I am indeed sorry for your loss, Mrs Penkevil. It is a difficult time for you."

Ruth had allowed her hand to lie slack in Ottilia's but she withdrew it. "Difficult? I should rather have called it a nightmare. It does not seem possible such a thing could happen to Hector."

The matron forestalled anything Ottilia might have said. "Well, it did happen, Ruth, and Lady Francis is here to find out why and how. Not to mention who."

The widow's blue eyes widened as they again met Ottilia's. "Is it so?"

"If I am able, yes."

The direct response had an odd effect. Ruth's face crumpled and she seized Ottilia's hands. "Oh, thank you! Thank you, a thousand times. I can know no peace if this horror is not fully explained."

"You won't be so thankful when she starts to question you," stated Mrs Poyle with some degree of relish which Ottilia could not but deprecate.

Ruth dropped her hands and put her own instead to her cheeks in a gesture of dismay. "Question me?"

Ottilia produced a smile. "When you feel able to respond to questions, I would appreciate your help, Mrs Penkevil." She took note of the flicker of fear that showed for an instant before the widow gave way to the anxiety natural to the occasion. "You, after all, must know Mr Penkevil best."

"Hector? Yes, oh, yes, but…" She faded out, seeming to try to fathom any hidden meaning in these words.

"When you are more yourself, ma'am, pray send to me and I will come."

CHAPTER SEVEN

"Will she send to you, do you think?"

"I am relying on Ruth's inevitable curiosity, Fan. I think she will."

Ottilia had been obliged to wait until dinner to relay the substance of her interview with the ladies at the Penkevil household. By the time all parties had returned to Ash Lodge, it was too late for any colloquy with her husband. There was no privacy to be had in the bedchamber they were occupying, one which had been her own in the past, what with Tyler assisting Francis and the presence of her own maid.

Since the whole household was in mourning, Patrick had vetoed any of the party making a change in dress, but a wash and brush-up was essential. Ottilia had Joanie redo her hair, exchange her day cap for a wisp of lace now edged in the black border Joanie had sewn for her, and set a warm shawl about her shoulders, which at least provided a touch of colour to leaven the prevailing black. Francis changed his black neckcloth for a pristine white one and wore a grey waistcoat he had purchased in Salisbury. When he was at last satisfied with the set of his new hairstyle, he grunted his assent to Ottilia's query as to whether he was ready.

"As ready as I'll ever be with this head. It is becoming a confounded nuisance." He waved off Tyler's attempt to brush his coat. "That will do, I thank you."

His mood was altogether propitious, Ottilia felt, despite his complaints of his hair. Encouraged, she began to hope indeed that he had truly embraced her return to that character which had caused so much grief between them in the summer. Dare she allow free rein to the inevitable build of intellectual stimulation that attacked her upon these occasions? At least she stood in no danger herself this time. Would it be —? Could it be as it had been between them in past adventures? Ottilia found she was cherishing a secret yearning for that shared involvement when the two of them threw about ideas and discussed possibilities as they worked to solve the puzzle.

The dining parlour was for once full of lively discussion. A counterpart in size of the parlour above it and as sparsely furnished, it boasted merely a polished table of several leaves, only two of which were in use, the whole covered in a white cloth, and a large sideboard, together with a serving stand.

Ottilia's brother and her two nephews were found to have similarly reduced their mourning, leaving off black neck-cloths for white ones. It struck Ottilia that the boys, with their shiny blond shoulder-length locks, which contrasted starkly against the black collars of their coats, were becoming uncommonly handsome. Ben in particular, the planes of his face now looking distinctly adult, more closely resembled his father than hitherto.

An odd frisson of pride mingled with poignancy attacked Ottilia. "They are growing up fast, Patrick. You will have proper men on your hands before too long."

Her brother looked up from his work of carving a joint where he stood at the head of the table. "I am all too aware of it." He cast a glance at his sons, seated side by side. "A good thing too. I may hand over this duty to you, Ben."

"Carving, Papa? Well, I'll try. But you are so practiced at chopping up bodies that —"

Ottilia cut him off. "Ben! Not at the table, if you please."

At which Tom chimed in. "Aren't we going to talk of the murder then?"

"Yes, I thought you wanted our report, Auntilla."

"Report, yes. Comparing cadavers to your papa's joint of beef, however, is quite unnecessary. I shan't be able to swallow a mouthful." All the males fell into laughter and Ottilia was delighted to see how her spouse took as much enjoyment in the mild jest as the rest. She nevertheless addressed her nephews with mock severity. "I am glad you find it amusing."

"I thought you had a stronger stomach, my dear sister."

"She does in general, Patrick. You must make allowance for her condition."

"I thank you, Fan." Ottilia eyed the youngsters. "For that I shall make you hold your report until I have made mine and heard from your uncle too."

Patrick had begun piling slices of beef onto plates. "Never fear, Ottilia. They will be far too busy stuffing themselves to speak for a space, in any event."

Ben, handing across the plates as he took them from his father, was indeed regarding the beef in a fashion distinctly predatory, making Ottilia laugh. He grinned. "Well, I'm hungry, Auntilla."

"So'm I," said Tom, setting his plate down and picking up his knife and fork.

Ben nudged him. "Vegetables, Tom. You should offer them to Auntilla before you start."

"You may wait for everyone to be served, Tom," said Patrick. "Pass Ottilia the gravy, will you, Fan?"

As usual when dining *en famille* at Ash Lodge, it was the custom for the diners to serve themselves once the footman and maid had delivered the various dishes and set them upon the table. They would return to clear and bring in the second course when the bell was rung.

When all the plates were larded to each diner's need, Patrick took up his utensils and the rest of the company followed suit. Ottilia, partaking sparingly of the beef, having passed to her spouse quite half of the quantity on her plate, began instead upon a generous portion of a side dish of leek and potato pie, one of the housekeeper's well-remembered specialities. She waited until she judged the first hunger of the male contingent had been satiated. Then she drew a breath and plunged in. "I had the luck to find Nancy Meerbrook with the Penkevil ladies today."

To her joy, Francis looked round with one of his teasing looks. "Ah, the gossips you were after."

"Indeed, Fan, and I may say both Mrs Poyle and this Nancy ran off at the mouth to some purpose." She relayed the gist of the discussion.

Her brother said nothing throughout, but during a lull, took what Ottilia judged to be a reluctant interest. "What does all this tell you then, my dear sister, if anything?"

Ottilia ignored the caveat. "There is room to suppose that any of the three might be involved."

"How?"

She smiled. "You are sceptical, Patrick, but this is how it is done. One questions and sifts until the right answer becomes clear."

"It always does become clear eventually." Francis, to her deep pleasure seconding her efforts. "But if you ask me how, I cannot tell you. Tillie sees things the rest of us are blind to."

Patrick had no comment to make on this, rather to her chagrin. "Well?"

Ottilia could not resist a dig. "You were present at Willow Court, Patrick. You have seen the pattern at work."

He made pretence of shuddering. "Don't remind me. A more repulsive set of individuals I hope I may never meet."

"You had best avoid Mrs Poyle and Nancy then. The two of them were at each other's throats throughout. I can find it in me to pity Mr Penkevil."

At this, a cry of protest came from Tom. "Don't, Auntilla! He was truly horrid. You should have seen what he did to poor Willy."

Ottilia's attention was arrested. "I heard about that from Mrs Poyle." She looked to her brother. "Was he severely injured, Patrick? She says you tended him."

Her brother's professional look overspread his countenance. "Willy's back was striped with several cuts. I had strong words with Penkevil."

"And he wasn't sorry," Tom growled.

"I fear that is true. I told him it was unbecoming in a magistrate. All he would say was that the boy was lucky he had not thrown him in gaol. He was more concerned about his so-called valuable horses than Willy's welfare."

"He does sound a very monster," Francis remarked.

"Just so, Fan. Mrs Poyle called him a beast. She was free with her criticisms and volubly pleased by his death. Which leads me to think her an unlikely candidate."

"Will you cross her off then, Auntilla?"

"Not yet, Ben. It could be a ploy to be thus open, though I doubt it. This Nancy, on the other hand, is a much more interesting proposition."

"How so, Tillie?"

"She is either very cunning or exceptionally naïve. Her slips, whether deliberate or genuine, threw suspicion upon Ruth. But then Nancy might equally be hand-in-glove with Alexander Penkevil, in whom she clearly sees a potential husband."

"What about Ruth?"

Was Patrick beginning to be intrigued? She was in no doubt now that Francis at least was fully at her back once more. "I shall know more when I have spoken to her direct, my dear brother, preferably with neither of the other two present." She bethought her of the task she had set her spouse at his request and noted that he had disposed of the bulk of his substantial meal. "If you are done, Fan, can you tell how you fared with Brigadier O'Turk?"

"Aha, my turn." Francis took up his glass and sipped wine before saying more.

Ottilia curbed a flicker of impatience. The last thing she wanted when he was being so supportive was to irk him into ill temper. She spoke mildly. "Was he forthcoming?"

Her husband gave a little grimace. "Forthright. He was very free with his opinions of Penkevil but he had not known of the death. When I spoke of murder, he assumed it had been a shooting."

"Why, Fan? Was it an effort to throw you off the scent, do you think?"

"Definitely not. He said it because he told Penkevil he would meet him with a gun if he again stepped on the brigadier's land."

When she had heard the full sum of her spouse's discourse with Brigadier O'Turk, Ottilia could not but agree with his supposition that the man was innocent.

"I thought you might see it my way, Tillie, but I told him we can't rule him out." Francis set down his glass and there was an oddly serious look in his face as he turned to meet her gaze. "He gave me a warning for you."

Ottilia's senses prickled. "What sort of warning?"

"That I have been unable to fathom. He said you are stirring up a hornet's nest and bade me tell you there are wheels within wheels."

"How cryptic. Intriguing, Fan. I wonder what he meant?"

"It is no use asking me. More he would not say."

Ottilia was silent for a moment, falling into that state of rumination these events engendered, only half aware of the ensuing discussion as the rest of the company tried to dissect these words.

"What does that mean, Papa?"

"Yes, you know these people best, Patrick. Have you a notion in your head?"

"I'll wager he does, don't you, Papa?"

"You would lose, Tom. I cannot imagine what Brig is talking about."

"Well, think, Patrick! Tillie has gone off into one of her reveries. Quick, before she comes up with the answer. You could beat her to the post."

This last snapped Ottilia's attention back and she had to laugh, rejoicing at the natural way he fell into the old habit of exchanging pleasantries. She entered a protest however. "Fie on you, Fan! Don't heed him, Patrick. Though I suspect I may well be obliged to rifle your store of knowledge."

"By all means do so, my dear sister."

"I will, but not now." She looked across to the two boys. "First, I wish to hear how Ben and Tom fared with Petrus Gubb."

The farmer, it appeared, had expressed himself as pleased as punch to hear that Penkevil was dead. "Although he said it a deal more rudely than that."

Ottilia hid a smile at Ben's adjusting his tale for her feminine ears. She doubted Petrus Gubb had said anything she had not heard before. "Then he did not know of the death until you told him?"

"He knew all right," said Tom in a smug tone. "He'd even heard Mr Penkevil was hung."

"But not that it was in fact a murder?"

Ben took this. "Well, his eyebrows flew up when we told him, so I can't think he did know, Auntilla."

"Well spotted, Ben."

"I spotted something too, Auntilla. Old Petrus vowed he'd shake the hand of the man who did it." Tom's eyes were bright with excitement. "Only how did he know it was a man?"

"How indeed." Ottilia exchanged a brief glance with her spouse whose eyebrow quirked and refrained from pointing out that this was hardly conclusive. "What else did he say? Did you ask him if he had been in those woods lately?"

Here Ben's face dropped. "We did and he took it ill. Demanded if we were accusing him."

"Of course, we said no. I told him we were asking everyone. Or you were, Auntilla."

"He didn't believe us," disclosed Ben. "He went on a rant and yelled loud enough to startle the birds."

Ottilia jumped on this. "Excellent. People are never so apt to speak the truth as when they lose their tempers. Did you catch anything he said that might be of use or interest?"

Tom rolled his eyes. "How could we, Auntilla, when old Petrus was threatening to set his dogs on us?"

"Ah, but you heard that. Think, boys! What else did he shout?"

For a moment neither spoke, both faces redolent of a concentrated effort of memory. Ottilia caught an amused look from her brother and smiled back. But she did not speak and was grateful neither of the men interrupted.

At length Ben brightened, looking across. "Is this any use, Auntilla? I'm pretty sure he listed some of the times Mr Penkevil fined him."

"Did he do so often?"

"According to old Petrus," chimed in Tom, "he was targeted non-stop."

"What sort of misdemeanours had he committed?"

"He will have it he did none of them," said Ben. "He says it's not his fault if one of his sheep wanders and he's entitled to shoot rabbits on his own farm. Oh, and the cattle never crossed some boundary or other. All manner of things he complained of, I can't recall the half of them." His face lit. "Oh, but I do remember one thing, Auntilla. He said if you were like to take Penkevil's place and blame him for everything, he would be ready for you."

"But I remember he insisted he didn't have anything to do with it, Ben. He repeated that just as we were leaving."

"That's true. I expect you think we ought to have stood our ground, but —"

"Certainly not," said Ottilia at once. "We cannot have the two of you savaged by dogs. You did very well. One thing we can be sure of is that Farmer Gubb had scores a-plenty to settle with Mr Penkevil."

CHAPTER EIGHT

Sunday intervening before further potential witnesses could be pursued, Ottilia elected to attend service at All Saints' church in Ebbesborn where the Reverend Alexander Penkevil presided. Francis was dragged thereto by his eager wife, who, it seemed to him, had availed herself full-heartedly of his willingness for her to pursue the business. He was conscious of a sliver of satisfaction when the reverend proved to be away.

"Ha, Tillie! So much for chivvying me to set out an hour before we need. We could have gone to St Mary's in Kington's Ash with the others."

She looked round from her study of a bill posted in the open church door. "It is not wasted, Fan."

A faintly anxious note caused him to moderate his tone. "What, when your quarry is absent?"

She gave him a deprecating look. "I ought to have expected it under the circumstances."

"Yes, you ought," Francis grumbled. "I'm hungry already."

"Fie, Fan, you have only just had breakfast."

"That was two hours ago or more."

Tillie touched a hand to his chest in the way she had and the mischief he found irresistible entered her face. "Your sacrifice will not be in vain, my dearest. Mr Penkevil's substitute is the Reverend Bruno Pidsea. According to the boys, his churchyard abuts the woods where they found Penkevil's body."

Unwilling interest slipped into his breast although he entered a caveat. "It doesn't necessarily follow he murdered the fellow."

"But he might have heard or seen something."

Francis drew her aside as an elderly couple sought to enter the church, nodding at them to pass. He received a frowning look for his pains.

"We are blocking the entrance, my dear one. Do you want to go in or not?"

"Yes, of course. It is growing cold."

"I'll wager it's a deal colder inside."

There was no satisfaction in finding he was right as he made his way down the aisle, his wife on his arm. He refrained from uttering the acid remark upon his tongue for he suspected Tillie was still a trifle wary of his moods, but the notion of an hour's sermon in the dank interior could not but weigh against the fruitless expedition.

"It is rather sparse of company for the occasion, do you not think, Fan?"

She had taken her place in one of the pews not too distant from the altar to which he had guided her, remarking sotto voce that they would be conspicuous in the front. Tillie was looking about the other pews where indeed the parishioners were dotted only here and there.

Francis grunted. "What's the occasion?"

"Don't be obtuse, my dearest. Their reverend's brother murdered? One would suppose they would flock to Sunday service."

"There is that." He flicked a glance to the lace-covered altar where a couple of tall candles provided a modicum of illumination. Apart from three or four wall sconces, this appeared to be the only source of light, the high stained-glass windows showing only grey from the dull day outside.

"It does seem odd. Unless they expected his absence. That notice may have been there since the event."

At this point, an organ somewhere in the upper regions started up and a youngish clergyman dressed in the robes required by his calling appeared from somewhere in the rear and stepped up to take his place behind a lectern that stood to one side.

He had pale locks framing an equally pasty complexion. His voice, however, when he began his opening prayer, proved to be rounded if a trifle high in pitch. Francis suppressed a sigh and resigned himself to a period of boredom.

As was to be expected, the Reverend Pidsea concentrated his remarks upon the evils of ignoring the Almighty's exhortations towards brotherly love. His aspect was solemn and he interwove several sighs into his expressions of regret for the wages of sin.

"There is amongst us, my brethren, somewhere in these our local parishes, one who has committed the gravest sin of all. Thou shalt not kill, so saith Our Lord. Yet one has done this heinous deed and I fear for his mortal soul."

His? Yes, a man must have carried out the strangling. But Penkevil was drugged, which argued a woman's hand was also possible. Were they looking for two persons? Tillie seemed to think it likely, what with the women involved in the Penkevil household.

His mind roved over the scene in the woods and the subsequent discoveries, seeking some indication he might have missed, the pastor's sermon a mere murmur in the background. At length his attention caught on the Reverend Bruno Pidsea again and he realised the clergyman was casting surreptitious glances in his direction. Or was he looking at Tillie? She was not acquainted with him, so he could not have divined her identity. More likely it was the presence of strangers in his congregation that captured his interest.

A whisper came from beside him. "He has noticed us."

"So I perceive."

When the sermon finally came to an end and the last hymn was sung, Tillie urged him to hang back as the reverend made his way down the aisle where he waited at the door to greet the churchgoers as they left.

"If we leave the last, we may accost him, Fan."

It did not take long for the meagre congregation to weave its way out of the church and Francis guided his wife along the aisle to be ready. At least they might remove from this damnably chilly interior.

Tillie did not wait for an introduction but accosted the fellow at once. "Mr Pidsea, I understand?"

The reverend's eyes flashed in recognition and he shoved his head forward, reminding Francis irresistibly of a tortoise. "I am he? I did wonder who were the strangers in our midst."

His questioning gaze encompassed Francis, who took it upon himself to perform the introductions. The name of Fanshawe did not appear to be familiar to him.

"Ah, yes? How do you do? May I bid you welcome to All Saints'? It is not my territory, of course, but perhaps you know that already?"

Tillie gave him one of her warm smiles. "Astute of you, sir. My errand was to the Reverend Alexander Penkevil, it is true, but you will do quite as well."

A gleam of amusement lit the Reverend Pidsea's eye. "I am quite at your service, my lady. Although I cannot imagine what your errand may be."

"I am looking into the matter of Mr Hector Penkevil's untimely death," said Tillie, wasting no words. Francis was conscious of a flitter of gratification to hear her so much like her normal self.

Her target exhibited surprise. "Indeed? That seems an odd circumstance."

Francis intervened. "It would not if you were aware of my wife's reputation, sir. She is adept at unravelling this kind of affair." He glanced at Tillie as he spoke and encountered the oddest expression in her face. Not mere astonishment, but something more he could not fathom. He gave her a reassuring smile and she turned back to the Reverend Pidsea.

"Would you object to my asking a few questions of you, sir?"

"Not in the least. Although I hardly think I may have anything of value to contribute."

Tillie's smile came again. "You might surprise yourself, Mr Pidsea. I have frequently found that people know a great deal more than they suppose. For instance, are you aware that the woods where Mr Penkevil was found abut your churchyard at St Leonard's?"

Pale eyebrows flew up. "He was found in those woods? Gracious me! I had no notion. All Alexander told me was that the unfortunate man was murdered and left for dead in the night hours."

Francis eyed the man closely as his wife related the details of their discovery, hoping to judge whether he spoke truth. So often witnesses were found to have lied or at least concealed important facts. But this Pidsea appeared genuine enough. He was certainly visibly upset at the tale.

"This is dreadful! I wish I had known this earlier. I might have offered Alexander a more generous sympathy. Much as his relationship with his brother was distant, such a taking off must necessarily distress him."

Tillie pounced on this just as Francis might expect. "Distant how, sir?"

The fellow reacted badly. "Why do you ask? You cannot suppose Alexander had anything to do with this murder?"

Tillie's clear gaze was upon him in a look Francis knew well. "That you jump to such a conclusion, Mr Pidsea, rather points to his involvement than otherwise."

The reverend raised horrified hands. "No! I never meant to imply that."

"But the notion crossed your mind."

"Only in the vaguest way, I assure you. It is only natural to pass under review any person nearly concerned with the deceased."

"Natural when the deceased has been unnaturally killed, yes." Tillie's voice softened in that way she used for persuading a witness. "Come now, Mr Pidsea, let us be frank. I have it from several sources already that these two brothers were at outs."

"Yes, but that does not mean —"

"I am not suggesting it does, sir. You have yourself just said that it makes sense to pass under review any person who might have a reason to dispose of the dead man."

"Indeed I said nothing of the kind!"

Francis cut in. "It's what you meant. Don't quibble, man."

He received a glance of dislike. "I fail to understand why you should expect me to condemn a man I both like and respect."

"Nobody asked you to condemn him," said Francis with impatience. "If you will come down off your high ropes, sir, we will make better progress."

His wife touched his arm. "Hush, Fan, let him be. Mr Pidsea's dismay is perfectly understandable." She turned back to the reverend. "May we begin anew? I should have explained at the outset that any questions I have are merely designed to widen my understanding of the individuals concerned. I am making no accusations and certainly would not do so without certain proof."

Reverend Pidsea looked a good deal mollified. He passed a hand over his brow and let out a somewhat overwrought breath. "Forgive me, my lady. I confess the business has unsettled me."

"I am not at all surprised." She gestured to one of the back pews. "May we sit awhile?"

So saying, she moved to take a seat there, patting the wooden bench beside her. As the reverend moved towards it, Francis received a glance from his wife that contained an unmistakeable message. She wished him to remain aloof, did she? He gave a faint nod and remained standing in the aisle as the clergyman slid into the pew beside Tillie.

"There, that is more comfortable, I hope."

The fellow did not, to Francis's eye, look in the least comfortable, and maintained a discreet silence.

"One thing you might help me with, Mr Pidsea. I gather the Reverend Penkevil was in Salisbury on the night his brother died. Is that true, do you know?"

Pidsea hesitated. "I cannot say for sure. I know he visits the bishop there and sometimes remains in Salisbury for a night or two."

"But you don't know if he was there on Wednesday last?"

"There is no reason for him to tell me, unless he wishes me to fill in for him here. We cover for each other at need, you must know. It is common practice amongst us clergymen."

Tillie picked up the point she had wanted to check from the first. "Then you must have been in your own vicarage on the fatal night."

"I imagine so. I have not been absent for many weeks."

"I wonder, did you hear anything unusual?"

"Such as?"

"Well, it is a remote possibility, I know, but you might have been awakened by some unusual noise. Or if you had been wakeful, you could have heard or seen something."

A faint laugh came from the reverend. "You mean had I been watching from the window? I regret to be obliged to disappoint you, my lady, but my bedroom window looks out upon my garden rather than the woods."

Francis was not surprised to receive a glance of exasperation from his darling wife. She was getting nowhere with this fellow. True to form, however, she did not abandon her efforts.

"I take it you heard nothing then?"

"Not that I recall."

"Are you a heavy sleeper, sir?"

He gave her an amused look. "No more so than the next man. If there had been any unusual noise, I imagine I might well have woken. An owl's cry would certainly not disturb me."

Francis stared at the man. Why mention an owl? Tillie took it up on the instant.

"Did you hear an owl? That night, I mean."

Pidsea blinked several times, looking baffled. "What is that to the purpose? I may have done."

"Did you?"

The repetition, said with more emphasis, produced an odd response. "Yes. At least ... which night was it? Wednesday, yes. I did hear an owl. Twice. It kept me awake for a short time, half expecting the bird might call again."

"Think now, if you please, sir. Did you hear anything else in that time?"

For several moments there was silence in the dimly lit church. Francis found he was holding his breath as the clergyman concentrated, his gaze fixed upon the wooden back of the pew in front. At last, he raised his head.

"Do you know, there was something."

"What sort of sound?"

"A grunt? Clearing a throat perhaps. I paid it no heed. I suppose I took it for one of the servants, stirring early."

Tillie jumped on this. "At what time was this? Can you make a guess?"

"Well after midnight. The church clock chimes the hour and I am sure I had heard it strike two." His pasty features registered puzzlement. "It cannot have been a servant at such an hour."

"No, indeed."

His gaze went to Tillie. "I am ashamed, ma'am. I apologise for my earlier remarks. I would never have guessed there was such a memory to be found."

"No apology is necessary, Mr Pidsea. It is often the case that these little moments seem trivial at the time, and then later turn out to have significance."

"Does it have significance?"

"It is very possible."

"How?"

"Only in that it suggests there was someone abroad in the early hours in, or at least near, the vicinity of the murder."

"Can that help you?"

"It might." Tillie's smile almost embraced the fellow. "These affairs are usually composed of a collection of small incidents that eventually, one hopes, add up to a whole."

Reverend Pidsea shook his head in a gesture redolent of disbelief. "It hardly seems credible you might make something out of nothing."

"Pardon me, sir, but it is not nothing. Moreover, you might, if you will, add a little something more. Tell me about Alexander Penkevil."

He almost shied away. "Are you at that again?"

"Not at all. I only wish to form a picture of the gentleman."

Pidsea stood up and shifted out of the pew. "In that case, my lady, I suggest you approach him direct. I cannot undertake to tell tales of my colleague."

Within an ace of objecting to the tenor of this speech, Francis desisted as his wife stood and held out her hand.

"Then I should not dream of asking you to go against your conscience, sir. I thank you for your time."

Farewells were speedily said and Francis took the matter up as he was escorting his wife to the waiting coach. "Why didn't you press him?"

He received one of her roguish looks. "I had no need to do so, my dearest dear. He told me quite enough with his refusal to speak on the matter."

"How so?"

"He made it clear there must be something to hide."

"Oh." A trifle disgruntled not to have seen this for himself, Francis helped her to enter the coach without speaking. Only when they were settled did he say what was on his mind. "You know, my dear one, it is quite a comedy to watch you returning to the game to which you are best suited."

She showed him an anxious face. "Is that why you touted my reputation to the man?"

"Don't I always?"

"Not lately, Fan."

"I told you I am reconciled."

She gave a little sigh. "You say that now, but it only needs for some danger to threaten and —"

"I won't change, Tillie." He took hold of her hand and squeezed. "If you want the truth, I took pleasure in your being your true self."

"I don't know whether to believe you, my darling lord."

He brought the hand to his lips and kissed it. "Well, you may. I don't promise not to get grumpy and impatient, but —"

"I wouldn't believe it if you did make such a promise. You are your mother all over again, you fiend of a husband."

Delight at the brighter teasing note made him laugh. "There's the woman I fell in love with. Which gives me tacit permission right this minute to protest that my stomach thinks my throat is cut."

"Have no fear, my dearest. Betty will have prepared for your gargantuan appetite."

"You may talk, woman, as gargantuan as you are becoming."

"I have an excuse." She turned in the seat and set her free hand to his chest. "In which regard, Fan, I fear I must consult Patrick. I believe Joanie and I may be out in our calculations."

Francis pressed the hand resting against his chest. "Aha! A far more interesting exploration for my brother-in-law than this infernal murder."

CHAPTER NINE

Doctor Patrick Hathaway, attending the sermon at St Mary's with his sons, had reason to feel relieved at his sister's choosing to hunt down Alexander Penkevil at Ebbesborn. Fond as he was of Ottilia, he could not have been easy while Averil was present in the church. Especially after the conversation he'd had with his brother-in-law on their excursion to Salisbury.

He had not intended to confide the whole to Francis, but the discussion man to man had veered in a dangerous direction and Patrick had felt impelled to explain himself.

"It is not that I don't grieve for Sophie, Fan."

His brother-in-law set down his cup and looked across the table where they sat in one of the booths in Patrick's favourite coffee house. "I am sure you do. I asked only because Tillie is worried about you."

Patrick had let forth a mirthless laugh. "Naturally she is. My sister no doubt expected to find me basking in a slough of woe."

"Hardly that, Patrick. She is merely concerned that you may end the worse for holding back."

A hollow opened in Patrick's chest. If Ottilia only knew! The months of disappointment, trying this or that, reading up on cases that sounded similar only to find his wife's symptoms matched but poorly. Watching her sink, knowing with all his skill he was powerless to halt the decline. Throughout, the niggle of conscience, the dichotomy wherein his need overcame the natural scruples which must arise for any man in his position.

Yet she, Averil, was the only leaven to mitigate the corroding sense of failure, the one bright spot in the overwhelming darkness. Irresistible, to partake of her sweetness when he could, to draw strength from her generous gift. She risked so much — gossip, censure from unforgiving critics who gave no quarter for circumstance. Worst of all, the continuance of the lie to the husband to whom she owed that duty, a lie Patrick knew he forced upon her by the very nature of their intimacy. No, Ottilia would never condone his conduct, the worse for setting Averil in jeopardy.

He made his answer at length. "It is guilt, not grief, that troubles me, if you want the truth."

"Because you could not save her?"

"Not on that account. Well, partly." Patrick sighed, setting his elbow on the table, and supporting his brow with one hand. A lifeline, to speak of this instead? "I regret that I failed to spot the cancer soon enough. Although, even if I had, there was nothing I could have done to avert Sophie's death. I gave her what relief I could, but…"

He was grateful to Francis for saying nothing, although his look was eloquent. They had sat for a time in silence, sipping the dark brew. Patrick would have left it at that, but his brother-in-law had brought up Ottilia again, plague take him!

"You should tell Tillie, Patrick. She would understand."

"That, yes."

Fan's questioning gaze made him uncomfortable. Goaded, he brought it out flat. "What Ottilia would fail to understand is my seeking consolation elsewhere." Defiance made him glare in response to the startled expression in Francis's eyes. "You are as disapproving as my sister would be, I see."

"By no means. I am not judging you. I am only surprised at your mentioning it."

Patrick had to laugh. "Confession, Fan. For the Lord's sake, don't tell Ottilia!"

Francis had regarded him with a lifted eyebrow. "You must learn to be more master of your eyes, my friend, if you don't wish her to notice."

Startled in his turn, Patrick eyed him. "What the deuce do you mean by that, man?"

Francis gave a rueful laugh. "I think my wife was too occupied to spot your wandering gaze at the funeral feast."

"But you did? Damn it, Fanshawe!"

"Who is the lady?"

Patrick let out a breath. "The wife of one of my patients."

"Do I take it your liaison is of long duration?"

It was oddly a relief to unburden his mind and Patrick spoke more freely. "Weeks, then months that turned into years. Don't judge me too harshly. Averil's husband is many years her senior and has been incapable, you might say, since well before we met." He drew a breath. "Sophie too … well, suffice to say we have slept apart for more years than I care to count."

"You have my sympathies, Patrick. That must have been difficult."

"Say rather impossible. Not that it is an adequate excuse." He fought down the rise of guilt. "I don't excuse myself, though I could offer up a plethora of reasoning to justify my actions. I don't, Lord knows. I had no will to resist and my eyes were and are open. But I know well my prude of a sister would never accept anything I might offer in mitigation." He gave Francis a straight look. "I must request you to respect my confidence, Fan."

His brother-in-law's smile was a trifle crooked. "I shall do so, of course. Yet I believe Tillie might surprise you. She is not near as prudish as she was."

"Ha!"

"It's true, Patrick. She has seen much of the seamier side of life in these years. She has been obliged to adjust her ideas. She is far more sympathetic to the exigencies that plague people less fortunately circumstanced."

Patrick remained unconvinced. "You will not persuade me that Ottilia could forgive me for playing my wife false."

"She would not condemn you, Patrick."

"Perhaps not, but she would think the worse of me."

He could not forget how Ottilia had looked to him for succour when her first husband died. Their father was long deceased, their mother living in her own parental home in Ireland. What else could he do, but invite Ottilia into his home? Not that it had been a hardship. She was a welcome addition to the household. He'd been grateful when she took over the care of his sons, Sophie's ill health having already manifested.

When his sister showed an interest in his professional work, her eagerness to learn touched him and he allowed her to assist where she could. Yet all that preceded the advent of Averil into his life. The reflection could not but obtrude that had Ottilia still been within the family, he might have refrained from beginning the affair in the first place. For fear of her acute mind and that too-sharp observational skill his sister had ever exhibited. As it was, he and Averil were far more circumspect whenever the boys were at home.

Anxiety loosened his tongue. "I cannot have Ottilia knowing how I have behaved, Fan. I am her big brother. Ottilia has ever looked up to me. It would hurt us both for her to discover I have feet of clay."

He had been thankful for Fan's assurance that he would keep his secret, yet he had sought for more. "If she questions you?"

"I shall say only that you are suffering from guilt more than grief. Tillie will take it as concerning Sophie's illness."

With which Patrick had been obliged to be content. He was rather sorry now that he had opened his budget. He cast a quick glance towards the pew where Averil sat alongside her elderly husband and caught her eye. She gave him one of her tiny smiles, causing a frisson to pass through him, before turning her eyes back to the pastor. They had not met in private since his wife's demise. Patrick had contrived but a quick word when he tended Ralph Deakin a couple of days after the funeral.

"My sister is here. I daren't make our usual rendezvous."

Averil had touched his arm briefly. "We will wait then, my love. Be patient."

Yet was she as impatient as he felt, to be attending church in Kington's Ash? The Deakin home being part way between here and Knighton, it was not unusual to see the couple in St Mary's when Ralph's health permitted. If he was too frail, Averil worshipped instead at Knighton since, as she said, it was better for her not to appear by herself where Patrick was to be found, for fear of gossiping tongues.

"I think there are one or two who suspect, Patrick. No, I don't know how, my dear, so it is of no use to ask me. It is inevitable, I fear, living as we do in such a close community. Let us ensure we meet only at home when you tend Ralph, or else in Salisbury, whenever I can contrive it."

Her common sense was one of the traits Patrick found soothing, a characteristic sadly lacking in his late wife. Sophie had been a mistake from the first. He had fallen in love with a pretty face and a charm of manner that ensnared him, blind to the gulf that lay between them. Once married, the essential differences between them showed up in glaring colour.

Sophie was a butterfly, unable to settle to a task without growing bored or impatient, where he was methodical and persistent. She loved company and grew to resent Patrick's frequent and necessary absences to attend his patients. She became fretful when he could not accompany her on visits to their acquaintance, frustrated as he believed, with the lack of company in a higher stratum of society than that to which he could aspire. Patrick, content with his circle of professional men with whom he could share intellectual interests, had no time for the frivolous social whirl his wife yearned to enjoy. Patrick had truly supposed Sophie's many ailments were largely imaginary, developed as an interest perhaps, or more likely a plea for his attention.

Matters improved when Ottilia came to live with the family, providing as she did a buffer between husband and wife. Sophie readily abandoned the upbringing of their sons to her sister-in-law, for which Patrick had found it hard to forgive her. Not that she did not love them, but she contented herself with cuddles and gestures of warmth provided they were well-behaved. But both Ben and Tom were rowdy rascals from birth, curious and possessed of inventive minds that strongly appealed to Patrick, but caused their mother to dispense with their company upon some trivial excuse. It was surprising how quickly Sophie could develop a headache the moment the boys became too vocal and excited.

All this had contributed, Patrick knew, to his proving vulnerable to Averil's very different appeal. Physically, she could not have been more so, her tendency to plumpness in contrast to Sophie's stylish figure. Averil, with her rounded countenance and button nose, had not his wife's prettiness, yet there was an indefinable quality about her which was infinitely alluring. Her better features lay in her soft curls tending to auburn and a pair of hazel eyes, their intelligence borne out as Patrick discovered how her thoughts on so many subjects chimed closely with his own. Their talks when he tended Ralph had grown longer, the attraction between them increasing. They both knew it. In the end, Patrick had been unable to resist acting upon it. Averil, bless her heart, had succumbed and that was that. By now, it was as if he could no more desist than he could cease to breathe.

On the thought, he looked across again and found her watching him. Longing seized him. If only this hellish murder had not descended upon them, Ottilia would have been soon gone and the boys back at school. Why the wretched man must needs get himself killed just at this time was a curse and an inconvenience of the highest order. Perhaps it might be politic to assist Ottilia's hunt for the perpetrator, if he could.

The sooner the business was settled, the better pleased he would be.

To Ottilia's surprise, over an impromptu luncheon of cold meats and pies, flanked with a selection of patties, cheesecakes and a rich plum cake, the whole set out upon the dining room table in an informal fashion, her brother enquired about her progress.

She set down the cheesecake with which she was merely toying, having consumed enough ham pie to satisfy a failing appetite. The further her pregnancy advanced, the less she felt like eating, although she did what she could manage by way of sustenance for her unborn child. "I did not think you wished to hear about my enquiries, my dear brother."

Patrick made a face. "Since I must needs endure them, I may as well partake of your conclusions."

"If I had any."

Her brother cast her a frowning look. "What, nothing at all?"

"Nothing yet. Or at least, not of value enough to form any conclusion."

Rather to her pleasure, Francis intervened. "She has garnered a few facts. Moreover, my love —" turning to throw her an encouraging smile — "you have indeed put two and two together in some respects."

Here her nephews, both of whom had been far too busily engaged in replenishing their adolescent stomachs to talk, became eager participants.

"What have you found, Auntilla?"

"Do you know who did it?"

Ottilia had to laugh. "Already? I have only just begun. There are several interested parties we have not yet accosted who might add to our little store of knowledge."

Tom became eager. "We can question some for you, Auntilla. Only say the word!"

His brother nudged him. "Don't be an ape, Tom. We don't know what to ask. We didn't even manage to ask Petrus all we were supposed to."

"You could hardly do so under the circumstances," Ottilia said by way of excuse. "But you do know people."

Tom jumped in. "Yes, we know everyone round about."

"But how will that help, Auntilla?" Ben spoke in a sober manner that struck Ottilia with a sense of his growing maturity. Was it from working with his father? She could perhaps make use of it.

"It will help if you will make me a list of your papa's patients, Ben. And Tom, you may add to each name anything you know about their activities."

"Like what, Auntilla?"

"How they spend their days; any interests they may have that might take them abroad; whether they have employment. That kind of thing."

Her two nephews exhibited elation at being given the task and at once requested permission to rise from the table in order to begin.

This being granted by their father, both lads sped away and Ottilia found Patrick's eye upon her. "Well, what, brother mine?"

He pursed his lips. "I should have thought I could more readily supply you with that sort of information."

"Just so, Patrick, but you are bound to discretion by the obligation of your calling, are you not? Besides, it will keep them occupied and may even provide some fresh insight."

"How so?"

Ottilia turned to her spouse who had put the question. "A child's view of the world is often more truthful than that of an adult, Fan, do you not think?"

"I suppose there is something in that. Not that I would call Ben a child. At his age, I was packed off to the Army."

Patrick asked the startled question in Ottilia's mind. Francis rarely spoke of his army days and never in any detail. "You did not then attend the university?"

"My father believed I would learn far more of what I needed to know by that means than by addling my brains with more Greek and Latin." Francis grimaced. "He was right. Martial training is a harsh school, but it equipped me for life. Had I not met and married Judith, I imagine I would be still in the military."

"Your first wife? Ottilia did tell me."

Feeling this line of discussion might prove a painful reminder of her brother's recent loss, Ottilia cut in. "I did, but let us not dwell upon the past. What you could tell me, if you will, Patrick, is what you know of Lady Carrefour's involvement with the late Mr Penkevil. She I know to have been one of your patients these many years."

Her brother was eyeing her with an expression she could not read. "Why would you wish to know of Lady Carrefour? Or indeed any of my more elderly patients. You surely cannot suppose she could have done away with Penkevil?"

Ottilia sighed. "One does not merely have to do with those who might have done the deed. Much of what one learns comes from those who are not involved at all. Esther Winning, for example, alerted me to Brigadier O'Turk's involvement and gave me an inkling of Margery Poyle's character. She it was indeed who suggested I ought to talk to Lady Carrefour."

Her brother had nothing to say to this, instead asking an unrelated question. "Did you talk to Alexander?"

Her husband took this. "We did not. She pumped the Reverend Bruno Pidsea, who heard an owl in the night and thinks he also heard someone grunting."

"On the night in question?" Patrick's surprise gave Ottilia a good deal of satisfaction.

"Just so, my dear brother. It may prove irrelevant, but at least we know that someone was abroad in the early hours."

"This is how she does it, Patrick. Piece by piece." She received one of her husband's quirking looks. "I can tell you, it often seems to me that Tillie garners a fount of useless information. But I am obliged to admit that most of it does slot into the particulars by the end."

"Thank you, Fan. I fear my brother remains sceptical, however."

Patrick apparently had no answer for this, instead asking, "What is it you wish to know about Lady Carrefour?"

Ottilia did not hesitate. "Had she any truck with the late Hector Penkevil?"

Patrick frowned. "How would I know that?"

"Oh, come, don't fob me off. Patients talk to you. Not merely of their ailments, before you claim as much. You have told me often and often how you have felt much like a priest confessor upon occasion."

A rather sheepish grin overspread her brother's features. "I might have known you would remember that."

"I remember also that you complained only the other day of both Mrs Poyle and Nancy Meerbrook chattering so much you could scarce get done with your examinations."

A snort greeted this reminder. "You don't suppose I pay the least attention to anything either of them says, do you?"

"Whether you consciously do, you will undoubtedly recall it if there is anything pertinent to be found. But at this present, I am only interested in what Lady Carrefour may have let fall."

Francis set down the glass from which he had been sipping wine and let out a bark of laughter. "You may as well surrender upon the instant, Patrick. I can vouch for it that Tillie won't break first."

"Be quiet, you fiend of a husband!" Ottilia ignored her spouse's quirked eyebrow and turned back to her brother at the head of the table. "Pay no heed. He delights in making game of me. Be sure I don't expect you to reveal anything of a confidential nature. But a matter that does not bear upon your patient's health need not be secret."

For a moment or two her brother did not reply, instead sipping at his own wine and studying the depleted platter upon which rested the remainder of a neglected slice of plum cake and crumbling pieces of pastry. At length he gave a resigned sigh. "Well, I suppose there is no harm in disclosing the one thing I do know of Lady Carrefour's dealings with Penkevil."

Careful not to appear too eager, Ottilia merely made an interrogatory noise. Patrick's gaze rose to meet hers.

"She was not left well provided for, you may recall."

"Very poorly provided for. Esther once told me the late Lord Carrefour was something of a gamester."

"So I believe. His heir did little to remedy the situation. She is obliged to manage on a meagre widow's jointure."

At this point, Francis cut in. "Are you going to tell us she applied to Penkevil for relief and was refused?"

"Not precisely."

Ottilia's interest quickened. "What then, Patrick?"

"Brig set up a fund."

"Brigadier O'Turk? Heavens!"

Patrick picked up the bottle and offered a refill to Francis before replenishing his own glass. Ottilia had confined her imbibing to water, wine having a deleterious effect upon her during pregnancy.

"You would not credit Brig with a compassionate heart, I dare say," her brother went on, "but he and Lady Carrefour are of the same generation and have been friends for an age."

"How was this fund managed then?"

"Brig managed it, which is probably why Penkevil was the only person applied to who refused to make a contribution. It was supposed to be secret, but Brig was too indignant to keep silent and the whole leaked out. Lady Carrefour was at first too proud to accept charity but Brig told her not to be a fool. This was a year or two before her mind began to fail so she fully understood she had been slighted. She talked of her gratitude, but it was plain from how she spoke of the matter to me that she was greatly hurt by Penkevil's reluctance. She avoided him thereafter."

Ottilia thought this over without speaking but her spouse took it up in a moment. "If you ask me, that increases the brigadier's store of resentment against the fellow. I am inclined to revise my opinion that he is innocent."

Ottilia let this pass, addressing her brother again. "Is that the sum of it, Patrick? Was there no other backlash?"

He set down his glass. "Not to my knowledge. Unless you would make something of Lady Carrefour openly quarrelling with Margery Poyle?"

CHAPTER TEN

The house occupied by Lady Carrefour might be considered adequate for an elderly dowager with a frail constitution, but it suited ill with her former status. Two small parlours below stairs were situated off a little square hall, with domestic quarters behind. As far as could be seen, the upper rooms were much the same size and, as Patrick had informed Ottilia, the four-poster in the lady's bedchamber left little space to manoeuvre. Most of her personal accoutrements were crammed into the second bedroom, leaving only a small accommodation for her maid to sleep within call. Ottilia could not think well of the current Lord Carrefour, who could leave his relative to live out her remaining years in virtual poverty.

Lady Carrefour was likely in better circumstances than Nancy Meerbrook, but the deprivations, after a life of ease, must irk.

Setting out for the house situated in the little village of St Martin as soon as her coachman and groom were ready for her on the Monday morning, Ottilia found her quarry in a parlour overstuffed with chairs, a sofa and occasional tables dotted with knick-knacks, playing cards and various impedimenta. She was apparently engaged in reading, but the spectacles were askew upon her nose, the open book stood in imminent danger of falling off her knee and the flustered manner of her greeting made it evident she had been dozing when Ottilia was announced.

"Gracious me, is it you indeed, my dear? Doctor Hathaway's little sister, is it not? Mrs — er…"

"Ottilia Fanshawe now, ma'am, though you may remember me as Mrs Grayshott." This, despite Lady Carrefour having met her at Sophie's funeral feast. She bent to take the old lady's hand which was like parchment, as bloodless as the withered cheeks illuminated by the meagre daylight afforded by the single front window, augmented with candles on the mantel even at the early hour of eleven of the clock.

"Yes, yes, you married again, did you not? Gracious me, I almost forgot." Lady Carrefour resettled her spectacles and peered at Ottilia. "Are you *enceinte*, my dear? Do sit down. I hope you are not gadding about in that state. Nothing could be more prejudicial."

Ottilia took the chair opposite, glad of the warmth from the fire. A brisk wind had even penetrated the carriage and the journey had been too short for hot bricks. "You need not fear for me, ma'am. I am positively hedged about with advice, from both my brother and my husband."

"Who is your husband?"

She had met Francis, but Ottilia obliged with his name and style to refresh her wayward memory. She was beginning to doubt of culling anything useful, although one might hope Lady Carrefour would vividly recall any grievance. She had to allow for the delay in her hostess requesting the hovering maid to produce suitable refreshment and was quick to suggest coffee. Not only did she prefer it, but Lady Carrefour's tea caddy was likely to be rarely unlocked. These preliminaries dispensed with, Ottilia came at once to the business of her visit.

"I dare say you have heard of Hector Penkevil's unfortunate death, ma'am?"

A change came over the elderly lady's features. The pale cheeks seemed to whiten still further and her lips, thinned no doubt by lack of teeth, became pinched. Her eyes signalled distress. Her voice was cold. "We have all heard of it, I imagine." She put up a hand to her lips, passing a finger across them in an agitated way. "One ought to feel sorry."

Ottilia pounced. "But you do not, do you, ma'am?"

A sudden snap in the old eyes reminded Ottilia of her mother-in-law. "I don't. A cruel end, but fitting. The Lord works in mysterious ways."

"True, ma'am, but in this case, I do not believe the Almighty had a hand in the event. Penkevil was murdered."

The finger moved in even greater agitation. "I heard it was so. Now, who was it brought the news? Ah yes, dear Brig. He visits me regularly, you know. Such a kind man. Many of our neighbours find him fearsome, but not I. He brings me a bottle from his cellars, you know. Most palatable. Gracious me, I should have offered you wine, my dear."

Ottilia waved a hand in dismissal. "I thank you, ma'am, but wine does not agree with me during pregnancy."

"Oh, that is a pity. Brig's wines are superior. I believe he only buys from France. Or is it Italy?"

It was unlikely Brigadier O'Turk could be importing his wine from France in these times, but Ottilia refrained from allowing herself to be sidetracked into a discussion of the hostilities, which now involved Spain who had departed the coalition earlier in the year to side with the French, as she had heard from Francis who liked to keep abreast of events abroad.

"Be that as it may, Lady Carrefour, might I ask you something?"

A bright smile greeted this request. "By all means, my dear. Say on."

It was plain the matter of Penkevil's murder had already passed from her mind and Ottilia suffered a slight pang of conscience at being obliged to bring the old lady back to it. She must, if she was to settle the business. She was already tardy, being now five days into the hunt.

"I understand you were not upon terms with Mr Penkevil, ma'am. Would you object to telling me the occasion of your quarrel with him?"

Lady Carrefour's hand went to her bosom and she frowned under the spectacles. "Quarrel? I certainly did not quarrel with the man. Indeed, I scarcely exchanged a word with him. Particularly after he made it his business to censure poor Brig."

"Censure him how, Lady Carrefour?"

"Oh, I don't know precisely. Some legal matter between them. Penkevil tried to bring him to court, I believe."

This was old news. Ottilia tried again. "What of Mrs Poyle?"

She had no need to ask further because Lady Carrefour's pallid cheek flew a trifle of colour and her eyes sparkled with indignation as she became positively voluble. "That graceless hussy? A grasping vulgarian, if ever I met one! Put on airs with me, would she? We all know from which puddle she came, with the audacity to aspire to a sphere to which she plainly does not belong."

Ottilia did not share Lady Carrefour's prejudice, but the indication of a breach was of interest.

The arrival of the maid with a tray interrupted the proceedings, much to Ottilia's annoyance. She could only hope the whole discussion would not fade from the old lady's mind as she fussed over the coffee, directing her maid to do what the girl was already doing as she strove to enquire of Ottilia's preferences and ensure they were met. By the time both women were served and the maid had withdrawn, Lady Carrefour's mood had indeed shifted once more.

"I hope it is to your taste, my dear. I do not myself take more than a lump or two of sugar, but coffee is quite bitter without it, do you not find?"

Ottilia agreed to this, declaring the brew to be acceptable and once again attempted to bring the discussion back to her purpose. Better to be direct. "You were telling me of your dispute with Mrs Poyle."

The indignation returned and Lady Carrefour set down her cup in the saucer she held in her lap. "That pretentious hussy? Do you know, she had the temerity to suggest that it was I who requested dear Brig to ask Penkevil to frank me. As if I would dream of begging for charity. Do you know what she said to me?"

"No, indeed." Ottilia infused eagerness into her voice. "I should be happy to hear it."

"If anyone was entitled to demand funds from Penkevil, she said, it was she. She berated me for trying to take the very bread from her mouth, if you please. The very bread from her mouth! As if I were a beggar!" Her voice became husky. "I may be purse-pinched, but I have still a trifle of pride. Carrefour did his best to make a beggar of me, but I can hold my head up high. I have n-never in my l-life p-pleaded for assistance. If it had not been for dear Brig, I w-would not have t-taken charity from anyone alive!"

A burst of sobs followed this little tirade and Lady Carrefour had recourse to a pocket handkerchief which she whipped from her sleeve and applied to her eyes.

Ottilia made soothing noises, reflecting meanwhile that Margery Poyle had been less than frank on her own account. Had she made a practice of demanding money from her son-in-law? She might well have contributed in no small degree to the destructive nature of his temperament.

The bout of crying did not long endure. Lady Carrefour, urged thereto by Ottilia, sipped her coffee, and very soon returned to her habitual amicable state. Ottilia dared swear that in a very few moments, in talking of other matters she took care to introduce, the old lady had forgotten all about it.

Her coffee drunk and set aside, she was making ready to take her leave when Lady Carrefour suddenly revisited the subject. "You do know, my dear, don't you, that Penkevil was obliged to marry that girl?"

Startled, Ottilia settled back into her chair. "Ruth? Was it so indeed?"

"Oh, yes, it was quite a scandal. Or it would have been if the knot had not been tied. That dreadful creature threatened to make known the girl's wrongs to the world."

"Margery Poyle, you mean? How do you know this, ma'am?" Why had not Esther said anything of it?

"We all knew it, my dear, and no one could doubt the truth of it when the child was born within six months of the wedding. They are all respectability now, you may be sure, but it was not always so. Putting on airs! I know what we'd have named her in my day, my dear."

Ottilia could not doubt it. The little burgeoning of sympathy she had felt for the victim dissipated. He had evidently seduced an innocent girl and tried to escape the consequences when she became with child. Otherwise, why should Mrs Poyle have pushed for marriage?

The revelation threw a good deal into question. Was this what Brigadier O'Turk had meant when he spoke of stirring up a hornet's nest? The complications were certainly mounting enough to justify his warning of wheels within wheels.

On her return to Ash Lodge, Ottilia was both gratified and surprised to find Ruth Penkevil awaiting her in the parlour. She was in company with Ben, who appeared to have been making painstaking conversation with the widow. He broke off what he was saying upon spying Ottilia. "Auntilla! Come in, do. Mrs Penkevil came to see Papa, but she wishes to talk to you so Papa suggested she might wait. He asked me to stay with her because he has a patient."

The blue eyes signalled the frantic condition, at variance with his words, into which he had been thrown by the task of entertaining Ruth Penkevil. Ottilia went at once to the rescue, moving directly to the visitor who had risen and was gazing at her in quite as disturbed a fashion as her nephew.

"You are very welcome, Mrs Penkevil, and I am sorry to have kept you waiting. Do sit down again." She turned to Ben, still hovering before the fire. "Thank you, Ben. Have you offered Mrs Penkevil refreshment?"

"Yes, but she doesn't want anything."

Here the widow herself intervened. "Nothing for me, I thank you, my lady." Her anxious glance encompassed Ben. "Only perhaps we may speak in private."

"Certainly. My nephew will leave us, won't you, Ben?"

There could be no doubt of his desire to do exactly that. He gave a brief bow, said something about finding his brother and left the room with alacrity. Ottilia suppressed her amusement and turned again to Ruth.

The widow had found time to array herself correctly in black, although the gown she wore looked to be in the fashion of an earlier year, its waist lower than was presently common and made of a sturdier material than the silks and lawns currently in vogue. Kerseymere, Ottilia guessed, which was both warm for the season with sleeves to the wrist and practical. A redingote of some dark stuff lay over the back of one of the straight chairs by the window, and a black bonnet rested on its seat.

Ottilia began in the conventional way. "How are you coping, Mrs Penkevil?"

"With difficulty." The widow put up a hand to fiddle with the light brown curls which brushed the neck of her gown. "I have not properly dressed my hair, do forgive me. I find it hard to deal with everyday matters."

"I am sure you do," said Ottilia, moving to the special chair and taking her seat with a sigh of thankfulness. The excursion, despite its brevity, had tired her. "I must thank you for taking the trouble to find me. I would have come to you, had you sent to me."

"Yes, you said so. There are reasons why … I did not want…"

"You did not want to speak before your mother?"

A tiny smile flickered and was gone again. "Nancy too." She rubbed her hands together. "You must not think I do not value her friendship, but Nancy is apt to take issue with Mama and … and…"

"And the two of them make things uncomfortable for you. I comprehend perfectly, my dear Mrs Penkevil. Or may I call you Ruth?"

The widow looked across, seeming relieved. "Oh, yes, do, if you please. To be addressed as Mrs Penkevil, under these cruel circumstances, feels quite horrid."

Ottilia let this pass. "You may call me Lady Fan if you choose. It is a sobriquet that helps a little with informality. I should much prefer it if we could dispense with all the shibboleths of politeness."

Ruth heaved a sigh. "Thank you. That is a relief. Everyone has been so kind, but to be obliged to respond suitably to expressions of pity has driven me nearly to screaming point."

"I can well imagine it." Ottilia did not feel it politic at this stage to enquire whether Ruth felt pity to be inappropriate. "I have no doubt you have also been subjected to a great deal of curiosity."

"Yes!" The widow threw up agitated hands. "They think I don't notice, but I see it in their eyes. That is why I wished to talk with you, my lady — I mean, Lady Fan. How can I avoid these horrid suspicions? Why should they believe I might have reason to do away with my husband?"

Ottilia went into the attack. "Have you any such reason?"

The shock hit hard. Ruth stared, hollow-eyed. Then her features crumpled and she put up her hands to shade her face. "You think it too!"

Was it an act? It looked real. Ottilia gentled her tone. "Not at all, Ruth. It is my business to ask such questions. If you answer truthfully, I can the more readily discover just who did murder your husband. Then all these terrible suspicions will be laid to rest."

At first, she did not think the words had gone home. Ruth continued to cover her face for several seconds. Then abruptly, her hands dropped and she met Ottilia's eyes. "I came to ask your brother for a potion to help me to sleep easier. I have had such nightmares."

Ottilia waited, but she said no more. A prompt was in order. "Did you understand what I said, Ruth? Will you answer truthfully anything I ask?"

She threw out a dismissive hand. "Yes, yes. I want only to be rid of the business." She paused and a flicker of some emotion crossed the pretty features. "One cannot go back."

What did that mean? "Let us go forward then."

The widow seemed to gather herself, setting her hands together in her lap and holding one set of fingertips so tightly that the skin stretched on the back of the hand. "What do you wish to know?"

Better not to revisit the pertinent question. Ottilia opened with what she had just learned from Lady Carrefour. "Forgive me, but is it true that Penkevil married you because he had got you with child?"

A gasp escaped the woman. "How did you come by that?"

"Is it true?"

The widow let her breath go again. "I suppose there is no point in concealment. It was a long time ago. Yes, I was pregnant with Jason when we married."

No choice but to push this through. "Was Hector unwilling at first?"

This time a hoarse laugh came, redolent of contempt. "You mean was he forced into offering for me because of the hue and cry Mama set up? So rumour has it, but Hector had promised me marriage before —" She broke off, putting a hand to her mouth as if to stop the words escaping.

Relentless, Ottilia supplied them. "Before you succumbed to his overtures of seduction."

Another laugh came, this time filled with an odd mixture of indignation and genuine amusement. "You do favour frankness indeed, Lady Fan." She let out a seeming groan. "Yes, he seduced me with promises which he later tried to recant. He offered money, but Mama would not have it so. No, Hector had no real wish to make me his wife."

"What was his reason, if I may be permitted the impertinence?"

Ruth sighed. "We are not of his class. At least, my father was a gentleman, but Mama…"

Mama managed her own marriage in much the same fashion? Ottilia let it ride. "Did Hector make an issue of your mother's original position in life?"

"Not overtly. Not at the time. Later, he developed a habit of needling Mama. Little pinpricks, designed to hurt. Not that Mama was innocent. They were prone to carp at each other." She gave herself a little shake. "With hindsight, I do not believe the matter of social position was a factor for him. The truth is he never intended marriage. He deceived me. I could wish I had known it earlier, or that I had not been with child. I might have refused to comply with Mama's insistence upon the union." She let forth a sigh which seemed very like frustration. "Mama could not forgive his early refusals and took umbrage at every opportunity."

Thus contributing to the difficulties of her daughter's marriage. Not to mention providing herself with a very good reason to be rid of her son-in-law. Pity for the widow could not but burgeon.

"Were you unhappy?"

"Oh, not unduly. Hector became resigned when I bore him an heir. He treated me well for the most part, but he did not love me."

"Did you love him?"

Ruth sighed. "I thought so. Later I realised I was mistaken."

Ah, was this the potential spur? "What made you realise it?"

The widow looked her full in the face and did not flinch. "I knew it when I met and grew to know Roland Huish."

Startled by the outright confession of her affections, Ottilia said nothing for a moment.

Ruth's mouth twitched and her brows drew together. "You bid me be truthful."

Ottilia shook herself into responding. "Yes, and I am grateful for it, if surprised."

The bravado collapsed and the widow sank a little, looking away. "It is good to stop dissembling."

"Who knows about your true sentiments, Ruth?"

Her head came up again. "Oh, no one, upon my honour! Not even Roland himself. He has professed his love for me, but I have never reciprocated. It would not be right. I have my children to think of."

"What of Hector? Did he suspect?"

A trill of somewhat hysterical laughter emanated from the widow. "Hector? Suspect? He would not have seen what was directly under his nose. Hector cared only about what concerned Hector. I — all around him — were merely there to fit into what suited his way of life. Only Jason perhaps impinged on his attention. He cared not the snap of his fingers for Ariadne, poor mite. As for me, as long as I did not make waves, nor support Mama's complaints, I was free to do as I pleased."

This did not tally with what Ottilia had so far heard. "Are you telling me, Ruth, that Hector has never mistreated you? He never raised a hand to you in anger, for instance?"

She received a questioning look. "Who told you he did?"

Ottilia did not enlighten her, instead pressing the matter. "It is so rumoured. Hector's reputation is one of ill temper, even vindictiveness."

The terms appeared to cause the widow to ruminate. Ottilia could not judge whether or not they were familiar. She waited and was rewarded at length with one of the tiny flickering smiles.

"He was not well liked. His conduct elsewhere did not accord with how he behaved at home."

"That sounds remarkably like an excuse. In my experience, an ill-tempered man is worse in his own home than when he goes abroad."

Ruth's fingers went to her brow and kneaded there. Ottilia did not suppose she had a headache. Was it prevarication? Working out how to answer?

Abruptly, the fingers released their hold and dropped to her lap again. Ruth's features grew taut, her gaze uncertain. "If I tell you that he berated me, even struck me once or twice, you will suppose that gives me a reason to take his life away, will you not? Coupled with my feelings for Roland, it is enough to damn me, no?"

Ottilia relaxed a little and smiled. "My dear girl, I could scarcely condemn you, or indeed anyone, without being certain of my facts. Yes, I say facts. If you tell me your husband was violent towards you, I will require you to give me specific instances. As for your having been responsible for Hector's taking off, I could not be certain of that without sifting and adding together facts which proved your hand in the business beyond doubt."

She noted a burgeoning of interest in the other's face. "It sounds to be complex in the extreme."

"It is. Very much so. Especially because people are apt to lie in order to escape suspicion."

That drew a laugh from the widow. "Caught! Very well, I will tell you it all."

The tale the widow then unfolded, in spurts of confession between little silences, was indeed enough to provide her with reason to rid herself of a husband who evidently was, if not downright cruel, uncaring, and apt to strike when roused.

Rather like an adder. Ruth had learned to let him alone but her mother had not been similarly circumspect, attacking especially when his mood was uncertain and driving him to retaliate. In general, in Ruth's direction.

"So often I begged Mama to desist since Hector invariably took out his annoyance on me, but she has never been one to mind her tongue."

An understatement. "Did these altercations happen often?"

"Between Hector and Mama? Only when he was at home for any length of time. Hector spent days at a time in Salisbury. He had often to attend at court in his judicial capacity. He said it was simpler to remain for the duration of a hearing or a series of cases." Ruth twisted her neck this way and that, as if to shift away stiffness. A sign of tension of which Ottilia took due note. "For my part, I believe he preferred to keep out of Mama's way."

She was not meeting Ottilia's eyes as she said this, glancing instead about the room. Did she in fact see anything? Or was she gazing inward? Was there doubt of Hector's alleged reason for remaining in Salisbury? Suspicion burgeoned. Ottilia did not hesitate. "Did you believe Hector had a mistress in Salisbury?"

The startled look in the eyes as they flicked to meet Ottilia's gave Ruth away. Her tone dropped to a hush. "How did you guess?"

Ottilia suppressed a smile. "A bow drawn at a venture."

To her surprise, the widow stared her out. "No. I made you realise it. How?"

"You have been direct and open, but at that moment you did not look at me."

Ruth nodded and the intensity of her gaze lessened. "Very good. Report does not lie."

"Report?"

"Of your capabilities." She sat up straighter in her chair and clasped her hands together in her lap. "You will solve this." It was a statement rather than a plea. "What else do you need to know?"

"Tell me about Roland Huish."

At that, Ruth let out a sighing breath. Once, twice, looking away. Her features were distressed when she turned her gaze back. "I hoped you would not ask."

"Yet you are going to tell me, are you not?"

"Yes. Yes, I must. I cannot have him suspected." Her eyes grew luminous. "His is a gentle soul. He did not deserve…" She faded out, alarm entering in.

Alerted, Ottilia struck. "There was something between Roland and Hector. Tell me."

The widow's hands came up, once again covering her face. A trifle of impatience went through Ottilia and she struggled not to sound tart. "Come, Ruth, out with it. What happened? Did they quarrel?"

The hands dropped and there was real anguish in both face and voice. "It was my fault. So foolish to speak of Roland in such terms before Hector."

"What terms?"

"Oh, of the beauty of his poetry, as comely as his person. I was enraptured and I failed to see the danger." She let out another of her despairing sighs. "That was before I knew him, before I developed… Oh, you cannot understand, no one can."

"Try me."

"I heard him recite at a soirée. The first time, I mean. It was magical, like being woken from a dreaming state into the world of the dream. When your life is dull beyond words, when no true joy or pleasure is granted to you, when you are rubbed daily by this or that little trouble, and then a new vista opens before you — you cannot imagine how such a change affected me."

On the contrary, Ottilia could almost envision it. Captive in an unsatisfactory marriage with a mother who made it her business to worsen the strife, small wonder Ruth had been dazzled by a handsome face and figure. A poet, no less. But this did not bring them any closer to the event. Moreover, there was an anomaly here.

"You blame yourself for praising Roland to your husband, but did you not claim that Hector was too self-absorbed to be jealous?"

The response was immediate and scornful. "Jealous? It had naught to do with jealousy. Hector was dog in the manger about all his possessions, of which he considered me to be one. A wife is but a chattel and that is precisely how Hector regarded me."

Compassion went through Ottilia. This was not how she experienced marriage. No man could be more forbearing or apt to allow his wife almost unlimited freedom than Francis. The heart squeezed in her bosom at the very thought of her darling lord's attitude towards her. Theirs was a partnership of equals. Even her first husband Jack, brief though their union had been until his untimely death in the American war, had respected her intellectual capabilities. Ruth's lot must have been pitiful indeed. Yet Ottilia was not convinced of her innocence and this Roland might yet prove the author of the plot to be rid of the encumbrance in his path.

"Very well, I take your point. What in fact did Hector do after you praised Roland?"

Ruth shifted with evident discomfort. "I do not know precisely how it came about. Hector found means to quarrel with Roland. They fought. Roland is no match for Hector. He is slight, where Hector is — *was* a larger man, well-muscled. Roland had the worst of it. He fell, and on his bad leg too. He could not walk again for days."

"He had an existing injury?"

"Roland limps. I do not know the origin of it, but he told me his disability arose in childhood."

Ottilia began to perceive the inception of Ruth's tendre for Roland Huish. The temptation to romanticise a man of his attributes must have been irresistible. To have her husband, whom she clearly disliked, then hurt that object in some sort of possessive rage, could only serve to stir her sympathies in the direction of the victim. From that to fancying herself to be in love was a small step. Ottilia must of course give her the benefit of the doubt. Her feelings might be quite genuine. Ruth certainly believed in them herself.

"How did it come about that Roland expressed his affection for you?"

Ruth's lips curved into a smile of tenderness. "I sought him out to apologise for Hector's despicable act, and to make him understand that some words of mine may have led to his being attacked. Roland would have none of it. He insisted the quarrel was of his making, that he had noticed how Hector treated me and had taken him to task."

Was that true? It sounded unlikely to Ottilia. But Ruth had not finished.

"He did not tell me that at the time, of course. Only later, when we became friends, did he venture. He was so very attentive, so kind."

Ottilia entered a caveat. "If Hector had an eye to his property as you say he thought of you, how did you contrive to meet with Roland?"

"Oh, openly at first. We are a small community here, one is bound to run into people. Later, as Roland became more urgent to meet me, we appointed a secret place."

Ottilia could not but wonder at the nature of these trysts. Ruth was, after all, a woman who had succumbed to seduction before. She let it go. There was matter enough here to ponder. She made to rise from her chair. "I must thank you for your candour, Ruth."

The widow stood up. "I have said enough to damn myself, have I not? Roland too."

A good ploy. Unless she was indeed innocent. Ottilia was inclined to lean towards that conclusion at this juncture. She chose not to answer the comment. "I am delighted you came. What you have told me is indeed useful."

Ruth came to her and held out a hand, her eyes once more intense. "Find your murderer soon, I charge you, Lady Fan. I don't think I can endure a lengthy period of this dreadful suspicion."

CHAPTER ELEVEN

The day being a trifle grey with a brisk wind blowing, Francis was relieved to dismount and leave his hired horse in the care of an ostler, happy to do his bidding upon receipt of the douceur handed across. Francis entered the White Horse through the back door and made his way along a dim corridor to the entrance hall where, as his ostler informant had advised, he might find the door to the tap.

The place was quiet, its regular clientele no doubt busy at their employments at such an hour of a winter's morning. All to the good. He might hope to question the landlord without fear of too much interruption.

He entered to the welcome sight of a good fire in an inglenook across the room, which added both warmth and light, the latter augmented by a couple of lanterns swinging from the higher of many beams. It was clean, the wooden chairs and benches in the style of pews gleaming with polish, although the inevitable aroma of stale drink was pervasive. A couple of elderly men sat near the inglenook, puffing at clay pipes, a set of abandoned dominoes scattered on the small table between them, and a man wearing an apron was engaged in wiping down a large table at the far end of the room. Otherwise, the place was empty.

Francis, surveyed with apparent interest by the only two customers, approached the counter, behind which were arrayed a variety of squat bottles, jugs and two large tapped barrels. The fellow in the apron saw him and came across.

He was a burly man of middle years, bare-headed and wearing no coat, sporting only a waistcoat over his shirt under the apron. He touched a hand to his forelock. "How may I serve yer honour?"

"Mr Hexworthy?"

The man's brows drew together. "Aye."

"You are the landlord here?"

The fellow's brow cleared. "Ah, you'll be wanting my brother, sir. I'm just the tapster." He took a few paces towards the back of the taproom and let out a bellow. "Jerry!"

An unidentifiable shout answered him from the nether regions in the back. The tapster gave forth another yell. "Gennelman wants yer!"

Resisting the impulse to put his hands over his ears, Francis instead stood back a pace or two. A chuckle from the area of the inglenook brought his head round.

One of the old gagers waved his pipe. "Could'a gone ter fetch him 'stead of yellin' his head off."

"That's Sid all over is that," offered the other.

Both gave forth a cackle, to which Francis grinned an acknowledgement. The first lifted a tankard in a salute and drank deep, what time a bustle from the back of the taproom produced the landlord. At least so Francis hoped as a thick-set fellow, dressed in a workaday suit of shag breeches, a brown frock coat over a nankeen waistcoat and sporting a scratch wig, came towards the counter, stopping to give some passing admonition in a low tone to his brother who had resumed his wiping with a large cloth.

He eyed Francis under his brows as he came up. "I'm Hexworthy, sir. What would you be wanting?"

No point beating about the bush. "I am Lord Francis Fanshawe and I am here to ask about your association with the late Justice Hector Penkevil."

The other man's face changed. At mention of Francis's name, his brows had risen, but they lowered again when the victim was mentioned, his features becoming distinctly disgruntled.

"Dead and gone, he is, my lord. Danged if I know what you want with me about it."

"Yes, he's dead. Did you know he was in fact killed?"

A look of belligerence at once entered in and a muttering was heard from the old fellows in the background. "I never had nowt to do with that."

Quelling his instinct to bark at the man, Francis tried what a soft approach might achieve. "I did not imply that you had, Mr Hexworthy. However, it may help our enquiries if you can furnish any information concerning your dealings with Penkevil."

The hostility did not abate. "How? Nor I don't understand why it's you as is enquiring. To my mind, it oughter be that there Sir Hugh Riccarton as is the other justice hereabouts."

Francis gave an inward sigh. Must his darling wife land him with the most recalcitrant witness? "That is so. Sir Hugh has requested me to make enquiries on his behalf."

"Why so?"

"Because I have some experience of dealing with matters in this line."

"What line would that be?"

"Murder."

The word affected his adversary powerfully. He reared back, slamming large hands down on the counter. "I ain't done for him. Why should I?"

Francis hit back with some asperity. "Why should you think I might suppose you had? Unless you had reason to wish to be rid of him?"

Hexworthy glared. "No, I ain't. A bit of a set-to don't mean nothing. 'Sides, Penkevil were one as could be said as argufying with one and all."

"So I understand. What was your particular argument?"

"I ain't saying." He thumped the counter with a closed fist. "You can't make me neither. If you think to bring the constables down on me, they'd best come prepared to fight."

Before Francis could think how to counter this defiant attitude, a new voice cut in, shrill and authoritative. "What's all the fuss now, Jerry? Who's this gentleman? Why're you giving him lip?"

The stout dame who had spoken had come up unseen and was now standing to the side of the counter, her gaze flicking between Francis and the landlord. She was gowned in an old-fashioned manner, but her purple gown in the low-waisted style of yesteryear was neat, a large bib apron overall and dark locks largely concealed by a frilled cap tied under the chin in a bow. This was clearly the landlord's wife and Francis, sensing relief in this potential ally, made haste to direct himself to her attention.

"Mrs Hexworthy, I presume?"

The plump features were questioning, but not yet amicable. "Matty Hexworthy, yes. Who might you be, sir?"

Francis repeated his name and style. Instant change came over the matron's features and she turned on her spouse. "Jerry Hexworthy, you'll be the death of me, you will. How could you treat his lordship to such a display? It's mad you are and no mistake." Without giving him an opportunity to respond beyond a protesting grunt to which she paid no heed whatsoever, she turned back to Francis. "I'm that sorry, my lord. He's not usual so cantankerous, be sure."

"I got reason, Matty! He —"

"Don't you be telling me he this or that, Jerry Hexworthy. I'll have it from his lordship myself and then judge if you was right. Not as you was, sure as check, for as there ain't no reason to treat shabby any customer as comes through our doors, let alone a lord."

"He ain't no customer," said the irrepressible Hexworthy.

Francis intervened before the two should come to blows. "It's true, Mrs Hexworthy. I am here to ask about your husband's dealings with the late Mr Penkevil."

"You see? What did I say, Matty?"

"You keep your tongue between your teeth, Jerry." And to Francis, "Well, my lord, I'll say as we're not sorry he's dead, and that's a fact."

Hexworthy pushed in again. "He's saying as Justice Penkevil were murdered, Matty."

This information did not appear to afford the dame any surprise. She did not answer her husband, addressing herself exclusively to Francis. "I heard that, but I didn't believe it. I favoured the story as it went that he took his own life. Are you saying 'tis true, my lord?"

"Yes. I was present with Doctor Hathaway when he made his examination of the body. We agreed that the circumstances could only point to Penkevil having been slain by another."

"Fancy! I'd never have credited it, not if it were any other as told me. Only I don't suppose as you'd say it if it weren't so."

"I would not."

"Well, there." Matty Hexworthy shook a pitying head. "Not as I'm surprised neither. You'd go the length and breadth of the county to find one single body as liked Hector Penkevil. There's few as will weep at his funeral."

"Matty, will you stop your gabbing? Don't you know as this lord of yourn wants ter say as we done it?"

Rather to Francis's surprise, the stout dame pooh-poohed the notion in no uncertain terms.

"You're not right in the head, Jerry Hexworthy. Why'd his lordship think as we done for that Penkevil? We don't have no quarrel with him."

This was a patent falsehood and Francis, who had warmed to the woman, began instead to wonder if he was being played for a fool. Tillie would be instantly suspicious. *Warily now, tread warily.*

"In that case, madam, you won't object to telling me anything you know of Penkevil. Did he frequent this inn, for instance?"

Mrs Hexworthy eyed him with an expression he could only stigmatize as guileless. She even smiled. "I ain't no madam, my lord. Matty's the name. Why don't I have Jerry here pour you a jug of our finest? Might as well be comfortable as not, eh?"

Francis thanked her and accepted the jug, filled with clear reluctance by her spouse from one of the barrels. He smiled at the woman in his turn. "May we all sit down perhaps?"

"Come you this way, my lord." The dame shifted into the back of the room, flicked her apron over the round table that had lately been wiped by the tapster, who had vanished during the late contretemps, and invited Francis to take one of the chairs set around it.

"Jerry, you sit and all!"

A clear command and the landlord obeyed it, if with obvious hesitance, waiting until both his wife and Francis were settled before perching on the edge of one of the remaining chairs.

Francis took a pull from the jug and pronounced the ale therein to be of superior quality. It went down well.

"We pride ourselves on the purity of our ale," Matty said in a confiding sort of way. "You won't find it watered down in this house and so I tell you."

A faint edge to this statement gave a clue to the possible subject of any dispute with Penkevil. Taking a leaf out of his wife's book, Francis jumped in feet first.

"Is that what Hector Penkevil accused you of, Matty?"

She looked both surprised and a trifle discomposed, throwing a glance at her husband, whose thick cheeks had grown ruddy along with the anger in his eyes. Then Matty's gaze returned to Francis.

"I'll be bound it's Jerry as give you to suppose it. Well, it's true. Penkevil swore as the ale were weak. Said he'd have us up for cheating the public."

"And did he?"

There was a pause. Hexworthy glared. Matty hesitated for a moment and then capitulated, setting her folded hands on the table. "May as well tell you now, for you're bound to find it out. Yes, my lord, he did. Sent Jerry a summons. We went along for what else can you do?" A steely glint came into the woman's eyes. "Only he erred bad, did Penkevil. If he'd stuck with the ale, we'd have had to pay a fine. But he didn't."

Intrigued, Francis demanded enlightenment.

"Got too clever for his own good. Brought out half a dozen of them green bottles in evidence, as he said. They was watered all right, all six when we duly tested them. Yes, and we had the witness test them and all."

"What witness was this?"

"He who brought them bottles and said he bought 'em from our house." A sly grin crept over Matty's face. "Only he didn't, not by a long chalk."

"How so? Could you prove otherwise?"

"We don't keep no bottles for wine. Them as wants wine, and there's few enough, brings their own jug or cask for us to fill from the barrel."

At last Hexworthy's belligerence was relaxing, for he let out a contemptuous laugh. "Penkevil didn't think of that, did he? He couldn't prove nowt against us and he were obliged to drop the case."

In which event, it seemed unlikely the couple could be bent upon revenge. Unless he had not been told the sum of it. Francis pursued it. "You were fortunate. Was there any other difficulty with Penkevil?"

The Hexworthy couple exchanged a glance, Jerry's easily read features now showing definite anxiety. Francis knew he had hit the mark and rejoiced. This was how Tillie must feel when she gauged it right. Matty's look was less clear, but he noted that she was biting her lip. Francis applied a goad. "You will do better to be open with me. We are questioning several people." He gave the wife a wry smile. "You must know well enough how village gossip travels, Matty."

She blew out her cheeks and let her breath go. "True enough, my lord, I do that. Well, it follows on from this dratted court business."

"What does?"

On a sudden, Jerry Hexworthy stood up, setting his hands on the table, and leaning over it. "Don't say nothing, Matty."

His wife slapped his arm. "Sit you down, Jerry Hexworthy. There ain't no manner of use going for to hide it. Best he hears it from us." She added as she turned back to Francis, "You'll only get a garbled tale otherwise."

"Very likely." He said no more, for Matty had clearly decided to make a clean breast of it and, equally clearly, she had the mastery of her husband.

She waited until that worthy had retaken his seat and then patted his arm in a comforting fashion. "That's better. Now then, my lord, what you'll hear ain't nowise reason to think as Jerry here had aught to do with that devil's passing."

Tillie would be the only judge of that, but Francis refrained from the comment. "Go on, Matty."

"Well, it were this way." She let out a sigh. "After that Penkevil tried to do us down, we vowed we wouldn't serve him nor none of his people in the White Horse."

"What is our right," put in Jerry with his usual belligerence. "No one can't dictate us as to who we'll serve and who we won't."

"That's right, Jerry. But Penkevil, my lord, wouldn't have it so. A feller come one day asking for a room for the night. A stranger here he were, only when Jerry were jawing with him over his ale, as he does with all, we found as he were here for Penkevil. A clerk come to do his accounts or some such."

Here the landlord took up the tale, his eyes a-smoulder. "I told him to his face we ain't got a room for him. Told him he could take his custom elsewhere."

Francis thought he knew what was coming. "He left?"

"He left all right," said Matty, "only what do you suppose happened next?"

"I have no notion," said Francis, in fact having a very fair notion. "Tell me."

In her turn, Matty's eyes spewed fire. "Penkevil arrives next day, saying as we had no right to refuse the fellow a room and we was running afoul of the law by it."

With his knowledge of the bylaws of the land, Francis was aware that in some areas an innkeeper with a free room could not refuse to house any traveller. He did not reveal his understanding. "How did you answer him?"

The landlord lifted his chin. "I showed him my fist and told him to get out of my house."

Matty clicked her tongue. "You oughtn't to have done that, Jerry, but never mind that now." She turned to Francis. "It's what Penkevil said next that riled us up proper, me and all."

"Well?"

"He told us to expect another summons. This time, he says, we wouldn't get away with it."

"Only he catched cold at that," put in Jerry with relish, "for afore he could issue any such, Penkevil were dead as a dodo."

"This becomes interesting." Ottilia brushed the last crumbs of the tartlet she had been consuming off her fingers and sat back in the chair.

Her brother gazed at her from his usual place at the head of the dining table. "Interesting? Confusing rather, I'd have said. Impossible even."

"Not for Auntilla," said Tom with his usual eagerness, pausing briefly in his munching of a second apple. "She always finds it out, don't she, Uncle Fan?"

"So far she has, yes."

To Ottilia's surprise, her older nephew, engaged in cracking a walnut, did not appear to share this confidence. "But this is altogether difficult, sir. I agree with Papa."

"I thank you, Ben. I am glad one at least of my sons has his head on right."

Tom cracked a laugh at this, but Ben's bright gaze sought Ottilia's as he emptied the walnut shell of its contents. "Why do you call it interesting, Auntilla?"

The exchange of the day's gathered information had been engaged in over dinner, not without a deal of exclamatory comment from its auditors. It lasted through the main course of roasts and pies and into the second, when fruit, nuts, cheese, and apricot tartlets had been supplied by the footman and maid. A habit of the Hathaway household which Ottilia had brought to her own in marriage. Since Francis was content with such fare, rarely interested in anything beyond his beloved meats, Ottilia had not felt the need to change on his account.

The discussion veered in several directions, Tom in particular, with the enthusiasm of youth, leaping from one conviction of guilt to another with each telling, but his brother's reception was altogether more thoughtful and Ottilia felt drawn to explain herself.

"We are accumulating suspects, Ben, but with no clear arrow pointing to the truth."

Her nephew reached for another walnut. "Have you then spoken to them all?"

"Pretty much, have we not, Tillie?"

"All except Alexander Penkevil, I think." She watched her spouse cut another slice off a crumbly white cheese, with a passing yen for a morsel of Cheddar. But her mind still roved the puzzle.

"After what Ruth Penkevil told you, my dear sister, I would have thought you would wish to speak to Roland Huish too."

"How right you are, Patrick." She smiled her thanks. "I am growing forgetful. I take it he is one of your patients?"

"I wrote him on the list, Auntilla," came from Tom in a reproachful spirit. "Did you not study it?"

"I have not yet had an opportunity, Tom. Don't think me ungrateful. I am very much wishing to look at it."

"Yes, and I'll wager you'll find even more suspects," her nephew declared with an air of triumph.

Francis groaned. "For pity's sake, do we need any more? It is bad enough as it is."

Ben, once more showing his maturity, again eyed Ottilia. "Who is it you do suspect, Auntilla?"

"You mean which two individuals may prove to be possible murderers?"

"Two?"

"Yes, Ben. I believe this murder was carried out in tandem."

"Why, though?"

"Because your papa found that the victim was fed valerian before he was killed."

Patrick here intervened, with a caution. "Probably valerian, it is not certain. Nor does it necessarily mean two persons were involved. One individual could have done both, could he not?"

"True. Yet do you not notice how our persons here are falling into pairs?"

"How, Auntilla?" Thus Ben, eager now.

"At the head, let us say, there is Ruth Penkevil and this Roland of hers. Then we have the Hexworthy couple. If Alexander Penkevil is involved, he might have been aided and abetted by Nancy Meerbrook. Yet either she or Ruth may as easily have worked with Mrs Poyle."

A scoffing sound came from Patrick. "You would say a conspiracy?"

"To be rid of a man who soured all their lives? I think it possible."

Francis entered a caveat. "What of the brigadier? He must have worked alone — if he did it, of which I am doubtful."

"If he did, it was for Lady Carrefour rather than himself."

"Good grief, Ottilia, you will scarcely suggest Lady Carrefour drugged the fellow!"

"I don't suggest it. Yet I would not rule it out altogether. In one of her lucid moments, if she remembered her grievance and Penkevil happened to be present, she might well put something in his drink."

"Now you are being ridiculous."

Ottilia could not forbear a mischievous look. "You may well say so, my dear brother. But for all that, we have in the past found solutions to be true which at first appeared wholly far-fetched."

Her husband gave a bark of laughter. "I can vouch for that. But don't include me in that *we* of yours, my dear one. I was ever sceptical in those instances."

Patrick remained unimpressed. "Well, if it proves out that Lady Carrefour did any such thing, I swear I shall take a bite out of the next corpse that comes my way."

His remark producing gales of laughter from his sons, the matter of Lady Carrefour was allowed to drop. When Tom at length recovered, he reminded Ottilia of the others in the case. "There's still old Petrus Gubb and our Willy Heath, Auntilla. Do you think they might be a pair too?"

Ottilia thought it unlikely but did not wish to depress her nephew's offering. "That is certainly a consideration, Tom. I shall bear it in mind." He looked gratified, but his older brother's serious mien drew Ottilia's attention. "What is it, Ben? Are you taking this to heart?"

He flushed. "No. At least, I'm only thinking, if it is one of Papa's patients, it might make others wary of coming here."

"Pooh, why should it?" scoffed Tom.

Ottilia looked to her brother. "Does that trouble you, Patrick?"

His lips twisted in a wry grin. "It does not." And to his elder son, "Don't fret, Ben. If anything, we will find ourselves inundated. People love nothing so much as scandal. I dare say I may grow rich on the back of this investigation."

This remark served to amuse the company all over again and Ottilia could not but rejoice to see the Hathaways in spirits.

When she was private again with Francis, she ventured to mention it as they were settling for sleep. "This new adventure at least seems to be serving the purpose of diverting Patrick and the boys from their grief, do you not think, my dearest?"

Her spouse turned his head and dropped a kiss on her hair, cuddling her closer. "You don't need a justification, my loved one. I am completely reconciled."

She let out a contented sigh. "I am glad, though I did not mean that precisely."

"What, then?"

"Well, as engaging as the hunt is, there are drawbacks. It is keeping us from our little ones and I do wonder how they are faring. I am surprised Mrs Bertram or even Hemp has not replied to your express telling them we are delayed."

"I told them not to bother unless anything urgent came up. I have no doubt both those imps are as lively as ever." His hand reached to stroke her large bump. "To be frank, I am the more concerned for the welfare of this new one. Are you sure this business is not too much for you?"

"I am tired, I admit. I will be good and rest, Fan, but now I have begun, I must see it through."

"However complex it proves to be."

Ottilia sighed. "That is just it, Fan. I'm afraid it is indeed much more complex than I at first supposed."

CHAPTER TWELVE

The letter was unsigned. It was addressed to Mrs Averil Deakin, who read its contents in a curious mingling of astonishment, distress and gathering wrath. The hand of the individual who had penned these startling words was obviously intended to be disguised since it was written in capitals.

From across the breakfast table, Averil's invalid husband made gentle enquiry. "What is it, dear girl? You look to be disturbed."

A flurry attacked Averil's pulse. How in the world to explain this without giving Ralph pain? In general, her elderly spouse paid little heed to what might be troubling her, his awareness of the world around him increasingly foggy. Lately, however, Ralph appeared to be a degree more alert. Averil could not help but wonder if the demise of Sophie Hathaway had propelled him into anxiety. Did he worry that she might seek her happiness at the expense of setting him adrift?

She opted for a version of the truth. "It is one of these nasty missives of the type I have received from time to time. Don't trouble your head over it, Ralph. I have a broad back."

Her husband, clad as was his custom in the mornings in a banyan over his breeches and a nightcap covering his bald pate, continued to regard her in that enigmatic fashion she knew well. Sometimes it denoted nothing more than vacancy of mind. Occasionally, he surprised her with a show of lucidity, as if he were still the erudite, professorial man she had married.

"You do not deserve it, dear girl. Do not allow it to upset you." With that, he applied himself to his plate again, forking scrambled egg into his mouth and chewing with concentrated attention.

Averil's eyes stung. She did deserve it, and she had long suspected that he knew. If he did, no word of blame or reproach had ever crossed his lips. Her husband's generosity of spirit was the real reason why she never would abandon him while he lived. She could not forget the early years, before his health and mind began to ail, when Ralph had showered her with kindness, given her carte blanche to live as she wished, and supplied her lack of education from the benefit of his large intellect. Almost twenty years her senior, and a somewhat reclusive widower, he had never stopped addressing her as "dear girl" as if she were still a youthful maid instead of a matron on the shady side of forty. A matron, moreover, whose illicit liaison was clearly known to the writer of this appalling letter.

"*Adulteress*," it began, "*your sinful way of life demands a price. Tell your partner in crime these words: Let the hunter known as Lady Fan who dwells in your house cease and desist forthwith. If she persists the consequence will hurt you all. Your hussy will be first to suffer Society's condemnation. Be warned.*"

The first flush of embarrassment left Averil, to be replaced with a lively fear for Patrick and his family. His last letter had given her to understand his sister's part in the aftermath of the Penkevil death. Lady Francis ought to be alerted to this threat at once. Only her inamorato had made it clear he did not wish his sister to know of their amour. What to do? She did not fear for herself, for what could this person do after all? Gossiping tongues could not hurt her.

She folded the sheet, pressing her finger to the broken wafer. Whoever had sent it had been too canny to use a seal, which might be recognised. Setting it to one side, she picked up her fork to resume eating and discovered she had lost her appetite. She set it down again and pushed the plate away, instead reaching for the teapot. Ralph, knowing her preference, had always insisted she drink as much tea as she chose, regardless of expense.

Sipping the brew, she tried to think how to act. She had thought of and discarded several possibilities before a notion more urgent than all the rest seeped into her brain. Lady Fan's hunt? It was almost a week since the slaying, was it not? Then the hand that had penned this threat must belong to the murderer!

Hesitation left her. Averil set down her near empty cup and rose. "Ralph dear, I must go out."

He looked up, a faint frown between his brows. "Must you, dear girl?"

"I hope not to be gone long." She picked up the hand bell and rang it. "Peter will see to your comfort and you may ask Molly for your hot milk if you wish for it."

He waved his fork in a vague fashion. "Do not worry over me, dear girl. I can perfectly well manage. Shall you read to me later?"

"Of course, dear." She went around the table, dropped a kiss on his brow and stroked his cheek. "We will continue with *Tristram Shandy* if you wish."

His rather rheumy eyes, pallid now they had lost their vibrancy, surveyed her. He surprised her yet again. "Is it that letter?"

She'd thought he must have forgotten. A flutter arose in her stomach. Yet it ought to be said. She did not want to lie to him. "Yes, dear. I must show it to Doctor Hathaway."

His eyelids flickered. "Does he come today?"

"No, dear. That is why I must go to him."

A little smile appeared. "Give him my best, dear girl. A good man that."

Averil agreed that Patrick was indeed a good man, relieved that Ralph's mind was not proving tenacious in this instance. She gave her directions to the servant who appeared in answer to the bell, and departed.

The words jumped out at Patrick as he read, his mind at once struggling to grapple with the implications. Averil's unexpected appearance had jarred him. His first thought had been relief that his sister had not yet come down to breakfast, his second that both his sons had long broken their fast and gone off to try what they could glean by way of clues. He was just rising from the table himself when Aaron entered.

"There's a lady to see you, sir."

"This early? A patient?"

"No, sir. She says it's urgent."

Impatience seized his breast. What now? Was it one of these witnesses? "Did she not ask for Lady Francis?"

The footman looked oddly sheepish. "It's you she asked for, sir."

Patrick gave a resigned sigh. "Where have you put her? In the parlour?"

"No, sir. She said she'd be better in your examining room."

"I thought you said she wasn't a patient?"

Aaron shuffled his feet. "She told me not to say, sir, but it's Mrs Deakin."

Averil here? At such a time? Anxiety invaded his breast as he left the dining parlour with alacrity and made his way towards the examining room. Was it Ralph? But Averil would send for him if her husband needed his services. She would scarcely leave him to come here. His heart warmed for her tact. She must have supposed Ottilia might be in the parlour.

He reached the hall and opened the door into the small lobby that served for a waiting room to his examining room. Averil was at the window, gazing out of the little casement which looked onto the back garden, but she turned upon his entrance, showing him a face of apology.

"I had to come, Patrick. This could not wait." She was holding an open sheet of paper and held it out to him. "I received it this morning. Read it!"

He eyed her a moment as he took the sheet. "You look dreadfully pale. Are you all right?"

"No." The little smile he knew so well appeared and was gone. "Read and you will see why."

The lack of preamble in her approach did not trouble him. Averil was ever direct. He turned his eyes to the sheet in his hand.

"Good grief!" The exclamation escaped him the moment he had mastered the contents. "Who the deuce wrote this?"

Averil's voice was a trifle shaky. "I did not think of it at first, but it must surely be the murderer. I set out the moment I realised it."

He nodded, his eyes running through the words all over again, the ramifications hitting him one after the other. "This is appalling. It must all come out if I show this to Ottilia. Damnation! That is the last thing I wanted. And he threatens to shame you publicly, the villain!"

"I imagine that is what he means." Her gaze searched his. "Is it a he? Does your sister have any notion?"

"Ottilia thinks there is a woman involved, so this might well have been penned by a female hand. Why had this to happen on my doorstep? And at such a time!"

"Let us not waste words upon what cannot be helped, Patrick. What are we going to do?"

"How the deuce do I know? This vile person —" striking the paper with the back of his hand — "seeks to threaten me, and you too, and I am perfectly sure it will have no effect upon Ottilia whatsoever. She won't stop."

"I should think not indeed." Averil laid a hand on his arm. "From what you have told me of your sister, I imagine this will make her doubly determined to find out the perpetrator."

Patrick took the hand and held it tightly. "I don't want her judging you, Averil."

Her smiled embraced him. "Better your sister than the world, don't you think?"

He groaned, feeling all the force of the reasons he had given to his brother-in-law for keeping his dealings with Averil secret from Ottilia. An idea occurred. "Wait! I'll see Fan first. He knows already."

"Lord Francis? You told him?"

Patrick sighed. "I more or less had to. He is pledged not to tell his wife."

"But he will now?"

"Let us find out."

With a hope of averting disaster he secretly considered vain, he bade Averil wait for him and hurried back to the dining room, hoping Francis might have come down ahead. Neither of the Fanshawes were yet there, but he found Aaron busy resetting viands and a fresh pot of coffee on the table.

"Ah, just the fellow I need. Go up to my sister's room, if you would, and ask Lord Francis to come down to the examining room. Don't say anything else, even if he asks why."

The footman bowed and went off, leaving Patrick thankful for his servant's bland demeanour. Returning to the examining room, where he found Averil had taken a seat in one of the few chairs kept in the lobby for patients who were awaiting his services, he relieved his feelings somewhat by folding and unfolding the letter over and over.

"With luck, Fan will take the hint and come without saying a word to Ottilia."

Averil said nothing, merely gathering her hands together in her lap in the way she had and keeping him under observation. Her restful ways were balm to him. On impulse, he said the words itching at his mind. "If this gets out, I won't let you suffer by it, my darling."

She wafted a hand. "Don't call me that. Habits are dangerous. You might slip in public."

"Maybe it won't matter if I do."

"It will matter. We will weather this. We cannot allow an evil mind to ruin our lives."

"Is that why you had rather face Ottilia? I'm not sure I agree with you."

Averil gave the little laugh he knew so well, a musical sound he cherished. "You have more to lose by her knowing. I am a stranger. We have no history together."

Her ready understanding was one of the things he admired. Averil was wont to say she had learned of Ralph, but Patrick believed it was innate in her to see the truth of feelings. In that she resembled Ottilia a little. The thought of his sister brought back all the dread of her condemnation.

Before he could express a craven wish to suppress the abominable letter, the door opened, producing his brother-in-law.

"Is anything amiss, Patrick?"

He drew a breath. "Very much so. But first let me make you known to Mrs Deakin. Averil, this is Lord Francis Fanshawe."

The name clearly registered with Francis, for one of his eyebrows quirked even as he made his bow. Averil responded with a curtsy and Patrick hastened to put his brother-in-law in possession of the facts.

Fan's face as he read the letter was a study. Patrick could have laughed had the matter not been so serious.

"You perceive the difficulty, Fan?"

Francis's gaze came up. "Vividly."

Patrick drew in a taut breath. "I suppose you have no bright notion in your head how I may avoid showing this to my sister?"

A scornful noise escaped Francis's lips. "Hardly, my friend." He set a hand to Patrick's shoulder for a moment. "I did say she may surprise you."

"It's not a test I had any desire to make, but it appears I have no choice." He turned to his secret paramour. "There is no need for you to run the gamut of her disapproval, Averil. You should leave."

She looked from him to Francis and back again. "This concerns me far more than you, Patrick. I had rather face the music at the outset."

"Are you certain?"

Averil's gaze went to Francis. "Your wife is no gorgon, from all I have heard, my lord?"

He laughed. "Far from it. In any event, she won't express her opinion to you."

"No, she will reserve it for me," said Patrick on a sour note. "*En avant* then."

Ottilia had been alerted by her husband's precipitate departure from the bedchamber without her, upon receipt of a message from Aaron which Francis took at the door. Tyler, who was assisting at his toilet as usual, had answered the knock and moved to murmur to his master.

Witness to this unusual proceeding as Joanie was dressing her hair, Ottilia was about to ask what was afoot when her spouse left the room, saying only, "Don't wait for my return, Tillie."

They had been preparing only in a leisurely way, Francis having decreed that a rest was in order since she had been active for several days without cease. "It will make no odds if you leave off questioning suspects for a day. You may do so with renewed vigour tomorrow."

Completing her own preparations, her mind now afire with speculation, Ottilia came downstairs with every expectation of finding a conference in train. She was unprepared, however, as she entered the dining parlour, for the presence of a stranger. Even more odd was the mien of her brother, whose gaze met hers with a sort of defiance in it as he moved to intercept her passage.

"We've something to show you, Ottilia. But first let me introduce you to my —" his hesitation spoke volumes — "my friend, Mrs Averil Deakin."

Her eyes went to the woman indicated, a lively notion already floating in her brain. Mrs Deakin was not a woman of stature, nor was she conventionally pretty. Yet her countenance was pleasingly formed, framed by a bonnet from which curls of faintly auburn hue escaped. Ottilia's immediate attention was drawn to a pair of intelligent hazel eyes which were appraising her in quite as measuring a fashion as she was using herself.

Amusement entered her breast and she smiled, moving to greet the woman, and holding out a hand. "How do you do? I gather this little emergency may be set down to your account?"

A tiny smile hovered on Mrs Deakin's lips, but her response was a surprise. "Or yours, Lady Francis."

"Averil!"

Ottilia caught Patrick's glance as he let out the murmured protest. Was it a warning? He looked to be both embarrassed and irritated. Before she could respond, Mrs Deakin spoke again.

"If there was no enquiry in the case, Patrick, no letter would have been sent."

Ottilia's interest pricked. "Letter? Has this to do with our murder then?"

"Give it to her, Patrick."

As of instinct, Ottilia looked to her spouse and he met her gaze, his own loaded with meaning. She gave a slight nod to indicate she had taken his intention and found her brother was holding out an open sheet of paper.

"Make of it what you will, my dear sister. I make no apology. Only pray don't direct your criticisms towards Averil."

Taken aback, and a little hurt, Ottilia did not immediately accept the proffered sheet. Certain little anomalies were chasing one another in her head, coalescing into the only possible conclusion. Patrick had a mistress and this was she.

Suppressing the inevitable shock, Ottilia took the sheet without looking at it, her eyes on her brother's. "Do you know me so little, Patrick?"

His features betrayed his inner disquiet as much as the hands he threw up. "I can't tell any more, Ottilia. Judge me if you will, but not Averil."

There was a silence. Ottilia was only half aware of Francis moving to her side. Her gaze went from Patrick to Averil Deakin and she found there the oddest combination of rebellion in the lifted chin, apology in the eyes and a quiet dignity that commanded her admiration. She broke the impasse. "It is not for me to judge either of you. Suffice it that you are my brother's friend, ma'am, and he has my affection and loyalty. That alone seals my lips."

Then, with deliberation, she turned her eyes on the paper and read its message. The words drove every other consideration from her mind except the puzzle of identity.

"What do you make of it, Tillie?"

She was still looking at the text, roving the capital letters and taking in the style of the language. She spoke almost absently. "I think this is penned by a woman."

"Why so?"

"Consider, Fan. A man would likely use a cruder appellation. We females learn to be circumspect in our language. None of the terms here, while insulting, are altogether pejorative. The worst she can venture is *hussy*, perhaps the mildest of epithets and common to female tongues. Even your mother is prone to use it indiscriminately, and she does not mean this by it."

She raised her eyes from the sheet to find Patrick frowning and the unfortunate victim of the letter half smiling.

"How right you are, ma'am. I had taken it as vitriol, but indeed these words are far less vile than they might have been."

"They are bad enough." Patrick's tone showed his underlying fury. "Moreover, their intent is evil."

"Or merely to avoid detection," said Francis, in a matter-of-fact way. Was he attempting to soothe her brother's ruffled feathers? Ottilia mentally blessed him for it, but returned to the matter at hand.

"The person who wrote this is well educated by the style. Which I think rules out Mrs Poyle. I imagine she would use a rougher approach, although the sentiments expressed might well come from someone of her temperament."

Mrs Deakin's interest was evidently stirred. "Do you count her among your suspects?"

"She and several others, yes." Becoming aware of the hollow in her stomach, she gestured to the table. "Should we not discuss the matter over breakfast? I am growing hungry."

"I have breakfasted," said her brother, "and Averil also, I believe." He glanced to Mrs Deakin as he spoke, and she nodded. "But we may join you. I'll take another cup of coffee. You prefer tea, Averil, yes?"

"I am content with coffee. But are you not expecting patients?"

"Not yet."

Ottilia had already taken her seat and was conferring with her spouse who had offered to serve her from the various dishes and accoutrements on the table. As Francis lifted the lid from one of the covered silver containers, she watched her brother surreptitiously as he guided Averil to the table and supplied her with coffee. Every motion spoke an intimate familiarity. It was in his hand at her back, in her smile and look of thanks as he set her chair, in the way he added cream and a lump of sugar to her coffee without querying her wants.

A pang smote Ottilia for her deceased sister-in-law. Had Sophie known of this, or even suspected? No need to question if it had been going on while Patrick's wife was alive. The ease of togetherness, likely unconscious in them both, told its own tale. She recognised the signs from her own relationship with Francis. They might have been taken for man and wife if one did not know the circumstances.

As she began upon her meal, her brother's earlier attitude impinged upon her consciousness. He thought she would condemn him for it, did he not? Well, in a way she did. But she had not lived with the family for years without realising the lack in Patrick's marriage. She wondered briefly what had moved Averil to betray her husband.

The thought was unpalatable and she pushed it away. Of more moment to concentrate upon the contents of this abominable letter. Its words returned in full measure, one phrase in particular. Impelled, she spoke it aloud. "Cease and desist?" A gurgle of laughter escaped her and she could not resist throwing a playful glance at Francis, now settling to his own substantial plate of beef and bacon. "Do you suppose I might comply, my dearest dear?"

She was treated to a flicker of his mobile eyebrow. "Pigs might fly rather."

Intriguingly, Averil came in on this. "I did not imagine you would, ma'am. Nor should you."

On impulse, Ottilia smiled. "Oh, let us not be so formal. Most people address me as Lady Fan, but Ottilia will suffice."

"That is kind, but perhaps I had best keep to Lady Francis or Lady Fan. People are apt to draw conclusions if one speaks with too much familiarity."

Ottilia agreed to it, beset by a riffle of compassion. Averil was being extraordinarily forbearing and calm about this business. Had she endured much the same sort of derogatory criticism before? It occurred to her that this woman's calm good sense must have come as something of a relief to her brother. Sophie's sensibility had, she knew, irked him often beyond bearing. He had ever cheerfully shouldered the burden his wife represented, which made it the more surprising that he had given in to temptation. If she was honest, she did feel a trifle of disappointment in one whom she had supposed cherished similar values to her own.

"What will you do, Ottilia?"

The question, coming from her brother pat upon her thoughts caused her to suppress them. "Nothing today, since Fan insists I must rest."

"Quite right too," came back from her doctor brother. "You have time to plan then."

"Indeed, but I don't yet know what I may do about this letter. I still need to track down Alexander Penkevil, but perhaps it might be well to revisit the women in the case. With adroit questioning, I might be able to judge the author of this effusion."

Averil's eyes were on her. "Will you accuse them?"

"Possibly, if I can perceive a glimmer of the individual's identity." A thought occurred and she eyed the visitor with some degree of speculation. "I wonder if it might be well to confront them with you in person?"

There was an instant response from both, speaking one over the other.

"Absolutely not, Ottilia —"

"If you think it might serve a useful purpose."

"— I forbid it!"

She had no need to address her brother's prohibition, for Averil did it for her.

"That is for me to decide, Patrick."

"I won't have you exposed to further insult."

"For my part, I should much like to meet this challenge head on."

"For God's sake, why, Averil? Why put yourself through unnecessary pain?"

To Ottilia's secret amusement Averil patted his arm in a motherly way. "You need not fret. No one will dare insult me to my face. Such underhand methods as these are all I have ever been obliged to endure."

Ottilia jumped on this. "You have had letters before?"

The hazel gaze came around to meet hers. "Now and then."

"Is it too much to expect that you may have kept them?"

"You mean you could have made comparison?" A little sigh came. "I have not. I consigned them to the fire."

"Understandably. Then, unless you have an excellent memory, we must start afresh with this one."

Averil's brows drew together. "I do recall one was also written in capitals. The others were not, but the hand had obviously been disguised by using the careful rounded letters of a child."

Hope rose again. "Then you have been targeted perhaps by the same person in the past. Can you say if any of these have looked at you askance or in any other way shown disapproval?"

She recited the list of the women she had so far questioned and was immediately gratified when Averil perked up.

"Indeed, yes! Nancy Meerbrook almost gave me the cut direct when we met at a concert. She was forestalled, however, because Ruth Penkevil, whom she accompanied, greeted me with civility."

Ottilia almost clapped her hands. "That sounds very like the Nancy I met. She shall be our first port of call. Tomorrow?" Recollecting that she had no notion of Averil's circumstances, she instantly added, "Or on a day which suits. Sooner rather than later."

Averil was already rising. "I can manage tomorrow. Provided Ralph does not have one of his turns, I may leave him in the care of our servants. They are very good with him."

"Excellent," said Ottilia, taking due note of her remarks about Mr Deakin. "Shall we say ten o'clock? I would prefer to catch Nancy before she has an opportunity to leave her lodging. Otherwise, we might be obliged to run the gamut with Mrs Poyle and Ruth as well. People are always more malleable if one can get them alone."

Ottilia found herself under curious regard from the hazel eyes. She raised enquiring eyebrows and Averil gave a little laugh.

"You must excuse me, Lady Fan. I had not bargained for your expertise in these affairs. I am humbled."

Embarrassed, Ottilia hastened to disclaim. "Pray don't be absurd, Mrs Deakin. My only knack, if you must have it, is in noticing what others might not." She threw a smiling glance at her brother. "I learned much of the wiles of individuals while caring for Patrick's enterprising sons."

"Ha! Mischievous imps they were too." Patrick rose from the table. "If you have decided your plans, ladies…"

Averil made her farewells, accepting Patrick's escort to see her out, leaving Ottilia with a burning question on her lips.

She waited only until the door closed behind the couple before tackling Francis. "What is the difficulty with her husband, Fan?"

He gave her a startled look, pausing as he was about to put a forkful of bacon into his mouth. "How the deuce should I know, Tillie? Ask Patrick."

Ottilia clicked her tongue. "Oh, come, Fan. Do you suppose I have not fathomed that he told you everything? I remember now how evasive you were when you returned from Salisbury."

"I was nothing of the kind."

"Esther Winning too," she pursued, ignoring his denial. "If I am not mistaken, she was within an ace of telling me the whole. I dare say she only refrained because it was so soon after Sophie's funeral."

Francis threw down his fork with an oath. "I give up! How in the world could you tell? I never opened my mouth on the subject."

Ottilia broke into giggles. "You did not need to, my dearest dear. I know you so well. Now tell me about Ralph Deakin, if you please."

He cast his gaze heavenwards, but complied, shoving his plate aside in favour of pouring coffee into his cup and sipping the black brew as he talked.

"He's an invalid, Patrick said, and many years his wife's senior. Apparently, they have not shared a bed for years. Nor, before you think the worse of your brother, my dear one, had he and Sophie."

Ottilia felt a sort of hush descend upon her. "Is that true?"

"It's why he succumbed, Patrick told me." He grimaced. "I can imagine his frustration. More power to him he did not take to a harlot."

She eyed him, the hush turning to ice in her breast. "Is that what you would do, Fan?"

He looked incredulous. "If I couldn't share your bed? I can't now, idiot wife of mine. At least, I can, but without loving you the way I wish to."

She winked wetness away. "Am I such an idiot?"

"If you suppose for one instant that I would betray you with another woman, yes, you wretch! How dare you even think it?"

She let out a breath on a suppressed sob. "I never have before."

Francis gave vent to another oath and got up, moving to take a seat closer. He slipped an arm about her and drew her to him. "You are a deal more upset by Patrick's defection than you allowed to appear, are you not, my loved one?"

"Yes." She let her head rest upon his shoulder. "More than I knew."

She felt his lips on her forehead and was comforted. In a moment or two, she sat up. She could not quite help the tremor in her smile as she looked into the beloved features. "Forgive me. I won't doubt you again."

That lopsided smile she cherished appeared. "You had better not, or it will be the worse for you."

Her characteristic laugh came. "Your word is my command, my darling lord."

"Then you'd best resume eating and conjure your indifferent face. I hear Patrick's footsteps returning."

CHAPTER THIRTEEN

Averil Deakin was prompt, arriving at Ash Lodge just as Ottilia finished the last of the roll she was consuming, lavishly larded with honey. She licked her fingers, smiling as she rose from her chair. "You took me at my word, Mrs Deakin."

The other laughed. "I was fortunate. My husband chose to remain in his bed for the day. He bid me remove and leave him in peace to his book."

Ottilia noted the implication. Then Francis had been right to suggest the couple did not share a bed. "Mr Deakin is a great reader?"

"He used to be. Now he invariably loses concentration and forgets what he is reading. I often find him merely staring at the same page, but it makes him happy."

Ottilia spoke on impulse. "How sad! I am so very sorry. Was he a scholar?"

"A most erudite one. I owe him my education." But Averil closed her lips in a way that signalled a reluctance to say more, instead gesturing to the other inhabitants of the parlour. "Do we go accompanied?"

Francis took this. He had risen upon her entrance, along with both Hathaway boys who had been breakfasting with the Fanshawes. "By no means, ma'am. I am pledged to go with Ben and Tom here to seek out a certain Farmer Gubb."

"Yes," said Tom with eagerness, "because he's too cross with Ben and me and Uncle Fan — I mean, Lord Francis — won't have to run away like we did."

To Ottilia's surprise, Averil went into a peal of laughter, which altered her whole countenance, making it bright with warmth. Abruptly she realised why this woman had attracted Patrick.

"Do not tell me you have run afoul of old Petrus, Tom. Did he shake his stick at you and threaten to set the dogs on?"

"Worse," said Ben. "He chased us and promised to thrash either of us if we so much as crossed into his farmland again."

Averil's smile was wide. "He would never do that, however much he said so. He is too much indebted to your papa, you must know."

"Indeed?" Ottilia's interest was piqued. "Upon what occasion?"

Averil turned to her, a look of prideful admiration in her face. "He saved Mrs Gubb's life. She would have died of a virulent fever otherwise."

Ottilia's brother, who had been standing at the door after escorting Averil into the room, at once disclaimed. "Nonsense. I did what any doctor must have done."

"And refused payment into the bargain."

"Well, the harvest was bad that year and Petrus had lost several pigs too. Besides, I was merely lucky that my methods worked. They are not uniformly successful."

Averil cried out at this, and was joined by both Ben and Tom in protest. Ottilia watched the argument in silence, taking in how both her nephews appeared to be comfortably at ease with Mrs Deakin. How long had this intimacy been in train to allow for bonding with her lover's sons? Ottilia was obliged to suppress a rise of disapproval. It was not for her to dictate upon her brother's affections. But need he have involved the boys with their mother alive and ailing?

The discussion was brought to a conclusion by Francis, who bade her nephews make ready. "I'm going to muffle up if you mean to drag me through an icy forest, and I dare say you ought to do the same." He turned to Ottilia. "Shall I bring down your cloak, my love? Williams ought to have the coach ready by this time."

Ottilia opted to fetch the cloak herself since she needed to make use of the chamber pot before leaving the house. She accompanied her spouse to their bedchamber therefore and took opportunity to vent her distress.

"I should much like to know when the boys have had time to become so well acquainted with Averil Deakin. One would think Patrick would have more conduct than to introduce them to his mistress."

Francis, engaged in wrapping a scarf about his throat, glanced across. "I thought you were a trifle discomposed."

"I am annoyed rather."

"So I perceive. I hardly dare venture to suggest it, but it's possible they became acquainted with the woman by other means. It's a small set of villages, Tillie."

"And Ralph Deakin is his patient, yes. But if you failed to notice how easy they were with her, Tom and Ben, I assure you I did not."

He did not reply and she rose with the usual effort entailed by the growing bump in her belly, and readjusted her clothing, feeling disgruntled.

Francis came across, holding out her cloak. He had already shrugged himself into his greatcoat. "Here. Turn round." She did so and he set the cloak about her shoulders, then turned her to face him again. He leaned in and she received a quick kiss. "Stop fretting, my loved one. There is nothing you can do and you ought not to show that face to Averil on this expedition of yours."

Ottilia sighed. "True. My irritation is not directed towards her."

She was treated to an enigmatic look. "Are you sure?"

Ottilia drew a breath. "Fiend! No, I'm not sure. I think I may hate her."

His hands cradled her face and the dark eyes softened. "You are incapable of hating anyone, sweetheart. Concentrate on the task in hand. You have a murderer to find."

The tumult in her breast subsided and she covered his hands with her own. "I do love you so very much, my darling lord."

"Likewise." He kissed her again and released her. "*En avant.* Those brats will be itching to be off."

Ottilia accompanied him to the door. "Pray don't let that farmer fellow intimidate you, Fan. He sounds a very tartar."

"Have no fear. This is where one's position in life becomes useful. He won't dare to gainsay me."

She laughed and allowed herself to be ushered downstairs where she found Averil conversing with Patrick, but quite ready to depart. It did not take many minutes to see off Francis and the boys and enter the waiting coach. Patrick having supplied Ryde with Nancy Meerbrook's direction, Ottilia settled back as the vehicle began to move, and turned to Averil, who was seated beside her.

"When did you move to this area? I am sure we did not meet while I was living at Ash Lodge."

"We did not." Averil spared her a glance before turning to look out of the window. "We lived beyond Knighton for many years, closer to Tony Stratford. When Ralph began to ail and we realised, his son and I, that his condition could only deteriorate, we thought it best to leave the estate in Max's hands and move to the cottage where it would be easier for me and specially selected servants to take care of him. It belongs to the family and was used by an aunt until her death. Your brother fortuitously had his practice in the vicinity."

Convenient, Ottilia thought, and immediately inwardly chided herself for lack of charity. "You don't miss the larger life?"

"To be truthful, I have no time to miss it. My participation even in the local social circle is necessarily minimal."

"Is Mr Deakin's estate extensive?"

"It is a fair size. I could not have Ralph losing his bearings there, you see. Nor could he tolerate his noisy grandchildren. He needs quiet. He becomes hopelessly confused if there is a cacophony and too many persons about him."

Ottilia's compassion was stirred. "It must be very hard for you."

She half expected Averil to disclaim, but her response was frank. "It is, but I can endure it for Ralph's sake. He has been nothing but generous and kind to me."

Yet you betrayed him. But Ottilia kept the thought to herself, instead casting about for some innocuous question. "I take it Max Deakin is your stepson?"

"Oh, yes. Max is close to my own age. His mother died several years before Ralph and I met and married."

Ottilia yearned to ask why Averil had married a man so much older than she, but she could not feel they were well enough acquainted for such a personal question. Had Averil been a suspect, she would not hesitate. Which thought led her back to her mission for the day. "How well do you know Nancy Meerbrook?"

"Hardly well at all. As I said, she made her disapproval plain." A tiny laugh escaped her. "I cannot imagine she will be pleased to see me."

Ottilia all but snorted. "I have no interest in pleasing her. On the contrary, I trust I may succeed in tripping her into being a deal more truthful than she was when I first accosted her."

At that moment, the coach began to slow and through the window on her side, Ottilia saw they had reached Aston village and were moving along the row of small houses that led in due course to the turning into Aston Park, the Penkevil home.

"Ah, I believe we are arriving. We should certainly find Nancy in one of these dwellings."

So it proved when the coach came to a standstill and Ryde appeared at the window. "It's that one, m'lady." He pointed to a small door within one of a tenement. "Will you come down?"

"Yes, if you please. Let down the steps, Ryde."

He opened the door and Ottilia was soon able to descend. Averil followed her and she beckoned her on, turning to walk down the short path to the door. She plied the knocker with energy and stood back to wait. The door opened within a moment or two and a maid appeared behind it, bobbing a curtsy.

"Is Miss Meerbrook at home?"

"Yes, ma'am. Who shall I say?"

Primed, the maid led them into a narrow hallway and opened the first door opposite a set of stairs. "Lady Francis Fanshawe and Mrs Deakin, miss," she announced, and stood aside to allow the visitors to enter.

Ottilia stepped through the aperture into a very small parlour and stopped short. Nancy Meerbrook, looking utterly taken aback and not a little apprehensive, was in the act of rising from a cosy sofa set against the far wall. By her side, and rising also, was a gentleman unknown to Ottilia. He was a man of medium height, a trifle portly and of a florid complexion. His country frockcoat was of a sober hue, worn over black breeches. Tellingly, his neck-cloth was likewise black and he was wearing the clerical bob wig.

Ottilia brightened. "Ah, the very reverend Alexander Penkevil, if I am not mistaken."

The gentleman's gaze widened and his stare was inimical. "You are the woman who has taken it upon herself to interfere in the matter of my brother's unfortunate demise."

Ottilia's hackles rose but she kept her tone noncommittal. "I am she. I take it you have some objection?"

"I have every objection. The matter is under the jurisdiction of Sir Hugh Riccarton. I fail to comprehend your interest."

Moving forward, Ottilia ignored the entirety of this speech and held out a hand. "I have been looking forward to making your acquaintance, sir. May I begin by commiserating with you upon your tragic loss?"

"What?" The cleric frowned, plainly taken aback. He took the hand in the briefest of salutes, harrumphed a little. His belligerent stance did not falter. "I suppose I must thank you, although as I understand it, you are responsible for creating unnecessary complications."

Ottilia faced him down. "Unnecessary? You do not then wish to discover the individual who took your brother's life?"

His nose lifted as he sniffed. "I have yet to learn that anyone did. Other than Hector himself. A conclusion more distressful to me than the one you saw fit to introduce."

"Then you ought to be grateful to me for sparing you that misery at least."

Here Nancy Meerbrook intervened. "Oh, do not say so! You have no notion how the poor dear reverend is suffering."

Ottilia watched in some amusement as the poor dear reverend twitched with evident embarrassment, flicking the woman an irritated glance.

"Nothing of the sort, Nan— Miss Meerbrook. I am merely exercised by the weight of responsibility that has landed upon my shoulders." He looked back at Ottilia. "It falls to me, ma'am, to take care of my brother's family as well as his affairs. One would think this was enough."

The reproachful look she received indicated how he blamed her for adding to his tribulations. Ottilia abandoned him temporarily, looking instead to Nancy. "May we sit? My condition is not best suited to standing about."

The reverend's gaze dropped to the mound beneath her gown and his brows flew up. "You are *enceinte*, ma'am? Yet you persist in interesting yourself in an affair such as this?"

"Pray take this chair, Lady Fan," said Nancy, moving to one set to one side of the fireplace and turning it so that it faced the sofa.

"Thank you. I believe Mrs Deakin would be glad of a seat too." She gestured towards Averil, who had remained standing just inside the door.

With a leap of satisfaction, she saw how Nancy started, her gaze flying to the other visitor. Had she failed to take in the second name? Overtaken by surprise — or shock? — at Ottilia's entrance perhaps.

Overcoming her evident reluctance to welcome the other woman, Nancy produced a second chair and set it beside Ottilia's. "You may sit here, Mrs Deakin."

The tone was distant and Ottilia could not forbear casting a speaking glance towards Averil. The other received it with a slight lift of her brows but she did not speak as she settled into the designated chair.

Ottilia watched Nancy retake her own seat on the sofa and discovered the reverend still standing, his frown now directed at Averil. She took the bull by the horns. "Will you now object also to Mrs Deakin's presence? I promise you there is reason enough for her having accompanied me."

Her quarry's gaze shifted to meet hers. "You are here to speak to Miss Meerbrook, I surmise. In which case, I shall —"

"Oh, don't go, sir. Your presence is fortuitous. I searched for you in All Saints' church on Sunday, but found only Mr Pidsea."

His look became disdainful. "Do you suppose I had not been informed? I cannot imagine what you want with me."

"Can you not?" Ottilia gave him a spurious smile. "Perhaps you are not aware that in events of this kind it is imperative to question the relatives."

"Of what kind, ma'am?"

She brought it out with a ring. "Murder, Mr Penkevil."

He flinched. "A crude term, ma'am."

"It is the correct one, sir."

"So you will have it. I refuse to believe such nonsense."

"Oh? I thought you said it was preferable to the notion of suicide."

This time he winced. "You call a spade a spade, do you?"

"Euphemisms are such a waste of time, do you not think? It is always better to face things squarely."

He made no reply to this but hovered, evidently irresolute. Ottilia waited, reflecting that his grief did not appear to be very great. Or was that fair? It was possible his hostility was a manifestation of precisely that. On the other hand, according to report, not much love had been lost between these brothers.

At length, and oddly, it was Averil who settled the matter, impatience in her tone. "Oh, do sit down, Reverend Penkevil. The sooner we begin, the sooner over. If you have all day, I most certainly do not."

Alexander Penkevil directed an austere look towards her, but Nancy Meerbrook tugged upon his sleeve and he gave forth a disgruntled harrumph. But he did sit down. Ottilia could have cheered. Instead, she slipped a hand into the pocket of her cloak and brought out the anonymous letter. Opening it, she held it up, the writing turned towards the couple, and addressed herself to Nancy.

"I wonder if you recognise this, Miss Meerbrook?"

If she did, she gave no sign, merely staring at the sheet in an attitude of concentration. Was there a faint rise of colour in her papery cheek? She did not give a direct answer.

"Why should I? What is it?"

"A letter, to be sure. It is unsigned. You will note that it is written in capital letters."

"What of it?" Nancy pursed her lips.

"It is an obvious effort to disguise the hand."

"Oh. Yes, I suppose it is." She fidgeted a moment, but Ottilia kept silent. Nancy spoke in a goaded voice. "Why do you show it to me? Do you think I wrote it?"

"Did you?"

Before Nancy could answer, the Reverend Penkevil held out an imperative hand. "Let me see that."

Ottilia gave it up to him and waited while he ran his eyes down the sheet, Nancy peering over his shoulder. It was plain the effusion was new to the reverend by the line between his brows as he drew them together. Ottilia glanced at Averil and found her watchful eyes on the pair seated upon the sofa.

Alexander Penkevil lowered the sheet and his gaze went to Averil. "This explains why you are present."

Ottilia jumped in. "You knew at once it must have been addressed to Mrs Deakin?"

His lip curled a little. "Obviously."

"Then perhaps you may also guess at who wrote it?"

"I have not the remotest conjecture."

Ottilia noted a certain stiffness at his jaw as he held out the sheet for her to take back. He did not look towards Nancy. Was it deliberate? Ottilia was inclined to think he suspected she had indeed authored the letter. Without his approval. It struck her that Nancy's description of him did not accord with his attitude. Kind and not given to disputation? If Ottilia read him aright, he was more likely to prove an officious prig. She had no difficulty in imagining he might well have disposed of his brother. How to proceed to question him without raising his ire? She opted for a soft approach.

"Well, let us leave that matter for the moment." She folded the sheet but kept it visible, held loosely between her fingers. She produced another spurious smile. "Given that I am pursuing this matter, sir, would it be too much to request a little information from you?"

His look suggested it would be altogether outrageous, but at least he did not bark again. "Of what nature?"

"Oh, nothing very dramatic, I assure you. I am merely desirous of discovering, if I can, what your brother's habits might have been to take him into the woods in the middle of the night."

Alexander Penkevil let out a scoffing sound. "This is your line of enquiry? Do you suppose Hector went there for any other purpose than to do away with himself?"

Ottilia quashed this without hesitation. "As he did not do away with himself, I could scarcely be thinking along those lines."

"What then?"

"Could he have met someone in that vicinity? Had he acquaintance living close by? The wood has several pathways through it. He might have taken a short cut."

Both her auditors were frowning now. Was this tack unexpected? Did either instead expect an accusation? A glance at Averil found her equally puzzled. Ottilia waited.

Nancy broke first. "I cannot think Mr Penkevil would visit anyone at such a late hour." She turned an imploring gaze upon the reverend. "Don't you agree?"

The reverend spared her a brief glance and turned his gaze back upon Ottilia. "There is no saying what my brother might have done. He was unpredictable."

Ottilia's senses prickled. "Was he so? In what respect?"

"In every respect, ma'am." Contempt was in both face and voice. "I will not pretend to any great affection between us. Since you have seen fit to pry into Hector's affairs, I make no doubt you will have garnered that much from gossiping tongues."

Ottilia ignored the studied insult of this address. "Come, sir, this is excellent. I am an advocate of frankness. How distant was your relationship with Hector?"

"Not distant at all." He harrumphed. "We saw a good deal of each other, despite our frequent disagreements."

"Yet you say you cannot predict his habits."

The barb evidently pierced his armour for his florid countenance grew redder still. "With a temperament so volatile, it is impossible to say what he might do. Nothing would surprise me. If you tell me he was creeping about at night for some nefarious purpose, I would not credit it. But he might well stamp out into the night in a fury." He passed a hand across his face in a manner Ottilia could not but deem agitated. "Mayhap he ran into some individual for whom he cherished a grudge. Hector would think nothing of going into the attack, especially if he was in one of his rages. His victim may have struck back. The whole business might have been accidental."

Ottilia did not immediately dismiss this unlikely theory though she took due note that the reverend's notion precluded Hector taking his own life. "You mean this person could have killed him by accident and then chosen to make it look like a suicide? Why not simply run away?"

"How the deuce do I know? If you find him, you may ask." He was breathing deeply, as if he must try to bring his own temper under control. Was the volatility common to both brothers? He resumed in a milder tone. "I wish you might find it to be some such occurrence."

"It would indeed be convenient, but unfortunately there is one factor that prevents your interesting theory from proving true. Your brother was drugged, sir. Therefore, it could not have happened as you describe."

Alexander stared, as did Nancy. "Is that certain?"

"My brother found traces of a soporific substance, most likely valerian, in the stomach."

"Doctor Hathaway?"

"Just so."

A defeated look came into the man's face. "Then it was deliberate."

"Although I am an advocate for keeping an open mind, it appears that it was deliberate and premeditated, sir. Someone, or perhaps more than one individual, would seem to have plotted this death and carried it through."

His gaze shot up, the eyes suddenly keen. "More than one?"

Not wishing to show her hand this early, Ottilia prevaricated. "It is one possibility we must take into account."

She reckoned without her host. Alexander Penkevil became steely. "Whom do you intend to accuse? You have already caused havoc within my brother's household with your questions. What, do you think Hector's closest family would seek to remove him? Poor Ruth, for instance? Or myself?" The inimical look he had worn at first returned. "You seek to put this upon me, do you?"

Nancy uttered a distressed cry. "She cannot, Alexander. I told her you would never do harm to your brother."

The reverend turned on her an infuriated look and she shrunk away. "You did so, did you? Yet you failed to warn me of what was going forward?"

Nancy quailed, her voice shaking. "I was going to this very morning. That is why I requested you to visit me. If Lady Fan had not arrived…"

Ottilia met the reproachful gaze the woman turned on her. "It seems I was opportune. Yet I wonder you have allowed several days to pass before informing Mr Penkevil of his danger."

There was a silence. Was it guilt flashing across Nancy's face? One could not tell with Alexander Penkevil. His countenance gave nothing away.

Averil chose to break the impasse. "That was adroit, Lady Fan."

The reverend was swift with a crushing retort. "Adroit? It is an insult! By heaven, I had not thought it possible you could suppose me capable of this deed! If you were not so quick to take Nancy up, I would have told you that I have been absent these many days. I told you my brother's death has brought a deal of work upon me. That, ma'am, is why you did not find me when you sought me at my church. Miss Meerbrook had no chance to inform me of what was in the wind prior to this morning. This is the first opportunity I have had to respond to her summons."

Ottilia took due note of the word, but chose not to take him up on the light it shed upon his relationship with Nancy Meerbrook if she was wont to demand his presence.

"I see. Well, that puts a different complexion on the matter."

"I should think so, ma'am! Now, if you have no further questions —"

"Oh, I am not done yet, Mr Penkevil."

His lips closed tightly together and Ottilia was almost sure she heard a grinding of teeth. She held up the letter still tucked between her fingers.

"We have not yet settled the question of who authored this effusion."

Alexander gave tongue again. "It has nothing to do with me."

"But it may well have to do with Nancy."

At this, the woman drew herself up. "Do you accuse me, Lady Fan?"

Ottilia deflected. "Can you think of anyone spiteful enough to have written it? Mrs Poyle perhaps?"

Nancy's breath came out in a whoosh. "Margery Poyle is capable of any spite. I should not be at all surprised if she wrote it."

Ottilia glanced to Alexander Penkevil and found him chewing his lip. "What do you think, sir? You must know Mrs Poyle very well."

He shifted his shoulders and glanced away, looking briefly at Averil. "I could not hazard a guess."

"Ruth then?"

The suggestion was productive of protest from both voices.

"Nonsense!"

"Ruth is never spiteful!"

"My sister-in-law is not the type to pen such a letter."

Ottilia gave an elaborate sigh. "Dear me, this leaves me in a little difficulty."

"I see no difficulty," said Alexander. "Anyone might have sent it."

"Perhaps. But you see, the person who wrote this did not seek to insult Mrs Deakin here. That was merely a ploy. Did you not read it properly, Mr Penkevil?"

"Of course I read it. Of what are you talking?"

Ottilia noted the faintly apprehensive look on Nancy's face. "The author wishes me to cease and desist. A desire that points to their having had a hand in the murder."

CHAPTER FOURTEEN

"You certainly shook them up, Lady Fan."

A little sound of laughter escaped the woman seated beside Averil in the carriage. She found it oddly attractive in this strange sister of Patrick's.

"Did I not? The dear reverend was disconcerted."

Averil's recollection was more of the other party. "Nancy looked as if she might burst into tears, I thought." She put the question puzzling her. "Why did you not pursue it?"

She thought Ottilia made a face in the dimness. "I had made him too angry."

"He would not answer you?"

"Just so. Or only in a belligerent style. I doubt he is a man easily shaken."

Averil's interest in the workings of Ottilia's mind increased. "How will you manage then?"

There came another laugh, one decidedly roguish. "I suspect it won't trouble my ingenuity unduly. Dear Alexander needs time to consider. In a calmer frame of mind, he will likely come to me."

Startled, Averil eyed her profile. "How in the world can you know that?"

"Well, he must do one of two things. Either he ignores me altogether or he chooses to convince me of his innocence — assuming he is innocent."

"Gracious, do you think he did it?"

"He is certainly in the running. Much depends upon the actuality of his association with Nancy Meerbrook."

"How so?"

"If she wrote that letter, she did so without Alexander's permission or approval. The most likely answer, I believe, is that Nancy indeed fears Alexander may have killed Hector, in which case she wrote that letter in a bid to protect him. However, should we suppose instead that the two of them were in it together, that begins to be interesting."

Averil felt as if her head was whirling. "You have lost me completely. You surely don't think this was a conspiracy?"

"I think it possible. A woman might have administered the drug which rendered Hector insensible, allowing the man in the case to carry out the murder."

Light began to dawn. "That is why you asked about Hector taking a short cut?"

"We have to account for his presence in the woods somehow. To move an unconscious man is a tricky undertaking, although it has been done with a corpse. A calming draught does not necessarily render a person unconscious immediately."

Averil's mind took a leap. "So he might be drugged in one place and then walk into the woods before he dropped."

Lady Fan gave her one of those smiles Averil found peculiarly warm. "There now. You are in a fair way to becoming adept."

She had to laugh. "Never. I do not pretend to any great understanding of such matters, although I am intrigued almost beyond bearing. You have done much in this line, I believe?"

"Too much, if my poor husband was to be honest. He dislikes it intensely, but he is disgracefully indulgent and I am a wretch to trouble him with these affairs."

A faint note of melancholy accompanied this remark. Self-reproach? Patrick had spoken once or twice of his sister's acute sense of ethics. With apprehension, it had to be said. Although so far Ottilia had uttered no word of blame. It was on the tip of Averil's tongue to introduce the subject of her illicit liaison, but her courage failed her. For all her friendliness, this woman had shown a frankly intimidating and ruthless side in her dealings with Alexander and Nancy. Averil had no wish to draw her fire.

Just then Ottilia spoke, throwing her out of her reverie. "I wonder, Averil, do you know anything of Roland Huish?"

Averil gathered her scattered thoughts. "The young fellow who walks with a limp? I have met him."

"What do you think of him?"

"In what respect? I cannot say I have thought about him in particular, other than noticing how he makes sheep's eyes at Ruth Penkevil."

"Yes, that is precisely the point. She is quite open about their affection for one another. Or she was with me."

"Then you very likely know as much as I do." She found she was making another leap. "Do you tell me you suspect a murderous partnership there too?"

"It is another option. I am inclined to acquit Ruth, but one should never allow liking to prejudice one's thinking."

"I don't see how you can avoid it."

"Very easily. The sad truth is that the most charming of rogues can prove to be guilty of heinous crimes. It is a matter of keeping perspective."

This point of view caused Averil to suffer a reversal of feeling. Could she trust Ottilia's manner towards her? She might be as friendly as she pleased and secretly condemn Averil's conduct. The thought caused her a pang and she sat mumchance for a while. Until Ottilia startled her with a pertinent question.

"What is it, Averil? What have I said to distress you?"

She disclaimed with haste. "Nothing at all. I am not distressed."

For a moment there was no response. Then a gloved hand stole across and took hers in a strong clasp. "Forgive me, but you are certainly upset. Pray don't deny it."

Averil allowed her hand to lie within Ottilia's as she gave out a sigh. "If you press me, I am a trifle shocked to hear you speak so readily of being able to accuse someone even though you like them. I could not do it."

The hand did not release hers, but Ottilia's tone dropped low. "You need not fear me, Averil."

To her own surprise, Averil experienced a little spurt of anger. "No? Will you claim that you do not blame either of us? Patrick is convinced you must."

At last the clasp on her hand loosened and Ottilia released her. "I have no right to do so, but I will admit that I am having a little difficulty in arriving at acceptance. But that is my difficulty and need not trouble either of you. Be assured I will never voice any criticism."

It was no comfort, but Averil felt obliged to acknowledge the effort. "I thank you for that at least."

She was prepared to let the matter drop, but she found she had not bargained for a woman as persistent as this one.

"One thing does puzzle me, if I may be so bold?"

"What thing?" Realising her own disgruntled note, Averil sought to amend it. "I mean, yes, you may ask."

"Why did you marry a man so much older than you? I ask only in a spirit of curiosity."

Averil's heart lightened. She had been afraid of a question as to why she and Patrick had become lovers. She answered with greater ease. "My brother and I had been orphaned quite suddenly. Our parents both fell victim to a virulent fever. The same which Petrus Gubb's wife suffered, although much later. It has been prevalent across the county off and on over the years. We had no Doctor Hathaway to effect a cure and we lost them both."

"How unfortunate! You were both young, I take it?"

"I was only a year or so past my majority. My brother was established in the clergy, having refused the opportunity to work in our father's legal practice. Papa's partner took it over, with the result that I was left with little choice. Either I battened upon my brother or applied for some sort of position. Before I was obliged to do either, Ralph rescued me from my predicament. He was long widowed and had been my father's client. I was happy enough to accept his offer and we were content. I could even describe our union as a happy one."

"Until his unlucky condition materialised, I take it?"

"Indeed. It was scarcely noticeable at first, except for the occasional moment of confusion. His memory began to fail and that distressed him. He became irritable and harder to manage. I was obliged to—" She broke off, forgetful of her company as she became lost in reminiscence.

But Ottilia did not leave it as she might have hoped. "Obliged to?"

Well, what did it matter, after all? A fleeting notion that this offered an extenuating circumstance that might reconcile prompted her tongue. "We had to separate at night. It had become untenable to sleep at his side. You may imagine the situation, I dare say."

"Readily."

Surprised by the response, Averil looked round and found sympathy in Ottilia's features. She felt at once grateful and repelled. "You need not feel sorry for me, Ottilia. It was no real hardship to make that change."

She let the implication lie, certain this quick-witted woman would have no difficulty in interpreting her words. Why she should reject an olive branch she could not think. To her chagrin, Ottilia supplied the reason.

"You believe I will judge you less harshly, do you not, and you don't like that. I promise you I was not looking for mitigation. I strongly doubt that either you or Patrick took this step for any other reason than a too strong attraction. One cannot explain these things. Francis and I fell utterly in love in the space of a week, and all while we were trying to prove the innocence of his brother, mark you. Believe me, Averil, if you can make my brother even half as happy as I am with my darling husband, I can only bless the day he found you."

Averil's eyes pricked and her throat tightened. She it was this time who sought for Ottilia's hand and squeezed. The answering pressure sent a wave of warmth through her bosom.

By dint of trading upon his title, Francis had effected an entrance into Petrus Gubb's house. The farmer ushered him in through the nearest door, throwing a dour warning at the Hathaway boys trailing behind.

"You can come in, but one word amiss, young fellers, and I'll be chasing you out with a broomstick."

Francis threw an amused glance over his shoulder at his wife's nephews, both of whom looked decidedly apprehensive. "Don't fret, Mr Gubb. I will keep them in order."

"Best you does, yer honour, for as I won't stand for boys questionin' me like I were a crim'nal. If it were my lad, I'd dust his jacket for him, but I make no doubt as the doctor spoils them rotten."

As he spoke, Petrus was moving towards a huge deal table surrounded by straight chairs and set in the middle of a spacious apartment that looked to be an adjunct to the kitchen premises further along. Through a wide aperture, Francis could partially spy a spit over a fire and another heavier wooden table at which a woman in an apron and mobcap, hands and arms floured to the elbow, was busy throwing and kneading dough, a plethora of pots, bowls, jugs, and bottles scattered about the tabletop. The main room boasted a massive hearth, several pine cupboards and shelved sideboards groaning with tableware, a row of pegs from which hung hats, coats, whips and other impedimenta, and a flagged floor covered in claw scratchings no doubt from the dogs now barking outside.

"Sit you down, yer honour. Them too." He jerked a thumb at the Hathaway boys. "I've to get them hounds to shut their noise."

He then returned to the door, opened it, and let out a piercing whistle. It was answered by a cacophony of barks, upon which Petrus yelled an uncouth command containing dire threats. A few more were needed before the dogs fell silent, what time Francis took a seat with his back to the hearth, glad of the heat emanating from a crackling fire behind. He eyed with suspicion a big jug with a dirty lip and several questionable tumblers that stood on the table.

"I hope to God he's not going to offer me a drink from that thing."

Tom snorted a laugh as he dropped into one of the many chairs, but Ben, following suit, hastened to reassure. "It's likely only barley water, sir."

"Well, I don't want it, whatever it is."

Tom piped up, sotto voce. "If he offers you wine, Uncle Fan, don't take it. It's homemade and you'll be drunk as a wheelbarrow after only one glass."

Francis made a silent vow to refuse all refreshments and was somewhat relieved when the farmer showed no disposition to proffer anything after he slammed the door and returned to the table, pulling out a chair opposite and plonking down.

"Pesky dogs. Wonder is I ain't deaf with them barking their heads off all day."

Francis made no reply to this but went directly to the meat of his visit. "I expect you've guessed why I've come, Mr Gubb."

"It's Petrus to you, yer honour. Don't feel right otherwise. Old Petrus they call me, and that's fair. I've more'n three score in my dish and I ain't about to miss the other ten."

This looked to be no idle boast. Petrus Gubb might be old, as evidenced by his rusty grey locks and weather-beaten face, but his lean legs, clad in homespun breeches, and the arms protruding from a woollen smock, were all muscle and sinew. Deep lines ran between nose and chin and below a pair of hawk-like eyes, keen and intelligent, but the skin was otherwise taut. Francis guessed he was a working farmer who did most of the chores himself, perhaps with a hand or two to help. A whiff of sweat bore out this supposition. One could not but admire the fellow. He did not seem a likely candidate for a murderer.

"You know why I'm here, Petrus?" Francis repeated.

"I guessed it soon as I seen them two along of you." The head jerk indicated the boys. "More of that there dead Penkevil, is it?"

"Precisely."

"Say on then." He spoke grudgingly, but at least there was no explosion.

"We are trying to find out whether anyone heard or saw anything on the night Penkevil was killed."

Petrus's brows drew together. "It were unlawful killin' then?"

"Yes, that is established."

Petrus slammed a closed fist down on the table. "Good riddance, I say. Not as I hold with killin' unlawful like for I don't. But if yer honour wants me to weep for Penkevil, you can whistle for it."

Francis seized the cue. "You didn't like him?"

"Find one as did and I'll shake yer hand. He were one as took advantage of his position, were Penkevil. I don't hold with such. A fair man I am and if a man treat me just, I'll do right by him. But if a man ups and takes his revenge by means of law that ain't right and I don't hold with such."

Francis could not but sympathise with this point of view. "Penkevil took revenge by means of the law on you, did he?"

"Didn't he! Fining me for pigs being out of their sty on market day, which as anyone knows they must for as if you sell one you've to take it to the buyer. Had to let one go for a song that day just to pay it. Lost my pig and my money. Nor he didn't stop there, Penkevil. Next thing he's having me for wandering sheep when all the world knows as you can't keep one from straying if the dogs are too busy herding the rest. Nor it weren't the sheep's fault. It were caught on a wire. And whose wire was that, I ask you? Strayed onto his land, he says. No other in the county puts a wire fence up when he don't have no animals hisself. And that wire got my sheep, it did. Caught in his wool and the animal couldn't get free and struggles so bad he's bleeding by the time Willy found him. And there's Penkevil, shouting and screaming about as the sheep's on his land, but do he do anythin' to help the animal? No, he don't. Leaves it to suffer while he goes off and writes his complaint. Shoves the thing at Willy when he see him untangling the sheep, yelling his threats all through." Petrus ended his tirade at last, breathing hard, eyes fierce, spittle gathering on his lips.

The boys had sat mumchance, wide-eyed and mouths hanging open. Francis was not similarly affected. He had made no attempt to interrupt, instead listening with a growing realisation that the fellow had all too strong a reason to be doing away with Penkevil. His passions were high enough. If he were not raging, he appeared to have nerve and calm enough to be able to plan and carry out the murder. Yet one point remained a question.

"Revenge for what, Petrus? What had you done to inspire this enmity in Penkevil?"

The farmer's head came up and he pointed into the aperture. "See that? See her there? My wife, that is. Only she were cook to old Mr Lucian Penkevil. When he died, she upped and married me and Penkevil were mad as mad to lose her. Best cook in the county is my Bessie."

Glancing into the other room, Francis saw that the woman in question had halted in her work, her hands on the dough but her head turned towards her husband in a listening attitude. Nevertheless, the tale sounded absurd and Francis did not hesitate to speak his mind. "You are telling me Penkevil took a pet because you married his cook? Why in the world could he not employ some other?"

Petrus signalled and his wife wiped her hands on her apron and came through into the main room. She was a plump piece with a comely face, a trifle dumpy, but with a confident mien and eyes quite as shrewd as her spouse. She was perhaps some dozen years younger than him.

She was eyeing Francis and bobbed a curtsy as she arrived at her husband's side. Petrus gave her no chance to speak.

"You tell him, Bess."

"Tell him what, my dear?" Her voice was pleasantly musical, calm, but in no way subservient.

"Why Penkevil were mad as you married me, o'course. Didn't you hear me, woman?"

"I heard you." She looked across at Francis. "There's not much to add, your honour. I'd been with the Penkevil family since I don't know when, but it were a bachelor household and they were suited with simple fare. But then young Mr Penkevil were put to having to marry and he said as I'd best learn to make them fancy meals for as he were bringing a wife and her mother into the house."

"But you preferred to marry Petrus?"

"I preferred not to change my ways as I'd been used to for years. Nor I didn't want to work no more for young Mr Penkevil. A terror he was from a child, sir. I couldn't abide him for my master. Not after old Mr Penkevil who were naught but good to them as served him. After Mrs Penkevil upped and died, he were lonely but for them two boys. He wouldn't marry again, he wouldn't. Nor no woman would have put up with them two, and I reckon he knew that. So when Petrus here asked me, I said yes."

Having stated there was little more to tell, Francis was amused to be given this history. But at this point, Petrus intervened.

"She said yes for her own reasons, as is right and proper. Only Penkevil would have it as I was a-luring of her. Luring! Weren't no need for no luring. Bess, I said, I've a mind to make you my wife. And Bess said as that would sit well with her and there we were. No luring with fine words, nor gold, nor nothing as Penkevil accused me of."

"Petrus, keep a still tongue in your head. His lordship don't want to hear nothing of that." She turned back to Francis.

"Truth is, sir, as Young Penkevil never were one to be forgiving. If he thought he were done down, he'd hit back, no question. Nasty, mean little boy he were and he weren't no different as a man."

With which, she dusted off her hands as if she was done with Penkevil himself and returned to her labours in the kitchen.

Armed with this background, Francis felt it behoved him to dig deeper. He did not mince his words. "You realise, Petrus, that all this but strengthens the case against you?"

The farmer snorted. "If case there be, I'll answer it, yer honour. I never touched him by way of killing, and that's the truth."

"Can anyone other than your wife vouch for it that you were not abroad upon the night Penkevil was killed?"

Petrus's mouth twisted into a near snarl. "Who said I weren't abroad?"

"Were you?"

"Aye, I were. I were up the White Horse till late and come home the worse for Bessie to curse me and threat me with a ladle." For the first time, Petrus laughed. A low, growling sort of sound in his throat which might have been taken otherwise but for the set of his open jaw and the sudden twinkle in his eyes.

Francis lost patience. "Are you trying to make game of me, Petrus? What, you were too drunk to have perpetrated this crime, is that it? That won't fadge. You can't prove it."

Petrus scowled. "Ask Bess."

"I need a witness other than your wife, I said." Recalling his own wife's tactics with the Reverend Bruno Pidsea, he tried another tack. "But let us leave that for the moment. You must have come home through the woods. Drunk or sober, you could have heard something or seen something. If you did, tell me now. Anything at all, even if it seems insignificant."

Petrus set his elbow on the table and his chin in his hand, regarding Francis in a ruminating way. "What time of night are you thinking?"

"Late." The murder likely took place in the early hours, but any little piece could be worth adding to the puzzle.

"I misremember what time I come home. Don't recall as I saw nor heard nowt unusual. Animals. Creeping."

"The animals?"

"Aye. Snuffling like they do."

"Did you have a lantern?"

"I know my ways well enough without a light."

Francis gave it up. If the fellow was guilty, he was giving nothing away. His report sounded reasonable enough. But Francis could not shake a conviction that Petrus had not told him everything. The man was sly, responding to questions in a way that might well obfuscate the truth.

Rising, Francis nodded to the boys. "Thank you for your time, Petrus. I may need to talk with you again." The older of the Hathaways was looking at him rather than the farmer. Was Ben trying to catch his eye? It would have to wait. But it occurred to him to take advantage while he might. "I might send the boys over with a question. If they come as my messengers, can I rely on you not to harm them?"

CHAPTER FIFTEEN

"Looking at this list of yours, Tom, it seems we have tackled every one of your papa's patients except Roland Huish."

Ottilia set the paper down and glanced around the table. As well as Patrick himself, who had finished his morning examinations, both investigating parties had returned in time to partake of the light repast provided by Betty. Ottilia had taken opportunity to pool their findings and institute a discussion on what to do next.

Averil Deakin, prevailed upon to remain both to eat and join in their talk, here entered a caveat. "You cannot have questioned Ralph."

Ottilia laughed. "I think we may acquit your husband of any involvement."

"I did not mean that."

"What, then?"

"He was very well acquainted with Mr Penkevil senior. I only wondered, since Lord Francis heard so much of the young Penkevils from Bess Gubb, if Ralph might have heard some similar tale."

"You mean for the purpose of corroboration?" Ottilia considered the question. "Do you think he will recall it?"

"He is better at recalling long past incidents than what happened yesterday."

"Perhaps you might ask him?" Ottilia smiled across at her brother. "Averil has joined our team, you must know."

Patrick cast a glance towards the heavens. "You mean you inveigled her into it."

Averil spared Ottilia having to protest. "No such thing, Patrick. The murderer involved me. It is only fitting that I help to unveil the miscreant."

"Miscreant? He is an evildoer."

"Or she."

Ottilia received a wry look from her brother. "You've thrown that theory at her too, have you?"

Before she could answer, Ben piped up. "You know, Auntilla, that might hold with Petrus Gubb too. Don't you think so, Uncle Fan?"

"Aha! You're thinking of that Bess," Tom said in glee. "I'll wager she was the one who drugged Mr Penkevil. She couldn't abide him, could she, Uncle Fan?"

Francis raised an eyebrow. "You have settled it between you. Why bring me into it at all?"

Both boys laughed and Tom turned to Ottilia. "You see, Auntilla? You had better arrest them without more ado."

"She will require more proofs than that, Tom." Francis caught Ottilia's eye. "Moreover, your aunt does not arrest anyone. She will leave that to the constables once she knows the culprit."

"Well, I do wish you will hurry up, Auntilla. Papa is threatening to send us back to school already."

Here Patrick entered the lists. "You can't be absent for much longer, Tom."

"I don't see why we can't just stay home till after Christmas. After all, there's not much left of term."

"Which is precisely why you must put in an appearance and show willing. Your masters will be a good deal more lenient with you than they would if you were absent until January."

This reference to their bereaved state caused Ottilia to glance at Averil as Tom entered a spirited defence of his argument for remaining at home. Had Sophie's death caused the couple to curtail their meetings? Or was it rather Ottilia's presence? Given the conversation they'd had earlier, she inclined to the latter theory. It could not but strike her that once she and Francis had returned home and the boys were at school, there must be ample opportunity for meetings, clandestine or otherwise.

Would Patrick entertain his mistress at Ash Lodge? Would he not have more regard for Averil's reputation than to risk servant gossip besmirching her good name? Dare she mention the matter to him? Better not. Patrick would take it amiss and assume disapproval on her part that she had already ceased to feel. Averil's story had invoked her sympathy. She could well understand how the liaison had come about. In a little corner of her heart, she suspected she had still a sliver of discontent for her brother's fall from grace. Suppress it she must. Besides, there was a far more urgent matter demanding her attention.

"No, Tom, and that is final." The exasperated note in her brother's voice prompted Ottilia to intervene.

"Come, Tom, let us return to the murder. If we bend our minds to solving the puzzle, we may do so in good time."

Her nephew looked disgruntled but the elder, who had taken no part in his brother's argument, became eager. "You said you had not yet spoken to Roland Huish, Auntilla. What will you ask him?"

Ottilia pondered. "I am not sure. It will depend upon his attitude. If he is amenable, I may be more direct."

"But not if he takes umbrage like Alexander Penkevil."

"Just so, Averil. Although I suspect that particular clergyman will come around."

"Why, Ottilia?" Patrick was frowning. "If, as you say, he was annoyed —"

Averil took this. "Your sister thinks he will either continue so or seek to deflect her suspicions from himself. For my part, I consider him too arrogant a man to be amenable to questioning."

"Yes, if he is innocent," Ottilia said. "Not that it would prove guilt if he does seek me out. But it must certainly demonstrate that there is more to be learned from him. I find it frankly absurd that he could dismiss any knowledge of his brother's movements on the basis that Hector was unpredictable. What besides is his actual relationship with Nancy? I am convinced she is the author of that letter. Alexander was angry with her for having penned it. That suggests there is more between them than we were privileged to witness."

Francis was eyeing her with one of his speculative expressions. Ottilia raised her brows in question and he smiled. "I am wondering if you favour those two over Ruth Penkevil and Roland Huish."

"I cannot say, Fan. There is certainly a more cogent reason for Ruth and Roland to be rid of Hector. The one flaw with Alexander and Nancy is that I cannot yet see any benefit for them, at least not as a couple."

"Do you discount Margery Poyle?"

"By no means. But again, what is her advantage? With Hector gone, who holds the purse strings? Certainly not Ruth."

"Presumably the trustees," Patrick suggested.

"Of which Alexander is one." Ottilia made a decision. "I think I must find out the other. Nancy mentioned a lawyer, but I forget the name."

Before Ottilia could formulate a plan to find out the second trustee, or indeed to locate Roland Huish, she was forestalled upon the Thursday morning by the appearance at Ash Lodge of Sir Hugh Riccarton, the magistrate nominally in charge of the Penkevil case.

A gentleman somewhat past his middle age, he was of stocky build and medium height, dressed in an older stylet than was current, the blue frock-coat nevertheless well-fitting with decorative buttons, over a striped waistcoat and buckskin breeches. His top boots were well polished and he sported a brown long bob, scorning the prevailing fashion among gentlemen for wearing their own hair. He greeted Ottilia in an avuncular fashion he claimed as the privilege of age, taking her hand in both his own and leaning down to plant a chaste salute upon her cheek.

"You'll not take it amiss now, you young spark," he observed to Francis as he straightened. "No need to be jealous of an old fellow like me, eh?"

Ottilia's spouse, who had shaken hands upon being introduced and was once again propping up the mantelpiece, as was his wont, cast a pointed glance towards his wife's fingers still in the justice's grasp.

"I won't be if you unhand her, sir."

Sir Hugh retained his hold, patting the fingers. "I'll do no such thing, my boy. Why, I've known Mrs Grayshott since I don't know when. Before you set eyes on her, I'll be bound."

"She has not been Mrs Grayshott for years, sir. The correct name is Lady Francis."

"Pooh! Lady Fiddlesticks. Nothing but a girl to me and ever will be."

Seeing how her husband was showing signs of pokering up, Ottilia intervened. "I wish you will stop teasing my poor husband, Sir Hugh. Pay him no heed, Fan. He delights in ruffling feathers, if he can."

Sir Hugh released her as he threw back his head and gave vent to a bark of laughter. "Don't spoil sport, my girl! If you'd left me to it, we'd have had pistols at dawn, I don't doubt."

"I thank you, but we need no more corpses. We have enough on our hands as it is."

Sir Hugh sobered, but there was a lurking twinkle in his eye. "True enough, my Lady Fan." He looked again at Francis. "That suit better with you, you young dog?"

To Ottilia's relief, her spouse chose to let this form of address pass unremarked. "Much better, I thank you. As my wife says, we would be better employed in discussing Penkevil's murder."

A pained look crossed Sir Hugh's face. "I could wish he hadn't got himself killed in such a fashion. Most inconsiderate to land the business on me. In general, you know, I have not been obliged to bestir myself."

"Because Penkevil chose to act himself?"

A sly grin crossed Sir Hugh's face. "Very assiduous was Hector. Who am I to stop him enjoying himself?"

Ottilia had to laugh. "You are perfectly dreadful, Sir Hugh." And to her husband, "Pray don't take anything he says at face value. He has stepped in now and then to rein in Penkevil's severity. It is no use arguing the point, Sir Hugh, because Esther Winning told me so."

The magistrate shook his head at her and smiled. "Ought to have known I'd not readily fool you, Lady Fan." He wagged a finger. "I shall have words with Esther."

"You will not indeed. She is my particular friend and has proved most helpful. Come now, cease your teasing, if you please."

He grinned. "Let's have it then. You've had a week, my Lady Fan. Where have you got to?"

Ottilia gestured for him to take a seat near her position in the late Sophie's comfortable chair, and gave a rapid relation of the activities so far and what had been discovered.

"I am hoping you may be able to tell me," she said, when she had done, "who is the trustee appointed alongside Alexander Penkevil."

"Nothing easier, my dear girl. It's one Theodore Hope. He's Penkevil's man of business."

"Yes, I had heard he is a lawyer. Where can I find him?"

"He has an office in Salisbury. Mind, Penkevil is by no means his only client. A busy man, Hope. Serves me, among others in the district. I can furnish you with his direction."

Ottilia thanked him. "Is he likely to be forthcoming?"

"I'll give you a note. He won't unlock if I don't tell him to."

"Then I am pleased you came before I sought to tackle the man. If you will vouch for me, we may visit him this very day."

Francis, whose ruffled temper appeared to have cooled, here cut in with a query of his own. "Can't you supply more detail for any of the others? It would speed things up if you share what you know."

To Ottilia's consternation, Sir Hugh's tendency to levity overtook him again.

"But where would be the fun in that, I ask you? No, no, let our Lady Fan here puzzle it all out for herself."

Receiving a speaking glance from her spouse, Ottilia again called the magistrate to order. "You are incorrigible, Sir Hugh. I do not doubt you came here for no other purpose."

He had the grace to laugh. "There's no fooling you, is there?" He threw another of his barbs at Francis. "How in

Hades do you keep her in check, eh, you young spark? Don't envy you that task."

"Enough, Sir Hugh! He has no need to employ any great restraint, I will have you know. We have a very good understanding, have we not, Fan?"

His eyebrow flickered but he addressed himself to the magistrate. "I let her have her head. It's the best way with a resty mount."

"Fiend, how dare you?" Ottilia shook an admonitory finger. "That will do, the pair of you." Although she was glad Francis chose to emulate Sir Hugh's light-hearted banter. "May we please return to the res?"

Sir Hugh smiled and spread his hands. "By all means. What can I tell you?"

Ottilia gathered the pieces of the puzzle together. "Are you well acquainted with Alexander Penkevil?"

"Not especially. Why?"

"I wondered what you think of him."

"In what respect?"

"I found him belligerent but a trifle pompous. He was disinclined to answer any of my questions."

Sir Hugh's brows rose. "You failed to persuade him? Now that does surprise me."

Ottilia took this head on. "Is that another tease or have you good reason to say so?"

Sir Hugh's smile was wry. "Touché! But, no. That particular parson has shown me nothing but courtesy. He's fairly learned and we have exchanged views on theocracy once or twice. In my experience, Penkevil belligerence has been confined to Hector."

Francis uttered the thought in Ottilia's mind. "Then either Alexander is a man of more than one face or he despises women." His gaze met Ottilia's. "What was he like towards Ruth Penkevil?"

"That is a point which might reward observation, Fan, thank you." And to the magistrate, "Did you ever see him in company with Ruth, Sir Hugh?"

"I dare say I did, but there was nothing untoward to notice. I cannot imagine he would behave ill towards his brother's wife. I certainly never heard that he disparaged the woman. I should doubt of his paying her undue attention, but as I say, I saw nothing in his conduct to deprecate. Alexander's company manners are certainly better than his brother's."

Ottilia leapt on this. "Now there I think you must be able to give a useful opinion. We have been regaled with tales which smack of prejudice on Hector's part, using his influential position for his own ends. Would you say that is a fair assessment of the man's conduct?"

Sir Hugh poked his chin in the air and gazed at the ceiling, a pose Ottilia recalled in him from past occasions when he needed to think. She refrained from hurrying him, remaining silent. He was a shrewd judge of character despite his apparent insouciance and his opinion would be valuable.

At length he lowered his chin and met her gaze. "Hector was always scrupulous in my presence. I cannot say I knew him to act to such advantage. However, as you have discovered, I felt obliged to take him to task upon several occasions for too harsh sentencing. Hector was never inclined to temper justice with mercy. Nor would he overlook such petty crimes as I should regard as mere peccadilloes. Especially where I might know that the perpetrator or his family would suffer unduly."

"Could you be specific perhaps, Sir Hugh?"

He blew out his cheeks. "Oh, take the matter of Willy Heath. The poor lad has no notion that it is poaching to pot a rabbit or a bird on another man's land. Willy is known to pick up one or t'other now and then to augment his rations. Brig turns a blind eye, but when Willy took one of Hector's pheasants, he had the boy up before him. A night in the lock-up would have done, but Hector fined him five pounds. Five pounds! The boy won't earn that in a twelvemonth."

Ottilia's senses prickled. "Willy could not have paid it. Who did?"

"Bruno Pidsea."

Ottilia's astonishment was mirrored in her spouse's face as she caught his glance. "That is most interesting."

"As I recall," said Francis, "the Reverend Bruno Pidsea gave us to understand that he had no quarrel with Hector."

"Indeed, Fan. Nor did he mention this act of charity."

Sir Hugh was frowning. "That's odd. Bruno has been quite a champion of Willy Heath. He even remonstrated with Hector when the man gave the boy a beating."

"We heard about that."

"We did, Fan, and from Patrick who tended Willy afterwards. But no one spoke of Bruno Pidsea's part in it."

"They might not know of it, my dear Lady Fan. I happened to be present when Bruno accosted Hector."

"Where did this meeting take place?"

"At Hector's home. We were in discussion in his library when Bruno charged in and delivered himself of a tirade of a sermon. He might have been in his pulpit."

A short laugh came from Francis. "From all we've learned of Penkevil, I'm surprised this Bruno didn't receive a blow."

Sir Hugh twinkled. "Likely he has my presence to thank for that. Hector was always circumspect in my company. He expended a good deal of hot air justifying his actions, addressing himself for the most part to me."

Intrigued, Ottilia sought for more. "Why was he so careful of you, Sir Hugh? Had you some hold over him?"

"I am the senior magistrate. Besides, he is aware I am acquainted with the Lord Chief Justice, with whom I am apt to correspond. Hector thought himself a big man in the district, but he was a sycophant with persons in power for all that. He'd not want to lose face with those who matter."

Ottilia tutted. "The more I hear of the man, the less I feel sympathy for his demise."

"In that, you are not alone. Hector had not the trick of endearing himself to others."

"Far from it, by all accounts," said Francis. "Unfortunately, this makes my wife's task all the trickier. There are too many persons who had reason to be rid of the wretched fellow."

Sir Hugh eyed Ottilia. "Do you favour one over another?"

"Not as yet. The reasons my husband mentions are somewhat flimsy for the most part. The one person with a cogent reason, who may truly benefit from the man's death, happens to be one I am least inclined to believe could be guilty."

"Are you thinking of Alexander?"

"No, Fan. I am referring to Hector's wife, Ruth."

Sir Hugh looked interested. "Why do you consider her innocent?"

"Because she did not hesitate to reveal the truth of her relationship with Roland Huish and she was quite frank about the difficulties in her marriage. In my experience, the guilty party is usually at pains to keep hidden anything that could make them suspect."

"Unless it's a ploy, Tillie. You've had individuals being apparently open with you before in hopes of pulling the wool over your eyes."

"Ruth Penkevil is no play-actress. I may be proved wrong, but at this present I believe she is genuine."

"I take it you've not yet spoken to Huish?"

"I have not, Sir Hugh. Do you know him well?"

"I've met the fellow. Namby-pamby sort of a fish, I thought him. Indeed, it was in my mind he might be one of these mollies." He then appeared to recollect himself, clearing his throat loudly. "Beg pardon, my dear. Shouldn't have spoken so free."

Ottilia threw an amused glance at Francis. "My husband will vouch for it that I am perfectly au fait with such matters."

"She has learned to be so, sir. When you delve into this kind of affair, you meet all sorts and conditions of persons. My wife has become somewhat inured, have you not, my love?"

"Indeed, Fan. I cannot think I am any longer in a way to be shocked by anything."

Sir Hugh's twinkle was back. "In that case, I needn't hesitate to mention Penkevil's propensity for visiting ladies of dubious virtue."

Ottilia refrained from pointing out that Ruth's virtue had been compromised before the marriage. "I had gathered as much."

Sir Hugh laughed out. "I ought to have guessed." He rose. "If you've pen and paper handy, before I leave you, I'll write that note for Theodore Hope."

CHAPTER SIXTEEN

The lawyer Theodore Hope proved to have chambers in the more prosperous area of Salisbury. Ottilia knew the town well from her early sojourn with the Hathaways and it had changed little in the intervening years. There were a few new buildings, a couple of shops she did not remember to have seen before, and the main thoroughfare seemed cleaner. For this, a plethora of boys diligently sweeping away the debris from the passage of horses was likely responsible. The coach turned off the main thoroughfare, proceeded a little way along a busy street and came to rest beside a large establishment given over, by the comings and goings of several clerks through its main door, to the use of offices. A porter, accosted by Francis, led the Fanshawes upstairs and to a door bearing a wooden plaque with "Theodore Hope, Legal Practitioner" inscribed upon it in gold lettering.

The porter opened the door upon his knock and ushered them in. Ottilia walked through ahead of her husband and found herself in a large apartment divided in two. A wooden rail separated the clerks seated at several desks from the area behind, where one elderly individual sat in solitary state on one side with a bank of cabinets on the other. This gentleman rose at once upon sighting the visitors and came through, bowing before them.

"Good day, sir, madam. How may I serve you?"

Ottilia glanced to Francis who at once took charge. "We wish to see Mr Hope. Is he within?"

The man gave them both an appraising look. He was spare, not tall, and he wore no wig, instead tying sparse grey locks in a queue behind. He was clad in black breeches and coat, neckcloth neatly tied, an inconspicuous attire that befit his station. His tone was polite but not servile. "May I ask who is desirous of seeing Mr Hope?"

"Tell him Lord and Lady Francis Fanshawe would appreciate a moment of his time."

Ottilia watched the change come over the clerk's thin face. She could not help reflecting how dependent she so often was upon rank. There could be no doubt that it opened doors one might otherwise find closed. Dislike trading upon it she might, but that it furthered the cause was undeniable.

"If you will give me a moment, my lord." The clerk bowed and went off through the far door, delivering a light knock before entering.

"You brought Sir Hugh's note, I trust?"

Ottilia glanced round at her husband's murmur. "I have it safe. At least we were not obliged to produce it for that clerk's edification."

Francis raised his brows. "I should hope not."

She smiled at the faintly haughty note, but said nothing as the clerk was seen to be returning.

"Mr Hope will be pleased to see you, my lord."

Her spouse nodded and gestured for her to go before him. Ottilia caught his muttered comment as she passed. "He likely thinks we want to commandeer his services."

All too probable. Ottilia thanked Sir Hugh's foresight in providing her with a terse instruction to the lawyer to aid her with whatever information she required.

The room she entered was furnished more like a library than an office, with bookcases lining the walls, a seating area to one side and a large desk to the rear, before which stood a man of large proportions with a belly to match. Mr Theodore Hope was clearly in prosperous circumstances, judging by his appearance. He wore a bagwig tied in a black bow framing a broad countenance with a prominent nose and a pair of interested eyes. A well-tailored coat of fine cloth in darkish hue was worn over a fancy striped waistcoat and buff breeches, with polished top-boots to his feet.

He came forward, smiling and holding out a hand. "My lord, my lady, welcome, welcome. How may I serve you?"

Ottilia allowed her husband the lead as he shook hands. "We are here on behalf of Sir Hugh Riccarton." He gestured. "My wife will show you his note."

Ottilia was already fishing the letter out of the pocket of her cloak. She held it out and Mr Hope, a faint frown between his brows, bowed as he took it from her.

"I will be happy to read it, but will your ladyship not take a seat?" He indicated the coterie of chairs to one side.

Ottilia moved to seat herself, watching as the lawyer spread open the sheet and ran his eyes down the message contained therein. By the time she was settled, he had finished and was already moving to join her, ushering Francis before him. He waited for her spouse to take a seat before himself occupying the third chair and leaning back at his ease, crossing one leg over the other, the letter held loosely in his fingers.

He eyed Ottilia with an expression hard to read. "This jogs my memory, my lady. I had heard of your interest in this affair. A terrible business."

Ottilia picked this up at once. "From whom did you hear it? The Reverend Alexander Penkevil perhaps?"

His brows rose. "Now how came you to guess that?"

Ottilia smiled. "As I understand you are joined with him in the trusteeship, it seemed a fair inference."

Theodore Hope's mouth turned down at the corners. "Yes, that is so, more's the pity."

Francis cut in. "Why so?"

"The boy is very young." The lawyer folded the sheet and slipped it into an inner pocket as he continued, "It will be a long road, I fear, until Jason Penkevil reaches his majority."

"Is the task likely to prove onerous then?"

"Somewhat, my lord. Mr Penkevil's affairs are, I regret to say, in something of a tangle."

Ottilia found she was not surprised to hear this. "Are you able to elaborate a little, sir?"

He coughed in a delicate fashion. "Since your enquiries are bound to elicit a good deal of private information, I dare say it will be appropriate for me to unbutton."

"Now that is excellent, Mr Hope," said Ottilia with enthusiasm. "Pray do unbutton. You will make my task much easier if you do."

He gave her a conspiratorial sort of smile. "Between you, me and the lamp post, my lady."

Francis evidently grew impatient. "Well, sir? What is this tangle?"

The lawyer sighed. "Mr Penkevil was not one to heed advice. He would ignore matters that I should much have preferred him to attend to instanter."

"Such as?"

"Such as, my lord, outstanding threats from merchants desirous of being paid." Mr Hope's tone grew a trifle acid. "Added to which, I was obliged to field several suits at law which Mr Penkevil refused to answer."

Ottilia pounced on this. "Who was suing him?"

"Brigadier O'Turk, with regard to alleged encroachment upon his lands. One Roland Huish for injuries he claims to have received at Mr Penkevil's hands. There is also a suit from the farmer, Petrus Gubb, but that cannot hold water and I should doubt anything would have come of it."

Francis took the last, his interest clearly aroused since he had conducted that interview. "On what specific complaint?"

"Oh, it is quite spurious. Petrus Gubb tried to act on his wife's behalf, claiming damages for harassment, but since Mr Penkevil was a minor at the time, the matter is not legally viable."

Ottilia received a frowning look from her spouse. "He never mentioned that to me, although his wife told me Penkevil the boy was a brute."

"So you said, Fan." Ottilia looked at Theodore Hope. "Did either of the two other cases come to court?"

"Heavens, no, my lady!" The lawyer laughed. "I am not an amateur. I have kept the correspondence going to and fro for years, demanding this or that specific detail. Now, of course, the suits will lapse."

Ottilia's instant thought went to her tongue. "Which benefits neither Brig nor Roland Huish to have Hector dead, since they cannot hope to be compensated."

Her spouse's brows snapped together. "Does that mean you can eliminate both?"

"It certainly reduces suspicion, but not quite yet. Mr Hope, how long have the suits from those two been extant?"

"Let me think." The lawyer pursed his lips, tapping a hand on the chair arm for a moment. "The O'Turk affair has been going on longest. About six years? The brigadier began it not long after Penkevil senior died. Huish put his claim in something in the region of two years ago, if I recall correctly."

Ottilia digested this. "Then it is fair to say perhaps that one or other of these gentlemen could have grown tired of using legal means and sought a more direct revenge."

"From my observation of O'Turk," said Francis, "I should doubt he would take the trouble. If the law suit was troublesome to Hector, I dare say that would satisfy him."

Ottilia looked back at the lawyer. "Was it troublesome to Hector? You said he would not take it seriously."

"Oh, he took is very seriously. He behaved in an infuriated fashion every time I brought the matter up. But he point-blank refused to settle as I advised. The best I could do was to prevaricate to prevent it coming to court."

"Would Hector have lost the case then, had it come to fruition?"

"He would have gained nothing. Any competent judge would have thrown it out. Neither plaintiff nor defendant could produce irrefutable documentation. The land in question had been in dispute for years beforehand. A mere strip of land too, not worth an expensive court case."

Except to Theodore Hope himself, whose bank balance had no doubt benefited in legal fees. But this thought Ottilia kept to herself. "What about the case of Roland Huish? Might he have won?"

"Again, proof was wanting. He could produce no witness to the assault. Nor could he prove his injury had not been sustained upon an earlier occasion. But he might have gained his point in a court of law had he had the luck to get a sympathetic judge."

"Which was why, I must suppose," cut in Francis on a wry note, "you chose to delay the case?"

Another of those sly smiles crossed Mr Hope's face. "As I said, my lord, I am a professional. My client was depending upon me."

Ottilia pursued a thought that had been niggling at the back of her mind. "You spoke of Hector not paying his bills. Did he pay yours?"

"Since he employed me to handle his financial affairs, my lady, I made certain that he did." He added, on a wry note, "Not, I may say, without several reminders. Upon occasion, I was obliged to tell Mr Penkevil I would no longer act for him if he did not comply with my demand for payment. He could not afford to lose me. None of my colleagues would have chosen to act for him. Indeed, one or two questioned why I took his custom. The answer, my lady, is that I had been his father's man of business for many years. Mr Penkevil senior knew his son. When he asked me to act for Hector Penkevil, he made me promise I would not abandon the boy. A promise I have frequently had cause to regret making."

The sour note served only to strengthen Ottilia's growing conviction that the world was well rid of Hector Penkevil. It made the task of discovering his murderer less palatable than she could have wished.

"It becomes difficult, Fan. I find my sympathies very much with the perpetrator. Not that I can approve of murder," she observed to her husband when they had left Theodore Hope and were on route to find Roland Huish.

"No, and this one is particularly unpleasant. There is no mitigating circumstance as it was clearly premeditated."

Ottilia thought for a moment, turning over the circumstances of the death in her mind. "Or was it?"

She found her spouse's questioning eyes on her even in the gloom of the interior of the coach. "What will you be at now,

Tillie? He was drugged and strangled, and then hung. Surely you can't be thinking any of that was accidental?"

"Not that, no. But two things now strike me. We know the hanging was an attempt to hide the crime after the event. You found that out."

"Go on."

"The drugging might not have been intended as a precursor to murder."

"What then?"

She heard the sceptical note and reached for his hand. "Bear with me, Fan."

He laced his fingers with hers. "I am all ears, my dear one."

"You are indulging me, you fiend."

"I am always willing to be convinced when you go off on one of your tangents, puzzling wife of mine. Continue."

"Very well then. Ruth or Margery might administer valerian only to calm the man down, do you not think? If his temper was riding high, for instance."

"So far, I follow. But there is a strangulation to be accounted for."

"Yes, and that was bungled. I submit that it might have been done in a fit of fury."

"But did not Patrick say Hector was strangled in his drugged state?"

Ottilia's mental shifts paused. "There is that. Let us think away from logic then."

"How, pray?"

"No, wait, Fan." She spoke slowly, thinking it through. "Suppose our murderer meets with Hector unexpectedly in the woods. They quarrel. The murderer loses control and tries to strangle Hector, at which point he succumbs to the sedative.

Our perpetrator then panics. He thinks Hector is dead at his hands. What does he do?"

"Puts a rope about the neck and strings him up? It won't fadge, Tillie. Where does he get his rope? Supposing he came unprepared, he won't have one upon his person."

Ottilia tsked. "I was forgetting the rope."

She felt him squeeze her hand. "You can't lessen the perpetrator's guilt, my dear one, however hard you try."

Ottilia sighed and sank into him, resting her head on his shoulder. "Perhaps you are right. But I do wonder if I misjudged the notion of there being two persons involved."

CHAPTER SEVENTEEN

Roland Huish was found at his lodgings, the address having been supplied by the lawyer Theodore Hope. Ruth's putative lover proved to be one of the prettiest young men Ottilia remembered to have seen. He was possessed of features more properly belonging to a feminine countenance. The Almighty had a distinct tendency to be indiscriminate in his endowments. Many a female might envy such lilting lips, the sculptured nose and beautifully rounded cheeks, the wide blue eyes framed with lashes dark and long. Matching locks, smooth as silk, fell across a white brow and brushed slim shoulders. His proportions were slight but perfectly formed, marred only by the pronounced limp that showed up as he set down a quill and rose from the chair where he was seated before a small bureau at which he had evidently been writing — poetry perhaps? — and approached his unexpected guests.

A manservant, presumably Mr Huish's valet, had announced the Fanshawes, having answered the door that let into the apartment which occupied the entirety of the first floor of a large house in Berwick St John.

"My lord, my lady, welcome." Roland Huish made a graceful bow and gestured to a sofa placed against the wall. "Will you not be seated?" He waited for Ottilia to take her place, glanced at Francis who chose to remain standing, and himself took up a stance at the mantel, resting his arm upon it.

The pose rendered him both poetically handsome and excessively romantic. Appropriate. Was it deliberate? Habitual? No surprise that Ruth, burdened with the brute Hector, had fallen head over heels. His voice had a mellow quality that perfectly complemented his looks.

"I am glad you have come, my lady. Ruth warned me you had the intention to visit me. I hope I may be successful in persuading you of my innocence."

Ottilia almost laughed out. "You are ready of tongue, sir. Do you perhaps anticipate my questions also?"

He gave a faint, sweet smile. "I might, ma'am. But pray do not hesitate to ask me anything you wish."

An explosive sound came from Francis. "She will, Huish, make no mistake. You may well be forearmed, but my wife will worm the truth out of you regardless."

This attack had little effect upon the young man, although he blinked at Francis, those preposterous eyelashes batting his cheeks. "I have no wish to conceal it, my lord."

"Well for you."

Ottilia ignored her spouse's grunted response and took her chance. "I take it you have been thoroughly primed by Ruth. She told you of our discussion?"

"In detail. She said she held nothing back and advised me to do likewise. I am at your service, my lady. What would you wish to know?"

If this was a bid to unsettle her, it would not succeed. Ottilia plunged in. "I would like to know more of your suit against Hector Penkevil. Let me understand one thing first, however. Did he attack you or, as you apparently told Ruth, did you take him to task because he treated Ruth badly?"

"Cruelly! Let us not mince our words, ma'am. He was a brute to her and I found it unendurable."

"Then it was your action to begin the fight?"

Huish sighed. "Not precisely. He confronted me with the nonsensical notion that I was deliberately flaunting my —

attributes, shall we say? He used a derogatory term. Flaunting them at Ruth in a bid to steal her from him. What would you? I retaliated."

"How, sir?"

"Oh, quite mildly, I fear. I said, if I remember it correctly, that if he cherished his wife more there would be no future in any flaunting of mine, or any other man's." He put a hand to his mouth, emitting a slight cough. "A mistake, as it turned out. Penkevil attacked me, causing considerable damage. That, ma'am, is why I sought redress by means of the law."

Ottilia digested this. Was the attack of a nature that might provoke a man to kill his adversary? She probed for more. "Do you claim the damage to your leg — forgive my mentioning it, if you please — is to be set to his account?"

Thick and perfectly arched brows rose. "My leg? No, no, not that, ma'am."

"Indeed? I understood Ruth to say as much."

A ripple crossed his countenance, of what emotion Ottilia found it difficult to judge. "It is what I allowed her to believe. The truth is not for Ruth's ears."

Ottilia senses prickled. What then? A tale too unpleasant for his inamorata? "What is the truth, Mr Huish?"

He did not answer directly. "I sustained no additional injury to my lame leg, although I might well have done."

"You became lame by some other means?"

"I was born so, ma'am. My left is the shorter by an inch or so. My bootmaker strives to improve my walk with built-up insoles, but he cannot wholly eradicate the limp."

A bid for sympathy? Yet the facts were stated in a matter-of-fact tone which made Ottilia discount that possibility. "How then did Hector injure you, sir?"

Intrigued to see a slight rise of colour enter the young man's cheek, Ottilia eyed him with new interest as he hesitated. She cast a quick glance at Francis and found him frowning. Her gaze returned as Roland Huish cleared his throat.

"In relating the facts, ma'am, I must beg for your discretion and indulgence. They are not pretty. Nor, had Ruth not given me to understand that you are neither mealy-mouthed nor readily put out of countenance, would I be as willing to disclose the nature of my hurts."

At this, Francis predictably lost patience. "Cut line, man! I will engage for it that nothing you have to say will disturb my wife. She is perfectly inured to mutilated bodies, of which she has seen too many to be troubled by them."

Ottilia could not repress a spurt of mirth. "A very odd idea of me you are giving poor Mr Huish, Fan." And to the blushing Roland, "I was used to learn of my brother, Doctor Patrick Hathaway, when I lived at Ash Lodge, sir. I have watched him cut up corpses. Do not fear me. However gruesome, I shall try my best not to be too much mortified."

Roland gave a little bow. "You are very good, ma'am. Gruesome is perhaps an inappropriate word. My injury is, let us rather say, indelicate."

Lively curiosity sent a raft of possibilities into Ottilia's mind. "Try me with it, Mr Huish."

Another little bow indicated acquiescence. "He began by knocking me down." Roland let out a soft sigh. "I am not a man of violence. Nor do I lay claim to the sort of superior strength a man ought to possess. My shortened leg, moreover, renders me vulnerable to that sort of attack. He struck me with his fist and I lost my balance and fell." Here he drew an obvious breath, his gaze dropping from Ottilia's. "Penkevil was not a man to lose an advantage. He used his booted feet to judicious effect."

In spite of all, Ottilia's imagination painted for her a shocking picture indeed. "He kicked you?"

"Several times. In an extremely sensitive area of my anatomy."

"Good Lord!" Thus Francis. "A brutish assault."

Huish raised his eyes again. "I thought so too, sir. At the time, I was of course in too much anguish to think of anything beyond the immediate effects, which were considerable." Once again, he cleared his throat. "By the time I came to myself again, at least enough for the coherence to protest, Penkevil was gone. A servant of the place came to my aid and called in a surgeon."

Appalled, Ottilia exchanged a glance with Francis, whose expression, and a flick of one eyebrow told her he fully understood the implications. She ventured a question. "Was the surgeon able to assist you, sir?"

A sad shake of the head. "He could do little more than recommend cold compresses, to ease the bruising, he said. Later, he confirmed what I learned to fear when once my agonies subsided."

"What was that, sir?" Despite a niggle of doubt, Ottilia's sympathies were stirred.

Another of those sweet, faint smiles appeared upon the pretty countenance. "If I say only that one item was crushed beyond repair, I hope you may understand me."

Ottilia thought she did, but she had to remove all doubt. "Let us be clear, Mr Huish. What precisely was the basis of your suit at law?"

The fine lips pouted for a space and for the first time a spark appeared in the blue gaze. "Due to the injury inflicted by Hector Penkevil, ma'am, I may never be able to — er — reproduce."

"Pardon me, but are you saying you cannot lie with a woman?"

He neither blushed nor flinched. "Not that. But such an act may never result in my siring offspring."

"It is not certain?"

"The percentage against is high, so my doctor informs me."

Motive enough for murder, but Ottilia made no mention of this, turning instead to his liaison with Ruth. If she wanted more detail concerning this alleged outcome of his injury, her spouse, or more probably Patrick, could supply it.

"You have been frank, sir. Pray continue to speak with all candour. When did your association with Ruth begin and how far has it progressed?"

He hesitated, one hand going up to flick the hair away from his brow in a gesture that Francis used upon the new cut, although her spouse was growing more used to the shorter style. It suited Roland Huish, lending him a captivating air. He sighed out the words as he spoke at last.

"We have been as friends for some two years, I think." His gaze slipped away, seeming to seek answers of empty spaces. "I say *as friends* advisedly. My wish had been for something more from the outset." The blue eyes returned to stare into Ottilia's, deep with feeling. To show sincerity? "I trust I am a man of honour. Ruth's tie with Penkevil, however uncouth, prevented my urging her to sin." He added in a low tone, and with a look of eloquent apology, "For some time at least."

Ottilia stifled the burgeoning amusement. He might have been upon the stage, so earnest was his manner, the choice of words reminiscent of theatrical dialogue. She took it up without compunction.

"Do I take it you did indeed so urge her? Before Hector's death?"

He threw back his head as if he had received a blow. "If only I had waited! But it is useless to be wishing that now. Too late, alas. Hindsight is a wonderful thing."

Not much to Ottilia's surprise, Francis lost patience. "Be damned to you for a play-actor, Huish! For pity's sake, cease this foolishness. Do you hope to enlist my wife's sympathies in this manner? It won't lessen her suspicions of you. Just answer the blasted question, man. You and Ruth have been lovers since when precisely?"

His irritation had little effect upon the poet, who wafted his hands in a despairing gesture. "Since the day I found her bruised and tearful. I begged her to leave him, but she would not. The children. One can appreciate a mother's reluctance. Ruth feared she must lose them if she fled, a woman ruined. I sought to comfort her. She responded in a way that … I could not help myself. Regret is useless."

Ottilia cut into the passionate utterances, her tone matter of fact. "When was this, sir?"

He sighed again. "In the summer." He gave a gentle laugh. "My summer madness."

Ignoring the manner of this speech, Ottilia pressed him, doing a rapid calculation in her head. "Several months then." Time enough to be making plans. "Do I understand correctly that you then continued in this illicit liaison, despite Hector's likely reaction should he discover it?"

Roland relaxed into himself, as if confession had relieved him. "I did, to my shame. Our trysts were carefully orchestrated. The danger to Ruth was all too real."

"To you too, one imagines," came in a snap from Francis. "Did you not fear Penkevil's revenge?"

The young man shrugged in a manner too nonchalant to be believed. "What more could he do to me after that first attack?"

"Kill you?"

Roland's gaze flicked to Francis and he stared as one bemused. "Call me out? I would have refused to meet him. He could prove nothing, after all."

Ottilia struck in. "From all we have learned, Hector acted upon the spur of the moment. You knew that, having been his victim."

A mirthless little laugh came. "Indeed, ma'am. I see what you would be at."

"Do you?"

"Shall I outline your thoughts, Lady Fan?"

Ottilia eyed him, intrigued. He was bolder than he appeared. "Pray do."

"I surmise that you believe I might have eliminated Hector Penkevil with the object of making Ruth a widow. Thus, she would be safe from his vengeance, as would I, and she might marry me honourably. Have I hit the mark?"

Ottilia exchanged a glance with her spouse, whose brows were flying. "It is certainly a possibility, Mr Huish."

He sighed and spread his hands, as if to say, 'You see how I strive to be truthful with you.' Then came another of those faint, sweet smiles. "At all events, I had rather you placed the blame on my shoulders than upon Ruth's."

Ottilia turned the tables. "I dare say she would say the same, sir. Did you agree together that your best policy must be honesty?"

That did surprise a laugh out of him, genuine, she felt sure. "Touché! We did, but only after Ruth had already spoken to you. Not that I expect you to believe it."

Ottilia did not enlighten him. "Where did you meet?"

"At a place provided by an elderly relative of mine. Lady Carrefour. Perhaps you know her?"

CHAPTER EIGHTEEN

"Lady Carrefour is your patient, Patrick. Did she never mention the connection with Roland Huish?"

Accosted by his sister immediately upon his return to his home from attending an elderly fellow whose demise was imminent, Patrick Hathaway found himself disgruntled. Must he be dragged back into this tiresome business when all he wanted was to collapse into his favourite chair with a glass of port and rest his tired eyes? Truth be told, all he really wanted was Averil's comforting bosom rather than the cushioned head-rest that did little to ease his aching brow. How long since he had last checked on Ralph Deakin? He had another call to make in Knighton, but might he fit in a short visit? The Deakin home was, after all, on the way. Seeing Averil, if only briefly, always brought balm.

But there was no speaking of that. His sister was eyeing him with expectance in those infuriatingly penetrating orbs. He tried to bend his mind to her question, the separate images of Lady Carrefour and Roland Huish rising in his head.

"Did she speak of it? I can't remember, Ottilia."

"Very well, but did you know?"

He put a hand to his head and closed his eyes, striving for patience. "Let me think."

Rescue came from an unexpected source. "Here, my friend. Get this down you."

He lifted his eyelids and found a glass in front of his face. Ruby liquid! Blessed be. He took it and threw a brief smile up at his brother-in-law. "You are a lifesaver, Fan."

As he drank, he caught Francis's murmur from across the room. "Leave the man alone, Tillie. Can't you see he's exhausted?"

There was a brief silence, and then his sister spoke up. "You are, of course, brother mine. Forgive me. I am being importunate, am I not?"

No surprise to hear the contrite note. Ottilia was ever quick to admit a fault. Too much so upon occasion. Patrick took another swallow and rested the glass in his lap, attempting a grin. "It was ever thus with you when you're chasing a scent." He transferred his gaze to Francis. "You would not credit the barrage of questions when she was on the trail of some disease or other. Questions, mark you, to which I often had no answer."

"No, but you were adept at directing me to a volume where I might find the answer."

Patrick sighed. "I cannot upon this occasion. I must rely upon memory. It is not precisely the sort of information I need enter into my notes."

To his chagrin, his sister returned to the burden of her query. "Roland said she was a relative. To what degree he did not say."

"But why is it of interest?"

Francis took this before his sister could respond. "It's this notion of conspiracy she has concocted. Though it strikes me as unlikely young Huish would entrust his schemes to the hands of a woman who is, by all accounts, halfway demented."

Ottilia cut in at this. "Not so, Fan. She is merely forgetful and a little confused perhaps."

"Much the same thing, Tillie. It's absurd to imagine she could be party to a scheme to be rid of Penkevil."

Patrick spoke his thought aloud. "But he might be moved to act on her behalf should he feel her to have been wronged. Assuming, of course, a closer relationship than I suspect to be the case."

A ripple of laughter came from his sister. "Dear me, brother mine, you appear to have caught the bug despite your dislike of my proceedings."

He had to laugh. "Hardly that. It is difficult to withstand a certain sense of intrigue perhaps."

"Ha! Precisely my trouble, my friend. I detest these shenanigans, yet time and again I find myself drawn in by the puzzle of it all." Francis turned to his wife. "What do you make of Patrick's theory, my dear one?"

Patrick eyed his sister's now thoughtful face with a smidgeon of apprehension. Ottilia was not going to try to drag him further into these deep waters, was she?

"I would not dismiss it utterly," she said at length, rather to Patrick's annoyance at the notion she would dismiss his contribution at all. "But on the whole, I imagine Roland's motives to be far more likely bound up with the trials of his inamorata. If he did it for anyone, it would be for Ruth."

"Then I fail to see why you bothered me about their relationship."

He was treated to one of Ottilia's mischievous looks. "I do believe it was you, Patrick, who taught me to explore every avenue before coming to a diagnosis. I always abide by your dictates, brother dear."

Patrick threw his eyes heavenwards and Francis, obviously no more convinced, burst into laughter.

"I wish I might see it, sister dear."

She smiled but entered a protest nevertheless. "In the main I do. Especially where medical matters are concerned. Indeed, I believe I am sadly lacking since leaving your tutelage. You must have advanced well beyond my knowledge by now."

Patrick chose not to answer this. A thought was stirring in his memory. "As it chances, I have recalled something."

Ottilia looked eager. "About Lady Carrefour and Roland?"

"A snippet only. Lady Carrefour was bemoaning her relative's neglect. The present Lord Carrefour, I mean. She often did so. I paid it little heed beyond murmuring sympathetically. On the occasion I am thinking of, if I remember it correctly, she compared him unfavourably with Huish."

"What did she say? Can you remember precisely?"

"Not precisely. She spoke along the lines that she wished her husband's heir had been as charming and graceful as his cousin."

"Well, that certainly describes Roland, but did she name him specifically?"

"I think so. Or at least, she spoke of his lameness and his poetry, asking if I had yet met him. It must have been when he first came to live in the area."

"Perhaps he then came because his aunt was living here?"

"There is no saying she is his aunt, Fan," Ottilia objected. "She said cousin, which could mean anything."

"Did he hope to batten upon her generosity?"

Patrick gave a short laugh. "If so, he will have caught cold at that. Lady Carrefour is left in near penury."

"As we have discovered," said Ottilia. "I think I will revisit her, if only to eliminate the possibility."

A measure of relief entered Patrick's breast. Perhaps now Ottilia would leave him out of it. Sounds betokening an arrival at Ash Lodge came to his ears and he gave an inward curse. "I hope to heaven that isn't another patient. I've only a brief respite before I must be off to Monk's Cottage."

He caught a questioning glance from his sister. Had Averil given Ottilia her direction? Impelled, he put in a spirited defence. "You need not look censorious, Ottilia. I am obliged to attend Ralph Deakin." Not that the opportunity was not convenient, but he was not going to add that.

For a wonder, Ottilia looked a trifle distressed. "I have said I will not judge you, Patrick. Why must you carp at me in that fashion?"

A glance at Francis found his brother-in-law assiduously regarding the ruby liquid in his own glass. Patrick sighed. "It was not meant, my dear sister. Set it down to my mood. I dislike losing patients and —"

"Who is it?"

"You likely won't remember old Silas."

"Oh, one of your charity cases?"

"John has been looking after his needs for some months, but he is despairing and wanted me to take a look. There is nothing I can do. It is a matter of days, I suspect."

To his surprise and gratification, Ottilia rose up out of Sophie's old chair and came across, setting her arms about him in a warm hug. Her voice was husky. "Forgive me, dearest brother. I am too apt to be single-minded with these hunts of mine."

Patrick returned the pressure of her arms as best he could for his seated position and the protuberance at her waist, then put her away from him, looking up into her face. "Must you weep, silly woman?" He patted her cheek. "There. You are pardoned."

He was about to recommend that she resumed her seat when the sound of the opening door arrested him. Ottilia straightened and looked around so that he was able to see past her.

Aaron was entering the room, a figure just visible in the doorway behind him. "Mr Penkevil to see you, sir."

For an incredulous second, Patrick half expected to see Hector's corpse below the countenance that appeared as the footman moved aside. He rose somewhat hurriedly to his feet. "Good God, Alexander, you startled me! I had never before realised how much you resembled your brother."

Ottilia, quite as startled as her brother, if for a different reason, watched with interest as Alexander Penkevil's features suffused with colour. For all she had spoken of expecting the cleric to seek her out, she was nevertheless surprised.

She moved to one side as he came forward, addressing himself to Patrick. "You are mistaken. We have never been considered much alike." Both gait and tone were as pompous as ever. Ottilia could not blame Patrick for the curtness of his response.

"Neither in temperament nor character perhaps, but you certainly share facial features." He gestured towards Ottilia. "Do I take it you are here to see my sister?"

Alexander favoured Ottilia with a slight inclination of the head. "Correct."

"You have not met her husband, I think. Lord Francis Fanshawe. Fan, this is the Reverend Alexander Penkevil."

Ottilia watched the two men exchange brief bows, noting how her husband's gaze took in the other. A faint twitch of the lip told her he had gauged the man's personality with ease. Francis despised men of his stamp. She trusted he would not allow his prejudice to appear.

She greeted the visitor in a neutral tone. "I am very pleased to see you, Mr Penkevil. I hoped you might visit me."

Alexander's nose went up. "Be assured, ma'am, that I do so only at the behest of Sir Hugh Riccarton. Had he not made the request, I should not have come here at all."

Ottilia did not see her spouse's bristles rise but she could feel his rising choler. By a fortunate chance, Patrick spoke before Francis could voice any objection to Alexander's manner of addressing her.

"I will leave you. These matters are better left to the Fanshawes alone."

He started across to the door, but Alexander detained him with a raised palm. "I should prefer you to remain, Doctor Hathaway. You are the only professional in this matter of my brother's demise."

The insulting nature of this remark had not the intended effect upon Ottilia. She could have laughed if not for the inevitable reaction from her husband, who stepped forward to confront the visitor.

"You are offensive, sir. I will thank you to adhere at least to a semblance of the rules of etiquette."

To Ottilia's relief, Patrick intervened, setting a hand on Francis's arm. "Steady, man! Save your energy for a more worthwhile battle." His gaze returned to Alexander's face. "I regret I cannot comply with your request, sir. My services are required elsewhere. I have done my part and I dare say you have seen my post-mortem report."

"I have and I dispute it."

"Then I suggest you pay another medical man to recheck my findings. Good day to you, Penkevil."

With which, he brushed past Alexander and left the parlour, closing the door behind him with exaggerated care.

Ottilia let out a light laugh. "My brother is in general slow to anger, Mr Penkevil, but you succeeded in enraging him in an instant." Ignoring the increasing colour in Alexander's face, she gave him a bright smile. "Shall we all sit down? Perhaps you would care for refreshment? Fan, will you do the honours, if you please?"

Her husband, tight-lipped, began to move towards the side table where a tray containing the decanters recently used was set out.

"Nothing for me, sir."

Not even a thank you? Francis turned short about and marched to the fireplace where he took a stiff stance, setting his elbow on the mantel. Ottilia gestured to Patrick's vacated chair. "Do take a seat, Mr Penkevil. It is foolish to be standing about in this way, do you not think?" She resumed her own chair in a pointed manner and waited while Alexander stood, irresolute, staring her out.

At length, he harrumphed a little and then set his person down in the indicated chair. His expression was anything but conciliatory. "Well?"

Ottilia was not going to make it easy. "Yes?"

"Riccarton said you had questions."

She eyed him a moment. Would a direct attack pierce his armour? She tried an oblique approach. "Do you believe Nancy wrote that letter?"

From his expression, he was clearly taken aback. Silently rejoicing, Ottilia awaited his response. He took his time. Then the nose went up again.

"If you will have it, it is just the sort of ill-considered act Nancy Meerbrook would undertake. If you are asking whether I know for a fact that she wrote it, the answer is no."

Ottilia was satisfied. It would appear that Nancy's overtures to this man would prove vain. "That is good enough. I did not suppose you instructed her to write it."

His brows rose. "Why should I do so?"

"Oh, if you'd had a hand in your brother's death, and —"

He sat up with a jerk. "Now we come to it. If you can supply a single reason why I should be complicit in a plot to kill my own brother — which I take it you imply — I should like to hear it."

Ottilia hit back. "You mean you see no way in which you might benefit? You are a trustee, are you not?"

"I am, and I resent the implication I would cheat my nephew of his inheritance."

"Did I say you would?"

Before he could answer, Francis took a hand, a very growl in his voice. "For pity's sake, will you cease this shilly-shally give and take! We all know what is meant here. It is not beyond the bounds of credibility that a trustee may enrich himself at the expense of his charge." He held up a hand as Alexander made to answer. "And don't bother mentioning the lawyer as a second trustee in the case. Yes, he might put a curb on your predations, should there be any, but he might equally let it pass. Theodore Hope is clearly none too keen on being saddled with what he considers an onerous task."

Alexander let out an explosive sound. "You deem the two of us to be unscrupulous, do you? Allow me to tell you —"

"I made no accusations. I am merely pointing out the possibility that gives my wife every reason to put you down on a list of suspects. Don't be so ready to show hackle, man! Have you no interest at all in finding out who killed your brother?"

"If anyone did."

"That is beyond doubt. You would do better to accept the fact and assist my wife."

The cleric took a visible breath and let it out in a sound of frustration. He turned his gaze on Ottilia. "I have said I would answer your questions. What more do you wish to know?"

She pondered. He had been frank in his condemnation of Nancy. "At the risk of drawing your fire, may I ask in what light you regard Nancy?"

He coloured a trifle. "I see no reason to answer that."

"I suggest she wrote the letter to Averil Deakin in concern for your welfare, Mr Penkevil. Had that not occurred to you?"

His brows drew together. "If you are insinuating what I suppose, I take it very ill, ma'am. Allow me to advise you that any regard I may have in that direction is but tepid. I should consider such an interference in my affairs as an impertinence."

No conspiracy here then? Still, his own actions were to be questioned. "Let us move on then, sir."

"If you must."

Ottilia looked him in the eye. "It is said you were in Salisbury on the night your brother met his unfortunate end. May I know what occupied you there?"

"You may not."

"Helpful."

The ironic inflexion made no impression upon him. "Show me how it may be relevant and I may reconsider."

Ottilia produced a spurious smile. "Your business, whatever it may have been, kept you away for one or two nights, I believe."

"What of it?"

"Well, there is no saying that you did not return upon the night in question, despatch your brother as planned, and return again to Salisbury."

A snort of derision escaped Alexander's lips. "Preposterous!"

"You would be astonished, I dare say, if we were to relate some of the more preposterous antics of those I have met in the past who were involved with murders."

"Involved how?"

"After the fact, Mr Penkevil. We need look no further than your brother's case, after all."

"You refer, I take it, to this idiotic notion that some person attempted to make a murder seem a suicide."

"Just so."

The reverend thrust his nose into the air. "Well, you will not put this nonsensical proposition upon me. I was in Salisbury. I did not return, and you may ask my servant who was woken by Hector hammering on my door at an unseasonable hour."

Startled, Ottilia exchanged a glance with her spouse, whose brows were flying. She turned back to Alexander, becoming a trifle tart. "Pray why did you not mention this circumstance at the outset, sir?"

He shrugged. "It is hardly relevant. The footman told Hector I was absent and he went on his way."

"If he was hammering on the door, did not your servant notice his condition?"

"He was somewhat the worse for wear. One is accustomed to that, I regret to say. Even had I been present, I doubt I should have been able to deflect him from his fell purpose."

Ottilia blew out a breath. "This is why you insist upon his having committed suicide, I take it?"

"Is it not obvious?"

"Not when Hector's body exhibited such bruises as indicated someone had squeezed him by the throat. Whether it was the same person who did the deed or another who came upon his unconscious body remains a question."

Alexander's features took on a look of distaste and he rose in rather a hurry. "Permit me to tell you that I find this line of discussion particularly disagreeable. I will not stay to be subject —"

"Murder is disagreeable, Mr Penkevil," Ottilia said, cutting him off. Francis had taken a step as if he meant to stop the cleric's retreat and she gave a slight shake of the head. Nothing was to be gained by manhandling the man. "That is why I am trying to discover what happened here. I understand your distaste and will try to be brief."

She waited to see what effect her words might have, not unhopeful. At length, the cleric shifted back to the chair and sat down heavily, letting out a sigh. He spoke in a tone of great weariness.

"Hector was trouble enough when alive. One had not looked for him to continue so in death."

"Then help me solve this, sir. The sooner we have an answer, the sooner the trouble will cease."

His gaze came up at that, his features redolent with both scorn and irritation. "When I am left to guard his family, bring up his boy and administer his estate? Hector mangled everything he touched. Can you truly suppose I would have disposed of him, knowing the shambles of his dealings must fall to my lot? I only wish I might escape it, but no. The wretched fellow must needs name me both executor and trustee and then die on me. As if I had nothing better to wish for!"

The bitterness was unmistakeable. Ottilia was inclined to believe him, but that did not mean she could refrain from further question. In this mood she dared hope he might prove more amenable.

"Why were you away in Salisbury, sir?"

A sigh came. "I was summoned thereto by my bishop. He had a few matters to go over with me pertaining to several of the parishes round about." A slight rise of colour mounted to his cheeks. "You must know I am in line to be named an honorary canon. If the bishop decides in my favour, I will be obliged to attend at the cathedral more often." The acrid note returned. "This, as you may suppose, makes me the more reluctant to take up the burden my brother saw fit to lay upon me."

Ottilia ignored the rider. "Did you stay with the bishop then?"

"He would not suffer me to return home for the night. As it chanced, we concluded our business by noon upon the following day, but he proposed a visit to a crony. I could scarce refuse."

"You remained for two nights."

"No, for I received an urgent missive containing the dread news before we could set out."

Ottilia's ears pricked up. "Who sent it?"

"My reverend colleague, Bruno Pidsea."

"A more irritating fellow I doubt I have met." The grumble came from her spouse, in the act, at Ottilia's suggestion, of pouring himself a second glass by way of calming his temper once the visitor had departed.

She attended with only half an ear as she tried to recall the interview with Reverend Pidsea. "Did not Bruno say that he learned the news from Alexander?"

"I don't remember."

The snap in her husband's voice sank Ottilia's spirits and she watched him down a swallow or two before speaking again. "Pray try to remember, my dearest. It may be important."

She received a sharp look. "Don't trouble to use your cajoling voice, Tillie. I'm out of temper."

"I had noticed." She pushed up from the chair and went to him, smiling as she set a hand to his chest. "A waste of energy, do you not think? He is not worth it, my darling lord."

For a moment, the brooding look persisted, the dark eyes hard. Then they softened, crinkling at the corners. His lip quirked. "Witch wife you are." He put his glass down on the mantel and set his hands on either cheek. "How is it the very sight of your face is enough to break my resolve?"

"Did you mean to scold me? You may, if you wish. Behold me all wifely meekness, dear husband."

His smile came at last. "Wretch! Be thankful you are *enceinte* or I'd deal otherwise with you."

Since he chose to kiss her, Ottilia was in no danger of taking his threat seriously. She returned the caress with interest, but afterwards he leaned back, a slight crease between his brows as he scanned her face.

"Speaking of which, how are you holding up? Are you unduly fatigued? No, don't fob me off. You look pale."

Ottilia folded her fingers over his hands and drew them down. "I confess I am a little tired."

"More or less than when you were carrying Luke?"

The concern in his tone touched her, but she had to shrug. "I cannot say with any certainty, Fan. Perhaps I was more careful then, anxious as I was to avoid a repeat of…" She faded out, unwilling to speak of that fateful first pregnancy.

"That will not happen again, my dear one."

She grimaced. "You can't know that."

"Are you fearful then?"

"No. At least, only if something brings it to mind. I promise you I have been well this time. It is not as if you don't harry me into resting. What with Patrick's commands into the bargain —"

"That is all very well, but you've been gadding about after this wretched murder for days now, and we are no further forward."

Ottilia suppressed a sharp rejoinder. Plainly, his mood was still ruffled. She chose a mild response. "Well, I think we have come some way towards a resolution, Fan." Her attention snapped back. "I must say that this Bruno Pidsea does keep coming up. Remember what Sir Hugh said of him?"

Francis was frowning now. "What do you mean?"

"Bruno took Hector to task for his treatment of Willy Heath. Now we hear that he sent to Alexander to apprise him of the death. I have a niggling suspicion that Bruno said it was the other way around."

Her spouse shifted a shoulder. "Even if he did, what does it prove?"

"Nothing immediately." Ottilia shifted away to the window, looking out in the direction of the woods where the body had been found. "I wonder…?"

In a moment, she discovered Francis at her elbow. "What do you wonder? Are you making one of your leaps?"

She threw him a smile. "I only wish I was. It occurs to me that there is one person I have not even thought to question."

"Who?"

"Willy Heath."

"What? You surely don't suspect the boy you said is a savant? Granted, Penkevil treated him badly. But one would suppose he hasn't the nous to carry out a plan of this nature."

"That I admit. Yet Bruno is a tenacious champion of the lad, and Bruno's name keeps cropping up."

CHAPTER NINETEEN

Averil waited for the moment her husband's wandering attention returned to her. She had persuaded him into the conservatory in hopes of drawing him into discussion of past and better times. In his day, Ralph Deakin had been a keen gardener, overseeing the blooming of exotic plants and guarding their fragile existences with jealous eyes. He had long ceased to hanker after the rare and beautiful, but the sight of verdant greenery still had the power to render his mood mellow. Sometimes also it would draw pockets of recollection from his fading store of memories.

His pleasure in his surroundings could not be in doubt. Large pots from which sprouted variegated leaves were set in clusters with wicker chairs placed strategically to provide the most attractive prospects and Ralph's gaze went from one to another, prompting anecdotes concerning the histories of his darlings. Averil was obliged to wait to put her careful questions until Ralph had finished eulogizing over a particularly lush fern.

"It is one of the rarer species, you know. I was lucky to find it before my rival did so."

A fortunate recollection. Averil seized the cue. "Ah, you are speaking of the older Penkevil, I think."

Ralph's gaze returned to her face. "That's right, dear girl. Lucian. He's dead now. Silly fellow."

Averil regarded his mildly amused expression with curiosity. "Silly for dying?"

A light laugh came. "He couldn't help that, dear girl. It comes to us all. No, no. Lucian fancied himself a horticulturalist, pottering about among his plants. It wasn't his only conceit either."

"Tell me about him, dear."

"Well, that's it. Not much else to him."

"What was his other conceit?"

"Ancient Greece. He thought if he gave his sons heroic names, they would grow up to match them. A vain hope. Dreadful boys, both of them. Particularly the elder."

"Hector?"

"There you are. Foolish name to give a lad. One might guess he would besmirch it at the first opportunity."

Averil rejoiced. How convenient Ralph should begin upon this subject. "Did he resemble his father?"

Ralph's gaze wandered away again. "The maidenhair symbolises purity and innocence, you know."

"Yes, Ralph dear, but you were speaking of Lucian Penkevil."

"Was I?" He sounded vague, his attention concentrated upon the plant.

Averil suppressed a sigh. Was that to be the full sum of it? Then Ralph spoke again.

"There was a deal of wrangling over the business, but for my part I was inclined to believe old Brig rather than the boy. Lied as fast as a dog will trot, did young Hector."

Trying to keep the eagerness she felt out of her voice, Averil pursued it. "What business was that, Ralph?"

"Hm?"

"The wrangling with Brig, dear."

"Oh, that. Hector went shooting on Brig's lands. Decimated his birds, so Brig said. Hector denied it. Claimed he had kept to Penkevil land. Both keepers backed their masters, so no one knows the truth of it, but Lucian stuck to it his son was telling the truth and Brig swore he'd shoot the boy if he saw him within a yard of his boundary."

"What was the outcome then? What happened?"

"Nothing at all. All hot air and sabre-rattling. Lucian thrashed the boy for all that, so he knew well Hector was guilty. Did it for spite. That's the sort of boy he was and Lucian knew it."

"Did he tell you so?"

"Grumbled it out in his cups. Couldn't hold his liquor. Both boys inherited his weak head. The younger abstained, but the elder became violent. Lucian bemoaned his ways often. He was used to say nothing would teach Hector. Born bad, like that foxglove there." A frown creased his brow. "Why do they keep foxgloves in here? You must tell them to pull them up, dear girl. It won't do for some poor fool to pick them in mistake for borage or comfrey."

He animadverted upon the carelessness of the gardeners for some time while Averil wondered whether to write to Lady Fan or make time to visit Ash Lodge again. The prospect of catching even a brief moment alone with Patrick sent flitters through her bosom.

The yearning had grown stronger since his wife's death. Guilt rose up. It was one thing to betray Ralph. Quite another to be envisioning the prospect of a legitimate future at her lover's side.

She contemplated her husband's gentle features, all smiles as he looked over his beloved vegetation. No, she would not dream of seeking her happiness at Ralph's expense. She held him in the deepest affection and the little niggle of fear at his loss — inevitable as he had said — sat like a pebble, scoring a corner of her heart. Had she not spent hours soothing Patrick for the self-same grief?

Too many believed him stoic, showing a courageous face to acquaintances and patients alike while he pursued his calling. Only she was permitted to witness the well of mingled guilt and despair that consumed him. Only she understood, too well for her own dread future, how the thought of his failure harrowed him. The more so because of the betrayal. Patrick could not forgive himself for his perceived neglect. His perception only. Averil knew, for she had listened often and long, how he had sought in vain for a cure, poring over his books well into the night when he ought to have been conserving his strength; writing endless queries to his colleagues, long letters describing Sophie's symptoms over years. All to be proved vain.

"I failed her, Averil. I did not soon enough take her complaints seriously. I grew too used to hear them and they drove me crazy. Pains here, aches there, until my patience was exhausted. If I had listened soon enough, I might have prevented —"

"But you might not, Patrick." She had berated him soundly for that one. "You can't know. It is foolish to torture yourself with regret for what cannot be known. Lash yourself for all else, if you must, but that I will not allow. You do not and cannot know whether you might have saved her."

Yet he had wept still. She hoped he was easing a little. He had seemed to be doing better when they met over the fateful anonymous letter, and perhaps the distraction of this murder was a blessing.

"I'm cold. This place has no heat."

Averil's attention snapped back to her spouse. Ralph was shivering despite the warm blanket she had taken care to wrap about his shoulders.

"We'll go inside, my dear. There's a good fire in the front parlour. Come, let me help you up."

His legs carried him but slowly and Averil was obliged to summon his valet to assist. She went ahead, sending a maid to bring hot coffee to the parlour and plumping the cushions in his chair set to catch the warmth from a cheerful fire. The room was somewhat higgledy-piggledy since it was largely their headquarters. Everything needed for Ralph's comfort was in general here, which resulted in surfaces covered with books, bottles and jars of cordials, lotions and potions, the unavoidable impedimenta of the invalid.

Once Ralph was warmed up and settled, a cup of coffee well sweetened with cream and sugar in his hand, Averil was again at leisure to indulge her thoughts. She was just deciding to forego the chance of seeing Patrick and instead put pen to paper concerning what she had learned of Penkevil senior when Peter, the household's invaluable footman and general factotum, entered the room.

"Doctor Hathaway, ma'am."

Averil jumped in her seat. As of instinct, her gaze went to Patrick's face as he entered and the quick, intimate smile he gave made her heart flip. She rose as he turned his eyes upon her husband, moving towards his chair.

"How do you do, Ralph? I have been remiss. I ought to have checked upon you days since."

Ralph was looking up at him without recognition. Averil saw his confusion and quickly supplied the lack. "It is Doctor Hathaway, Ralph dear. Your physician, remember? He has come to see how you are faring."

Light entered her husband's eyes and he gave the smile that endeared him to all. "Of course, of course I remember." He turned to Averil. "The best doctor hereabouts, dear girl, did you know?"

"Yes, dear, that's why I like him to take care of you."

His brows rose. "Take care of me? I'm not ill, dear girl. Did she send to you? I was a trifle cold among the plants, but I am perfectly warm again."

Averil exchanged a glance with Patrick, who gave a slight nod. Thankfully, he was well used to Ralph's ways and spoke in the reassuring tone Averil was aware he used with all his patients.

"I can see you are well indeed, sir. Since I am here, though, perhaps I may take a look at you? We ought to keep an eye on that chest of yours, especially if you have felt the cold."

Ralph flapped his hands where they rested in his lap. "Do as you please then. Fuss, fuss, fuss. The dear girl thinks me weaker than I am, but so it is always when a man reaches my time of life. You wait, Hathaway. Your wife will do the same by you when you reach my years."

Averil noted with a sinking heart the little flinch these words caused. There was no point in reminding Ralph that Patrick's wife had died. Why force him to an apology when he would have forgotten again in a moment?

"Do let Patrick examine you, Ralph dear. I will retire while he does so."

"Yes, yes, you go, dear girl." He raised his arms. "Have at me then, dear fellow."

Averil caught Patrick's eye as she made to leave, giving him a significant look and a tiny jerk of the head. He would read the message readily, but she was reassured by the slight nod he gave that he had understood.

She left the parlour and headed instead for the small apartment she used for a study. From this haven, she directed the household, wrote her letters, and savoured the odd moment of solitude. Patrick knew to find her here and they might seize a few moments of privacy.

Anticipation curled her stomach as she waited, too restless to take up any of the several tasks she had set herself among the papers piled on her desk and awaiting attention.

She was obliged to dawdle for some fifteen minutes before Patrick put in an appearance. He came in and closed the door, standing before it and gazing at her with hunger in his eyes.

"I've missed you."

Affection swelled in her bosom. His directness was one of the characteristics she loved in him. "Likewise." She smiled at him. "We must endure for a little longer."

A grimace crossed his face and he came for her. Averil melted into his arms for one blessed moment, allowed the kiss and then gently prized herself away. "Be patient, dear love."

He hesitated, the grey eyes warm on hers. A little sigh came and he shifted away. "Ralph's chest is crackling. Have you any of the syrup remaining, the one I left the last time?"

Averil forced her roving mind to behave. "Half the bottle, I believe."

"Feed him a spoonful three times a day. Five days should be enough. I'll check on him again after that."

She agreed to this programme in an automatic fashion. When they were private like this, his physical presence almost overwhelmed her, so tall and loose-limbed as he was, his face strikingly attractive — oddly familiar and alien at the same time. She spoke on the thought. "How like is your sister to you! For an instant then, I saw her face in yours."

His countenance creased in laughter. "Ottilia would not thank you for it. She is softer in looks by far than I. Nor can I lay claim to her vaunted charm. She would ensnare a snake, my sister."

A faintly bitter note made Averil eye him with concern. "Have you quarrelled?"

He shifted in a way that signified discomfort. "Not precisely. It galls me how she delights in this wretched murder."

The mention of it recalled her earlier exchange with Ralph to Averil's mind. "At the risk of dismaying you further, I have something to add to Lady Fan's store of knowledge."

Patrick cast his gaze heavenwards. "Not you too!"

She was betrayed into a laugh. "Well, I did confess to being intrigued by her manner of tackling the business. But you need not be troubled. I promised Ottilia I would enquire of Ralph what he might know of Penkevil senior and indeed he did let fall a snippet that may be of interest."

She relayed the tale of Hector's trespass upon the brigadier's lands and the outcome thereof. Patrick did not look to be edified by it, but he consented to tell his sister.

"Ottilia seems to feel that any little piece may add to her puzzle, so I dare say she will be only too happy to include your contribution."

Noting his clear reluctance to become involved in any way, Averil stepped up to him and laid a hand on his arm. "Better to help her, I suggest, my dear, than to rail at what cannot be avoided. The more we assist, the sooner Lady Fan may draw her conclusions."

"We?" Patrick's mouth twisted and a gleam came into his eye. "You propose to become even more involved, do you?"

"I don't see why I should not. After all, such an opportunity as this is unlikely to come in my way again."

"I'm glad you regard it as an opportunity. To do precisely what remains a question."

She had to laugh. "That I don't know, but we shall see. I cannot do much, tied as I am to Ralph's convenience, but I dare say I may prove a useful adjunct if I set my mind to it."

He was smiling at last in genuine amusement. "You are capable of anything once you set your mind to it. Just don't drag me into it, that's all I ask."

"You won't object if I visit Ash Lodge?"

"You know well I would love to see you there — permanently."

She made a quick negative gesture. "None of that. Not yet awhile. I won't wish him away."

Patrick did not meet her eyes. "I should not have spoken of it. Forgive me."

She made no answer beyond a slight shake of the head. It was a discussion she could not enter into and he knew it well.

"I had better go." He moved to the door. "I'll tell Ottilia your news and warn her to expect you."

Averil, her heart wrung, reached him before he opened the door. "Don't leave like this!"

He turned with a rueful look. "I need you too much, Averil."

"I know. It is so with me also." She reached up and touched his face. "Let us be circumspect awhile. Matters will settle in due course and we will find our time together again."

He caught her hand and pressed her fingers to his lips. The fierce caress pierced her, but in seconds and before she could speak, he was gone.

CHAPTER TWENTY

To Ottilia's intense gratification, she found Brigadier O'Turk with Lady Carrefour when she dropped in upon that elderly dame for the second time on Friday morning.

"Why, this is providential, Brig! How do you do?"

Her aged acquaintance stared her out for a moment before replying in the terse manner habitual to him. "It's you, is it, you brassy chit? Didn't recognise you for a moment. Blame that." He pointed at her vanished waist. "Breeding, are ye? Got a quiverful of brats already, I'll wager."

Ottilia laughed as she came forward and held out her hand. "Only two, and one of those is not my own. But she is loved and precious to me for all that."

Brigadier O'Turk ignored the hand and instead patted her cheek. "Don't seem a day older now I look at you." Then he bent a frown upon her. "Why'd you send that husband of yours instead of coming to me yourself?"

Ottilia did not beat about the bush. "Because I thought he would get more out of you than you would willingly proffer to me."

"Ha! Always were an impertinent minx. How that young feller bears with you beats me."

Devilry entered Ottilia's breast. "It flummoxes me too, sir. I am fortunate beyond my deserts." She turned from him then to attend her hostess, who was staring up at her in puzzlement from her chair by the fire. "I trust I find you well, ma'am?"

Lady Carrefour blinked up at her. "Who are you?"

Brigadier O'Turk intervened before Ottilia could answer. "She's the Hathaway chit, Sal. Married off a few years back. Name escapes me, but —"

"I am Lady Francis Fanshawe, ma'am, but pray address me as Ottilia. Or Lady Fan, if you prefer."

A snorting laugh came from Brigadier O'Turk. "Lady Fan! What sort of a sobriquet is that? No, don't tell me. Don't want to know. Heard quite enough of it hereabouts." On a sudden, he glared at her. "Ye've not solved it or you wouldn't be here badgering. What's to do?"

Ottilia seized her chance. "I am so glad you asked, sir. I have a question for Lady Carrefour, but let me first put one to you."

"Well? Well? Speak up, girl!"

"I will if you will give me an opportunity."

"Yes, very well. Spit it out."

Ottilia suppressed an urge to respond in a like manner. "Is it true that Hector once shot birds on your land, resulting in a quarrel between you and Mr Penkevil senior?"

For a moment or two, Brigadier O'Turk merely stared, his brows drawing together. Then he snuffed in a breath. "Where'd you get hold of that old tale?"

She bypassed the question. "It was so then, was it?"

Brigadier O'Turk gave forth an explosive sound. "Young scoundrel damned near ruined my sport that year, saving your presence, Sal." He turned as he spoke to proffer a tiny bow towards Lady Carrefour.

No apology for his language was apparently due to herself, Ottilia noted with faint amusement. "I understand he did it for spite?"

"Did it because he was an evil brat and a worse man. Only wish I had been the one to rid the world of his presence."

"Were you?"

The direct attack did not fluster the old man in the least. "Wouldn't tell you if I was, would I? Stupid question to ask."

Ottilia had to smile. "It does occasionally elicit a result. Unlike you, sir, some are apt to become defensive if they think I am accusing them."

He evidently had nothing to say to this, instead turning the subject. "What do you want with Sally? If you must needs trouble her, say your piece and be done."

During this exchange, Ottilia had not failed to watch Lady Carrefour surreptitiously. The elderly dame's gaze had followed from one to the other. Had she understood the implications? It was hard to judge whether or no her vagueness was in play.

Ottilia turned to face her again. "Will you tell me, if you please, in what relation you stand to Roland Huish?"

The name sparked recognition, for Lady Carrefour's eyes lit. "He is a poet, you know."

"So I believe. He told me that you are related."

"What the deuce has that to say to anything, even if they are?" Brigadier O'Turk was in again. "Going to trace down every family tree, are you?"

Ottilia strove for patience. "That would be a waste of time. Come, sir, you surely don't need me to explain. I am very sure you are fully cognizant of all the possible ramifications of this business. After all, did you not warn my husband that there are wheels within wheels?"

Brigadier O'Turk had the grace to look sheepish, his cheeks darkening a trifle. He rallied quickly. "Don't mean I have to put up with you turning the screw on Sally here."

Exasperated, Ottilia became tart. "How in the world can I be said to be turning the screw on her, Brig? I merely wish to know in what relationship she stands with Roland Huish. Is that so problematic?"

The old man did not yield. "Ah, but why? What is it you think to make of such information?"

"That I cannot tell until I have it. Really, I begin to regret that I found you here after all. You have given me next to nothing on your own account, and now you are interfering with my attempt to acquire a little piece of information."

"Ye've yet to explain why you want it."

Ottilia gave a heartfelt sigh. "If you must have it, there is every reason to suppose Roland might have been involved in this murder."

Brigadier O'Turk continued obstinate. "Granted. Still don't tell me why being Sal's relative has any bearing on the case."

"Very likely it does not, but —"

"Then you don't need to know."

Ottilia summoned every ounce of patience remaining to her in preparation for continuing the battle, when Lady Carrefour spoke up.

"Roland is my godson."

Relief swept through Ottilia. "Ah, so that is it. Is he also related to you by blood?"

"A cousin of sorts." Lady Carrefour wafted a wavering hand in a hopeless sort of gesture. "I wish I might be a better godmother. The dear boy looked to me for succour, but I am powerless to assist him."

Ottilia pounced on this, moving to the side of the old lady's chair. "In what way did he need succour, ma'am?"

To her chagrin, Brigadier O'Turk intervened again. "Ye need not say any more, Sal."

Ottilia, reading Lady Carrefour's condition, guessed that she was lost in reminiscence. She dropped to her haunches beside the chair and took the woman's restless hand in her own, speaking with gentleness.

"Go on, ma'am. What help did Roland need from you? Was it money?"

The elder lady sighed. "At first. I could only give him a little. He understood my predicament. Dear Roland. He said I must not think of putting myself in difficulties." Her tone changed. "But he fell into the toils of that creature! I warned him. He would not listen."

"You mean Ruth Penkevil?"

No direct answer was forthcoming. "He was a bad man." She looked up. "Wasn't he, Brig? You knew him best, my dear. A bad man. Thank heavens he's gone. But I couldn't help poor Roland. He is besotted."

A murmur filtered down to Ottilia. "Pay no heed. She don't know what she says half the time."

Ottilia ignored the brigadier's warning. "You are speaking of Hector Penkevil." She dared a throw. "Lady Carrefour, do you fear that Roland killed him?"

The old lady snatched her hand away, but only so that she might cover her eyes. She was shuddering, uttering breathy little cries of distress.

Brigadier O'Turk's infuriated whisper reached Ottilia. "Now see what you've done! What did you want to go asking her that for?"

He moved across to a side table and Ottilia watched him pour a measure of dark liquid into a glass. She rose to her feet and gave place as he brought it across.

"Sal! Drink this!"

The peremptory tone had its effect. Lady Carrefour dropped her hand and obediently drank from the glass as the brigadier held it to her lips. A few sips appeared to restore her. She waved the glass away and looked up at Ottilia, her brows drawing together.

"Who is this? Did you say I had a visitor, Brig? Why did they not announce her?"

Ottilia did not trouble to re-introduce herself. There was no more to be got out of her hostess. She waited while a maid was summoned and then made her farewells.

To her surprise, Brigadier O'Turk followed her from the room and she paused at the head of the stairs. "You are leaving too?"

"Not yet." He eyed her with a touch of suspicion. "What d'ye mean to do with that?"

"I have no notion. What would you advise?"

"Already told you not to heed her. Erratic is Sally."

"But not necessarily untruthful. In her lucid moments she is perfectly able to recall the reality of what has taken place, do you not think?"

He grunted. "Maybe so."

Ottilia took her chance. "You were quick to tell my husband I am stirring up a hornet's nest. Have I plumbed the depths of the wheels within wheels, do you think?"

Brigadier O'Turk blew out his cheeks. "Ye've discovered how too many persons had reason to wish that scoundrel underground, I surmise. Have you looked to the clergy?"

"Alexander?"

"Pooh! Too full of his own importance to be worth bothering with. He ain't the only benighted parson nursing a grudge."

"I asked him outright if he was referring to Bruno Pidsea, Fan, but he would say no more. For the life of me, I cannot think the beating of Willy Heath a sufficient reason for Bruno to resort to murder."

"If he thinks you still suspect him, Brig might have pointed to the clergy to put you off the scent."

Ottilia considered her spouse's words as she settled into her chair and took up the cup of coffee he had thoughtfully arranged to be provided upon her return to Ash Lodge. "I am much inclined to cross Brig off the list in any event. If he meant to eliminate Hector, he would not have done it in an underhand fashion."

"I agree with you." Francis was leaning his elbow on the mantel. "Although according to your report, he seems to be uncommonly attached to this Lady Carrefour."

"It is an old friendship, I believe. I doubt Brig would go so far as to take revenge on her behalf."

"Not Roland either?"

"Not on his godmother's account, no."

"You still consider him a possible accessory with Ruth Penkevil then?"

Ottilia regarded him with question, but Francis was not looking at her. He had caught sight of his reflection in the mirror above the fireplace and was flicking at his hair, which had indeed an unruly lock with a tendency to fall across his cheek.

Ottilia clicked her tongue. "Are you still at odds with it, Fan? Why don't you grow it out then?"

He brushed the lock back and turned his head, the dark eyes faintly rueful. "I'm finding I prefer the style, if only it would remain in place. Besides, I am reliably informed that shorter hair is in fashion."

"Who so informed you?"

"Your nephew Ben. He says all the older boys are following the *ton* in wearing their hair shorter."

Ottilia laughed. "Speaking of my nephews, I have not seen them since last night's dinner. Nor were they about yesterday. I wonder what they are up to?"

"Instead of assisting your enquiries. Quite so."

"Well, if I am honest there is little they can do that would be of much use."

Hardly were the words out of her mouth than the door opened to admit the two Hathaway boys, both in a high state of excitement.

Tom bounced up to Ottilia. "We've been tracking down the suspects, Auntilla."

She regarded him with an indulgent smile. "Have you indeed? Which ones in particular?"

"All of them."

"Not all of them, Tom. Don't be such an ass." Ben elbowed his brother out of the way. "We thought it would be useful if we found out more about who was where and what they did that day. You know the style of thing, Auntilla."

Before Ottilia could respond, Francis cut in. "Your aunt has already asked them all that, boys."

He was instantly confronted by Tom, who loped across to the fireplace. "Them, yes, Uncle Fan. But we've found witnesses who know different."

"We've seen the suspects too," put in Ben. "Some of them."

Ottilia's senses prickled. "That is indeed intriguing. Whom did you tackle and what have you found out?"

Ben took this. "The best one, we think, is the Hexworthies."

"They lied to you, Uncle Fan," said Tom with relish.

Francis straightened. "Say on."

Ben took up the tale. "You said they claimed they refused to serve Mr Penkevil."

"But they did serve him," said Tom. "At least, their tapster did. That Hector was in there that night and he took a drink of rum."

Ottilia's mind was working and she exchanged a glance with her spouse who looked to have made the same jump. Caution prompted her question. "Did the tapster pour it himself?"

Tom looked blank, but Ben's features became filled with consternation. "We didn't think to ask. Is it important?"

She smiled her reassurance. "It may well be, but leave that for now. This finding is very useful and I thank you for it."

Tom, once more exhibiting suppressed excitement, returned to her chair. "That's not all, Auntilla. We followed Roland Huish and he met secretly with Mrs Penkevil."

No surprise there, but Ottilia was moved to slight anxiety. "You were spying on them? I hope to heaven you were not seen. What my brother would say if you were caught in the act —"

"We didn't spy," said Tom, indignant. "We happened to be in the vicinity of Berwick St John and we spotted Roland."

Francis's amused tones came. "Oh, you just happened to be there, did you? I thought you said you'd been tracking suspects."

"Shut it, Tom," said Ben, sotto voce, digging his brother in the ribs. Then he faced Ottilia squarely. "It's true we were spying, Auntilla, but it was all in a good cause. Papa will understand that."

"Will he indeed?"

Her brother's voice, coming all of a sudden from the doorway, made Ottilia jump. Wary of his uncertain mood these days, she spoke up at once.

"I didn't tell them to do this, Patrick, but it may be set to my account. They were trying to help."

Her brother strolled into the room, his gaze on his sons, who looked both guilty and, in Ben's case, a trifle apprehensive. Patrick wafted a hand as he headed for the fireplace, joining Francis at the mantel. "Don't mind me. Carry on with your report."

At first it did not seem to Ottilia as if either of her nephews felt able to comply with this airy request. She could have wished Patrick had not chosen this precise moment to enter the parlour, but at least his mood seemed propitious. But this was valuable information, for Ruth had not been entirely truthful when she spoke of her dealings with Roland Huish. She made up her mind.

"Where did this meeting between Roland and Ruth Penkevil take place?"

Although Ben kept an eye on his father, Tom, nothing loath, plunged in again. "That's the odd thing, Auntilla. It was a cottage, not far from Roland's lodging."

"We think Mrs Penkevil came in a gig," put in Ben, relaxing a trifle by his demeanour, "for there was a boy looking after the horse around the back."

"You went round the back?" Ottilia's mind jumped. "Pray don't tell me you tried to look in at the windows."

Tom's cheeks reddened and Ben looked sheepish, throwing a glance at his father before he spoke. "We did. At least, we wanted to hear what was said, if we could."

"Yes, because they might have confessed about the murder, Auntilla. You would not have had us miss that."

Francis lifted an eyebrow. "You need not fret about that. Your aunt has been guilty of the self-same thing. She even used a glass against a door to overhear a private conversation."

Ottilia was obliged to stifle a wicked giggle, not quite successfully. "It is not conduct I would advise you to emulate, either of you. However, since you did make the attempt —" throwing an apologetic look to Patrick — "were you able to hear anything?"

Ben looked regretful. "Nothing of any value, Auntilla."

"No, it was all mushy love talk," came disgustedly from Tom. "How they had missed each other and all that."

"One thing though, Auntilla. I thought I heard Mrs Penkevil saying it was too soon to be thinking of showing their affection in public. She didn't want a scandal on their hands, she said."

"Yes, because being a widow was difficult enough," added Tom, "and that's when Roland spoke of you, Auntilla, saying they must wait until Lady Fan was done with it all."

To Ottilia's chagrin, her brother chimed in. "That's what we are all waiting for."

"I am doing my best, brother dear." But she could not avoid the stray suspicion that Patrick's impatience stemmed more from his interest in Averil than in the solution to the puzzle of the murder. It struck her that the discussion of Ruth and Roland's clandestine meeting might well prick at a chord with him. She wondered fleetingly, and not for the first time, where precisely the couple had conducted their lover's tryst.

Ben's voice recalled her attention. "We found out something more, Auntilla. I asked the boy about the cottage and —"

"Guess who owns it?" Tom's blue eyes were alight. "Lord Carrefour!"

Not quite as astonished as both her brother and spouse appeared, Ottilia was conscious of satisfaction. "That tallies with the Carrefour connection. But if Lord Carrefour owns it, how —?"

"What Tom means is it's on his lands. The boy lives there with his sister and she works up at the manor."

"Yet that does not explain how Lady Carrefour had access to the place. Roland said she provided a place where they might meet."

"She likely knows the girl, Tillie," said Francis. "There is no saying the present Lord Carrefour has any knowledge of his cottage being used for clandestine meetings."

"Very true, Fan." She turned back to the boys. "This is all very helpful. Did you happen to follow anyone else or question other witnesses?"

Tom grimaced. "Well, we caught that old biddy who is mother to Mrs Penkevil —"

"Mrs Poyle?"

"Yes, her."

"What do you mean, you caught her?"

"Not caught hold of her, Auntilla, I don't mean that."

Ben struck in. "You're just confusing her, Tom. It was like this, Auntilla. We saw her in Aston on our way back and so we followed to see where she might go."

"But she just went into the shop there and got some black ribbon. She gabbled away to the shopkeeper, pretending she was sorry that Hector died — as if anyone would believe it because we all know she couldn't abide him — and never said anything to the purpose at all."

"How disappointing. Never mind. At least we know she is pretending to be sorry for the death. I doubt anyone would have the temerity to ask her about the murder."

"No, and we couldn't either," said Ben with regret. "But we did ask the shopkeeper when Mrs Poyle last came in and it was on that day."

"Before the murder happened, you mean?"

"Yes, because she might have bought valerian there. He sells all sorts of stuff there, including potions."

Francis intervened. "Don't say you asked the fellow if Mrs Poyle had bought the drug?"

Tom became scornful. "We ain't daft, Uncle Fan, are we, Papa? We were cleverer than that."

"Indeed? What then?"

Ben took the question. "We just asked if the shopkeeper had any stock of it. I pretended I was asking because we were running out at your examining room, Papa."

"So he never suspected it had anything to do with Mrs Poyle or the murder."

Patrick snorted. "I should hope it is not generally known that valerian was involved. We must trust the shopkeeper won't put two and two together."

Ottilia hastened to deflect the discussion. "Is that the sum of your activities?"

"Pretty well," said Ben. "When we were coming back here, we did see old Petrus and Willy heading off together, but we steered clear."

"He don't like us above half, old Petrus," Tom put in on a gloomy note. "We didn't want to fall foul of him."

"Very wise." Ottilia spoke absently, a niggling idea chasing through her mind. "I don't suppose you know where they were headed?" she asked, almost without realising it.

"No, and we dared not ask," said Tom with feeling.

Ben was regarding Ottilia with a slight line pulled between his brows. "Is it important?"

"I do not know, to tell you the truth. I am tracing an idea, that is all."

"Well, it's not to say they meant to go there but the path they were on leads to St Leonard's, the Reverend Pidsea's church."

CHAPTER TWENTY-ONE

Averil arrived in the early afternoon upon the following day while Patrick was out on his rounds. Ottilia was alone, her nephews having elected to accompany Francis on an expedition to once again tackle the Hexworthy couple. After greetings were exchanged and Averil had taken a seat, Ottilia was intrigued to discover her guest had chosen her time on purpose.

"I knew Patrick would not be here at this hour. He does not mind my participating, provided I do not drag him into the business."

Ottilia eyed her with a lurking smile. "Do I take it you mean to offer your assistance?"

"If I can be of use. I don't feel the little I managed to elicit from Ralph is enough to claim being involved."

"It is helpful information, however, since it builds my picture of Hector. I taxed Brig with it, but he tended to dismiss the incident as of scant importance. He did say he wished he had been the one to end Hector's life, but I don't believe he meant it. His anxiety centred on trying to stop me questioning Lady Carrefour."

"Then what can I do, Lady Fan? I wish I might assist in some material fashion."

Ottilia waved this away. "You already have, Averil. You brought that letter, after all."

"I could not have done otherwise. Come, I know you lived here for some years, but I may be more familiar with the recent period. Is there anything you need to know? Some person I could question, or introduce to you?"

Her eagerness touched Ottilia, although she could think of no immediate necessity. "Let me mull it over. I don't doubt something will come up." She made a move to get up out of the comfortable special chair. "Meanwhile, I must revisit Ruth Penkevil today or the Sabbath will be upon me. If you have the time, would you care to accompany me?"

They had not been many minutes upon the road in Ottilia's coach when a thought occurred. "How well do you know the Reverend Bruno Pidsea, Averil?"

"Quite well, as it chances. He has been Ralph's spiritual adviser for several years. Ralph preferred his style to the man at Knighton which was our nearest church, and so we used to attend St Leonard's at Burchall before we moved. Ralph does not do well in the carriage except on very good days, and the road to Kington's Ash is better laid. It is quite rough going to Burchall and Ralph could not walk. Bruno used to dine with us when we had company."

Alert now, Ottilia probed for more. "Lately though? Have your dealings with him ceased?"

"We see less of him. Indeed, we don't mingle much these days in light of Ralph's condition. But Bruno is a conscientious man. He seems to feel it incumbent upon him to keep acquaintance with Ralph, even though we no longer count as his parishioners as we don't attend his services."

"He visits your husband?"

"Now and then. Not since Hector Penkevil's death. The last time was perhaps two or three weeks before."

Ottilia thought for a moment. "Then you won't be familiar with his present demeanour. Tell me, Averil. What sort of a man is he in your estimation? I grant you conscientious, as you said. Compassionate? I understand him to have been a champion of Willy Heath."

"Bruno has a good deal of humanity. He feels for his fellow man. To my mind, his calling is a vocation. Unlike many clerics, who I am very sure choose the church in hopes of an easy sinecure, in preference to the dangers of the armed services or the complexity of the law and politics."

Ottilia was moved to laughter. "You sound a very cynic, Averil."

"Do I? Perhaps I am so. My brother made just such a choice. Papa wanted to buy him a commission as he did not choose to become a lawyer, but Edwin would have none of it. His clerical life consists of carousing with his cronies, growing fat on good food and leaving far too many services to his deputy. I am out of all patience with him. I know for a fact too many of his colleagues behave in much the same fashion. A man like Bruno Pidsea is an exception."

Which did not speak much to his candidacy for a murderer. But this thought Ottilia kept to herself. She would not dismiss the notion out of hand. Even a paragon might be provoked to violence, given the right circumstances. The trouble was, she could see no circumstance that might so provoke the Reverend Bruno Pidsea. The only quarrel he appeared to have with the dead man was Hector's brutality towards Willy Heath, which was long past. Inconceivable that episode could move him to murder at this juncture. Yet Bruno was too much in evidence to be discounted.

The coach was slowing and a glance out of the window as it made the turn showed Ottilia it was entering the Penkevil estate. She shelved the Bruno matter for the moment, turning her attention to what she wanted to find out from Ruth Penkevil.

The widow was discovered in company with her mother and the two young children. Jason Penkevil proved to be a serious little boy engaged in attempting an inexpert pencil sketch of his grandmother, while Ariadne, not much older than Ottilia's toddler son at home in Flitteris, was playing with a kitten. Neither looked to be in mourning for a father who had been, by all accounts, too strict and remote a man to be much missed.

Ottilia could not but reflect upon the very different atmosphere at home, where her darling lord's loving influence was truly felt. Pretty adored Francis and Luke was rapidly learning to emulate his adoptive sister in twisting their father around his tiny finger. This pair might well be the better for their lack since Ruth was clearly a fond mother and even Margery Poyle seemed a different creature in their presence. She made no objection when Ruth suggested she should retire with the children.

"Come, little ones, come with Grandmama. I want my portrait finished, Jason love. Ariadne, take up kitty and come along to the nursery."

She ushered the children out and held back a moment, speaking in a hushed tone. "I'll be back directly, Lady Fan, if you've questions for me. Moreover, I want to know your findings, as does Ruth, so I'll thank you to give us a round tale."

She whisked away before Ottilia could answer, but Ruth took up the point upon the instant as she moved to tug at the bell-pull. "Pay her no mind, ma'am, for I doubt you've come with any answers. It's more questions, I expect. Let me send for tea first."

Ottilia would have preferred coffee, but she accepted the offer and an invitation to be seated. She waved Averil to join her as she settled into a convenient sofa placed to take advantage of the fire. She had been pleased to see the natural manner of Ruth's greeting of Averil Deakin, perhaps in some sympathy (assuming she knew at least as much as Nancy) for a woman who had also strayed from her marital vows.

The parlour was a cosier apartment than she might have expected. There were two of these small sofas and several well-cushioned chairs, a neat feminine writing bureau in one corner, a small filled bookcase against one wall and a round table near the window embrasure with straight chairs set about it. The walls were papered in a cheerful pattern of tiny flowerets and leaves, and the drapery at the window was of a frivolous gauzy material. Ottilia suspected this was Ruth's particular domain, its informality at variance with the more traditional drawing-room into which she had been shown upon the last occasion.

Once the servant who came in answer to the bell had been given instruction, Ruth seated herself in a chair opposite the sofa and gave a smile Ottilia could only regard as tentative.

"How can I help, Lady Fan?"

Ottilia did not hesitate. "I take it you are aware that I have spoken to Roland Huish?"

Ruth did not even blush. "Yes, he told me the substance of your discussion."

"Ah, then you will not be surprised to hear that I have learned of his relationship to Lady Carrefour. Was it by her agency that you and Roland are able to use one of Lord Carrefour's cottages?"

That did bring a trifle of colour to Ruth's cheek, her eyes widening as she stared at Ottilia for a moment. "I heard you were adept, but I had no notion you could be so thorough."

Ottilia did not feel it necessary to speak of the antics of her nephews, instead turning the widow's surprise to her advantage. "It is wiser to be frank with me."

"But I have been. I have told you all you wished to know."

The plaintive note put Ottilia on alert. Was Ruth indeed hiding something? She held the woman's gaze. "Have you?"

Ruth looked away, fidgeting with the folds of her black satin petticoats. She'd had time, it seemed, to equip herself better for the mourning state which no doubt would, for the sake of appearances, last a full year. The gown was clearly new. It was modestly high over the bosom, plain in style with long sleeves, but with a plaiting of white lace around the neck and wrists, the whole covered over with a caped velvet neckerchief, defiantly colourful in soft mauve.

Ottilia waited. She glanced around at Averil beside her and found that lady's gaze glued upon Ruth. She had obviously not missed the implication. A fleeting thought obtruded that Averil was far more suited to Patrick than had been poor Sophie. Ottilia dismissed it, feeling disloyal to her deceased sister-in-law. She had often found herself impatient with Sophie's megrims, a pinprick to her ever-fertile conscience.

Ruth gave a sigh, drawing Ottilia's attention back to the matter at hand. "There is one little thing I have held back."

In addition to lying about reciprocating Roland's love even in the physical sense? But Ottilia let this pass. Instead, she proffered encouragement. "Yes? You need not fear to tell me."

Ruth twisted her fingers together and did not meet Ottilia's eyes. "We quarrelled that night."

"You and Hector?"

The widow squirmed a little. "It was quite a scene, if I am to be truthful. He was growing close to violence. I know the signs. I forget now what set him off — so much has happened…"

She faded out, but Ottilia made no move to intervene. Let Ruth tell it in her own time. In a moment, her strategy proved out as the widow resumed, a little more confident now.

"When he reached that point, it was my practice to back down, even apologise, take the blame, make myself wrong. Whatever might serve to appease him and save myself from his wrath. That night —" a snatched breath like a sob escaping — "was different. I was different. Buoyed, I think, from a meeting with Roland. He had been so very sweet and warm to me, so tender. I could not endure the contrast."

She hesitated again. Ottilia applied a prompt. "You fought back?"

"Not precisely. That would have enraged him. A sort of calm came over me. I warned him that if he laid a hand on me, I would leave him. He scoffed at it, taunted me with the scandal, but I did not break. I said I was ready to become an outcast, that I would endure the scandal more readily than his cruelties." The words were coming fluently now, as if once started on her confession, she could not stop. "I said I would make him a laughing stock — that hit him hard for he prides himself on his dignity and status. I said — God help me! — that I wished him dead."

Small wonder she had held off revealing that snippet. Ottilia watched as Ruth put a hand to her mouth as if to punish her lips for speaking such words. Her voice had grown breathy and moisture stood in her eyes. At last she looked across, a plea in her face.

"At that moment, I meant it. If he had stayed, I might have retracted it as I did when I calmed down. But Hector stormed off. I thought — afterwards, when I had to relive that quarrel

— I thought he did not know how to react. I had never defied him before, never shown my teeth." Tears were trickling down her cheeks but she disregarded their passage. "The next thing I learned was that he had died in the woods. You may imagine how this news affected me."

Ottilia could well imagine it. Ruth's collapse and lamentations, for a husband she could not have valued, were now explained.

Fortune favoured Francis. The White Horse was not busy, the bulk of its likely clientele not yet released from their labours. As upon the last occasion, the elderly fellows seated close to the fire were dawdling in a game over a pint — cribbage this time. Neither of the Hexworthy couple was present, but the man who had described himself as the landlord's brother was behind the counter, in a desultory fashion wiping down its surface with a rag.

Ben leaned close. "That's the tapster we talked to, sir."

"Capital. Let me tackle him before I get to Jerry and his wife."

"Jerry?"

"The landlord. They are brothers."

"Are they? Then I'm astonished he told a different tale."

Francis was eyeing the muscular tapster, who looked to be in a morose mood. He had not even noticed their entrance. "He may not be in their confidence. All to the good." He raised his voice and stepped up to the counter, rapping his knuckles on the wood. "Ho, there!"

The tapster jerked back, looking up. "Hey?" His glance went past Francis to the two lads a little way behind and recognition brought a frown to his brow. "You two again? What d'you want this time?"

Francis rapped the wood again. "They are with me. I want you, Hexworthy."

The tapster blinked, bringing his gaze back to Francis. A second or two passed before the frown vanished. "Oh, it's you, yer honour. You'll be wanting Jerry, I expect."

"Presently. It's you I need first."

Thick brows drew together again and the tapster's mouth turned down. "Ain't my place, as I've been told all over again. Keep mum, I been told, if I want to keep a roof over me head. 'Keep mum, Sid,' he says. So that's that. I ain't saying nowt."

Francis took instant advantage. "Ah, so you've been raked over the coals for revealing that Hector Penkevil did indeed come into this tavern on the night he died."

The effect was almost comical. Sid's countenance fell, eyes popping, mouth slack and the red-veined cheeks grew pale. He raised a pointing hand that shook slightly, indicating the boys. "Them two yourn, are they? Told on me, did they?"

"They are my nephews and they are working with me to solve this murder. Pay attention, man! I've a question for you."

"I told you, I won't say nowt else. You talk to Jerry. I'll fetch him straight."

Francis moved quickly to bar the way as Sid made to head off to the rear of the stale-smelling taproom. "No, you don't. Ben, flank me!"

Not only Ben, but Tom too, hastened to join him, the latter raising his fists in a pugnacious fashion that amused Francis. He did not think the tapster would attempt to lay hands on him, but Sid was a big man and the reinforcements should at least provide a deterrent. The tapster hesitated, evidently weighing up his options. Then he slumped back in a defeated fashion, leaning against the counter.

"Get on and say it then." His tone had lost some of its belligerence, sounding merely sulky.

Francis straightened, signing to the two boys to drop back. Both obeyed, although Tom's fists were still clenched and Ben's focus remained on the tapster.

"It is a simple question, Sid. Was it you who poured the rum for Penkevil?"

The tapster hunched his shoulders. "I were in the act of. Only Matty come in and seen me."

"Did she stop you?"

"Made a grab for the cup. Made me spill the bottle, silly wench. I had to set it down and the cup too. Matty went for it but Penkevil got there first and he threw it down his throat afore she could stop him." Once started on his story, the tapster seemingly could not hold back, as if he was reliving the scene. "Matty got mad, yelling at him as he could drink the whole bottle for all of her. Then she seized up the bottle and she pours another tot. Penkevil ups and says he don't want it, nor he won't pay for it neither."

"Did he pay for the one tot?"

"Threw coins on the counter. But Matty picked them up and threw 'em back. Went all over the floor and she yells at him to pick up his rubbish." A sort of growling laugh came. "Penkevil ain't one to lose his brass so he scrabbles on the floor for 'em. Next I know, Matty goes around with the totted-up cup and pushes it into his hand, bidding him drink up and get out."

Francis's mind was running ahead, but he must get the full tale to be certain. "Did Penkevil drink it?"

"He were that mad by then, he grabs it off Matty and tosses off the rum and walks out cool as you please."

"That was the end of it?"

"Not by a long chalk. By that time Jerry arrived, hearing all the rumpus, and when he hears Matty's tale, he hares off after Penkevil."

Francis heard Ben gasp behind him. Glancing round, he saw Tom's eyes blazing with excitement and took immediate precaution, sotto voce. "Quiet, both of you!" Then, to the tapster, "Did Jerry catch him?"

Sid slumped again. "Nah. He were back in minutes, saying it were too dark to see. Not that no one cared after that for all the kickup as went on. Jerry and Matty at it hammer and tongs. Then they starts on me. I had enough so I scarpered. Don't know what happened after and neither of 'em will say." He gave a great sigh. "May as well pack up now, for he'll boot me out for telling it all, sure as check."

Francis could sympathise, but he had a task to perform. "Never mind that now. We are looking into an unlawful killing, Hexworthy, so be sure your assistance is of value. Will you fetch your brother out now, if you please?"

He stood aside to let the man through and the boys followed suit. Sid went with lagging steps towards the rear door, what time the two elderly customers set up a cackle, drawing Francis's attention. He turned.

"Anything to say?"

The one with a long pipe set beside his tankard waved a hand. "Jest as we seen it all, yer honour."

"You witnessed the incident?"

"We and the rest," said the other man, stroking his chin. "Talk o' the village it were, not to mention as him upped and died after, what we heard next day."

The first old fellow peered at Francis with a curious mien. "Odd as it ain't the magistrate askin'. Be you a law officer, yer honour?"

"I am not. I am assisting Sir Hugh Riccarton, however." He took a step towards the pair. "Would you say Sid's account of what happened is accurate?"

Both nodded, the one who had spoken second piping up. "What we seen seems as he said it true. Though it ain't like Matty to get in a pelt."

"Peaceable she is, Matty, usual like."

A thought occurred. "At what hour did all this happen, do you recall?"

The second man looked to the first, who scratched his chin, ruminating. "I'd say as it were near midnight, or mebbe a bit after." He glanced at his companion, who nodded and murmured agreement. His informant looked back to Francis. "Aye, t'would be about that, as we reckon it, yer honour."

There was time for no more as the murmur of voices from the rear produced Matty Hexworthy herself, closely followed by her husband Jerry. Of Sid there was no sign.

The landlord's wife looked both harassed and embarrassed, but Jerry's stance as he arrived in front of Francis was decidedly aggressive.

"We told all last time. No need to come badgering again."

The lack of either greeting or even lip service to his status made Francis's hackles rise, but he maintained an even tone. "It would appear otherwise, Hexworthy. Indeed, as I recall, you were adamant Hector Penkevil was not welcome at the White Horse, but in fact he came on the night he died."

"What's it to you if he did?"

Fortunately for his temper, Francis was forestalled in any reply by Matty, the wife.

"Now you just shut your noise, Jerry. 'Tis too late for that." She turned back to Francis, apology in her voice. "We oughtn't to have misled your lordship, only it weren't a tale to make me proud. I don't like to fall foul of anyone, but that Penkevil fair had me riled."

"So I understand. But you see, this puts us in a little difficulty."

"How so, sir?"

She looked apprehensive now, but the aggression increased in her husband's features. He grew red in the face. "Are you up for saying as we done it? We ain't had nothing to do with that man a-dying."

He received an elbow in the ribs. "Hush, Jerry! Let his lordship say his piece. What's this difficulty then, sir?"

Was this an attempt at appeasement? Her subservient manner was almost grovelling. Francis hardened his tone. "You gave Penkevil a second tot of rum, yes?"

She coloured a trifle. "I were that mad, your lordship, I couldn't help myself."

Francis hit hard. "Did you put anything else into that drink?"

Was the puzzlement in her face genuine? "What do you mean? I poured from the bottle. I weren't in no case to be thinking of putting in nothing but the liquor. Why? What's the trouble, your lordship?"

He did not answer this, instead changing tack. "How did Penkevil seem that night?"

The confusion deepened. "I don't understand."

"Was he his normal self?"

"Not after he'd had two tots of rum, I shouldn't think."

"But they would not have shown any effect so quickly. Are you inferring that he was in any way incapacitated?"

Jerry frowned. "Eh? What do you mean?"

Francis was moved to elaborate. "Did he seem, for example, the worse for liquor?"

Matty's brow cleared. "Ah. Well, I can't say as I thought as much at the time. After, I took it as the rum weren't the first drink he'd had. He were slurring a bit and when he went for to pick up them coins, he dropped one or two and almost fell over as I yelled him to stand up." She sniffed. "I shouldn't have spoke that strong, only what did he want to come here for asking for rum? Not as we serve it to many. The gin goes fast enough, but not rum."

Francis took her back to the point. "He was slurring his words, you say? Anything else?"

"Well, when I think back, he were none too steady when he walked out."

"He weren't that bad off though," cut in Jerry, "for as I couldn't catch him. He was well away towards the woods by the time I got after him."

Francis hesitated, thinking. It began to seem as if the drug had not been administered in the rum. Indeed, it scarcely seemed credible that Matty, in the throes of a temper tantrum, would think of troubling to add valerian to his drink. Which meant it had been given to Hector before he arrived at the White Horse. If he was slurring and unsteady, perhaps the effects were already beginning to be apparent. The liquor might well have hastened the drop into unconsciousness.

He made up his mind. "Very well. For the moment, I will accept what you say. But be advised, both of you, that any further prevarication will go ill with Sir Hugh Riccarton. If there is anything else you have not told me, I advise you to speak now."

"They were adamant they had told all, Tillie."

Ottilia had listened with interest to her spouse's report. "I am inclined to accept that, from all you have said."

The two parties had almost coincided on returning to Ash Lodge and, the dinner hour being not far distant, Averil was persuaded to remain to partake of the meal. Both tales having been related over the course of spooning Spanish Green pottage and consuming the pot-roasted chicken with a side of green beans and potatoes, the discussion during the usual dessert of fruit, cheese and tarts veered onto a dissection of what had been learned.

Ottilia had taken care to thank Tom and Ben once again for their discovery, seeing how it had led to so much more detail concerning the fatal night. But the puzzle had intensified.

"We are left with the question of who did actually administer this wretched valerian."

"Well, not the Hexworthies, I submit," offered Francis.

"Not Ruth Penkevil either, if I may make the suggestion," said Averil, surprising Ottilia with her further insight. "By her account, she was not in any state to be thinking of drugging her husband either."

"How right you are, Averil." Ottilia glanced around the table. "Ruth spoke of being calm as she defied Hector, but unless she did not tell it all, she had no time to be preparing such a drink. Nor, by her account, was Hector in any mood to have taken it from her hand. He would more likely have refused it or flung it away."

Ben chimed in. "But he must have gone off to the White Horse afterwards because he was in a fury."

"Yes," said the eager Tom, "because that's what men do when they are angry. They have a drink. Don't they, Papa?"

Patrick shrugged. "It is one method of cooling off, yes."

"Only Hector did not cool off." Ottilia was thinking aloud. "He ran into Matty and became even more infuriated. But this business of the valerian becomes problematic. We know he went to Ebbesborn before ending up at the White Horse, but he only saw the footman, so that does not help us. Did someone else in his household contaminate his drink?"

"Margery Poyle?"

"Yes, Averil, for want of any other. But, why? Did you establish what time he got to the inn, Fan?"

"It was near midnight or a bit after, according to the two old gagers who witnessed the whole, and Penkevil was headed for the woods, presumably on his way home."

"Then who was it Bruno Pidsea heard? That was around two in the morning. If Hector was already in the woods, and likely unconscious by then, any noise heard at Bruno's vicarage must be irrelevant."

"If indeed he did hear anything other than the owl, Tillie. Didn't he merely speak of a grunt? It could well have been some animal."

"Or," Ottilia said slowly, "he made up the whole."

Her auditors, to a man, were silent. Looking round, she perceived every face staring at her and laughed out. "Have I shocked you all?"

The answers came almost in chorus.

"Yes!"

"Why Bruno?"

"How could it be him?"

"He's a parson, Auntilla."

"He wouldn't lie."

This last caught her attention. "Pardon me, but why in the world should you imagine a parson would not lie, Ben? In my experience, position has no bearing on whether a man — or indeed a woman — will lie. If there is something to hide in order to escape detection, no one is immune to that temptation, I fear."

She regretted her words at once, for both Averil and her brother avoided her gaze, the latter taking refuge in his wine, his inamorata studiously regarding the peeled walnuts on her plate. Feeling the least said was a better policy, Ottilia hastened to change tack. "What we need to do is concentrate our attention on who planted the drug."

Neither of her nephews had apparently noticed the altered atmosphere and Ben spoke up, a sudden thought having clearly occurred. "Could Hector have taken the valerian himself?"

This had the effect of drawing attention off Ottilia, rather to her relief, and onto her nephew.

"That's a capital notion, Ben," approved his young brother.

"It is certainly worth consideration. What do you think, Tillie?"

She looked to Patrick. "He had no habit of drug taking, had he?"

"Not to my knowledge. I think the Poyle woman would have spoken of it if he had."

Tom argued the point. "She might not know. In any case, Papa, maybe Hector had the headache and took it for that."

"He'd have taken laudanum for a headache, don't you think so, Papa?"

"Yes, Ben, much more likely. Moreover, if Hector was a habitual drug taker, it would be laudanum rather than valerian."

"Besides, when might he have taken it, Tom?" Francis asked. "According to your aunt's account, he stormed off from his house. He is not likely to have stopped to take a headache remedy."

"But your informants, Lord Francis, did say he seemed to be in what could be a drugged state when he went to the White Horse."

Ottilia almost applauded. "Well said, Averil. If, as Alexander claims, Hector went to his brother's house at Ebbesborn first, that would provide sufficient time for the drug to have begun to take effect. Add the rum he consumed at the White Horse and it is scarcely surprising he succumbed. I begin to think he must have been at least half unconscious when the murderer came upon him. Or had he followed Hector throughout, waiting his chance?"

CHAPTER TWENTY-TWO

No credible solution to the puzzle entered Ottilia's mind over the ensuing hours. She was obliged to rest upon the following day, foregoing Sunday service, her exertions having tired her out unduly, to the consternation of her lord.

"You are doing nothing until you have recruited your strength, my dear one. Stay in bed for the morning at least. Your nephews and I will hold the fort and if there is any questioning to be done —"

"I can think of nothing at this present, my dearest dear."

"Then you need only rest. I will have Joanie bring you breakfast on a tray."

"Coffee and a roll is all I require, I thank you."

He frowned down at her. "You need more than that. Have an egg."

Ottilia sighed. "I have no appetite, but let Joanie add my favourite cheese. I will make an effort to manage that."

He agreed to this, but when her maid presently came up with a laden tray, Ottilia discovered her husband had sent up a sandwich of two slices of bread with several of bacon between.

"His lordship insisted, my lady, and he said to be sure and see you eat it. Won't you try a bit, my lady?"

To gratify her maid, and indeed Francis, she managed to consume one half, along with bites of cheese, the whole washed down with coffee. The pleasure of the last made her sigh in content and she settled back upon her pillows with a second cup in hand as Joanie removed the debris.

Despite her present inertia, she found her mind roving the puzzle, to which a solution seemed no nearer. Brigadier

O'Turk discounted, along with Lady Carrefour, left Ruth, Roland, and Alexander as the principal suspects, none of whom struck Ottilia as likely candidates. Mrs Poyle and Nancy she regarded only on the side. Nancy was spiteful enough to have sent the latter to Averil, but her relations with Alexander did not, from his perspective in any event, appear to warrant the elimination of Hector. Mrs Poyle, in Ottilia's estimation, was all talk and no action. If anything, she might be complicit in the drugging, but there was yet to materialise any real motive for so doing.

Then there was Bruno Pidsea, whose name persisted in cropping up. Yet why in the world should he kill Hector? Admittedly, he quarrelled with the man over Willy Heath's beating, but that could not justify murder. On an analytical level, Ottilia wanted to cross Bruno off the list, but a niggle of doubt persisted. She mistrusted the notion of operating on instinct, but a thread of question followed the cleric. Even Brigadier O'Turk had pointed a finger at the clergy. Although he had dismissed Alexander, who at least had reason to be ridding the world of his abominable brother.

The Hexworthies were out of count. She allowed that Francis would judge with some accuracy. He so often chimed with her thoughts and occasionally beat her to the post. Francis did not trust either Jerry or Matty, that was plain, since they had already proven to be ready to withhold vital information. But if he believed the tapster's account to be reliable, then Jerry Hexworthy was not absent for long enough when he chased after Hector to have had time to carry out this elaborate scheme. Which left Petrus Gubb.

She hardly knew what to make of the farmer. Again, she had not met the man herself, although she had known him by reputation when she lived here. She must go by her husband's assessment and he was not wholly convinced that Petrus Gubb was innocent. He had certainly been abroad that night. As certainly he had come home by way of the woods. That, however, did not mean he necessarily followed a path that would take him past the place where Hector's body was found, since there were several passages criss-crossing each other. But he could have done so.

She recalled her nephews saying that Petrus and Willy were seen heading in the direction of Bruno Pidsea's church.

Ottilia's senses prickled. It was not in the least logical, yet she could not shake a feeling she was on the edge of realisation.

Willy Heath now. No one had questioned him. If they did, what could they ask? His grudges, if any, were already known. Besides the beating, he was fined a ludicrous sum for alleged poaching. Yet Ottilia knew Willy for a gentle and timid fellow. His wits were wanting, but his ability with numbers was legendary, as if his brain moved like lightning. For anything else, it was slow to the point of sludgy. No, Willy would not be capable of planning a killing.

Nevertheless, it might pay to have Ben and Tom ask him at the least if he knew anything of what had occurred that night. Willy was apt to appear unexpectedly. He might well have heard or seen something that day, or even afterwards, which had no significance for him, but might shed light on the puzzle for a mind more used to looking at an overall picture.

She was just deciding to ring the bell and have Joanie summon the boys when there was a knock at the door and her brother's voice was heard without.

"Ottilia! Are you awake? May I enter?"

"Come in, Patrick." The door opened and his tall figure filled the aperture. "You are all back from church then." Ottilia cast him an impish look. "Fortunately, I was awake. Otherwise, you would have woken me."

His countenance relaxed into a grin and she rejoiced. He had been altogether too solemn lately, so unlike the easy-going brother she knew and loved.

"Fan said you have been downing your wicked habit, so I guessed you would be awake. Coffee acts opposite to a soporific."

She laughed. "There speaks the doctor. Do you mean to scold me? I cannot abandon my addiction, no matter how much you tell me it is not good for my constitution."

Patrick approached the bed. "I doubt it will do you any harm." His look became rueful. "Don't get upon your high ropes, sister mine."

She raised her brows. "Why should I if you are not going to start doctoring me?"

"Ah, but I am. Fan asked me to take a look at you."

Ottilia suppressed an instant rise of irritation, only now taking in that her brother had his bag with him. "My darling lord frets too much. I am merely tired, brother dear."

He perched on the edge of the bed, setting the bag on the floor. "It's not that. He wants to be reassured that your pregnancy is progressing as it should."

A frisson of alarm shot through Ottilia. "There is no reason to be concerned, is there? I carried Luke with no ill effects."

"Yes, but you were resting more. This business —"

"If you are going to say I am doing too much gadding about, don't waste your breath. I am feeling perfectly well."

"I understand that." The grey eyes, the mirror of her own, gazed steadily. "Did I not say there is no need to fly up into the boughs?"

With difficulty, Ottilia held her tongue on a sharp retort, instead trying for a light note. "Well, I hate being cosseted, as well you know."

"I am aware, yes."

"Fan knows it too. I can't think why he is making such a fuss."

A twisted smile crossed her brother's lips. "Will you bite my head off if I point out that it is not Fan who is making all the fuss?"

Ottilia's sense of humour got the better of her. "Touché, you fiend of a brother!" She sighed out a resigned breath. "Very well, do your worst."

"I had rather do my best, if you don't object. You are my beloved sister, after all."

Ottilia melted, catching at his hand and squeezing it. "A shrew of a sister, poor you. Forgive me, brother mine."

"Willingly." He became professional. "Now, before we begin, let me say that I was already thinking I ought to check you over. Fan has merely pushed me into seizing the moment."

A feather brushed Ottilia's heart. "You were thinking of it? Why, Patrick?"

"Because your belly seems rather bigger than is usual at this stage. I suspect you may be carrying twins."

His mind reeling, Francis could only gaze at his brother-in-law for what felt like an age. At length, as Patrick said nothing more, he found his voice again. "She is having twins? Are you certain?"

The solemn expression in Patrick's face relaxed and he gave a twisted smile. "Ottilia asked the self-same question. I can only tell you what I told her. I am as certain as I can be without seeing the infants after birth."

"But…" Words failed Francis again.

In a daze, he watched his brother-in-law cross to the side table where a tray with decanters had been placed earlier. Patrick came across with a glass in which he had poured a measure of golden liquid. "Brandy. Drink it down." He grinned. "Doctor's orders."

A laugh escaped Francis and he took the glass and put it to his lips with a hand that he found was not quite steady. Liquid fire enveloped his throat and burned its way down his gullet. The effect was almost instantaneous. His mind began to clear and his racing pulse slowed a little. Absently, he handed the empty glass back and gazed upon his brother-in-law's back as he moved to set it down on the tray.

"How can you be so certain, Patrick? Not that I'm doubting you."

Patrick turned, his brows lifting. "I wouldn't blame you if you did. Doctoring is far from an exact science. We need a better method of listening to internal sounds than direct contact by ear, but one may rely upon a good deal of experience. I heard what at first seemed to be a double heartbeat, which might have indicated an arrhythmic disorder — often temporary in the foetus, so you need have no fears about that."

Francis had not been aware of the change in himself beyond a faint rise of apprehension, always present where his darling wife's health was concerned. But Patrick must have seen it in his face. "It was not a disorder then?"

"No, for the beats became quite distinct. There are two of them. Mind, I was expecting as much. Some might say I heard what I thought to hear."

Francis shrugged this away. "I know you for a competent doctor, Patrick. I believe you." He drew in a breath and sighed it out. "Not that it makes it any easier to take in."

Patrick laughed. "You are as horrified as Ottilia."

Sudden energy overtook Francis and he closed in a little. "With reason. It was hard enough for Ottilia to bring one infant into the world. How the deuce will she manage two? Isn't it dangerous? She will be exhausted!"

Patrick laid a soothing hand on his shoulder for a moment. "There is no need to panic, Fan. Yes, it will exhaust her. She will need a longer period of recuperation after her confinement. But she is otherwise well. Her physical condition this time is excellent."

"But all this running around after murderers! She ought to be resting more."

"Yes, I've told her so. But she also needs exercise. The programme remains the same. Gentle walks, good food, plenty of rest, more as her pregnancy progresses for she will find it harder to get about."

Francis cast up his eyes. "How in heaven's name am I to keep her from overdoing it? A more stubborn woman than your sister I have yet to meet."

To his intense irritation, Patrick gave forth another laugh. "Don't I know it. But let me ease your mind. It's far better for her to be engaged in what interests her than to be moping because she may not do what she wants. Better for the infants also."

The word caught Francis's attention and he groaned. "Infants plural, for pity's sake! It's enough trouble coping with one, let alone two. Lord, we will have to employ yet another nurse. Hepsie can't be expected to manage two babes and Doro has her hands full with Luke. Not to mention she and

Hemp expect to leave us once they've tied the knot. And what about the wet nurse? We'll need two of those as well. Dear God, I may end in Bedlam at this rate!" He eyed his brother-in-law with disfavour. "It's well for you to laugh your head off, Patrick, but this is nothing short of a nightmare."

It was some time before he could contemplate the prospect without a feeling of panic. Presently, however, when his brother-in-law left him to go down to his study, it occurred to Francis that Ottilia might well be experiencing much the same reaction. He ought, moreover, to have gone to her directly upon hearing the news. He began to make his way upstairs to their allotted bedchamber, reflecting that it was as well perhaps. Better he had overcome his first dismay before seeing Tillie. At least he might allay her alarms without adding his own to distress her.

At first sight, as he entered to find her sitting up against banked pillows, Ottilia appeared to be calmer than he felt. She looked across, question apparent in the beloved features. "Patrick told you?"

"Obviously." Francis went across and plonked onto the edge of the bed, taking hold of the hand his darling wife immediately held out. He lifted it to his lips and kissed it. "You look to be over the first shock."

A smile wavered. "What about you, Fan?"

"I am still in a trifle of a daze, if you want the truth."

Her fingers tightened about his hand. "It is frightening, is it not?"

"Very." He reached to stroke her face. "We will become accustomed. Patrick is confident all will be well."

She wafted her free hand. "That, yes. Let us hope I don't succumb under the effort of birthing."

His heart missed a beat. "Don't even say that, Tillie."

"I know you dislike it, my dearest dear, but I prefer to face the possibility squarely."

Francis infinitely preferred otherwise, but he refrained from saying so. "You will get through it, my loved one. You managed Luke superbly."

"True and I am well."

"Precisely. We must remain optimistic."

To his consternation she sighed deeply, releasing his hand. "On that note, perhaps. Only what in the world are we to do, Fan? Two babies at once! How shall we manage?"

He blew out a breath. "I've been thinking of that too. We'll need an extra nurse as well as two wetnurses. And we can't delay any longer in finding a governess for Pretty. You won't be able to teach her and she is already beyond Hepsie's capabilities."

"Can we afford it, Fan?"

"Yes, if we make savings elsewhere. The rents are doing well since Pether had those cottages renovated." He recaptured her hand. "We must afford it. We will manage, my loved one."

"I suppose we have no choice."

For the first time, the perceived burden lifted a little and he leaned over to pat her bulging stomach. "Indeed not, with this pair of dictators in the saddle."

To his joy, his wife's infectious gurgle came. "We will be mere cyphers, my dearest, with four of them to run rings around us."

"Not they. Pretty will have them trained in no time. Luke is already under her rule." She laughed and Francis was moved to kiss her. "Better now?"

Her smile warmed him. "Much better."

"Then stop fretting over what may come and bend your mind to solving this wretched murder. I am under strict instructions from your brother to keep you actively entertained."

Come Monday, fortune favoured Ottilia when she set out upon her third visit to the Penkevil residence. A bonus, since she had felt a trifle of chagrin when her darling lord insisted upon keeping her company.

"I am disinclined to let you out of my sight after Patrick's diagnosis."

She had entered a mild protest. "It is hardly a diagnosis, Fan. Moreover, he may be wrong."

"He seemed pretty certain. In any event, we will take no chances."

"I am no worse today for knowing I am carrying twins, my dearest. Physically at least." Mentally was another matter, but this she kept to herself. Francis was anxious enough.

He was not persuaded. "Nevertheless, it pays to take extra care. I am coming with you."

Ottilia knew better than to argue when her spouse was in this frame of mind. "Very well, if you insist. You might entertain Ruth while I buttonhole Mrs Poyle."

Francis quirked an eyebrow. "If that is an attempt to put me off, spare your breath."

She laughed and capitulated. "I surrender."

"So I should hope, recalcitrant wretch. Any other wife would be only too happy to have her husband dancing attendance."

"Any other wife would be meekly staying home, would she not? I cannot think how you have borne with this one all these years."

She was treated to a mock-fierce look. "Get yourself down to the carriage, woman, before I deal with you as you richly deserve."

Ottilia bubbled over and complied. In truth, it was both balm and irksome to have him so attentive. His presence could not but give her pleasure, but to be hedged with concern served only to keep her vulnerability at the forefront of her mind. Strange that she could face down villains without flinching, yet any reference to her own state of health made her cringe. Ottilia could not decide if she was foolhardy or merely a coward. To be busy about her investigation was a relief.

As it chanced, Ruth was from home. Meeting with Roland again? It mattered little and relieved Francis of the necessity of keeping the widow company while Ottilia questioned her mother. After performing the necessary introduction, she wasted no time. "I am fortunate to find you alone, Mrs Poyle."

The other woman looked eager. "Well, for my part, I'm happy you came back, Lady Fan. I'd hoped to hear your findings the last time, only you'd gone by the time I managed to get away from the children."

Ottilia had taken care to seat herself in a chair near to Mrs Poyle's and at a little distance from her spouse, who had opted to take a stance by the window and was looking out. She used a tone low enough to persuade the elder dame that their conversation might be private.

"I cannot yet tell you very much, I fear. Did Ruth happen to mention to you what we discussed that day?"

Mrs Poyle pursed her lips. "She don't tell me anything, that one. Not that I don't know what she's up to."

"She told me that she quarrelled with Hector on the night he died."

"Ah, did she?" A faint colour rose in Mrs Poyle's cheek and she glanced away.

"You heard it perhaps?"

Came a shift of the shoulders and a swift look towards the silent Francis. "I expect the whole house heard it. Not that anyone would be surprised. Always raising his voice, was Hector."

Ottilia took due note of the build of belligerence in her tone and the way she kept avoiding looking at her questioner directly. "On this occasion, as I understand it, Ruth did not cower. She said she threatened to leave Hector if he raised a hand to her."

Mrs Poyle rubbed her hands over the bombazine of her black gown. Her discomfort was evident. She had undoubtedly been listening to the exchange.

Ottilia pushed. "You heard it all, did you not?"

The matron gave a frustrated kind of sigh. "Not as I wanted to, I can tell you that. It ain't pleasant hearing your daughter harangued by as mean a beast as you could hope to find."

Ottilia was tempted to ask why she had thrust her daughter into marriage with the man, only she knew the answer to that. No doubt she had not fathomed Hector's true character. Even if she had, could any other solution have offered when Ruth was with child?

She returned to the attack. "Did it strike you that this quarrel was different, as Ruth claims?"

Mrs Poyle gave a little shiver. "She oughtn't to have provoked him. Though I was used to wish Ruth would, it never did to stand up to him. I know. I couldn't help myself often and often, even though I knew he took it out on my girl."

Time to strike. "Is that why you administered valerian to Hector?"

The elder woman's cheeks paled and her eyes popped wide open. Her voice was hushed. "How did you know?"

Aware that Francis had turned as she made her attack, Ottilia kept her gaze on the matron. "I cannot otherwise account for Hector's condition before he died. He was slurring and unsteady when he went to the White Horse. That episode followed his quarrel with Ruth. After that, he directed his steps through the wood and never came out again. It follows that the drug must have been given to him in this house."

Mrs Poyle sunk in her seat, throwing her hands over her face. Her voice came muffled. "I never meant to kill him. I only wanted to calm him down. Never thought it would serve to hasten his end…" She dropped her hands, and Ottilia saw fear in the eyes. "When we heard from Doctor Hathaway, at first it seemed it weren't my blame. Except he said the drug had likely addled his mind, even if it weren't directly the cause of him dying. I never meant his death, I swear it." Her voice gained strength. "Not as I'm sorry he's dead and I don't care who hears me say it."

Her husband's voice came from behind Ottilia. "You have made that abundantly clear. Nor are you alone in that sentiment."

"Well, God save us, I weren't the only one who hated him!" Mrs Poyle's brief spurt of defiance collapsed. She looked to Ottilia. "What happens now? Will Sir Hugh haul me off to gaol?"

Ottilia ignored this. "Tell me precisely what happened, if you please."

The elder dame blew out a breath. "I'll try, though it's all got a bit blurry, to be truthful."

"Let us begin with overhearing the quarrel."

"Well, I did hear it." A sheepish look came over her face. "If you must have it, I listened at the door."

"So I supposed."

Mrs Poyle sniffed. "What would you? She's my daughter, when all is said and done."

"Go on."

"Well, when I heard her getting all uppity with him, it worried me sick, I don't mind telling you." As if the fear of being found out was no longer an issue, she gained in confidence as she spoke. "I was afraid he'd go off drinking like he was used to do, then come back in his cups and use his fists on her. All very fine to talk high like she was, but she was no match for Hector when he was roused."

"She took him aback perhaps?"

"Well, that's it, ain't it? There wasn't a doubt in my mind he'd go off into a tantrum when he thought about it. He'd never have let her leave him. Couldn't have stood the humiliation. Proud man, he was, Hector."

This was no news to Ottilia. Francis, moving into the fray, took the words out of her mouth, although with a deal more impatience than she would have displayed.

"Cut line, woman! We all know what sort of a man he was. How did you give him this drug? That's what my wife wants to know."

Mrs Poyle gave him a resentful look. "I'm just coming to it, my lord, if you'll have a little patience."

Ottilia saw retaliation in her spouse's eye and quickly intervened. "Do continue, Mrs Poyle. I confess it puzzles me how you persuaded Hector to take a dose of valerian."

A scornful little laugh escaped the matron. "Nothing easier, Lady Fan. I fetched him a measure of brandy and stirred the powder into that. He was rampaging about in his bedchamber, swearing and cursing."

"He did not go out immediately then."

"He would've, once he'd tugged on his boots and got his greatcoat on. I knew I hadn't much time. I gave the glass to his valet and told him to take it in. I know Hector drank it. Haugh caught him as he came out of his room and I saw him knock it back and give Haugh the empty glass."

Ottilia had still an unanswered question. "What did you hope for, Mrs Poyle? You say you did not intend his death."

"I didn't, I'll swear it again and again. It was to calm him, make him too drowsy to act against Ruth. To tell true, I hoped he'd go to one of his harlots and leave my girl alone."

Francis did not question anything further until they were back in the privacy of the carriage. Then he surprised Ottilia. "Why didn't you reassure the woman that she was not responsible for killing Hector?"

Ottilia chuckled. "It won't do her any harm to feel remorseful. Besides, in a way she is."

"Not directly."

"I don't know that as yet. If the notions in my head are correct, the sedative, combined with rather more alcohol than is perhaps wise, may well turn out to have been the catalyst."

A grunt came from beside her. "Do you mean to elucidate?"

"It is still surmise, Fan."

"Well?"

Ottilia sought for his hand and slipped hers into it. "If it proves out, there has been some sort of conspiracy. Margery Poyle was not party to it, except by default."

CHAPTER TWENTY-THREE

On the pretext of taking her necessary walk, having rested for the remainder of the day after her visit to Mrs Poyle, Ottilia managed to persuade her now more than ever careful spouse to allow a stroll with her nephews in search of Willy Heath.

"If you don't locate him within the half hour, back you come, Tillie."

"Very well, but don't look for us before at least an hour has passed."

"An hour!"

"Well, we must come back again, must we not?"

"Hm. I dare say, but —"

"Have no fear, my dearest. I will not overtax myself. We will take it gently and I will rest at need."

Francis, who had come to see the party off, still looked dubious. "I ought to come with you."

"There is no need, I promise." They were in the hall, Ottilia clad in her warm cloak, Ben and Tom similarly wrapped up in greatcoats and already awaiting her by the front door. She lowered her voice. "I have paid scant attention to the boys and I need to find out how they are truly faring. They won't speak of their mother if you are with me."

Her spouse continued disgruntled. "Very well, but I don't like it."

Ottilia set a hand to his chest. "You vowed to begin preparations, did you not, Fan? Is not this a good opportunity to write those letters. You said the family lawyer was best placed to look for a governess for Pretty."

He gave a non-committal grunt. "I can write to Jardine any time."

"The sooner the better, do you not think? And Mr Pether will know which of our tenants are likely to give birth in good time. You know I could not do without a wet nurse for Luke, and we need two, Fan."

Her husband let out a frustrated breath. "Yes, very well, I'll write the letters. But don't be late back!" He walked across to her waiting nephews. "Take good care of her, you two."

They chorused agreement.

"We will, Uncle Fan."

"You may rely on us, sir."

Ottilia was relieved to get out into the fresh air. The day promised to be fine, if cold, with only a light frost left from the night's chill lending a sparkle to the bare trees. Ottilia breathed in and felt an immediate lightening of the oppression that had settled on her spirits ever since her brother's thunderbolt. It was a relief to shake off the inevitable apprehensions and blow away the cobwebbing strands of uncertain dreams that had troubled her sleep. Waking, she found her mind dwelling not on the preparations for the accommodation of two additions to the family, but on those she ought to put in place to ensure that family survived well after her death.

Nothing of that had she confided to her darling lord, already disturbed enough on her account. If Francis knew she was contemplating her demise in childbed, he would be distraught beyond reason. To prevent his guessing at her state of mind, she had opted to induce her spouse to allow her go on this mission accompanied only by Ben and Tom. Their welfare was an excuse, but she nevertheless made a tactful effort in that direction.

Tom was his usual careless self, but Ben, maturing fast, had taken his uncle's words to heart.

"Careful of that fallen branch, Auntilla. Tom, don't go so fast!"

His brother was leaping over the branch. He paused and looked back. "I'm the vanguard. I can get rid of all the obstacles."

"Jumping over it is not exactly getting rid of it, you ass!"

Ottilia intervened. "We will stick to the path, if you please, Tom."

"Yes, go round. I'll meet you on the other side." With which, he took off at speed, his noisy progress brushing dried twigs off branches as he passed.

Ben gave forth a sound of annoyance and took the lead. "This way, Auntilla. The path skirts those trees. It's a little further, but at least you'll be safe."

Ottilia thanked him, taking care where she set her booted feet. As they progressed along the well-worn path, she essayed a light question. "Are you growing a little reconciled, Ben? I have not asked you and I am sorry for that."

She caught a serious look in his face as he glanced at her. "About Mama? I think it will be some time before I am reconciled, Auntilla. I miss her a great deal."

"I am sure you must, my dear. Sophie would not wish you to grieve too much."

Ben guided her across a patch of frosted grass. "Do you know, I don't believe it has quite sunk in that she is gone forever. I expect every day to see her sitting in her chair."

A pang smote Ottilia. "Does it trouble you that I have been using it?"

Ben stopped still and looked at her, consternation in his face. "I didn't mean that, Auntilla. Mama would wish you to make use of it. It's just that I keep picturing her there. Though Papa says she had not been able to come down to the parlour for many weeks."

Ottilia knew not how to answer. She felt an access of fresh guilt. How had she been so careless as to ignore Ben's likely reaction to her appropriation of his mother's chair? She was glad to be spared the necessity to speak of it when Tom's voice up ahead interrupted the discussion.

"Come along, slowpokes! We must hurry if we are to catch Willy." He appeared out of the trees further along the path, and waved.

Ottilia did not increase her pace, though her interest quickened. "I thought Tom said Willy could be found in the fields alongside Petrus Gubb's farm."

"True, but he is in the habit of going off to St Leonard's."

"The Reverend Pidsea's church? Every day?"

"Most days in winter. Petrus has less work for him in the cold months, but for a bit of ploughing when the soil isn't too hard, though he helps with the animals. Mr Pidsea pays him to do a bit of sweeping and that. Willy adds up his accounts too, but that's only quarterly, so the reverend finds odd jobs for him. It's just a reason to give him money, we think."

Bruno Pidsea once again rising to the surface. Ottilia's mind began to turn again upon the puzzle. A known champion of Willy Heath, it now appeared he had taken the lad under his wing, as had Petrus Gubb. The niggle of an idea that had been bothering her was turning into a thread.

It was not many minutes before the spread of farming land took over from the woods. Ottilia paused for a breather, looking over the open country, just now sparse of greenery and frosted here and there. Petrus Gubb's farm was a huddle of buildings off to one side, the separated fields occupied by a scattering of sheep in one and a few cattle in another. Three more were, so Ben informed her, cultivated with crops that had been recently gathered and were now in preparation for resowing.

"It looks like Willy's already gone," Tom observed, "or he'd be in there with the plough. I'll nip down to the farm and check. He might be feeding the pigs."

He was off on the words. Ottilia moved back to the edge of the wood and sat down on a convenient stump she had spied as they came through.

"How far is it to St Leonard's, Ben?"

He made his way back to her from the path. "Less than a mile. This path leads right to it, but it meanders through the woods again. Should you go back instead?"

Ottilia quashed the notion at once. She was feeling so much lighter, she was reluctant to return too soon, afraid her mind would betray her again. "We have come this far. I have time enough before your uncle begins to fret. It would be a shame to miss the chance to question Willy."

Ben eyed her for a moment. "What made you want to question him now?"

Ottilia made light of it, unwilling to speak of her largely unformed ideas at this stage. "We have asked everyone else and I am still in the dark. Willy wanders a good deal, does he not? He might have seen or heard something out of the ordinary."

Ben was frowning. "I doubt he'd think anything was unusual. He doesn't follow logic like others do. Willy just accepts life as he sees it. At least, that's how it seems to me."

"I expect you are right, Ben. It does no harm to ask though. I find people often see more than they realise themselves."

The sound of running feet took her attention, Ben also turning to look.

"Here's Tom back." He called out as his brother neared. "Not there?"

"No sign of him," yelled Tom. He staggered to a halt on the path as he arrived parallel to where Ottilia was seated. "We'd best go to Pidsea's church, Auntilla."

She nodded. "Get your breath back first. I can do with another moment or two myself."

Presently, as she noted Tom hopping with impatience despite still catching his breath, Ottilia reached out to Ben. "Lend me your arm, my dear. I'm too bulky to get up without something to push against."

This done, the party proceeded along the path. As predicted, it wound through the woods. Ottilia noticed the slighter tread of other worn routes criss-crossing the main one.

She gestured. "Who uses these?"

"Oh, the locals," said Tom, who this time chose to remain with Ottilia, although a little way ahead. "Short cuts, Auntilla. They're fine if you know the woods. Better stick to the path, though, because you might trip on a root or something."

Ottilia had no intention of deviating from the path, but she kept to herself the reflection that several persons, including the parson, Petrus Gubb and Willy Heath — not to mention both Hexworthies and Hector Penkevil — must all be well acquainted with these woods. The White Horse, Gubb's farm and St Leonard's where Bruno presided all bordered the woods, forming something of a triangle, the farmlands edging Aston Park, the Penkevil property that lay below the village of Aston. Brigadier O'Turk's lands were on the other side of Penkevil's property which made the woods a less likely haunt for him.

The church spire was soon sighted in between the trees and within minutes the entire building was visible, bordered at the wooded edge by a low wall that gave onto the graveyard.

"We'll go by the gate, Auntilla," said Ben.

"She'd better," Tom chimed in with a laugh. "Imagine Uncle Fan's face if she went climbing over the wall."

"I thank you, Tom. I am certainly in no condition to be trying any such feat. Where is the gate?"

Ben was already leading the way, the path following along the wall to where a gap became visible. He unhooked the latch to an iron gate and pushed it open for Ottilia to go through.

She paused on the other side, looking over the headstones that stood in neat rows along the graveyard. "Where should we look for Willy, do you think?"

"In the church is most likely," said Tom. "Else he'd be out here, sweeping the paths between the graves."

Ottilia became eager. "*En avant*, then. Lead the way, Tom."

Nothing loath, her nephew began to weave a path between the graves, calling back as he went. "This is the quickest way. The side door is usually open."

From the outside, St Leonard's church was a rather beautiful old building, its windows, though few and narrow, featuring stonework arches. The door Tom approached was of carved ancient oak decorated with an intricate design of ironwork curlicues. It proved to be unlocked, as her nephew had anticipated, and Ottilia entered an interior that at first sight appeared extremely dark. But that proved to be misleading, the effect of coming in from the brightness outside. As her eyes became accustomed to the dimness, she saw that the interior fulfilled the promise of the outside and that ornate door. The pillared arches mirrored the windows, narrow ribbons of light showing up the yellowed patina of time. The pews, of darkened wood, must have remained unchanged for centuries.

"He's here all right."

Tom's voice echoed through the building and Ottilia saw the slim figure of Willy Heath standing by the front pew before the altar. He was holding a cloth aloft and she guessed he must have been engaged in polishing the wooden back of the pew when he was surprised by their arrival.

"Hoy there, Willy!" Tom moved into the aisle as he called out.

But Willy was not looking at him. His gaze was fixed on Ottilia and he followed her progress as she moved along the short corridor between pews to reach the aisle. His gaze did not waver as she neared and it struck Ottilia that he looked unnaturally tense. His face had less of the vacant appearance she remembered from her days of living in the area. He was observably older, perhaps a trifle gaunt in the face, his cheeks dipping in below the bone.

Ottilia began on a light note. "I am happy to have caught you, Willy."

His answer came, gruff with a smidgeon of a shake. "Why'd you catch me?"

Before she could answer, Tom cut in, bright and cheerful. "It's Lady Fan, Willy. You remember. She came to see Mr Penkevil's corpse."

Was it a trick of the uncertain light coming from the few high windows or did his features pale a little?

"I seen her. Left me to guard him."

"No, Willy. That was our papa's notion," Ben said on a soothing note. "She just wants to ask you a couple of questions."

Willy's gaze jerked towards Ben and back again to Ottilia. "Don't know no questions."

This could go on for minutes. He was clearly frightened, but of what she could not tell. "There is no need to fear me, Willy."

He did not respond directly. "Been asking questions all about. I heard."

"What did you hear?"

"Petrus said. Likewise the reverend. Said you a-going to ask me. Don't know no questions."

Ottilia tried for a simpler way to go about discovery. "You are very good at noticing things, Willy. You were in the woods when the boys found the body. I think you noticed the body that morning."

"He were dead. I seen he were dead."

Before Tom and Ben found it? Or earlier still? She tried a throw, gently persuasive. "There now, I knew you were good at noticing. I expect you noticed something the night before too."

"I seen —" Willy broke off, jerking a step backwards.

He had seen something then. Ottilia flipped the idea in her mind, turning it to the likeliest statement. He responded better if she did not make it a question.

"You saw Mr Penkevil in the woods."

Willy was staring at her in a kind of fascination. Did he think she had second sight? He clearly had seen Hector. She pursued it.

"He was unlike you had seen him before. He seemed as if he was drunk." Willy made no answer. Ottilia tried again. "You see, Willy, he was not drunk. He was drugged."

Oddly, the boy flinched. Did he know something of the drugging? Or was it news to him? How to find out without questioning?

"Such drugs make a person sleepy. Mr Penkevil was getting sleepy and that made him stagger." No apparent reaction. "He could have fallen unconscious in the woods."

That elicited a hoarse protest. "He were dead. I seen him."

Ottilia's senses prickled. "You saw him dead in the morning."

"No! In the night he were dead." His voice rose. "He were on the ground and he were dead as a dead pig!"

Without warning, Willy turned and fled, along the altar to the side aisle, where he turned the corner, loping down the length of the church.

"Go after him, Ben!"

Tom had stood staring for a moment, but he leapt to the chase even as Ottilia spoke, haring off in pursuit, Ben close behind.

Ottilia began to move, as quickly as her constricted movements allowed, rather lumbering than running, back down the aisle towards the main entrance. She could hear better than she could see, the several sets of footsteps echoing in the vaulted reaches of the church. She gained the end of the pews as a clattering sound came, as of persons going up or down steps. Was there an upper floor? Had Willy gone up the tower? Her mind raced even as she made her way towards the corner of the church where the figures of her nephews had vanished into the shadows.

Willy knew more about the night of the murder than anyone else. He had been there. He had seen the body. Small wonder he was fearful. Had he thought to tell anyone? To whom might he have gone? Why did that person, assuming Willy had gone for help, not raise the alarm there and then? And what of the false hanging? She had not supposed Willy capable of putting such an action into effect, let alone thinking of it. He must have introduced another person and that person had not come forward. Or, if already questioned, had withheld the information.

It was darker in the corner than in the well of the church. She could make out a couple of openings in the stone by blacker shadows. Ottilia moved to the wall and used it for support and as a guide, setting her hand on the cold stone.

There was silence now. Was Willy hiding close by? Where were the boys? Nothing for it but to call out. "Ben! Tom! Where are you?"

One of them answered, a sepulchral voice that echoed into the church. "Coming, Auntilla! Wait there!"

Had it come from one of the openings? Footsteps clanged. Ottilia felt her way along the wall until she encountered air. She halted, waiting, listening as the footsteps grew louder.

To her relief, Tom's face appeared in the aperture next to her, a white oval only but thankfully recognizable. She let her breath go, only now realising she had been holding it. "Have you lost him?"

Tom dropped to a whisper. "Ben is searching the crypt. We think he's hiding down there."

"There's a crypt?"

"Well, kind of. It used to be for bodies, but they moved them all years ago. Pidsea uses it for storage. He's got trunks and crates down there, all sorts of rubbish."

"With plenty of places to hide, I don't doubt."

Tom made a move in the direction of the main doors. "Ben said to bring a candle. There's two big ones by the door. I only hope there's a flint so's I can light one."

Ottilia hoped so too. She followed her nephew, thankful to be in the lighter section. "Are you sure he went down into the crypt? What about the tower?"

"You can't get to the tower from this end." He had reached the main door by this time. "Ah, here we go." Ottilia heard a scraping and Tom turned with a large, thick candle in hand. "Can you hold this, Auntilla, while I find the flint?"

She accepted the charge, feeling a trifle uneasy. But light would be welcome. She toyed with the notion of opening the main doors to flood the interior with light, but that would not aid her nephews in their search below stairs.

A light sprang up and Tom's triumphant voice came. "Good old Pidsea! He had a flint and tapers handy." He came across with the lit spill and Ottilia held the candle steady as he applied it to the wick. It took a moment or two to catch, but a welcome glow spread a circle of brightness around them both.

"Thank goodness. I never thought I'd be happy to see your face, Tom."

Her nephew let out a smothered guffaw, but his excitement was almost palpable. "Give it to me, Auntilla. I'd best get down to Ben. We'll find Willy and bring him back up."

The thought of waiting alone in the cold, dark church did not recommend itself to Ottilia. "I had much rather come with you, Tom."

"You'll only scare him more, Auntilla. Besides, Uncle Fan wouldn't like you going down that stair."

This was undeniable, but Ottilia would much prefer to be doing than enduring the anxiety of not knowing what in the world was happening. She ignored Tom's warning.

"I am coming with you. Shall we take the second candle?"

But Tom was already moving towards the entrance to the stairway that evidently led down to the crypt. Ottilia, taking advantage of the flare of light from his candle, hastened after him.

The stair, when she began her descent, lit from below by Tom who held the candle high for her, proved to be not nearly as difficult as anticipated. The steps were shallow and wound only once before arriving at a wooden door which was partially ajar.

Tom called out in a hoarse whisper as they reached it. "Ben! Got the candle."

"I can see that," came the older boy's voice. "Bring it in."

Ottilia followed Tom into the crypt, looking about as he raised the candle high. There were indeed places enough for a slim lad to hide, what with the buttresses to one side and a collection of heavy wood crates and leather trunks. Her attention was drawn to Ben.

"Auntilla! You shouldn't have come down here. It's dusty and horrid!"

She was decidedly regretting her decision. "So I perceive. Perhaps I had best go back up."

"Shall I light you, Auntilla?"

"Just hold the candle in the doorway while I climb the stairs. I will call down when I am safe."

She moved as she spoke back towards the door. It slammed shut before she could reach the narrow aperture. A thunk sounded as the latch dropped home.

CHAPTER TWENTY-FOUR

Averil had been unable to shake from her mind the snippet of discussion with Lady Fan concerning Bruno Pidsea. She had been so distracted by Ruth Penkevil's revealing of her quarrel with her husband, she forgot to ask the reason for Ottilia's enquiry. If she had understood something of the character of Patrick's sister from the few times they had met, it was that she did not ask questions which had no underlying origin. The supposition was inevitable. Did she think Bruno was somehow involved in the murder?

After turning it this way and that, Averil at last decided that here was a way she might be of use. Her acquaintance with Bruno was of long-standing. It would not occur to him to question her motive. She had to admit to a slight feeling of guilt at her own duplicity, but was it not imperative to solve the murder? Even Patrick would admit to that since he was anxious to see an end which enabled them to resume their former meetings.

She was obliged to scold herself for a more selfish wish of contributing to Lady Fan's quest. Not that she was not as eager as her lover, but the prospect of involvement could not but excite her.

She seized the first available respite when Ralph was clearly in for a good day and might be left in the competent hands of Molly and Peter. The day was fine enough and Averil chose to tool the gig herself. Arrived at St Leonard's, she took the drive to the reverend's nearby house and left the carriage in the charge of her groom.

Bruno came hurriedly into his parlour, whither a servant had led Averil before summoning the master from his study.

"Mrs Deakin! Averil! How good it is to see you again!" He took her hand in both his own, making a little bow as he squeezed her fingers before releasing them. "It has been an age, has it not?"

Averil could not help but respond to his smile. "Indeed it has. We do not get about much these days."

His expression changed. "You do not bring fell tidings, I hope? Is Ralph —?"

"He is well. At least, as well as he ever can be. Today is a good day, so I have seized the chance to come away. I hope I have not disturbed your labours."

He ushered her towards a couple of chairs set to catch the warmth from the fire. "I was merely studying a text for my next sermon. Sit down, my dear, do."

Averil took one of the Chippendale chairs indicated. They were square-backed of carved wood with only the seat upholstered, typical of a bachelor household. The parlour was sparsely furnished and lacked the touch of a feminine hand. Bruno had never married and Averil believed he was wedded to his calling. He was a hospitable host, however, as she remembered, and was already moving to the bell-pull. "A little wine to warm you, my dear? Or would you prefer coffee?"

Averil waved the offer away. "Nothing, I thank you. I have not long broken my fast. Besides, I hope not to detain you for long."

Bruno returned to the fire and hovered by the second chair. "Is there some matter upon which you seek advice or help? You must know I am always at your service, Averil."

She was touched, but hesitated. How to begin? She bethought her of the poisonous letter she had received. "It is not precisely a service, but I am a little troubled."

He sat down at once, leaning forward and resting his arms across his knees in an attitude of listening. "Say on, my dear. Is it Ralph?"

"Not directly." Averil emitted a sigh. "I know you will not judge me and I am very sure you must have heard the rumours." She looked directly into his face but found nothing but interest and concern in the pallid features. "I received a rather unpleasant letter, the substance of which, although names were not mentioned, was that if I did not wish to become the subject of vulgar gossip concerning my personal life, I should persuade Lady Francis Fanshawe to abandon her purpose."

Bruno's pose changed as he straightened, pursing his lips. "Ah. This very troublesome murder, is it?"

Averil adopted a conciliatory air. "I am afraid so. I felt obliged to take it along to Lady Fan. She is convinced it was written by Nancy Meerbrook."

He became brisk. "Have you the letter?"

"I left it with Lady Francis. She seemed to feel it might be useful."

For a moment he said nothing, a ruminating look in his face. "Did you hope I might assist you in uncovering the perpetrator?"

Surprise made Averil laugh out. "Hardly. It is not within my province. I understand Lady Francis is more than capable of finding him."

"I meant the letter writer."

"Oh. Of course, how silly." She leaned a little towards him. "But do you not find it all very intriguing? Not so much the letter, but this business of Hector Penkevil's death. It seems to have upset everyone hereabouts."

An austere note appeared in the reverend's voice. "Because they cannot control their morbid curiosity."

Averil smiled. "Do you mean to scold me, Bruno?"

"Not at all. Some ill-disposed person involved you. One can understand your interest."

"Thank you. I collect you find it distasteful?"

"Infinitely. I am sorry for the fellow to be dying in such a way, but I am the more concerned for his immortal soul. I fear he will be unwelcome in Heaven."

Averil caught an edge to his tone and took it up at once. "I imagine you are not the only one wishing him a sojourn in Hell."

"I certainly don't wish for it. I would not wish fire and brimstone upon anyone, despite the reflection Penkevil has come by his deserts." Bruno drew in a breath that seemed taut. "It does not become me to say so. I trust you will not repeat it, Averil."

"I should not dream of it." She pushed for more, hoping to take advantage of what she took to be suppressed anger. "You do seem hot against him, Bruno. Has he harmed you?"

"I should not have allowed him to do so. His sins against the weaker among us I cannot forgive."

Dare she throw this open? "You are talking of Willy Heath." She held her breath, watching as his jaw clenched tighter. But it seemed the resentment he harboured would not be contained.

"He treated the boy with cruelty. Willy needs compassion, not punishment. What he does is done from a childish innocence and ignorance. There is no malice aforethought in Willy. He fell into vengeful error, yes, but Hector Penkevil may take blame for that."

Vengeful? Averil's heartbeat quickened. What did that betoken? Oh, for Lady Fan's quickness! She would know just how to ask to come at the deeper meaning. Supposing there was one.

She hesitated too long. A scuffing from without drew both her own and Bruno's attention. Next instant, the door opened and Willy Heath himself slunk into the room.

Bruno rose, moving a step or two in the direction of the doorway. "Willy? What do you want here?"

The lad's gaze was fixed on the reverend. Averil thought he likely did not even notice her presence. He spoke in a jerky fashion. "I done it."

"You have finished the chores I set you?"

"Done I am. Got to go. Got to get back to Gubb's place."

"Already? Did you polish the brass cross?" Bruno went towards him but Willy shunted back into the doorway.

"Done I am. Can't stay. Going now."

He turned on the words and exited the room in somewhat of a rush.

Averil regarded Bruno as he stood looking at the empty doorway for a moment. Then he went over and shut the door again before returning to the fire.

She waited, but he said nothing, only standing in a brown study. "Is he always as abrupt?"

Bruno half started, as if he had forgotten she was there. "Willy? In his speech, yes. But…" He faded out.

"Did he seem upset to you? I thought he looked quite agitated."

He was frowning as he retook his seat. "I agree. Something must have startled him." He looked up and his face cleared. "Well, there is no saying with Willy. Life does not look to him as it does to us. Anything might have triggered a reaction." He grimaced. "The only oddity is in his not telling me what troubles him."

"He usually does?"

"He is in the habit of running to me when circumstances become too much for him. He relies on my aid."

"Then why did he not say anything just now?"

Bruno shrugged. "Your presence may have made him reticent."

She was sure Willy had not even noticed her, but ought she to say so? Her mind was running over everything Bruno had said about his relationship with Willy. Impulse seized her tongue. "Bruno, do you truly not know anything about what happened that night?"

Was it instinct, or was he merely being over-protective? Francis could not decide. Yet a half-formed sense that something was not right drove him to follow his heart rather than his head. His letters written and despatched with the footman, he chafed at his wife's continued absence.

Ottilia had warned him not to look for her in under an hour. The wooden case clock on the mantel in the parlour informed him that the writing had occupied him for a good twenty minutes beyond the allotted hour, yet there was no sign of his darling wife.

Inevitable images of fell accidents travelled through his mind, but common sense prevailed. If any such had occurred, one of the boys would have run home for help. The likeliest explanation was that Ottilia had not found the lad Willy at the farm and had opted to look elsewhere. Or the questioning was taking longer than one might anticipate. Absurd to suppose anything untoward had occurred. Yet a frisson of apprehension would not be quieted. Francis chose to act.

Pausing only to inform his brother-in-law, busy in his examining room, that he was going in search of Ottilia and the boys, he went by way of the stables and collected his groom.

"Not that I am in need of reinforcements, but it's well to be prepared."

Ryde grunted assent. "It's like her ladyship to get herself in trouble, m'lord."

"I don't know that she is in any sort of trouble. I just don't like her being out on her own." He set off at a brisk pace, following the path he had trodden before that led to the farm. "We'll try Farmer Gubb's place to begin with. She thought to find the fellow Heath there."

Ryde was following close. "Is that the young lad as was guarding the body with Master Tom?"

This set Francis thinking. "I don't suppose you noticed anything when you relieved those two that day?"

"Such as, m'lord?"

"I don't know. You're usually fly to anything odd, Ryde."

A hoarse laugh came from his henchman. "Odder than the lad himself? A funny one he was, m'lord. Muttering away and counting."

"Apparently he's a savant with figures."

"I don't know about that, m'lord, but he said nothing when we told him he could go. Leastways, he were still muttering under his breath, but off he went straight and made no goodbyes, not even to Master Tom."

Francis paid scant attention, his interest in Willy Heath but tepid. "About the body or the surrounding woods is what I mean. I assume you had a good look around?"

"There was time enough, but can't say as I noticed anything particular. No more'n you did yourself. That rope never hung the man as it weren't tied off proper."

Ryde said nothing more for a moment and Francis was conscious of a tinge of disappointment as he trod the well-worn path. His groom had been with him since his army days and Francis knew he was generally observant. But presently, Ryde spoke again. "Now you say, m'lord, mebbe there was one thing."

"Say on."

"I didn't think much to it at the time since you and her ladyship, together with the doctor and them resty boys of his, had trampled all over. Still, it might be as the ground were more flattened about the corpse than you'd expect."

Alert now, Francis flicked him a glance. "Signifying what, Ryde?"

"I couldn't say for certain, but I'm thinking one man alone wouldn't have broke as many twigs or pressed fallen leaves so deep into the ground, mixed up in the ice like they were."

His mind leaping, Francis tried to re-envisage the area around the body as he had first seen it. Caution won. "It is a well-used path."

"True, m'lord, but the body weren't on the main path. It was a tributary, I'd guess. I remember we had to come off it and Master Ben led us well into the trees before we found the spot."

Francis considered this. "You are thinking there was more than one perpetrator."

"I don't say that, m'lord. Mebbe there were another party present."

A surge of irritation went through Francis. "If you are right, it means somebody has been lying to us."

"Or didn't tell all."

"Yes, that is a habit with these wretched witnesses. Lord, I wish we hadn't been obliged to come here just at this juncture!"

He might have deepened in dissatisfaction had the path not at this point come out into the wooded edge giving on to the farm fields. Francis halted, throwing a glance about which failed to produce any sight of Ottilia or the boys.

"We'd best go on down to the farm."

A short brisk walk brought them within sight of the huddle of buildings beyond a wide gate that made up Petrus Gubb's holding. There was no immediate sign of Willy Heath, but in a moment, Francis spied Petrus himself exiting a large shed, a shovel slung over his shoulder. He hailed the man. "Hoy there!"

Petrus halted and glanced across. Even at a distance his face visibly turned surly. He threw down the shovel and trudged in the direction of the gate. "What is it this time?"

Relieved the fellow had rid himself of a potential weapon, Francis wasted no courtesies. "I want Willy Heath. Is he here?"

Petrus hawked and spat, leaning his forearms along the top of the gate. "No, he ain't. Already told that whippersnapper o' yourn."

"You mean one of Doctor Hathaway's boys? When did he come here?"

"Afore. Think I got leisure ter watch the clock? Working man, I am."

Francis suppressed his irritation. "Approximately."

"I dunno. Hour agone mebbe."

An hour since? Then where in heaven's name were they all? He fixed Petrus with the eye of command. "Tell me this at least. Where might Willy Heath be at this time of day?"

To his surprise, a rather dour grin appeared in the farmer's face. "You could try looking behind yourself."

Francis turned on his heel. Willy was on the path, walking towards them.

He took a couple more steps and then froze, staring. Francis muttered a curse and made a motion in the lad's direction. "Wait there, boy! I want you."

Willy backed a step, threw up defensive hands and took off into the woods.

"The devil! After him, Ryde!"

The conviction that something had gone awry solidified as Francis ran. His groom was already heading into the woods, having gone in pursuit almost before the order.

Francis kept to the path, his gaze hunting the figure now darting between the trees. The bareness of winter made him easier to spot, but if he got too far within the thicker part of the woods, it could get tricky. Ryde was gaining on the boy and Francis slowed. The groom's bulk was deceptive. Older by some years he might be, but his calling demanded a level of fitness even Francis did not match. If he rode as often as his groom and spent his days brushing, harnessing and polishing saddles, he might rival his strength.

The fleeting thoughts left him as he noticed lumbering footsteps behind. He flicked a glance back. Petrus Gubb was following.

A shout drew his attention back. "Got him, m'lord."

Willy was struggling in the groom's grip. To no avail. Francis came to a halt in the path as he watched Ryde begin to drag the boy back through the trees.

The farmer also stopped, out of breath, his eyes on the struggling pair. "Why'd he grab him like that? He'll have me to reckon with if he hurts Willy."

There was some justification for Petrus Gubb's concern since the lad was squealing incoherently in protest. Francis chose to be dismissive. "He won't suffer."

"Why'd you want him? What's he done? Ain't no reason to go punishing the lad."

"Nobody is going to punish him." Although the urge to shake Willy until his teeth rattled was strong. That he had run told its own tale. Tillie must have spoken to him at least.

Francis strove for a measure of calm as Ryde brought his prisoner closer. No sense in scaring the boy more. Unless he chose to be recalcitrant.

His groom was attempting to soothe. "Quieten down, lad, do. No one's going to hurt you. His lordship only wants to ask you something."

At that, Willy cried out in something of a squeak. "Don't know no questions!"

"Quiet! Just you stop your noise and listen."

Francis spoke sotto voce. "Gently, Ryde. Don't frighten the boy more."

"Well, I ain't letting go of him, m'lord. A wily little devil, he is."

Francis found the boy's eyes on him, huge in a face now white. His suspicion deepened, but he maintained a cool front. "You know my wife, Lady Fan, don't you?"

Willy shook his head in a wild fashion. Much to Francis's annoyance, Petrus intervened.

"Let the lad alone! He don't know that Lady Fan any more'n me."

"Ah, but he does. She examined the body, Willy. You were there, remember?"

"No questions." The boy dragged against Ryde's grasp. "Don't know no questions."

Francis became stern. "This will avail you nothing, boy. You're going nowhere until I get answers. My wife went in search of you. Did you meet her?"

"Oy! Don't you go a-bullying of him!"

Francis lost patience. "Oh, be quiet, man! The boy knows something, can't you see that?"

Petrus Gubb's gaze veered to Willy Heath. "Well, if he do, you won't get nothing out of him thataway."

"Very well then, try if you can do better."

Petrus grunted and stepped in. "Well, son? You seen the leddy? Tell if you did. I won't let 'em hurt you none."

Willy's gaze went from the farmer to Francis and back again. He grew a touch calmer, but his voice shook. "In church. Seen her in church." Then he reached out in a claw-like manner and seized a fold of the farmer's smock. "Didn't say nothing, master. Don't know no questions. Didn't say."

His mind seizing for an instant, Francis eyed the lad's terrified expression. Then he flipped his gaze to Petrus Gubb. The farmer's brows had drawn close together, his eyes fierce below. Frowning the boy down?

Conviction gripped Francis. There was something here to find out, and both Petrus and Willy were party to that knowledge. He rapped a question.

"Which church?"

Petrus's gaze switched to his and Francis saw his lips tighten. He looked instead at Willy, sharpened his tone. "Come on, boy. Which church?"

"Reverend Pidsea." He threw a hand to his mouth, his eyes popping above it.

Francis hesitated no longer. "Lead the way there. Now!"

Willy began squirming again to be free, shutting his eyes tight.

Francis cursed. "Then you, Petrus. We need you as well in any event."

"For why? Ain't got nothing to say."

"Don't waste my time! I have to find my wife and you know where this blasted church is." Better at this juncture to say nothing of his suspicions.

"What if I do?"

"You can see the boy isn't going to cooperate, can't you? All I want is to discover my Lady Fan safe and sound. She is with child. I want to be sure she has taken no sort of hurt. Will you help me?"

Petrus grunted, eyeing him. Francis kept his features neutral. It would not do for the farmer to realise he had slipped up with that frowning look at Willy. Time enough to sift possibilities once he had Tillie back under his care.

After a moment that seemed endless, Petrus uttered one of his grunts. "S'pose I can spare a bit of time." With which, he pushed past and went off along the path.

Francis dropped his voice to a murmur. "Bring the boy, Ryde. Don't let go of him."

"Rely on me for that, m'lord." He shifted his grip and urged Willy forward.

Francis cast an eye over the boy. He was pale still and he looked scared, but at least he was quiescent now. Satisfied, Francis hastened to catch up with the farmer.

CHAPTER TWENTY-FIVE

The trunk Ottilia was using for a seat was growing increasingly uncomfortable. She was able to rest her back against the edge of the buttress, but even through the thickness of her cloak the stone struck chill. Still worse was the rattling and the thump of the blows her nephew persisted in giving the unyielding door.

"Tom, pray cease! You are giving me a headache."

Her nephew, little more than a silhouette in the meagre glow, left off hitting at the wood and looked round. "Someone's got to hear it in the end, Auntilla. Shall I yell again instead."

His brother answered this before Ottilia could open her mouth. "Leave off, Tom. There's no one to hear you. Willy is long gone."

Tom left the door and came to the crate where Ben was perched, guarding the flame of the big candle set down beside him. "Pidsea is bound to come in sooner or later. He'll be giving a service."

"Not till the evening."

Her younger nephew's grimace showed even in candlelight. "If we have to wait that long, I'll die of starvation."

Ottilia intervened. "I am sure we will be rescued long before then. Your uncle is likely on the hunt for us even now."

She spoke with a confidence she was far from feeling. Francis could be depended upon to look for her, but without Willy's testimony how would he know where to find them? Willy was certain to be hiding somewhere after giving himself away. It would not occur to the poor boy that his very act of locking the door to the crypt stamped him with guilt. Not to mention running off in the first place when she questioned him. What precisely he had done she could not be certain, but she was in no doubt he had seen Hector's body the night before it was discovered by her nephews.

She'd had time enough, incarcerated in this cold underground chamber which smelled of must and mold and felt distinctly damp, to wrap her mind around the little Willy had let fall. The formless ideas she'd had were taking on shape and substance. If she had not completely fathomed the events of that night, she was reasonably sure she was close to so doing. That Bruno Pidsea was involved could not be in doubt. Whether another had been instrumental in what Ottilia now believed to be a definite conspiracy of sorts was still a question.

Ben interrupted her train of thought. "Even if Uncle Francis traces us here, Auntilla, he won't think of looking in the crypt."

"That's why I need to keep shouting and banging," piped up Tom. "Once he gets into the church, he's bound to hear it."

Ben did not answer this, instead regarding Ottilia with that still unfamiliar seriousness of an adult. "Willy's involved in the murder, isn't he, Auntilla?"

Tom gaped. "What, do you think he did it, Ben?"

"I don't know what to think. I'm not the expert."

"Auntilla? Was it Willy?"

She knew not how to answer. She chose prevarication. "I cannot tell you at this moment, Tom. It would be pure speculation."

"Yes, but your speculations are generally right, Auntilla," said Ben. "For my part, I wouldn't think Willy was capable of murdering anyone."

Tom became eager. "Yes, but you don't know that. Hector was horrid to him, after all. He had as good a reason as anyone to take revenge."

"As I said, pure speculation, Tom. We must deal only with facts and probabilities. Pray be quiet now. I am trying to think."

Both her nephews subsided, but as they chose to stare at her in undisguised anticipation, Ottilia was unable to concentrate and could not withstand a burst of laughter. "Desist, the pair of you! You are gazing at me as if I were a wizard about to produce a piece of magic."

"Well, but you do, Auntilla. You always get the answer."

"Not by way of magic, Tom. It is all a matter of sifting and marrying up the various factors. As I am missing several at this point, I fear I am unable to satisfy you."

Tom heaved a disappointed sigh and plonked down on a nearby trunk.

In the ensuing silence, Ottilia tried once more to focus her mind on the puzzle. The discomforts of her position intruded too acutely to allow for any clarity of thought. She let out an exclamation of annoyance. "It is too bad of Willy. I am too cold, too uncomfortable and beginning to be hungry as well." She did not add that the babes growing within her were pressing on her bladder. Nor that her most urgent desire was for a cup of her favourite beverage, incompatible as that was with the more mundane need.

Ben suddenly sat up, cocking his head in a listening attitude. He spoke in a lowered tone. "Listen! It sounds like someone is in the church."

Tom darted to the door and put his ear to it. Ottilia held her breath, listening hard too.

A faint scraping sound came to her ears and Tom looked round. "Ben's right! Someone is out there. I'd best shout again."

Before Ottilia could give a warning to consider whether this was wise, her nephew raised his voice.

"Hey, out there! Is anyone there? Can you hear me?" He set to with his fists, hammering an accompaniment on the door as he continued to call out. "Hey! In the crypt! We're locked in! Do you hear?"

Ottilia signed to Ben, who took up the candle and went to join his brother, giving him a buffet on the shoulder.

"Hush! Let's see if they heard you."

In the silence that followed there was no answering sound for a moment or two. Then came the distinct thud of footsteps. Caution urged Ottilia to push herself to her feet. There was no saying who was out there. They had not spoken. What if it were one of the conspirators? And what if he had a weapon? She called out in an urgent whisper. "Boys, come away from the door!"

Both of them looked round, question visible in their faces, lit by Ben's candle.

"We don't know who it is. Come away!"

Ben pulled Tom back with him and Ottilia joined them, moving just behind the pair and setting a hand to each shoulder. The footsteps were louder now but slow and cautious. Whoever was there was taking as much precaution as Ottilia herself.

The steps ceased. A scraping sound as of the latch rising was at the same time welcome and productive of a sliver of apprehension. Came an odd click and Ottilia watched as the door was pushed slowly open and a figure appeared in the aperture. A distinctly feminine voice called softly. "Is that you, Tom?"

Ottilia let her breath go in a long sigh. "Averil! Thank heavens!"

CHAPTER TWENTY-SIX

A maid was removing the chamber pot, covered over with a towel. The door closed behind her and Averil watched as Ottilia resettled her clothing, shaking out her petticoats and smoothing them over the bump. She did not look too much the worse for her sojourn in the crypt, apart from a trifle of dishevelment.

Averil moved to Bruno Pidsea's dressing stand, hunting among the accoutrements there. "You may wish to rearrange your hair too, if we can find a brush."

The apartment was distinctly masculine. A carpet of oriental design provided the only leaven to the austerity of dark furniture and white-washed walls. Apart from the dominating four-poster, curtained in blue, there was a plain press, a wooden chest and the dressing stand with a mirror above, a small shelf, upon which stood a few items of toiletry, and jug and basin below. Averil poured hot water supplied by the maid into the basin.

"Here, Ottilia, you will feel the better for a wash."

She stood aside as Ottilia thanked her, coming up to make use of the water. There had been little time for discussion as Averil ushered the trio she had freed out of the church and across to Bruno's house. Ottilia had signified her urgent need and it was of more moment to secure relief for her than to enter into much more than a brief explanation of their presence in the crypt, along with the lucky chance that had brought Averil to the rescue.

"I left Bruno only a few moments ago. I wanted a little quiet prayer in the church I know well. Or that is what I said." She lowered her voice not to be heard by the Hathaway boys then walking a little ahead. "To be honest with you, Ottilia, what he told me of the night of the murder was disturbing and I needed to think."

Ottilia had instantly picked up on it. "He told you something pertinent?"

"Somewhat. But let us procure you relief first. I am very sure you must be in need of rest too."

Ottilia did not deny it and Averil hastened to bring her into the warmth of Bruno's parlour. She brushed aside his surprise and made known Ottilia's requirements. A maid soon arrived to lead the women upstairs to his bedchamber.

"The spare one is ill-prepared, so best to make use of mine."

Ottilia thanked him, but she was plainly in no condition to bandy words and the parting admonition was left to Averil.

"Could you order coffee, Bruno? Lady Fan would be glad of it. We will leave the boys to tell you what happened."

As it chanced, once her most pressing need was dealt with, Ottilia seemed to revive. Her ablutions dealt with, she evidently recalled Averil's mention of dressing her hair, peering into the looking glass.

"It is not too disarranged. I think I can do without a hairbrush." She prinked a little, replacing a few strands that had escaped their moorings. Then she turned and Averil found herself the recipient of a warm smile. "Thank you for helping me. I could not have managed without you."

"No, one can't rise with ease when one is *enceinte*."

Ottilia's brows drew together. "You have been pregnant? What happened, Averil?"

An old wound resurfaced for a moment. "I suffered a miscarriage. Ralph and I never did manage to produce a child of our own."

Her hands were taken in a comforting clasp. "I am so sorry. I do understand for I lost my first-born."

Averil pressed the hands holding hers and then released them. "I know. Patrick told me. But you are doing well this time."

"And I succeeded with Luke. I only hope it may go as smoothly with these two."

Averil blinked. "Twins?"

Ottilia's infectious laugh rang out. "My wretched brother says so. I do not know whether to be glad or sorry that he found it out."

Suppressing a feeling of jealousy, Averil said all that was suitable. Thankfully, Ottilia did not dwell on the subject.

"You said Bruno had revealed something to you about the night of the murder, Averil. Does it concern Willy?"

"You guessed that? Because he locked you into the crypt?"

"Just so. Although, if truth be told, I have been a trifle suspicious of Bruno's stated evidence for some days. He does keep cropping up."

Anxiety grew in Averil. "But it is Willy you suspect of the murder, is it not? After all, if he ran away from you as you said —"

"Together with his making us prisoner. Yes, it does rather point the finger, but one should not jump to conclusions. All I can feel certain of is that Willy did indeed see the body that night." Her clear gaze seemed to search Averil's. "Did he run to Bruno for help?"

Averil was startled into a mirthless laugh. "How came you to realise that?"

Ottilia's smile came. "It seems logical that if Willy was in trouble, or shocked perhaps, he would seek out his champion for support or guidance."

Averil blew out a breath. "Well, he did. Bruno gave me no details. He said only that Willy came to him in the night, severely frightened, and that he counselled him not to speak of it to a soul."

Ottilia clicked her tongue. "Barely credible. What frightened him?"

"Bruno would not say."

"No, because it bears upon the killing and he knows it."

Averil hesitated. She was fond of Bruno, but he had clearly concealed information and this was a case of murder.

Ottilia evidently picked up on it. "What troubles you, Averil? Is there something more?"

Averil drew a breath. "It is a word Bruno used. Before he told me that Willy had come to him that night."

She was treated to an understanding sort of look. "What word? Pray don't fear to tell me. If it helps, I am fairly certain Bruno's part did not include despatching Hector Penkevil."

Averil capitulated. "Make of it what you will, but he spoke of Willy acting vengefully."

"Ah, did he?"

A secretive smile crept into Ottilia's face and Averil began to feel a trifle disgruntled. "It means something? I collect you don't mean to tell me."

Ottilia touched a hand to her arm and the smile became warm. "It is only a vague picture surfacing in my mind. Forgive me, I cannot say more at this juncture. I trust I may soon satisfy your curiosity." Then she became brisk and moved towards the door. "I think it is high time the Reverend Pidsea disclosed the truth."

Averil did not move. "Do you mean to accuse him?"

Ottilia turned back, her fingers already around the doorhandle. "I never accuse. I may put to him a hypothesis and see how he takes it." She opened the door. "Come, Averil. The coffee you requested must have arrived by this time and I am positively gasping."

The church, as far as Francis could make out in the dark interior from his position by the side door through which the party had entered, was free of any sign of inhabitants. Such light as was afforded by the windows was poor and a scattering of candle sconces attached to pillars and walls gave notice of how the place was lit during services. It was also icy cold. If Ottilia was still here, she would by this time be frozen.

Francis turned on Willy. "Where is she? You said she was in the church."

He found himself blocked by the farmer. "Here, yer honour, ain't got no call speaking harsh to the lad."

Francis suppressed a desire to land the man a blow to the jaw. "Then you ask him, for I am fast losing patience. Where is my wife?"

Petrus turned surly. "Willy ain't her keeper."

"I told you. She had the intention of seeking him out and he says he saw her here."

He looked once more to the boy who was fidgeting, casting glances towards the front of the building and then back again to Ryde. The groom was standing close beside Willy, his stance alert. Suspicion burgeoned.

"What are you looking for, boy? What is down that way?"

Willy cast him a fearful glance and abruptly took to his heels, fleeing down the side aisle towards the entrance.

"Ryde!"

The groom needed no urging. He sped off in pursuit, closely followed by Petrus Gubb.

"Hoy, you leave him be! Let the lad alone!"

Francis made his way down the aisle in less of a rush. He could rely on Ryde absolutely. Willy would not get away.

As he arrived at the last of the pews, it became evident that the boy was not attempting to escape the church. Three sets of footsteps, which had echoed in the vast open space, now dropped in volume to a duller thudding across the way at the other side of the building.

As he kept on the move, Francis peered through a gloom which had enveloped the figures. He could just make out a darker shadow that signified an opening in the wall ahead.

Ryde's voice came at him from somewhere below ground. "Here, m'lord! You'd best see this." Treading with caution, Francis approached the shadow. "Mind the stair, m'lord!"

By what little light that came from the narrow windows behind the altar and those above the front door, he was just able to make out the shallow stairway. He found all three males crowded around a door at the bottom.

"The boy says this door was latched, m'lord, but it's open now. Nobody inside."

A horrid spectre rose within Francis. "Should there have been?"

"He won't say, but that's what I'm guessing, m'lord. There's a smell of burnt wax and remains of a fat candle standing on one of those chests."

"Are you telling me her ladyship was locked in down here?"

"It's what I'm thinking. Probably had them lads with her. Doubt they'd leave her alone, m'lord."

Francis, his eyes adjusted now, located Willy, and seized him by the edges of his coat. "Answer me this, boy! Did you lock her inside?"

Petrus pulled the lad away. "Let him be! Why'd he do any such?"

"If he didn't, what possessed him to come running down here?"

"Likely he meant to hide. It's what he does when he's scared like. That it, Willy lad?"

Francis tried to see the boy's expression, but his face was a mere pale oval. Was he shaking though? He made no answer to the farmer's question.

"He works fer the reverend, see," went on Petrus. "Only if someone come in as he don't know, he hides hisself down here in the crypt. At the farm, he'd took and climb up to the hayloft."

It was plausible, but Francis was not convinced. "Yet he did see my wife in the church, for he told us so."

"Likely she asked him questions. He don't like questions, Willy. Likely he ran and hid hisself so's he wouldn't have to answer."

Francis let out an exasperated sound. "This is all very fine talking but it brings me no closer to locating my wife's present whereabouts."

Ryde had one hand still about Willy's arm. He did not release the boy as he spoke. "Her ladyship might have returned to the Lodge, m'lord."

"She could not have done. She would have met us on the way. Unless there is another route back. Petrus?"

The farmer shrugged. "Not if you ain't one as knows the pathways through the wood."

"I suppose it's feasible Ben and Tom are acquainted with them, but they wouldn't take their aunt other than by the main route."

"Then she's still here, m'lord."

"Yes, but where?"

There was silence for a space. Frustration surged through Francis. If Ottilia had not managed to get anything out of Willy Heath, she must have chosen to continue her hunt in some other direction. He tried to recall her musings on the murder in hopes of lighting upon a method she might have taken.

Ryde interrupted his thoughts. "We'd best go back up into the church, m'lord. Too crowded down here and this fellow is wriggling to be free."

"Don't you let go of him!"

Francis turned and started back up the stair. In a moment the whole party had returned to the main hall of the church where there was thankfully sufficient light at least to see faces clearly again.

"What do you mean to do now, m'lord?"

Before Francis could answer, Petrus Gubb took hold of Willy's shoulder. "You don't need him no more, yer honour. Let me take him back to the farm."

In two minds, Francis almost gave permission. Just then, a loud clang from the main doors at the front produced a sudden access of brightness as one side was pushed inward.

Two figures slid into sight, clear in the illumination coming in from outside.

"There you are, Uncle Fan!"

Francis walked quickly forward. "Tom? Ben, is that you? Where the deuce is your aunt?"

"She's safe, sir, never fear." The boys strode up, Ben halting before Francis. "She's over at the vicarage."

Tom meanwhile, continued on past, crying out in a fury. "There's that pest of a Willy! How dared you lock us in? Auntilla might have been damaged!"

Francis spun. "Hold him, Ryde!"

The groom had anticipated him. Willy was struggling in his grasp, squealing as he had done when captured in the woods. The farmer took hold of the lad as well, trying to prize him from Ryde's grip.

"Leave be, Petrus!" Francis strode back to the group. "So it was your doing, boy. Is that why you were running to the farm? You endangered my wife by incarcerating her in a blasted crypt, of all things!"

Willy had stopped struggling, instead cringing towards Petrus, in whom he clearly saw salvation. Savage as his feelings were towards the boy, Francis remembered he had not all his wits. "Don't fret. I'm not going to lay violent hands on you."

His elbow was being nudged and he turned to find Ben at his side. "Sir, come away a moment!" Francis allowed himself to be manoeuvred a little apart, what time Ben spoke in a lowered voice. "I believe Auntilla thinks Willy knows something about the murder."

Francis almost snorted. "Since he saw fit to lock you all in the crypt, I'm damned sure he does."

"Auntilla did question him, sort of, and he got scared and ran off. We chased him, but he fooled us."

"Did she get anything out of him?"

Tom, popping up beside them, took this. "He kept saying Hector was dead in the night, so Auntilla thinks he was there."

Ben entered a caveat. "Yes, but I told her I don't think he's capable of killing anyone."

Francis was unimpressed. "If he can think of pretending to hide and then locking the door on you, he's capable of making an even more elaborate plan."

"He didn't plan it, though, Uncle Fan," argued Tom. "He did it on the spur of the moment, because he was scared of Auntilla finding out."

Francis held up his hands. "It is useless to speculate. I want to see your aunt at the earliest possible moment."

"That's why we came hunting for you, sir," said Ben. "Auntilla was sure you would have come after us. She's talking to Mr Pidsea."

"Yes, and she told us to come and find you."

Relief swept through Francis. "Well, thank the Lord you did. Where is this vicarage?"

Tom headed at once for the door. "Follow us!"

Francis made to accompany the elder of his nephews and threw a command over his shoulder. "Bring the boy, Ryde."

The farmer intervened again, cutting in between Francis and Ryde with his prisoner. "Hoy! What you want with Willy now? If yer thinking of basting him like that Penkevil done —"

"Nothing of the kind." Halting, Francis turned back. "I don't yet know what my wife may be thinking, but I am very sure she will wish to talk to Willy again. At the very least, he should beg her pardon for this prank." A thought occurred and he acted on it almost without consciously realising its implication. Making a sudden spring, he seized the farmer's coat and held fast.

"Hoy! Leave go of me!"

"By no means. It strikes me you know a sight more about this affair than you've seen fit to reveal."

The farmer pulled back. "Dang it, leave me be! I said my piece and that's that."

Aware of his nephews, who had returned and were hovering a few steps away, Francis gave a curt command. "Boys, relieve me here a moment!"

Both Ben and Tom moved with alacrity, the latter eager as he leapt to grab at the farmer's arm. "Got him, sir!"

His brother took the other side, making sure to hold the man by both shoulder and arm. They were both a good deal slighter than the farmer, but Francis supposed it was surprise at the sudden attack that held him frozen an instant before he began to tug his limbs away, grunting protests the while.

"Get off of me, you whippersnappers! I'll baste the pair of you, see if I don't."

Francis had wasted no time but dove a hand into the capacious pocket of his greatcoat and brought out his pistol. He cocked the gun and aimed it at the farmer's middle. "Stand where you are!"

Petrus Gubb froze, staring at the muzzle of the pistol.

"You can let go now, boys. As for you, Petrus, start walking."

CHAPTER TWENTY-SEVEN

Ottilia held off her attack until she was fortified with her favourite beverage and had sent her nephews off to look for Francis. She occupied herself in thanking Bruno Pidsea for his hospitality and assuring him, in answer to an anxious query, that she was none the worse for her adventure in the crypt.

"Willy must have been frightened, my lady. He is apt to act irrationally under stress."

Ottilia held her tongue on a sharp retort. She did not for a moment believe that Willy's action sprang from an irrational mind. Fearful he most certainly was. But luring them in the right direction for the crypt and locking the door had been a deliberate act. Which did not augur well for his innocence in the matter of Hector's death.

Bruno Pidsea was distinctly more ill-at-ease than he had been upon the last occasion of questioning. Was he regretting having said as much to Averil? Or did he wonder whether or not she had revealed his remarks to Ottilia?

She set down her empty cup.

He fixed his gaze upon her. "I take it you have further questions for me?"

Ottilia eyed him a moment. She opted for an attack direct. "Did you suppose I should not find out?"

His lips tightened briefly, a spark flaring in his eye. "You will have to excuse me, my lady. I do not understand you. Find out what?"

Ottilia gave a spurious smile. "Come, come, sir, you are not a fool. Let us throw off the gloves."

He did not speak, but merely looked a question. Was he determined to hold his nerve? She chose a light tone. "I fear you made a slip, Mr Pidsea, at our first meeting."

"Did I? How so?"

He appeared calm, but she thought his gaze became a trifle fixed. "You said you learned of Hector's death from Alexander, whereas his version is that he received an express from you." His gaze widened slightly and Ottilia felt a sliver of triumph. "Which was it, sir?"

A slight cough came and Bruno looked away. "I may have forgot it in the press of circumstance."

Ottilia almost laughed out. "Spurious, but let that be for now. I have more."

She waited, but he did not speak, his gaze returning to hers in that curiously glassy manner, his jaw visibly tight. She took the bull by the horns.

"You gave me to understand, my dear sir, that you knew nothing of what occurred on the night Hector was killed. You even spoke of hearing an owl. Perhaps you did, but not from the confines of your house, I suggest. Now it appears that Willy came to you in the hours of darkness, severely shocked by something he had witnessed. It happens that the one thing Willy told me before he saw fit to incarcerate us in your crypt, is that Hector was, as he put it, dead in the night. There would seem to be a logical connection there, do you not think?"

The reverend shot a look at Averil, who raised deprecating hands. "I could not let it pass, Bruno. You must see that."

His jaw was held so tight as his gaze returned to Ottilia that his chin trembled an instant. Then he let his breath go in a long sigh and his whole stance collapsed. Defeat was in his voice. "He did come to me, yes. He was distressed. It is true he saw Hector's body lying in the woods."

Ottilia took due note of the body's position, but she did not at once take it up. "Did Willy think to check on Hector's condition?"

"He did what anyone might do." Bruno's gaze shifted away. "Willy thought he was drunk at first. He said he shook him a little."

Or worse? But Ottilia held her tongue on the words. Bruno was no longer meeting her gaze. She could not trust his words. "Anything else?"

"Willy listened for his heart. At that point, he became convinced Hector was dead and that's when he came running to me."

In a severely frightened state? Merely from finding the man dead? Ottilia withheld these reflections. "What did you do, sir?"

"I calmed him as best I could."

"You did not think to verify his story for yourself?"

Bruno's gaze caught hers fleetingly and again wandered away. His answer came after a hesitant moment. Thinking how best to evade the truth? "It took me some time to drag a coherent tale from Willy, as you may imagine. He was distraught."

Distraught now? Earlier it was merely distressed. Ottilia held her tongue, waiting.

"By the time I was able to go and see for myself, there was no body."

Momentarily startled, Ottilia frowned. "It had gone?"

Bruno shifted. Discomfort? "Or I mistook the place."

"You left Willy here?"

"I could not subject him to a second sight of what had upset him so much. In the light of subsequent discovery, I must blame myself for not making more of an effort, but I confess the less time I was obliged to remain in the woods on a cold night the better."

Ottilia watched him for a moment in silence. The impression of a man in acute discomfort remained. He was certainly holding back. A slight movement to her right drew her gaze to Averil. Ottilia received a questioning glance and brushed a warning finger across her lips. Averil gave a slight nod in response and returned her gaze to Bruno.

Ottilia broke the rising tension. "Why did you not see fit to tell me all this at the outset, Mr Pidsea?"

A strangled sound escaped him. "To protect Willy, of course. I could not have the boy involved."

Time to turn the screw. "You protected him to a far greater degree, did you not, sir?"

That brought his gaze to bear upon her. "What can you possibly mean?"

"I mean, Mr Pidsea, that your story is almost a complete fabrication."

His cheeks suffused with colour. "You dare to give me the lie?"

Averil was on her feet. "Oh, Ottilia, pray be careful what you say!"

Ottilia ignored her, addressing herself exclusively to Bruno. "You speak of Willy coming to you in a distraught condition. You say it took you long to calm him, and yet you left him at your house while you investigated. I have heard much of your character, sir, and this does not ring with who you are."

"I cannot imagine why you should think so."

He was on the defensive now. Ottilia pressed the attack. "When you heard of Willy's beating, you stormed in upon a private meeting and did not mince your words as you berated Hector Penkevil. It does not accord with the man of action you have shown yourself to be that you would refrain, in this instance, from an immediate investigation. Logic dictates that you would have taken Willy with you to show you what he had found. Furthermore, you are scarcely the man to have abandoned the search for this body even had you gone alone. Having found it, you are equally not the man to have refrained from reporting the matter to the authorities. Very likely that very night. I submit that, had you discovered Hector to be dead — and had Willy's involvement not been in question — you would have set out, regardless of the time, to inform Sir Hugh Riccarton."

Bruno was staring at her in a kind of stupor. Before he could respond, to her intense annoyance, the door was thrust open and both her nephews bounced into the room, closely followed by Petrus Gubb with Francis behind him.

"We found him, Auntilla!"

"So I see, Tom." Ottilia rose from the chair as she took in the pistol in her husband's hand. "What in the world —?" She broke off at the further entrance of Francis's groom with Willy Heath in tow.

Ryde shoved the boy into the room and shut the door behind him, standing before it like a gaoler.

Willy ran to Bruno, crying out broken words between hiccupping sobs. "Save me! Done for … if you don't…"

The reverend, with what Ottilia considered great presence of mind, smothered Willy's cries against his shoulder, hushing him the while. But the lad had said enough. Ottilia's suspicions began to solidify.

She had no chance to voice them, even had she wished to at that moment, for Francis came up. He caught at her shoulder with his free hand, looking closely into her face.

"Are you well, my dear one? Would to God you had not suffered such an ordeal!"

Ottilia smiled at him, setting her hands to his chest. "It was of no great moment, I promise you. I am well rested now." She lowered her voice. "I believe I have the answers. You have come *á propos*."

His hand left her shoulder and cradled her cheek, his face softening as he smiled at her. "I knew you would." He added sotto voce, "Don't ask me how for I don't know, but I am convinced Petrus is involved too."

"I presume that is why you brought him here at gunpoint."

"Precisely." But he uncocked the pistol and slipped it back into his pocket, rather to Ottilia's relief.

She looked past him to where the farmer was now in a huddle with Bruno and Willy. "This becomes interesting indeed. It explains a part that I still found perplexing. I think we ought not to give them time to concoct any more lies."

He grinned. "Confound them then, my battle-axe of a wife."

"Battle-axe? You fiend, how dare you?"

"In a purely warlike comparison, my darling. I didn't mean you look like one."

Ottilia let out a stifled laugh. "Well for you, horrid creature."

He smiled and released her. As he stepped aside, Ottilia noted that her nephews were deep in a low-toned conversation with Averil. Pumping her for what had occurred so far, no doubt. It was heartwarming to see how well the boys got along with her, and perhaps the acquaintance was more innocent than she had at first supposed. Francis was right in that the local society was limited and one necessarily knew most in the circle. Perhaps Ben had also accompanied his father, in his apprentice capacity, on visits to Ralph Deakin. Ottilia nevertheless felt a pang for her lost sister-in-law. Poor Sophie could never have entered into a discussion of this kind. She was far too self-absorbed.

But the business at hand could not be further delayed. The trio over by the mantel were ripe for her to unravel the true facts of the fateful night.

She raised her voice. "If you please, everyone!"

The hubbub, of which Ottilia had been only half aware, ceased. All eyes became trained upon her. She turned to her nephews. "Sit, you two, and keep quiet." And to the trio by the mantel, "I have a few more questions for you all."

Bruno stepped forward, waving Petrus and Willy to one side. "Enough has been said, my lady."

"You are mistaken, sir. We are just arriving at what must be said."

His face changed, something almost a snarl crossing it. "Will you have done? Has there not been harm enough?"

Ottilia's response was forestalled as Francis stepped in. "Keep a civil tongue in your head when you address my wife, Pidsea, or you will have me to reckon with."

Ottilia moved to his side, setting a hand on his arm. "Thank you, Fan, but it is natural for Mr Pidsea to feel alarm." She turned back to Bruno. "After all, you have done your utmost to protect Willy, have you not? It is unfortunate for you all that I happened to be visiting at this time, I fear. All would have gone just as you hoped otherwise. A verdict of suicide or accidental death."

Bruno did not speak, but there was both resentment and dismay in his face. Ottilia's gaze turned on the farmer. "I had not got so far as to include you, Petrus —"

"Gracious! He was involved too?"

Ottilia passed over Averil's interruption. "It seems you have been just as anxious as Mr Pidsea here to protect Willy. I expect it was your notion to fake the hanging. It was always a puzzle how the murderer could have had a rope handy just at the right moment."

The silence was palpable. Petrus Gubb was staring at her in a species of shock. Ottilia spared a glance for Willy. Misery warred with terror in the lad's face.

Compassion stirred and she was hardly conscious of the smile she gave. "Poor boy. Temptation? Or was it simply pure rage that made you take revenge?"

At that, Bruno burst out. "Willy did not kill the man!"

Ottilia increased the pressure. "He strangled him. The marks on Hector's neck were unmistakeable."

"You have it wrong!"

"Why? Willy is strong enough to inflict such damage."

Bruno threw up his hands, his tone rising. "He thought the evil wretch was already dead!"

Ottilia let out a satisfied little sigh. "Now we come to it."

There was a breathless pause punctuated by gasps from her nephews. Bruno set an elbow on the mantel and dropped his forehead into his cupped palm. Willy collapsed to the floor, crouching, his hands over his head. Only Petrus stood his ground, belligerence in his stance taking the place of his earlier shock.

A mutter came from beside Ottilia. "This becomes more confusing by the moment."

She dropped her voice to a murmur. "On the contrary, Fan. To me, it is becoming clearer."

"Well, I wish you'd explain."

"Bear with me, I am about to do so." She put out a hand towards Bruno and raised her voice. "Mr Pidsea, I believe the time has come for frankness, but I fear I have been standing too long. I can just as well continue this while seated, do you not think?"

He turned haggard eyes towards her. "Do as you wish. I have nothing more to say."

Ottilia let out a light laugh. "I sincerely doubt that." She turned. "Fan, your arm, if you please."

He set his arm around her at once, guiding her back to the chair she had vacated, remaining beside it. Ottilia took time to look across to her cohorts. Averil was looking stunned, but both Tom and Ben were eager, the younger boy's eyes bright with excitement.

Ottilia smiled at them. "You may both have your say later. For this present, pray let me finish this."

They nodded in tandem and she trained her gaze back upon the huddled form of Willy Heath, addressing her remarks mainly to Bruno, however.

"Willy came to you because he believed he had killed Hector. As you say, he did not intend it. He thought he was behind the fair. Shall I say what I think happened, Willy?"

He peeped at her through his fingers but said never a word. Instead, Petrus spoke up, his tone a growl. "You don't know how it were, missus. Say nowt and yer won't hurt no one."

Ottilia gave a little sigh. "I wish it were that simple. A great many people are under suspicion. They are the subject of gossip."

"Whose blame is that then? Nowt would've been said if you'd left well alone."

"Hold your tongue, Petrus!" Thus Francis.

Ottilia threw up a deprecating hand. The man's anger was understandable. Her spouse subsided, but she could feel his choler still. Francis was ever prone to leap to her defence.

She held the farmer's eye. "Only the truth can make things right, Petrus."

"Who says it's true then?"

"I am trusting you all will, once I have outlined the facts as I suppose they occurred." She paused, but no retort was forthcoming. Once more, she looked to Willy Heath. "When you came upon Hector, he had fallen unconscious because he was drugged." This brought the boy's head up in a sharp movement. "You thought he was dead because you had no means of discovering whether he was still alive. His breathing must have been too shallow to be detectable and his heartbeat would have been slow. I do not believe you had any thought of killing him, Willy, but your thirst for revenge got the better of you, did it not? You put your hands about his throat and squeezed." She glanced towards Bruno. "An inept strangling, as it happens, which probably would have failed in any event." Her gaze went back to Willy. "And then he moved. Or perhaps opened his eyes."

Several mouths in the company gave vent to gasping breaths while Willy shuddered. Ottilia knew she had hit home. She softened her voice. "That was what terrified you so. That was why you ran to Bruno. Am I correct, Mr Pidsea?"

He only nodded, his face strained and paler than ever.

"The rest is easy enough to guess at. You accompanied Willy back to the place and met Petrus on the way. Or had he come upon the body in your absence perhaps?"

Bruno's voice was devoid of expression. "He was already there."

"Tried to revive him, didn't I?" Petrus showed a combination of antagonism and regret. "Shook him and yelled at him to wake, but he were ripe fer the diet of worms. Nowt a body could do."

Ottilia put up a finger. "This marks the point of conspiracy."

Silence once more. Bruno and Petrus exchanged a glance. Willy hid his face in his knees again.

"Go on, Lady Fan." This from Averil, and a glance showed her grim and almost forbidding.

"It is simple enough, I think. Some sort of conference ensued. Willy's fingers had left marks. Best to make it look like suicide, no? Petrus fetched a rope. That must have been a painful wait for the other two. Perhaps you took time for comforting Willy. At the scene, and not at this house as you attempted to make us believe."

He put up a protest, for all he spoke in a defeated fashion. "What else could we have done?"

Francis made an exasperated sound. "I can think of half a dozen alternative courses of action, any one of which would not have resulted in this mess."

"Willy would have taken the blame. Was that fair? Who would believe he had not intended harm to Penkevil? I could not risk it. We had to conceal his part."

Ottilia snapped. "Yet it did not remain concealed, Mr Pidsea. Yes, I know you blame me for that, but the evidence on Hector's body would have been discovered at autopsy. The same questions would have been raised. I merely raised them earlier."

"Without yer meddlin' none 'ud think to put it on Willy here." Petrus was in again.

Ottilia hit back strongly. "Without my meddling, an innocent party might have taken the blame. As it stands…" She faded out, thinking.

For several moments, no one spoke that Ottilia was aware of as she turned the matter over in her mind. Francis interrupted her train of thought.

"As it stands what? You can't leave it there."

Ottilia looked up at him and smiled. "It has just clicked into place." Her gaze roved the three conspirators. "It is a good thing we have uncovered it all because I think I see a way through."

Bruno lifted his head, straightening. "Is it to keep Willy safe?"

"Perhaps not entirely, but we may save him from the gallows at least."

"How?"

Ottilia glanced at Willy, whose now intent stare was disconcerting. Training her gaze upward, she found Petrus frowning, leaning a little forward as if he was eager to hear more, his stance thus a trifle less aggressive.

"Let's have it then, my love," prompted Francis.

"I believe I may be able to persuade Sir Hugh that this was an accident. It would appear that Hector died at some point between Willy leaving him and Petrus coming across his body. Willy's actions may have sped up the process, but his attempt at strangling could not have been conclusive as it was poorly done at best. If memory serves me from all I learned of my brother, the combination of the valerian, alcohol and the freezing cold would have brought about his death regardless of Willy's intervention."

"Will that convince Sir Hugh, do you think, Tillie?"

"I think he will be well-disposed enough towards Willy to be lenient. There must be an inquest, of course, but Sir Hugh would be able to direct the jury towards a less harsh verdict."

"Manslaughter?"

"At worst, Fan. At best, we might hope the jury will bring in accidental death."

She saw that Willy was looking confused and Petrus still frowning, but there was a glimmering of relief and hope in Bruno's face.

Ottilia made haste to sound a warning. "It is vital that all three of you tell the truth when you give evidence. Do not attempt to flummery the jury. Only then can you hope to enlist their sympathies for Willy's plight."

To her surprise, Averil spoke up. "There is no fear of that failing. The jury is bound to consist of those who know Willy well. He is uniformly liked in these parts. They will be only too eager to set him free."

CHAPTER TWENTY-EIGHT

Obliged to bite her tongue due to the presence up behind of her groom, Averil tooled the gig in the direction of Ash Lodge with impatience in her heart and a spurious series of innocuous remarks on her tongue. Ottilia, who had accepted the proffered lift, responded just as spuriously, Averil suspected, to her queries about the Fanshawe family's welfare.

When they arrived, Averil climbed down from the gig and handed the reins to her groom. "Walk them, Saul. I shall not be long."

"Will you not at least partake of refreshment, Averil?"

"I must go back to Ralph." She lowered her voice. "I am only coming in for the chance to express my admiration."

She received a deprecating look and a dismissive wave of the hand as she followed Ottilia into the hall. "Pray don't! It is of all things what I most dislike. You will only put me out of countenance."

Averil halted. "Then at least allow me to say how much I appreciate having been allowed to be in at the finish."

Ottilia turned back, smiling. "I could not have coped without you."

"Yes, you could. I expect you could cope without anyone at all."

"Not so. I rely absolutely upon Francis for one. And if you had not wormed out of Bruno the truth about Willy coming to him, my task would have been much more difficult."

Averil let the matter drop. It was plain Ottilia did not relish praise for her prowess. "Then it remains only for me to wish you well with your confinement. No doubt I will hear from Patrick that everything has gone smoothly."

To her surprise, Ottilia came close and caught her up in a warm hug. She was released, but for her hands which were strongly clasped. "I hope he may. I hope too that you and my brother may escape censure from the gossips. People are only too eager to cast stones, despite knowing nothing of the circumstances."

Heat ran up into Averil's cheeks and she tried to smile. "You do favour plain speaking."

The hands tightened. "Well, we ought to be sisters and I am determined not to be censorious." Ottilia let go at last, rather to Averil's relief, and an arch look came into her face. "May I be impertinent?"

Averil was betrayed into a laugh. "Do you need my permission?"

The grey eyes, so like to Patrick's, positively danced. "Asking awkward questions is rather my stock in trade, I fear, but this is sheer curiosity."

"Go on."

"Where do you contrive to meet?"

Taken aback, Averil could not withhold an exclamatory sound, half laughter, half astonishment. "I beg your pardon?"

Ottilia gave a smile that was somewhat sheepish. "Well, Ruth and Roland have acquired for their trysts the use of a cottage owned by the present Lord Carrefour, so…"

Averil laughed out. "You are incorrigible, Ottilia. For your information, we have no secret cottage, nor indeed any particular place of rendezvous. We contrive it when and where we can, which is not often."

Lady Fan looked rueful. "I am suitably chastened." She held out a hand. "Farewell, my dear, in case we do not meet for some time. I hope we will. I like you very much, you know, Averil." With which, Ottilia turned from her and directed her steps towards the stairway without looking back.

Averil watched her climb, a little glow of pleasure burgeoning in her bosom. Then she turned for Patrick's examining room. If he was home, it would take up but a moment to refresh her heart merely with a sight of his face.

Sir Hugh Riccarton was prompt to respond to Ottilia's note informing him that the matter was now resolved, arriving upon the following day to listen to her account. His customary twinkle of humour was lacking, however, by the time she concluded, and Ottilia regarded his serious mien with a riffle of doubt. She essayed a tentative probe.

"You do not appear to be much edified by my argument, sir."

The magistrate looked across from his position by the mantel. "I concede the boy's part in this muddle may be tackled with leniency. But what of the other two? Have you thought of that, ma'am?"

His more formal address dismayed Ottilia, but she rallied. "I have, sir, and I realise it is impossible for you to condone an accessory to attempted murder."

"*Attempted* if the jury accepts your brother's cautious or prevaricating conclusions. Moreover, it's two accessories. You've said yourself the pair of them conspired to conceal Willy's action."

Ottilia sighed. "Just so. A sillier scheme one could scarcely imagine, especially when they made such a botch of faking a suicide."

Sir Hugh eyed her, a frown appearing between his brows. "What have you in your head? I tell you now, I am in no mind to allow either one of them to evade the consequences altogether."

"No, that would make a mockery of the law indeed."

"What, then?"

She tried a smile but received no answering glimmer from the magistrate. "I am wondering if a pithy reprimand from the bench —" She saw an even pithier response in his eye and hastened to add a qualifier. "That is to say, once the jury have dealt with Willy's case and assuming the verdict is brought in accidental death…"

His gaze narrowed, but Ottilia thought she detected a slight softening there. "Well?"

"A denouncement of their conduct from your lips would ensure a high degree of public and unwelcome notoriety for Bruno Pidsea and Petrus Gubb, do you not think?"

"That goes without saying. The moment this news is out Bruno at least may look to be pilloried by his peers. Lord knows how the bishop will take it!"

"That is my point, sir. Even without a legal sentence, Bruno is likely to endure a severe reprimand from his superiors, if he is not dismissed from his post."

At last Sir Hugh's usual manner reappeared. "The bishop won't go that far. Probably write it off as a foolish error of judgement."

"Which indeed it was."

He bent a severe gaze upon her, but Ottilia was not fooled. He had definitely weakened. "You are determined to get those two out of being properly punished, are you not, you wilful female? I can't think how that husband of yours is still sane."

Ottilia was betrayed into a ripple of amusement. "Because he long ago divined my failings and married me in spite of them."

"The more fool he." But the twinkle was back in his eye and Ottilia was gratified. He came away from the mantel. "I ought to thank you, I suppose, but I shan't since you will no doubt be off home, leaving me to pick up the pieces."

Ottilia rose and took the hand he held out. "No thanks are necessary and I will at least do Ruth Penkevil the courtesy of informing her she is no longer under suspicion. Unless you prefer to undertake that duty yourself?"

He threw up a hand. "Go to it, my dear Lady Fan. Save me one task at least. You've landed me with quite enough to do, I thank you."

Mischief burgeoned. "Well, I will not be sorry to leave you to clear up the aftermath. It is only right that you bestir yourself now that I have done your work for you."

"And in a matter of two weeks only," said Sir Hugh on a spurious note of admiration.

"I am flattered you appreciate my skill, sir."

Sir Hugh laughed out as she made a demure little curtsy. "Impertinent chit! Admit it now. You would not have missed it for the world."

"It was an interesting puzzle and it has served a useful purpose at a difficult time."

He pressed the hand he was still holding. "A distraction? Yes, I dare say. How is Doctor Hathaway coping, by the by?"

Ottilia answered suitably and the magistrate spent a few minutes chatting on subjects unrelated to the case before taking his leave.

No sooner had he departed than the Hathaway boys bounced into the parlour.

"Did he take your word, Auntilla?"

"Is he going to let Willy off? He ought, for Willy didn't mean it."

"What will happen to old Petrus and Reverend Pidsea?"

Ottilia cut into the plethora of questions. "That is just the point we were discussing, Ben, before Sir Hugh left."

"May we know the outcome?"

"Is he going to throw Petrus in gaol?" Tom asked, not without a certain relish.

"I am hoping I have averted that repercussion. It does depend on whether a jury will indeed take the view that the death was accidental."

"Oh, they are bound to, Auntilla. Like Mrs Deakin said, everyone will be on Willy's side."

Ben took issue with this. "You can't be sure, Tom." He raised a warning finger. "And don't go thinking of going around telling people that's what they must do."

"'Course not," said Tom, indignant. "I didn't even think of doing so."

"No, well, don't think of it now just because I mentioned it."

"If I do, it'll be your fault. It was your idea, not mine."

Ottilia intervened as Ben began upon a heated rejoinder. "Enough! Quiet! Neither of you must interfere with the course of the law."

Tom let forth a snort. "How can you say so, Auntilla, when it's just what you did yourself?"

"I most certainly did not. A suggestion to the magistrate is not the same as suborning potential members of the jury into voting the way you wish them to."

Tom glowered a trifle, but Ben cuffed him. "Stop looking like that. You know very well Papa would be furious if you tried anything of that nature. It would embarrass him besides. He's got a reputation to consider and we have a duty to uphold it."

Patrick's voice spoke from the doorway. "I am glad at least one of my sons takes that view." He strolled into the room, followed in short order by Francis.

Ottilia's gaze immediately went to her spouse and she tuned out the ensuing protest entered into by her younger nephew. Her husband's lip quivered and the smile in his eyes warmed her heart.

"You will be relieved to know, my dearest," she said as he came up, "that Sir Hugh has sanctioned our departure."

"Capital." He continued in a lowered tone and with a glance at the three Hathaways, still engaged in hot argument. "Has your brother sanctioned it too?"

"I am sure he will be only too happy to see the back of me." Ottilia raised her voice to penetrate the hubbub. "Will you not, brother mine?"

Patrick hushed his sons and turned his head. "Will I not what, dear sister?"

"Be happy to wave me off home."

His sons cut in before he could respond.

"Oh, no, Auntilla!"

"Are you going indeed? We will miss you terribly."

A pang smote Ottilia and her voice went a trifle husky. "Will you? That is good to hear. Yet I don't hope to be missed so much once you are back at school."

Tom's face dropped. "School!" He turned at once to his father. "Do we have to go back, Papa? It's nearly the —"

"No, it is not nearly the end of term," cut in his father. "I'm sending you both back tomorrow."

Tom groaned, but his brother nudged him. "Don't plague Papa. We've had a splendid adventure, Tom, thanks to Auntilla." Ben turned to Ottilia. "When will we see you again?"

Recalling the boys' recent loss, her heart played traitor and she had difficulty in answering. Thankfully, her spouse took in her condition.

"You had best visit us. Pretty will be in alt to see her big cousins, and I dare say Luke will follow you about like a tantony pig."

Ben laughed. "We'll take him on, don't you worry, sir."

Tom instantly brightened. "May we go, Papa? Soon, if you please!"

Patrick put up a warning finger. "We'll have to see." He threw a glance at Ottilia. "You can't want this pair driving you demented at this juncture."

It struck her that it might do her brother a service, leaving him free to continue his liaison with Averil. It was besides a point with her to ensure her nephews were recovering from the grief of losing their mother. The thoughts relieved the pressure in her chest and she found her voice was free once more. "They never drive me demented. I would love to have them with us. Fan?"

Her spouse gave her a reassuring smile and looked to his brother-in-law. "Send them to us at Easter, Patrick, after the twins are born."

Ben blinked. "Twins!"

Tom's jaw dropped. "You've got two in there?"

Ottilia laughed, setting her hands on the bump. "So your papa tells me. I assure you it is as much of a shock to me."

The ensuing exclamatory comments served to make her feel a deal more reconciled to the prospect of the coming births. The boys were unanimous in approval, engaging at once in speculation as to the possible sex of the babies. Realising she had never given the matter a thought, Ottilia took it up with Francis when they were alone together.

"I know it is a fait accompli, my dearest, but have you a preference?"

He was sitting up in bed, waiting while Ottilia put her hair through her nightly brushing routine. "Preference for what, my enigmatic one?"

"I am not being enigmatic." She ran the brush through and set it down. "I am talking of these babes." She rose, blew out the candle and moved to her side of the four-poster. "Boy or girl? Or should I say two of either sex?" A thought struck as she climbed into the bed and pulled the curtains together on her side. "What if there is one of each?"

Francis banked her pillows. "Boy and girl?"

"It would perfectly round up our family, do you not think?"

Francis drew her to rest against him. "The only preference I have is for you to come through safely."

Ottilia snuggled into him. "And the babies too."

He stroked the bump. "And the babies too."

She received a kiss with pleasure and sighed in content. "It will be good to be home again, my darling lord."

"Indeed, my adored one." His tone changed. "And I may say it is my fervent hope that ill-disposed persons will refrain from murdering anyone in Lady Fan's vicinity for the foreseeable future."

Ottilia was at once beset with an attack of the giggles, impossible to control. Her amusement infected Francis, thankfully allowing her to release in laughter the deep-seated anxiety she had suffered since the exigencies of the summer. Her heart warmed, renewing, for the first time in what seemed an age, the loving affinity she shared with her spouse.

A NOTE TO THE READER

Dear Reader

In the 18th century, as Doctor Patrick Hathaway says, doctoring was not an exact science. As I had planned on the discovery that Ottilia was carrying twins, it was obvious her brother would be doing the discovering. The only problem was how?

I had seen images of tubes being held to the body by doctors, so I was all set to have Patrick use this method. On research, however, I discovered that the first of these "stethoscopes" was not invented until 1816! By a Frenchman at that, physician René Laënnec. Prior to this, doctors had to use their ears, which is what Patrick does to hear the heartbeats of the infants.

This highlights one of the difficulties that besets the historical mystery novelist. What was the medical knowledge at the time? How much can our sleuth (or indeed any doctor in the story) deduce from the condition of the corpse?

What I find surprising is just how much was known by the medical profession. The practice of cutting up corpses in order to learn about anatomy was essential. Hence, the illegal trade of grave robbing in order to provide medical men with said bodies, assuming there weren't enough legitimate corpses to go round. Not that studying anatomy in this way was new at the time, ancient civilisations being just as curious.

Indeed, in a Korean series I watched recently based in centuries old China, the physicians were apparently able to judge a person's physical condition just by feeling their pulse. They could tell if a woman was pregnant, for example. This kind of diagnosis is still done by Chinese doctors, so one must assume it has always been pretty accurate.

The 18th century was in general a time of great experimentation and discovery in all sorts of scientific fields, so it is no surprise to find that physicians were as capable as their instruments allowed. Later research showed that they did get some things wrong. These days, what with cameras and scans, keyhole surgery and AI, doctoring has become far more expert and efficient so that the errors of the past tend to be glaring.

Who was it said that the past is another country? As a historical novelist, it is actually quite useful to remember that. They did things differently there, it is true. But thankfully, the basic human condition does not change very much. In that past country, people still ran the gamut of emotions in response to personal events, reacted in the same fashion and gave themselves away with little clues of behaviour that spoke volumes to the observant. Which is very convenient for Ottilia's particular skill!

I do hope you have enjoyed Lady Fan's latest foray into the world of puzzling mysteries, and if you would consider leaving a review, it would be much appreciated and very helpful. Do feel free to contact me on **elizabeth@elizabethbailey.co.uk** or find me on **Facebook**, **Twitter**, **Goodreads**, or my website **elizabethbailey.co.uk**. You might like to browse all things Lady Fan at **ladyfan.uk** too.

Elizabeth Bailey

Sapere Books is an exciting new publisher of brilliant fiction and popular history.

To find out more about our latest releases and our monthly bargain books visit our website: **saperebooks.com**

Printed in Great Britain
by Amazon